I0822267

Keeper's Reign

The Final Keeper Trilogy

Book One

Chronicles from Alku

Recommended Reading Order

Keeper's Reign - Book 1

First Published by Eliza's Imaginary Adventures LLC 2023

This book contains explicit language and sexual content.

ISBN Print Paperback: 979-8-9893984-1-6 ISBN IngramSpark Print Paperback: 979-8-3485-3759-3 ISBN EPUB: 979-8-9893984-0-9

Contents

Foreword

"You've been alone too long, my dear. You have a family here who loves you and another spread over the country. Never forget that."

Well, it's been a long road to get here. Like, seriously long. Keeper's Reign started as a short story that blew past short and waved as it went by. It was the first thing I wrote for me, and that made all the difference. That was ten years ago. I spent two years writing other books after that, but then 2016 happened, and I couldn't bring myself to write again. I thought I never would.

Thankfully, I was wrong.

One ordinary day in November of 2022, I was driving home, and the name "Spayn" (pronounced Spain) popped into my head, and the love story of Spence and Xayn was screaming at me to be written. A month later, it was complete, and I had my mojo back!

It's been less than a year, and in that time, I've now expanded the Alku universe to ten books and still have imaginary friends screaming at me to tell their stories.

I genuinely hope you love the people of Alku as much as I do, and I promise there is much more to come. 1,000,000 words and counting, so grab a cup of tea and a squishy chair and settle in.

From my world to yours,
Eliza

For my family.

Grandma Connie and Gram (also a Connie). The memories I have of you both will make me smile until I join you, where you're likely chasing after my grandfathers and trying to keep them out of trouble. Good luck with that, by the way. I love you both, and don't worry, Gram, Onnie loves your cookies just as much as Mom and I do.

Grandpa Pinki. Your 'beautiful granddaughter' loves you and I promise you a basketball game when I join you too.

Mom and Bubby. Honestly, there's too much to say, and I could write you a whole book of thank yous... Oh, I guess I wrote you ten. I love you, Tory and Lewis. Thank you for listening to me babble about Alku for hours and for helping me make up new words.

Vin. Thank you for bringing me tea, reminding me to eat, and tolerating my incredibly loud mechanical keyboard. Rainbow LEDs make the stories better. Prove me wrong. While I know the stories I tell are not your cup of tea, I appreciate your technical support and your introducing me to Campfire. I will never be able to thank you for that. I love you.

Last but not least...Andi.
Damn. It's been ten years since we met in a NaNoWriMo room and began running sprints together. You are truly one of those people that my life would be bleaker without. Your foul mouth, dark humor, and endless support have gotten me through more than just writing issues over the years. The holidays we spent on Animal Crossing during the pandemic are some of the best memories I have.
I cannot thank you enough. Truly.

You are my Soul's Mate, and I love you.
...Even if we both named a main character, Gabe, independently.

Pronunciation Guide
Warning!
This page contains possible spoilers!

Names:

Eliza Leone : e-lie-za lee-o-knee

Onnie Moore : on-ee more

Abbot Moore : ab-ot more

Danella Vansand : dan-ella van-sand

Maldwyn : maald-win

Locations:

Alku : al-coo

Tiefen Hool : tee-fen who-oo-l

Nisi Dakry : nye-sigh dack-ry

Species / Races:

Sanguiste : sang-whist

Paranam : para-nam

Transmogromorph : trans-mog-row-morph

Atarga : ah-tar-guh

Qondo : con-doe

Nymph : nim-pfh

Mechanite : meh-caw-night

Zwerkalt : zwer-cult

Ceirnes : see-sins

Items:

Custos regni : cus-toes wren-ee

Chapter 1: Impatience

October 2021 - Alku | Onnie Moore

Onnie stopped on the cobblestone sidewalk and looked at a wooden sign above her that swayed gently in the soft breeze. *The Book Nook* was burned into the wood and was surrounded by an intricate curling design that reminded her of steam rising from a cup. Below the sign was a wooden door painted a cheerful green, and there was a considerable terracotta pot filled with flowers to the right of it. The smell of fresh flowers and foliage drifted off them, and Onnie smiled down at them. She looked over her shoulder at the building across the street that was bursting with flowers and then back down to the terracotta pot, assuming they were probably tended to by that florist. Like most of the town, the bookshop was a single-story building with old-fashioned windows and walls made of sturdy red brick that looked to have survived many rainy seasons.

Lifting her face to the sky, Onnie smiled and hiked her messenger bag higher on her shoulder. A few fluffy clouds were floating around the grey-blue expanse, and a light fog seemed to have followed her down the street this morning as she walked. The city of Alku was cold, green, and wet. The exact opposite of what she was used to in Los

Angeles, and she was no longer unsure if she would like the change of scenery.

Now that she stood before her family's legacy, she closed her eyes and let the feeling of belonging wash over her. Onnie was ready to explore her new life in the new city she would now call home. She took a deep breath, filling her lungs with the moist Washington air, and rested her palm on the store's door. She softly ran her fingers over its surface, the grain in the wood still pronounced enough to feel through the layers of paint. It radiated warmth, and the contrast with the weather around her made her grin. It felt cozy, even from the outside. With one last breath, she pushed open the welcoming wooden door and stepped inside.

Onnie blinked as her eyes tried to adjust to the dim interior of the bookshop. Everywhere she looked, there were books. They were stacked in piles along the walls, filling a mismatched army of shelves, and some were even under glass in cases. Considering the size of the building and the number of books Onnie could see just from where she stood, there had to be thousands. Her Grandfather's explanation of the shop had been far too modest.

"I'll be right with you," an older woman said from further inside the shop, and Onnie didn't answer her, instead wandering to a nearby shelf.

"Where is it, Rebecca? I need that book." A deep male voice said in frustration.

Onnie quickly ducked behind a row of shelves and out of the central aisle. The last thing she needed on her first day in Alku was to walk in on some altercation. She moved to get away from drama. However, she wasn't above eavesdropping to learn a bit more about her new town.

She made her way down the aisle, out of sight and in the direction of the two strangers. When she judged herself to be approximately even with the front counter, she removed a thick scroll from the center of a backless shelf, creating a gap. Careful not to push anything off the stack and onto the floor on the other side, she peered through.

Presumably, the older woman was Rebecca, who was currently frowning at the man at the counter. She was well dressed with a classic feel to her. Two pins tipped with pearls that matched the string around her long, delicate neck set her silver hair in a perfect chignon. She wore a conservative knee-length cream skirt with a black sweater and a purple shawl over one shoulder.

"It still hasn't come forward, Gabriel. You know how this place works. The book will show itself when you are ready for it."

The man was leaning on the marble counter, not talking with Rebecca, just staring at her. His hair was a rich chocolate brown, which had fallen forward, obscuring his features from where Onnie was spying. His workout shorts exposed the legs of a marathon runner, lean and powerful while not being bulky or overly lumbering. His fleece jacket outlined that his arms and torso were just as slim and fit.

What was most striking about the stranger was his height. He must have been at least six and a half feet tall, which, compared to her five foot four inches, was a literal giant. As Onnie's eyes wandered over the stranger, she couldn't help but blush at his perfectly sculpted backside, but the man's frustrated voice broke her ogling.

"I'm ready, Rebecca. When I'm not teaching, I do nothing but train, day in and day out! I can do this. Tell her to give me the damn book." The man sighed heavily. "You know how important it is that we do it before he gets any worse."

"You know I cannot force her to do anything she does not wish to do, Gabriel. You must wait and trust her to provide it when the time is right. Besides, the next one isn't ready yet. You must both be." Rebecca said quietly.

The woman glanced to the shelf Onnie was hidden behind, and

though she knew she was fully concealed, Onnie shivered and covered her mouth to quiet her breath anyway.

"We're running out of time." He ran his fingers through his hair in frustration, giving Onnie her first glimpse at his straight nose and chiseled jawline. "But you're right. She's never been wrong before."

The woman smiled. "Continue your training. I will call you when it comes forward," Rebecca rested her hand on the man's forearm, "You have my word."

Gabriel sighed and raised his hands in surrender. "Fine, Bec, fine. You win. Call me the moment that book shows up." He nodded once. "Tell the old man I said hello."

"I will. Take care of yourself, Gabe." Rebecca placed her hand on his cheek, her eyes filled with tenderness. "You're not eating enough again."

Pulling her small hand from his whiskery jaw, Gabriel sighed. "See you later, Bec."

Gabriel turned and shoved his fists into the front pockets of his coat as he stepped forward. Out of the corner of his eye, his sight connected with Onnie's, and she knew she'd been caught. She heard the man's breath catch as he stopped short to look at her, a look of surprise plain on his expression.

Onnie stumbled back, embarrassed at being caught eavesdropping, and quickly replaced the scroll on the shelf. Her heart raced, but she turned her back in the man's direction and pretended to busy herself with whatever the closest book was to her hand. It looked like she'd found a New Age section or something, the text describing rituals and protection spells.

She absentmindedly flipped through the book, still in her hand, but her mind was elsewhere. From the sounds of it, that man was looking for a particular book and not having any luck. Rebecca had mentioned another woman was also looking for it, so maybe another clerk wasn't working today.

Another stab of worry hit Onnie. Her Grandfather hadn't mentioned that he needed not one but two people to help run the store for him. He apparently hadn't told her everything, and a sense of dread rippled up her body.

When she looked around at the stacks of books that covered most of the surfaces in the shop, Onnie noticed just how cluttered and disorderly the store seemed. While it did add a nice touch of ambiance, it must be nearly impossible for the staff to find anything, that man's situation being a perfect example. The clutter made Onnie wonder how long it had been since her Grandfather had been in the bookshop and just how far the place had slipped in his absence.

A bell chimed in the distance, and Onnie was pulled from her head. She replaced the book she'd been holding on the shelf and wandered back to where she'd come in from. When she saw she was alone in the central aisle, it looked like the man had left the shop and the older woman had disappeared.

"Hello?" Onnie called deeper into the store, the stacks of books seeming to steal her words and muffle them. "I'm Onnie. Abbot was expecting me."

Aimlessly, Onnie wandered the central aisle of the shop and then over to the other side of the room while she waited for the woman to reappear. The left side of the shop seemed to be home to modern titles. Tall shelves were filled to overflowing with paperbacks, all organized and marked with handwritten genre cards. As with everywhere else, even more books lay piled on the floor.

The top shelf of each bookcase was bursting with hardbacks with gleaming spines in a multitude of colors. As Onnie looked closer, she recognized some authors and noticed that each shelf displayed only a single copy of each book. When she located one of her favorite romance authors, she skimmed the titles and saw that a version of each book they'd written was present. She was baffled by the sheer quantity and variety of books, and when she thought of the bookkeeping needed to manage a collection like the one she walked among, her heart started to race.

Her exploration drew her back over to the right side of the shop. In contrast, this side of the room had sturdier hand-carved shelves. Each was filled with a muted rainbow of leather-bound tomes neatly lined up, and not a speck of dust to be found. Tucked amongst these shelves were rare, hand-inked texts and delicately bound journals on velvet beds within glass cases. Onnie's jaw dropped when she saw a hand-painted copy of Le Morte d'Arthur open under glass. When she saw what looked to be an ancient copy of the Quran a few cases away, she grinned so hard her cheeks started to ache.

Deeper within the store, a kettle whistled, and Onnie ceased her drooling and pulled herself from the antiquity section. As she walked further into the bookshop, she looked around the end of the shelves, trying to see how many rows there were, but the shop seemed to go on forever. Shelf after shelf, stack after stack, each merging together, mimicking the sea stretching to the horizon.

Opposite the shop's door stood an imposing counter at the end of the center aisle. Made of glossy cherry wood and carved exquisitely, the object was one hell of a centerpiece. Crystals were inset into the carvings, gold leaf highlighted a few areas, and all of it formed the base for a solid slab of peach marble to rest on. On one end sat a cash register from a time long since passed. The brass was polished to a mirror finish, and the round buttons looked satisfying to press. The other end of the counter was home to a large hurricane lamp, the wick lit and providing the counter area a warm glow.

As Onnie reached the counter, still wide-eyed with wonder, she met the sparkling eyes of the older woman as she emerged from a backroom directly behind the front counter.

"You must be Connie," the older woman said with a pleasant smile.

"Uh, Onnie, actually, no one really calls me Connie," she replied, struggling to keep her eyes on the woman as they wanted to continue their roaming. "And you are?"

"Oh!" The woman stepped forward and offered her pale, thin hand to Onnie over the counter. "I'm Rebecca. Your Grandfather is a dear friend of mine, and I mind the shop for him on some of his worse days."

Onnie shifted her bag and reached out to shake the cold, well-manicured hand that the woman offered.

"You weren't supposed to be here until the day after tomorrow. Abbot will be so disappointed to have missed welcoming you home and being here when you met his shop for the first time!" The woman paused and looked at Onnie before saying, "Oh, but listen to me prattle on," Rebecca waved her hand as if to shoo away her babbling, "I swear, an old woman like me, you give me an inch, and I'll talk your ear off. Would you care for some tea? I just pulled the kettle off."

Onnie stared, her jaw slightly open, at the excitable older woman for another second before she caught her rudeness and answered with a stuttering, "Y-yes, please."

Rebecca chuckled quietly and hurried off to the backroom she'd come from earlier, leaving Onnie alone once more.

She mulled over Rebecca's comment about her Grandfather's worse days and wondered if he had minimized his condition when he'd told her of it. She wondered just how sick he really was. Abbot mentioned that he wasn't sure how much longer he would be able to run the day-to-day shop activities, and that's why he'd asked her if she'd like to move to Alku and inherit it one day. He had mentioned that he was slowing down, but he didn't tell her that he was already unable to run it.

Troubling thoughts aside, there was also the comment about Abbot being happy to have Onnie home. She'd just arrived in Alku, and before that, she'd never even visited Washington. No one in her family had been to the state after her Mom and Grandmother had left long before Onnie was born. Her Grandfather hadn't seemed senile when they'd spoken, but she was starting to become a bit more concerned for his health than she'd initially been.

The delicate clinking of china drifted from the backroom and signaled Rebecca's imminent return. She emerged smiling as she carried a silver serving tray with an antique tea set atop it. There were cups, saucers, and a large teapot with steam floating up from its spout. A small bowl held little pale purple sugar cubes and small metal tongs. On a matching plate, there were bite-sized biscotti that smelled freshly baked, lilac napkins folded beside them.

"Here we are now, dear. Why don't we sit and have a warm cup of tea? I'll try my best to answer any questions you may have. Then, when you see your Grandfather tomorrow, you two can chat. I bet you have a lot of catching up to do."

"He won't be coming into the shop today?"

"No, dear, it's his rest day," Rebecca answered with a smile. "Come with me." Rebecca turned and walked to the rare books side of the shop and, with just a few quick steps, disappeared behind one of the large shelves. Onnie followed the woman, and when they passed the shelf stuffed full of aging paper scrolls she'd hidden behind earlier, she blushed but continued to weave between rows of bookcases.

Rebecca gave Onnie a strange feeling, even though nothing was outwardly wrong with her. She just seemed...too put together. Onnie brushed it off as her being weary from the drive and assumed the woman's overly friendly attitude and high energy level were the issues.

Both qualities Onnie was unused to receiving from strangers. She followed after Rebecca anyway, trusting that her Grandfather wouldn't employ anyone too unsavory. She hoped.

After Onnie had zigzagged past a few more shelves, the room opened into a quaint sitting area with four different wingback chairs surrounding an oversized ottoman. The atmosphere of the tucked-away space was cozy and restful. Fewer lamps were in this section of the shop, and their soft glow made Onnie feel relaxed and sleepy.

Rebecca had already made herself comfortable in an emerald green wingback and placed the tea tray on the ottoman before her.

"Come sit over here, dear. This tea won't drink itself," Rebecca said, smiling warmly while she filled two cups with a red liquid. "Don't be shy, sit. You haven't been in Alku long enough to be immune to the fog's chill. Some tea will do you good."

Onnie stepped forward slowly but stopped and turned to look back over her shoulder at the front of the store, her brow creasing with her frown.

"Don't fret, dear. I'll know if we have a customer," said Rebecca reassuringly before gesturing to the comfortable-looking chair beside her.

Onnie lowered her bag to the floor near the empty chair and slowly sank into it, accepting the steaming cup of potent-smelling tea outstretched to her. She leaned forward, brought the cup to her nose, inhaled the tea's pungent aroma, and smiled. She recognized hibiscus and elderberries, but there were a few other elements that she couldn't quite place.

"There now, that's better, isn't it? Drink up while it's hot." Rebecca said before sipping from her cup and watching Onnie do the same. "How was your trip? Your Grandfather told me you were driving the distance by yourself."

Onnie lowered her cup back into its saucer and cleared her throat softly. "Yes, I drove alone. It was fun." Onnie grinned as she recalled the past few days, "I enjoyed my mini adventure. I loved Oregon and its greenness, and the mountain pass was breathtaking."

"How lovely. Did you manage to get all of your belongings moved safely as well?" inquired Rebecca as she picked up a biscotti, dunked it into her tea, and swirled the cookie around a few times.

"Everything I own fits in my car with me. A new life, new possessions, and all that." Onnie blew on her tea, more out of habit than necessity. She could tell by the china's temperature that it was already perfect. "Mom gave me the idea. Actually, she figured it would be a good way to start over."

"Oh, and how is Tory doing?" Rebecca asked, leaning forward with interest. "I have not spoken to her in quite a few years."

"She's great!" Onnie said with unstifled enthusiasm. "Happily living in Maine with Lewis in their dream home. She misses my brothers and me, though."

"I bet she does," Rebecca said, resting her hand on Onnie's knee and giving it a soft squeeze. After letting go, she sat back in her chair and resumed swirling her biscotti in her tea. "Your mother was always such a lovely girl. She used to run up and down the rows here, laughing and giggling. She liked to pretend she was a princess trapped in a tower by a wizard."

Rebecca took a bite of the soggy cookie. "Would you tell her hello for me?" Her face lit up as she spoke. There was a clear connection between her and the little princess in the tower from all those years ago.

"Yes, of course." Onnie agreed, skipping over the fact that her mother had never mentioned Rebecca before. "Mom always told us how much she loved Grandpa's shop. She was excited when I told her I had decided to move to Alku." Onnie reached for a biscotti as she spoke. "When was the last—"

Rebecca lifted her hand suddenly, cutting Onnie short. After a brief pause, she stood and placed her cup on the spindly table beside her chair. “I’ll be right back, my dear.” Rebecca walked past the corner shelf and off toward the front of the shop.

Left alone in the cozy space, Onnie continued to sip her tea slowly while mulling over everything she’d learned in such a short time. She had come into the bookshop this morning hoping to see her Grandfather and learn more about the shop. Now, she was more worried than excited.

On the rare occasions that Onnie’s grandmother told her stories about Abbot, they were always filled with a spry man covered in ink up to his wrists and smudged across his brow. He’d sounded hard-working and dedicated, so much so that it was a huge factor in her grandparent’s separation.

Apparently, the only vacation he’d ever taken was to attend Onnie’s high school graduation. She still had no idea why he wanted to be there. He didn’t go to any of her brother’s graduations, and he never attended any of their college ones either. Grandfather had called her Mom the week before her graduation ceremony, told her he was coming to town to meet his grandchildren, and asked if she had a spare ticket for the ceremony.

Since Onnie had first met him, they had spoken a few times around the holidays, but nothing more than familial pleasantries. All these years later, Onnie was ready to get to know him and catch up on lost time. Not to mention learning where he had been for the last twenty-six years of her life.

With Rebecca off doing whatever she was doing and Onnie’s mind increasing her anxiety, Onnie switched her focus to the cozy space around her. She rested her saucer on her lap, cradled her warm teacup in her hands, and began to admire the two antique lamps standing between the pairs of oversized chairs. Even though both lamps were on, they did little to light the space, and Onnie enjoyed the intimate atmosphere they created. She lifted her hand, slowly ran her finger along the edge of a glass shade, and enjoyed its soft sound.

She skimmed her eyes along the bookshelves nearest to the sitting space and noticed that between every few shelves, a lamp was tucked, providing the only source of light for customers to browse by. Not having any modern fluorescent lights made the space personal and homey. And antiquated. The space felt old as if it were sun-bleached curtains that had drifted in the breeze for too many seasons.

As she continued her visual tour, Onnie leaned back and wiggled further into the cushions. The combination of squishy chairs, soft lighting, and the plush carpet was well balanced by the multitude of shelves with their harsh edges and sharp corners positioned throughout the quiet space.

As Onnie took a few deep breaths, trepidation about her choice to move began to vanish. The Book Nook was a warm and cozy place. She could envision herself coming to the shop in the mornings happy and ready to work.

The sound of footsteps chased Onnie's thoughts away as Rebecca came around a shelf and smiled. "My apologies. How is your tea? Would you like me to top it off to warm it up a bit? Mine must be cold by now as well."

Onnie smiled as she regained her composure. "Yes, please, thank you." Pushing her anxiety aside, Onnie offered her cup to Rebecca.

Rebecca gingerly took the cup, poured more tea into it, and handed it back. She poured more into her own cup and then settled back into her temporarily vacated chair, sipping her tea with a contented sigh.

"Now, where were we, dear?" Rebecca looked at her with a warm smile and a knowing twinkle in her eye.

Chapter 2: Awe

October 2021 - Alku | Onnie Moore

A light rain sprinkled down around Onnie's car as she pulled into her new apartment complex and parked in the vacant spot in front of her cottage. There were only two options for a rental property in Alku: leasing directly from a homeowner or the mini cottages she'd chosen. There was one property manager for all of the locations, and clusters of homes were dotted around Alku. Within each grouping of houses, they were spaced a ways from each other but still close enough together that they felt related.

As soon as she saw them, she loved the idea of living in one, so she signed the lease through email while still in California. Now, she was more than ready to pick up her keys, so she skipped to the front door, smiling like a fool the entire way to the lockbox. Just around the corner from the front door were the electric meters, and on one, there was a small box that she quickly punched the code she'd been given. It clicked open, and she retrieved two house keys and relocked the box before returning to the door.

She slipped her key in the lock and grinned when she saw the interior for the first time. It was perfect. All of the cottages were different from one another and had varying sizes. She'd chosen one of the smallest ones, but even still, it was far too big for her. She stepped into the tiled entryway, eyeing the hooks on the wall for coats and the stone vase in the corner for umbrellas.

Further inside was a carpeted living room with windows on one side of the room looking out into the front yard and a wood-burning fireplace on the other wall. Past that was a small eating area and a substantial kitchen for a single bedroom. The countertops were crisp and white, with stainless steel appliances and a friendly magnet on the refrigerator. Off the kitchen was a set of double doors for the back porch.

The interior walls were a soft cream color that matched the exterior's trim that lined the edges of the light blue siding. Onnie could see only grass and trees from her patio, with only the slightest hint of another cottage in the distance.

Before she got lost exploring the rest of the space, she set her keys on the counter and returned to her car to bring in the food and drinks she had left over from the trip. Everything else could wait until after she explored the town a bit. After a few minutes, Onnie had her things in the fridge and unpacked her tea and cocoa collection onto the counter in a corner.

Finally, she wandered down the long hallway that backed up against the kitchen. She passed a bathroom door for guests and knew that another door led directly into it from the bedroom. Her room had four doors, two on each side of a corner. One for the walk-in closet, a small laundry room next to it, the entrance from the hallway, and the adjoining bathroom. At the opposite end of the room was a large bay window with a small bench that looked out onto the same trees as the patio.

The apartment was light and airy while feeling warm and inviting despite its small square footage. The images online hadn't done the place justice, and Onnie was exceptionally happy with how things had turned out.

With her full tour completed, Onnie grabbed her suitcase from her car and wandered into her new bathroom to freshen up from her long night of driving. When she saw her reflection in the white-framed mirror, she flinched and swung the suitcase onto the counter.

"What a great first impression I must have made on Rebecca. I should have stopped for coffee and a shower before going to the bookshop."

Seeing how crumpled she'd become from the two days of driving and sleeping in her car, she grabbed a fresh pair of skinny jeans and a long sweatshirt from her suitcase and quickly changed. She momentarily slipped her tennis shoes back on and ran to her car to grab her only pair of boots from the trunk. She figured she should at least try to dress appropriately for the weather, even if she was mostly clueless.

Back in front of the bathroom mirror, Onnie's waist-length raven hair was currently sticking out of its braid in every which direction. She loved the dark locks she'd inherited from her mother and grandmother, but unlike theirs, she had her father's straight hair instead of curly. So, while her mother and grandmother were always trying new ways to tame their curly hair, she was always tucking hers into a braid to keep out of her way and give it a bit of body when it was undone. She loved how her hair looked braided and how easy it was to deal with, so she'd kept it long most of her life.

Today, there was no saving the rumpled mess of tangles it had become after twenty-five hours in a car, some of which was from her time sleeping in the backseat. So, she threw her hair into a bun and called it good. She quickly brushed her teeth, applied lip balm, and spritzed on her rose perfume.

She scooped up her jacket and bag with a quick nod of approval to her reflection. The thought of any more driving made her groan, so she decided on a foot tour of Alku instead. She left her car keys and one copy of the house key on the kitchen counter and dug through her bag for her ribbon. Shoved down at the bottom was a long, black ribbon she threaded her new house key onto and then tied the ends in a knot.

She locked her new apartment and stuck the key into her bag before striding down the front walk, nearly bursting with excitement. She set herself down the sidewalk path that led back into town and began her walk, taking in everything around her as she went. L.A. wasn't the city for commuting on foot, everything was too spread out for that, but as she had driven through Alku, she noticed a few places she wanted to explore.

The bulk of the town centered around an expansive park area, with streets that fanned out from the center like the roots and rings of a tree. Her apartment was on one of the northern ones, and the bookshop was on one of the southwest.

Alku was situated at the bottom of a valley, surrounded by forests that climbed the encompassing mountains like moss on a rock. Green cocooned the town on all sides, and the only way in or out of Alku was a tunnel through the base of one of the mountains. Once you were in the city proper, it leveled out and was mostly flat and forested, with the cleared heart of town in the center. Some lakes, fields, and clusters of settlements were scattered throughout too.

As Onnie came around one of the cobbled street corners, she crossed the main street and stepped onto the curb at the edge of the park in the center of the town. She tried to remember exactly where she'd seen the coffee shop as she drove in that morning but could only remember it was across from the park. Without many other options, she took a small winding mulch path through the trees, shrubs, and the last of the fall flowers. When she emerged on the other side of the park, she was pleased to see a modern storefront a few buildings away.

Onnie jogged across the cobblestones and stopped outside the coffee shop, A Shot in the Dark, to pick up a local newspaper from a stand by the door. The door for the shop was iron and glass, nestled between two large bay windows and surrounded by red brick. Another wooden sign hung over the doorway, and flower boxes were lined up below the windows. The shop's exterior was incredibly modern compared to those around it and everywhere else she'd seen so far, but even with that difference, it still seemed to fit in perfectly with its oddity.

Onnie pulled open the weighty door and noted that the interior was much the same as the exterior. A mix of metals, woods, and brick, all of it coming together to create a modern loft vibe that was still warm and inviting. Leather couches and armchairs were scattered throughout the room, with a mix of wooden tables around them. Brightly colored prints and paintings of forests lined the walls, bringing the outside in and adding a bit of color.

People were gathered in small groups, chatting happily, and the baristas smiled at their customers with genuine interest as they made small talk while they brewed the order's coffee.

Onnie was grinning ear to ear by the time she made it up to the counter to order. A man with dark skin and the most beautiful set of golden-colored eyes she'd ever seen exited the back room and switched with the young woman at the register before Onnie had had a chance to order.

"Hello, what can I get for you this fine misty morning?" The man said with a friendly smile.

Onnie struggled not to stare, his golden-flecked eyes captivating. "Cinnamon latte and a cheese-filled croissant, please," she said politely.

"Of course." The man tapped on the register's screen several times and then picked up a cup and a black marker, "Name?"

"Onnie." The man's hand faltered briefly, and Onnie chuckled,

"Connie without the C." She added, assuming he was hung up on the spelling like most coffee shops in her past had been. Her name wasn't difficult, but it was rarely shortened and threw people off.

"Ah, I see." The man said quickly, writing her name and passing it to a woman who had come to fetch it from her place at the coffee maker. He cleared his throat softly at the woman, "It's pronounced, Onnie."

The young woman's eyes went wide, and she looked at Onnie and quickly turned and rushed to complete her order.

"Let me get that pastry for you, too." The man said, drawing Onnie's attention back to him. "My name's Anton, by the way. I own the shop, so I assume we'll see a lot of each other in the future."

Onnie smiled and nodded, "Definitely. If everything tastes as good as it smells, you've made a patron for life."

Anton grinned and handed her the paper bag with a soft, crinkling noise. "I assure you, it does."

Onnie handed him her credit card, and after he rang it up, the woman making her coffee brought it over. "Thank you both."

"It's a pleasure. Please let us know if you have any questions or need anything." Anton smiled, and the woman beside him followed suit and tipped forward in a slight bow.

"Ah...sure, thanks again," Onnie said before she crossed the room to an overstuffed armchair in the corner and flopped down less than gracefully. She chalked the pair's overly friendly demeanor up to the small-town stereotype and noted she'd have to get used to it eventually, but for now, she wanted coffee.

Absentmindedly, she flipped through the paper she'd picked up earlier as she ate her croissant. A few pages in, she stopped, noticing an article about her Grandfather's bookshop. There was a picture of a middle-aged woman standing with him in front of a school, and children surrounded them, each child's gaze locked on something different, and only one of them looking at the camera. Onnie read through the article and smiled to herself.

"Abbot's a great man. He's done a lot for this town and for those children especially," said a young woman as she sat down in a matching armchair next to Onnie's.

Onnie looked up, startled out of her reading by the stranger.

"Hello," the woman stuck out her right hand covered in silver rings and bangle bracelets, a gentle tinkling sound coinciding with the motion. "I'm Dany."

Onnie reached up and clasped the woman's hand in a relaxed shake. "Hi, I'm Onnie."

"Nice to meet you. Sorry for intruding, but I've never seen you in here before, and it's a small town, so I figured you're new here and could use a friend." Dany said before taking a sip of her coffee.

"Do you always make it a habit of befriending strangers?" Onnie asked with speculation in her voice. After all, people didn't stop and talk to strangers where she'd lived her life until now, let alone offer friendship.

Onnie smiled behind her coffee and tried to hide her apparent observations of Dany. The young woman wore leather pants tucked into chocolate-brown boots that rose past her knees. A dark purple shirt billowed around her and most likely hid a gorgeous figure beneath it. The woman looked like she'd just stepped off the runway in New York, not into a coffee shop in some remote town with less than a thousand residents. As Onnie's eyes made it up to Dany's heart-shaped face, framed by loose waves of violet hair, she knew she'd been caught gawking at the woman.

"As I said, small town," Dany replied with a warm smile. "So, are you visiting or something more permanent?"

Onnie folded the newspaper and slipped it into her bag to finish reading it later. "Ah, more permanent. I just moved here from Southern California. This morning, actually."

"Oh!" Dany said with a start of excitement. "You're Abbot's granddaughter! No wonder you were reading the article about him!"

"Ah, yeah. I am. How did you know?" Onnie frowned.

"Everybody knows you're coming to live here. Gossip travels quickly in small towns," she winked at Onnie.

"That explains the odd comment from the owner earlier, then," Onnie mumbled to herself.

"Sadly, I don't have time to stay and chat right now, but you call me if you need anything. Honestly." She stood and handed Onnie a business card before reaching behind her to drop her coffee cup in the garbage can. "Coffee buddy, tour guide, girl's night out with plenty of wine. Anything." She smiled brightly and raised her hand in a small wave, her bracelets offering their own goodbye, "See ya'!"

Onnie watched Dany walk to the coffee shop's door, stopping and turning with the door half open.

"It was a real honor to meet you, Onnie." With one last smile, Dany sauntered out of the coffee shop and left Onnie blinking in surprise, her mouth open.

When she regained her composure and looked around the bustling coffee shop, she was startled to see a few other people staring at her. Uncomfortable with all the attention, she quickly slipped her bag back over her shoulder and made her way to the exit.

Once outside again, she closed her eyes, took a deep breath of the clean air, and smiled. She drank the last few sips of her coffee, tossing the empty cup and pastry bag into a bin, and now that she felt fueled and ready for the day, she set out to explore her new home.

With nowhere to be and no idea what to do for the day, Onnie made her way down each spoke of the cobbled main street as a tourist would.

She wandered down a narrow road lined with antique shops, a classic barber shop, and a dog groomer. As she passed the quaintest antique stores, an older woman stopped beating a rug with a gnarled wooden broom and waved to Onnie fondly before returning to her task.

Just across the street from The Book Nook was a small florist with an older woman on a porch, covered with potting soil up to her elbows, planting bulbs. The lady smiled and raised her hand in greeting as Onnie passed. The red brick building looked like it was held up and together by plant vines and roots rather than mortar. Flowers burst from windows, filled planters and pots, and ivy wound up the pillars and around the banisters. Even better than the view was the smell, though, and Onnie was already looking forward to passing the shop daily to get to work.

A few streets over, there was a shopping section containing small clothing boutiques, an antique movie theater, a shoe store with a cobbler, and a shop that looked filled with home goods. A small storefront window and a black door leading into an occult shop were tucked between two buildings. Candles and crystals filled the window, and Onnie made a mental note to stop past it on a later day.

Each business had a wooden sign above their door, some painted, some raw wood, and others with unique plays on the wood theme. All the buildings were red brick, and each had some form of plant life out front in colorful pots or rustic barrels.

Ignoring the somehow remarkable uniformity yet uniqueness of everything in the town, Onnie had yet to see someone frowning. Or angry. Everyone looked genuinely happy.

After a few hours of walking, Onnie bought a bottle of water from a place called the Day Night Cafe. It was another business she decided she'd need to try in the future. It was a quaint and picturesque representation of a small-town eatery with its small bistro tables, soft colors, and a menu full of variety.

Taking her water with her, she crossed the main street to sit on a bench in the park she'd cut through earlier and people-watch. The city's inhabitants milled around her as they went about their business for the day. Alku looked like a diverse place, considering its small population. Moms with strollers walked the street towards the park, and men in business suits left the barber shop clean-shaven. When she thought about living in L.A., she had always felt like a minuscule fish in an endless ocean. Here, she felt a bit bigger. As if maybe there was enough room in this pond for her to make a few waves and not just follow the school.

It wasn't just the people that felt more approachable, though. The red brick buildings and old-fashioned cobbled streets paired with the homey touches and happy people. It was at that moment that she could finally see herself settling down.

Onnie drank the last of her water and popped it into a trashcan beneath one of the tall antique street lamps. She approached another grassy area that looked like it backed up against the town's school buildings. It wasn't a sports field, but she imagined they might use it as extra play space when needed. Along its edge, a series of trails and bike paths led off in one direction, and more followed a small street headed in the other. It looked like some of the trails led into a forest, and Onnie promised herself she'd further explore them while wearing her running shoes.

As she followed the sidewalk around the school, she noticed a small doorway leading into a sizable five-story building tucked away behind a fire station. Unlike the other buildings in Alku, this one lacked a wooden sign. Instead, a large bronze plate adorned the front wall. The brick was clean and bright, and there were no planters, just a tiny drop slot under the sign. Onnie beamed at the community library but knew if she ventured inside, she might never leave. There was still more exploring for her to do, and she begrudgingly pulled herself away.

The rest of the afternoon, she wandered the streets without direction and lingered at whatever drew her attention. A few people stopped her in the streets to introduce themselves, and she began to feel more comfortable with all of the welcome. Yet, she quickly became exhausted by all of the small talk she wasn't used to doing.

The cloud cover turned the sky dark early, and she stared at it. Alku's weather was vastly different from L.A.'s, and Onnie hoped she wouldn't be caught in a storm she wasn't prepared for. Either way, she wasn't quite finished, so she welcomed the air's chill and sat on a bench holding a cup of hot cocoa as she watched the last kids leaving their after-school programs.

Onnie recognized the one child from the newspaper article who had been looking into the camera as the little girl dashed away from the other kids and over to her Mom to hug her. Then Onnie saw the woman she'd met this morning, Dany, wave to a group of students with their parents before she ducked into the school's gymnasium.

Onnie had only been in Alku for one day, and everyone's genuine respect and affection for each other gave her hope for a future she never knew she'd wanted. She felt herself wanting to fit in. To belong.

It was fully dark when Onnie slipped back into her cottage and flopped her body onto her empty living room floor. She pulled her phone from her bag and checked her messages. There was one from her brother Jace and three from her Mom. She ignored her brother and planned to call him in the morning, but she quickly texted her Mom to tell her she was safe and sound and apologized for not saying so sooner. Truthfully, Onnie had completely forgotten once she'd started wandering the town. Not only had she missed a few calls, but she hadn't even managed to tell anyone she'd made it to the town safely.

Onnie pulled herself off the floor and wandered around her apartment, dragging her fingers along the surfaces as she passed them. Her childhood was filled with too many homes to count, and because of that, she'd learned never to get attached to the places she lived. They were always just that, places. Once her brothers had grown up and left for college, their houses felt even less like homes without their energy. When it was her turn for college, her parents left too, moving across the country to Maine.

Over time, Onnie had slowly become accustomed to living alone, and you didn't need much when you were alone. She survived with the bare minimum, and that made it easier when the time came to leave again. Which she always did.

She didn't begrudge her brothers for finding happiness or even her Mom for finally chasing her dream to live in Maine, but Onnie's last few years had been lonely, and she never found a place she felt like she fit in well enough to put down permanent roots.

As she walked through her tiny living room and into the most extensive kitchen she'd ever called her own, she leaned on the breakfast bar to stare out of the patio doors.

"Maybe this can be that place?" she said aloud, looking around the empty space filled with nothing but cream coloring for personality. "I could buy a plant or something." she laughed softly, the sound echoing off the bare walls and making her jump.

She was suddenly humming with energy, and she shook off her daydreams and made her way to her car to finish unloading the rest of her boxes. She tucked her limited amount of cooking paraphernalia into one of the cupboards and stacked a few piles of books in a corner by the front window. When pleased with her progress, she wandered down the small hallway and into her new bedroom.

Onnie could feel the day catching up to her, and she changed into sweats and a t-shirt before taking what little remaining toiletries she had into the bathroom and setting them on the sink. Then she inflated her air mattress on the bedroom floor, unzipped her sleeping bag so it laid flat, and used it to cover the plastic material. Her handmade quilt was next, and she flopped on top of it.

She rechecked her phone before getting back up, switching off the light, and forcing herself to get into bed and sleep a bit before her early morning.

After just a few minutes of tossing and turning, she was sufficiently snuggled into her blankets, and all she saw was the inside of her eyelids.

Chapter 3: Joy

October 2021 - Alku | Onnie Moore

Onnie stepped out onto her front porch and into the crisp fall air, pulling her front door closed behind her. She shivered before quickly pulling her light canvas coat tighter around herself. The air felt nippy, and she didn't mind the temperature at just a few degrees over sixty, but with a suitcase of clothes more suited for a desert festival, she wished it was closer to eighty degrees and far less damp.

Already missing the half-empty mug of tea she'd left inside, Onnie pulled out her phone and opened the directions and accompanying map to her Grandfather's house.

"Looks like he's west of City Center Park and four blocks north, which makes him…two blocks west and another two south from here and along the lake. Sweet." Onnie mumbled to herself as she clicked off her phone and slipped her hands into her coat pockets.

She couldn't help smiling as she began her walk and watched people milling around as she went. A group of bicyclists and a few cars passed her by, but most people she noticed were on foot as she was, and she wondered if that also held true in the rainier season.

A block into her walk, Onnie's pocket vibrated, and she checked the caller ID. With a grin, she answered, "What's up, big brother?"

"Hey, Missy. I believe you owe me an explanation for that driving stunt you pulled." Anthony's deep voice rumbled over the phone as he chuckled.

"Driving stunt, who me? I've done nothing," she snickered. She loved picking on Anthony, and it was way too easy.

"You should have called. I would have driven with you."

"Anthony, you live a million miles away. You weren't around the corner, or I would have."

Anthony sighed, "I'd have been there."

Onnie frowned at the worried note in her brother's voice. "I know you would have been, but I'm fine, Anthony, really. I got in early, stopped by to see the bookshop, and then went to my apartment."

"I know. I called Mom, and she said you made it safely. Otherwise, I would have called yesterday."

"You still could have…." Onnie said with a frown.

"Once I knew you were safe, I gave you space to settle in."

Onnie snorted, "A whole twenty-four hours; patience is not your strongest quality."

"You are so lucky I have a meeting in a few minutes." His voice teased, telling her she'd placated him enough, and he was starting to relax.

"Thanks for worrying…really." Onnie looked at the street signs on the corner. "Um, can you give me a second? I need to check something on my phone."

"Sure, kiddo," Anthony replied.

Onnie pulled her phone from her ear and quickly flipped back into her email to check the map. She continued to look where she was walking from under her lashes, ensuring she didn't run into anyone while her head was down. "One more block," she mumbled as she returned to her phone call. Before she looked up, she felt someone shove into her left shoulder with enough force to knock her back a step.

"Hey! Watch where—" Onnie scolded the man's back as he continued down the street opposite her direction. "Stupid punk." She returned her phone to her ear, where Anthony was chattering away again.

"Onnie, what happened? Are you okay?" His voice was full of panic.

"Sheesh, Anthony, I'm fine. Just some jerk in all black late for something more important than using his manners to apologize for running into me." Onnie straightened her coat and resumed her walk.

"You sure?" Anthony asked, his voice marginally less erratic.

"Yeah, Mom, peachy keen."

"Now, you be a good little sister and call your big brother if you need me, okay? I mean it, Onnie." she smiled as the humor returned to Anthony's voice. "Anytime, day or night, seriously."

Onnie could picture him pacing in his office, shaking his finger at an invisible her. "Don't you shake that finger at me. Only Mom's allowed to do that."

"How'd you—" he groaned, "Aw, hell, I'm getting old."

"Yup!" she smiled broadly.

"Don't tell Lizzy."

"Your secret's safe with me. So long as you promise to send me your munchkins for a few days over summer vacation." Anthony's two kids were ten and thirteen, the perfect age for some shenanigans.

"How about I promise to work on Lizzy for you instead? You know she doesn't want them to fly alone."

"I'll come pick them up. Don't worry, I don't want the boys flying alone either." Onnie stopped and looked up at a cute house set back from the street.

"Yeah, I know." Anthony sighed, "I'll work on her."

"Thanks, but hey, I'm at Grandpa's. Can I call you in a few days?"

"Sure thing, Missy, be safe, okay? We love you."

"Love you too. Tell everyone I said hello."

"Will do. Bye."

"Bye." Onnie hung up and smiled at the caller ID image that lingered on the screen. She missed her family.

She returned her focus to the house she stood in front of and the family within it and took a deep breath. A brick driveway, wide enough for two cars on one side of the property, and a thinner matching walkway disappeared behind a few trees. Bushy shrubs blocked the view from the street into the windows, and behind it, a creeping ground cover was where most homes had a grass lawn. Smaller plants and straggling fall bulbs lined the sidewalk and walkway, making everything feel manicured and looked after.

She slipped her cell phone into her pocket and followed the path up to the porch. After a few steps up, the front door finally came into view. Two smaller planters flanked it, each with a braided jasmine plant that crept up the front of the house and around the overhang above her.

Onnie knocked softly on the door and tried to stand up straighter, her nerves finally starting to get the better of her. After a few moments, a thin teenager opened the front door, dressed in black with a ring through his eyebrow and multiple in his ears.

"Ah...." Onnie said as she went to pull her phone back out to check the address.

"Hey! You must be Onnie. It's really great to meet you finally!" the young man grinned from ear to ear, his face brightening. "Come on, your Grandfather is this way." He said before stepping aside to let her into the house and closing the door behind her.

"Yeah, I am. And you are?"

The teenage boy stopped and turned around, offering his hand. "Oh, sorry. I forgot I know all about you, but you have no idea who I am."

Onnie shook her head once. "Nope, sorry," she took his hand and shook it.

"I'm Sam. Nice to meet you."

"Pleased to meet you too, Sam," Onnie said before following him through an entryway, past a living room with a large fireplace, and across the kitchen before exiting the back porch.

Her Grandfather's house was immaculate and stunning. The front garden was inviting while still providing privacy, and the interior was cozy and warm. She'd not seen a spec of dust nor a knickknack out of place as they'd rushed through the space. Nothing came even close to what she saw once she stepped out onto the deck in the back. Onnie was knocked speechless. An expansive deck ran the length of the house, with large windows letting in the light and the view of the mirror-like water from the lake and the many tall evergreens around it. Nearly centered in the deck was a dock, about fifteen yards or so in length, jutting out into the water.

"I'll give you two some space." Sam said with a smile, "Call if you need anything."

"Thanks," Onnie nodded, and Sam closed the door, no doubt keeping the warm in for later.

Onnie returned her gaze to the dock, where she found her Grandfather. He was bundled up on the end, feeding ducks with a slight smile on his face. He looked diminished and withered, unlike when she'd seen him eight years ago. His hair was white and wispy around his face, and his skin clung to his bones, but only just. She slipped her bag off her shoulder and scuffed her shoes along the wood to make noise and not startle the happy man out of his daydreams.

"Ah, Grandpa?" She said as she poked her head around his chair.

Thankfully, he looked warmly dressed in a red wool sweater and flannel pants, a blanket tucked over his legs. Her Grandfather looked up and grinned. "Onnie! My dear, look at you!"

"Hi, Grandpa," Onnie said, returning his smile.

"Well, don't just stand there! It's been too long!" The old man pulled off the blanket on his lap and held out his hand, waving it at Onnie. "Help me up, child. I want a hug from my beautiful Granddaughter!"

Onnie chuckled at the older man's spirit before grasping one of his thin, gnarled hands gently in her own and placing her other hand on his elbow. She slowly pulled him to his feet, where he teetered briefly but quickly regained his balance.

"Come on now. I want that hug."

Onnie bent forward and hugged the man before her, her eyes glittering with amusement. "Well, you're certainly not lacking any spirit, Grandpa."

With a peck on Onnie's lowered cheek, the older man straightened up and held her at arm's length. "Now, who said I lacked spirit? This old man isn't down for the count yet!"

"That's not what I—"

"Don't you worry, dear. I know you didn't mean any offense. Run back up to the porch and grab another chair. I'll hold your bag." Reaching out, he took it from her, and as he settled back into his seat, he placed the bag across his lap. She left him smiling to himself as she made her way back up to the house and grabbed a matching chair for herself.

She sat the chair next to her Grandfather's and tucked her legs up into it as she sat down. "Here, I can take that back. It's heavy." She carefully retook her bag, set it on the floor beside her, and began to fiddle with the end of her long braid while he resituated beneath the blanket.

"Rebecca said you stopped by the bookshop yesterday morning. I'm sorry. Had I known you had come up to Alku early, I would have been there to greet you."

"It's okay. I could leave a day early, and my apartment here was ready, so I figured it wouldn't hurt to have some extra time on the drive up."

"Of course, what a sensible thing to do, and I get to see you earlier. What a pleasant surprise!"

Onnie chuckled softly, "Less sensible and more impatience, but I won't tell if you won't."

Abbot snorted at her and shook his head, "Secret's safe with me. Would you like something to drink? Tea, maybe? It's a bit cold out here this afternoon. October is always a bit chilly, but this year has been more damp than usual."

"Sure, thanks. If you tell me where to look, I can go get it." Onnie offered as she began to stand.

Abbot reached his hand out and placed it on her forearm, "It's okay. I can have Sam get it for us."

Onnie settled back into her chair as the older man grabbed a bell from atop a tiny table on the other side of him and gave it a quick ring. "Rebecca's idea," he said, raising his eyebrows to the bell. "She figured it would keep me from having to get up or holler for Sam. He, on the other hand, finds it hilarious."

"You rang, Sire." Sam purred in a wickedly sarcastic tone from over Onnie's shoulder, making her jump.

"Yikes! Damn, dude, you scared me half to death!" Onnie said, clutching her chest.

"Whoops, sorry," Sam said with a quick laugh and an apologetic grin before looking back at the old man. "What's up, Abbot?"

"Would you bring us some tea, please?" Abbot asked, smiling but still shaking his head at the young man.

"Sure thing. Red tin?"

"That's the one. Thank you, my boy," Abbot said with a wink and a fondness in his voice that made Onnie instantly jealous of the young man.

Sam nodded once to her before he walked back up to the house.

"What is he, part ninja?" Onnie said, still with a racing heart and cheeks that were slightly pink from embarrassment.

As Sam's figure walked away, Abbot laughed deeply and watched him go. A melancholy had crept into his features, and a frown tugged on his lips despite his laughter.

"Not a ninja, but he's had quite a long time to practice, yes." After a few more seconds, he shook his head and looked back at her. "So, tell me about your adventure so far, and don't leave anything out!"

At some point during the recounting of her short time in Alku, Sam brought a chair down to the dock for himself and joined in on their conversation. Her Grandfather frowned when Onnie mentioned that she had so little and needed only her car to move it all. He quietly ripped a chunk off the stale slice of bread in his hands and threw it to a nearby duck.

"I don't like you having so little to your name, child. My intention was not to make you discard your old life when moving to Alku, only to move it to a new location." Abbot's brow furrowed, and Onnie could see he was uncomfortable, and likely guilt weighed on him.

"Please, Grandpa, don't worry about it. I'm happy with my choice. The move was quick and easy, and now I get to splurge and buy some neat new things. I'm excited, not upset or sad."

Sam nodded in agreement with Onnie before throwing a chunk of bread to the duck furthest from the rest. "Actually, it sounds kinda cool, Abbot. Onnie de-fragged her hard drive. Ditch the old, sort the current, and make space for the new."

Abbot chuckled and tossed a piece of bread at Sam instead of the ducks, "That boy, there's a smart one. Too smart for his own good sometimes."

"Seems like it, though technology and I are not friends, so I only followed half of what he said," Onnie added, throwing her bread at the ducks instead of Sam. "Sounded right, though."

"Well, as long as you're happy then, my dear," Abbot said before sipping his tea.

Onnie nodded and looked at Sam over her teacup. "So, how do you know my Grandfather?"

Sam smiled before pulling another slice of bread from the bag on his lap. "Oh, I've known Abbot forever. He's also friends with my parents."

"Made friends with you first, though," Abbot said fondly.

"True."

"Sam has taught me many things about the people of this town, and we'd often get into trouble together." Abbot chuckled and pointed to Sam. "Some things never change. I still get scolded from time to time with this young man."

Again, Onnie felt a pang of envy that so many others had shared her Grandfather's life with him while she was barely aware he existed for most of hers.

Sam snorted and rolled his eyes at Abbot. "When Abbot needs help —"

"Or a babysitter," Abbot interjected.

Sam stuck his tongue out at the older man before continuing. "I come help out."

Onnie raised her teacup to Sam before saying, "Well, you certainly know how to make a good cup of tea."

"Lots of practice," Sam said with a weak glower in Abbot's direction.

The three of them sipped their tea and finished sharing their bread with the ducks in a mix of comfortable silence and light-hearted conversation. Onnie liked Sam. He came across as a good kid and made Abbot laugh, which seemed to remove a few years from his wrinkled features every time he did. She was enjoying her time, spectating their wit and words as they ribbed each other like childhood friends.

"Hello there!" Rebecca's voice came from the kitchen window behind the three of them. "What are you all doing out there? It's freezing today!"

Abbot looked over his shoulder and yelled back to Rebecca. "Why hello, dear, we'll be right in. Welcome home."

Abbot passed his teacup to Sam, who gathered all the dishes on a serving tray and returned to the house. Onnie stared out over the lake in awe. She hadn't realized that Rebecca lived with Abbot on top of watching the bookshop for him, but now that she thought about it, Rebecca's attitude towards Abbot had been rather affectionate the day prior.

"Come on, my girl," her Grandfather said as he folded his blanket and slung it over his shoulder, "we'd best get in there before too much longer. Rebecca's a fantastic cook, and I'd hate to miss dinner. We're eating a bit early tonight."

Onnie forced a smile and helped the unsteady man to stand once more. She watched his back as he slowly shuffled toward the house, and her smile faded. There was so much more to the story of her Grandfather, the bookshop, and Alku than she'd first understood, and it both excited and concerned her. Rebecca greeted Abbot at the door, and he kissed her cheek as she took the blanket from him. When the older woman looked at Onnie, her expression said she knew what Onnie had been thinking. After Rebecca and Abbot left the doorway,

Onnie took a deep breath and grabbed her bag before following everyone inside.

Warmth wrapped around Onnie as she stepped into the house and hastily closed the door behind her, enough cool air having already crept in while she'd dawdled.

"Hello, Onnie dear, are you staying for dinner?" Rebecca asked from behind the kitchen counter that doubled as counter seating.

"Ah, I—" Onnie began.

"Yes, she is darling. Sam is as well, isn't that right, my boy." Abbot said before patting Onnie on the cheek and heading into the living room.

Onnie glanced at Sam, who just shrugged and followed Abbot out of the room. "If it's not too much trouble," she told Rebecca. "I can help if you'd like."

"Of course, it's no trouble." Rebecca sliced potatoes into a pot of boiling water before drying her hands on a dish towel and picking up a tea tray. She handed it to Onnie and began to shoo her from the kitchen. "You can help me by taking that with you and spending time with those two. Keep them out of my hair, and I'll manage."

"If you're sure," Onnie said before entering the other room, a contented Rebecca returning to the stove.

Her Grandfather was sitting on an antique couch watching Sam stoke the fire he'd lit in the fireplace. The floral scent of the tea Onnie carried must have drifted to Abbot's nose, and he inhaled deeply before turning to smile up at her.

"Oh, wonderful! You've brought fresh tea. Just sit it here, Onnie." Abbot scooched forward on the couch and patted the coffee table. "You better watch out, young man. Onnie may steal your babysitting job."

Sam feigned surprise, and Onnie laughed at the two of them. They were so comfortable around each other, and when she looked at her

Grandfather, she longed for that kind of relationship with someone as well.

"Thank you for the tea, Bec," Abbot called into the kitchen.

"Of course. Do you need anything else? Dinner will be ready shortly." Rebecca's voice drifted in from the kitchen.

Abbot poured three cups of hot water from the pot and added bags to each before he passed one to Sam across the table. "No, we're okay. Thank you."

Onnie accepted a teacup and then crossed the room to sit on the hearth before the fire, but she was careful not to block any heat headed to the other two. She warmed her hands on the delicate china and tipped her head down to inhale the steam. Smiling, she took a small sip before looking up to meet Abbot's gaze, which sparkled.

"Delicious, isn't it?" he asked, sipping from his cup.

Onnie nodded as Sam sighed. "It always smells like it would taste good. You're lucky, Onnie."

"Aren't you drinking it too?" Onnie said with raised brows.

"Naw, not allowed," Sam said before becoming a shade pale.

Abbot cleared his throat and looked over the coffee table at Sam sternly. "Sam's allergic to one of the herbs in it. He's drinking chai instead."

Sam nodded once quickly before setting his cup down and standing up. "I'm going to see if Rebecca needs any help."

Abbot returned to his tea as Onnie watched Sam flee the living room.

"Drink up, Onnie, before it gets cold."

Onnie took another sip and, after a few moments of silence, placed her cup on the table and held her hands up to warm them with the fire instead of the china. "So, I really like The Book Nook. It's cozy, and I couldn't believe how many books there are."

"Yes, it's quite a lovely shop."

"When would you like me to start working? I don't have anything to do, so I can start—"

Abbot lowered his cup and closed his eyes. "My dear, please, ask Rebecca all your questions. She keeps our shop company far more often than I do these days. She'll know best."

"Alright, I didn't mean any—" Interrupted again, Rebecca's voice came from the dining room off the kitchen.

"Dinner's ready, you two. Come and sit down. Sam has set the table."

"It smells fantastic, Bec. We're on our way," Abbot said before shuffling to the front of the couch and pushing himself up to his feet. "Come now, Onnie, best not to let it get cold."

With that, Abbot turned and walked away. Onnie watched as her Grandfather carried his weary bones into the other room and left her alone—just her, her tea, and a confusing mix of emotions.

Chapter 4: Content

October 2021 - Alku | Onnie Moore

It had been a week since Onnie had moved her life to Alku and first walked into the bookshop her Grandfather owned. She spent nearly every evening with him and Rebecca, sharing meals in their home and swapping stories around a pot or two of tea. The three of them developed a quiet routine, and Rebecca no longer called to ask if Onnie was coming to dinner, but there was always a place set for her and extra food when she arrived after work.

Work at the bookshop had settled into a familiar pattern as well. Every morning, Onnie would arrive early to clean and ready the shop for the day. She would dust and sweep the store and the sidewalk outside, tidy up loose books that had been pulled out and put back incorrectly the day before, and polish a piece of furniture or two now that she had them all on a rotation. The flowers out front never needed watering, thanks to Mother Nature's help, but Onnie made sure to inspect for weeds and check if anything needed tending to.

By the time she was ready to open, the old register had also been stocked with enough change for the day, and the beautiful tea set was washed and prepared for use while the kettle bubbled away in the back room. Just as Rebecca had that first day, Onnie often served tea to customers on the ottoman near the four wingback chairs.

When it came time to handle the business side of running a bookshop, Rebecca had given Onnie the short version of everything she would need, and after that, she passed over the reins. That had been five days ago. At first, Onnie was overwhelmed, but Rebecca throwing her into the deep end forced her to learn much about caring for the shop quickly. Onnie hadn't worked in retail before, let alone owned or managed a shop, so she quickly had to learn how to balance the day's sales, where to deposit money every evening, and how to pay the various bills the shop accrued.

Every day, the people living in Alku came to introduce themselves and occasionally pick up something new to read, but the tourists surprised Onnie the most. Apparently, The Book Nook was a must-see on the Alku vacation destination list. She'd seen so many tourists enter the shop in her short time managing it, but every time, she warmed when their eyes went wide and then struggled to keep up with how quickly they wanted to see everything.

Between the excitable guests, Onnie tried maintaining the store's clean, tidy, organized, haphazard vibe. One of the days, she updated some of the paper genre cards that labeled the shelves. Another day, she'd removed every lampshade and cleaned them inside and out, their glass clear and twinkling with renewed vigor.

However, there were still some aspects she was unsure how to do and arguably were some of the most important. Many of them were management tasks that would need to be done at some point in the future, but she'd rather have been prepared in advance. She still had no idea how to order stock, which suppliers to contact for new releases, or how she would even begin hunting down the rare books that filled the right side of the store.

She found herself frustrated by her Grandfather's lack of interest and Rebecca's lack of explanations. Onnie didn't understand why her Grandfather was so adamant about not discussing anything relating to the store with her, and considering she'd moved her life to Alku to help him, she felt she had a right to be annoyed. The least he could do was answer a few questions, but she already knew she'd get no help from him, so she made a mental note to ask Rebecca after dinner.

Onnie's phone vibrated from where it sat on the marble counter and interrupted her internal grumblings. She had a new email, and when she saw a delivery confirmation from a small furniture store near her cottage, she grinned. Yesterday, on her way home from an early dinner at her Grandfather's, Onnie had decided to take a different street home. She walked past a store filled with yarn, the local clinic, and a little shop that sold handmade items for the first time. In the latter's front window was an overstuffed chocolate leather armchair that looked worn in all the right places and practically begged for a blanket and a good book. With the quilt her mother had made, Onnie knew it would be the perfect place to cozy up. The shop's owner graciously offered to deliver it directly to Onnie's apartment tonight, and judging by the email, Onnie needed to call Rebecca and see if she was free to come in and close the bookshop this evening.

Onnie set her phone back on the marble, picked up a rag and a bottle of wood polish, and began to rub the delicately carved designs on the front of the counter. A few minutes into her caretaking, a soft bell chimed in a distant corner of the shop, and when Onnie looked towards the front of the room, Rebecca was closing the door behind herself.

"Good morning, Onnie!" Rebecca said with a charming smile as she began unwrapping her scarf. It was expertly woven around her neck and head to protect her immaculate up-do from the damp air. "How are you this fine morning?"

Startled, Onnie stood and sputtered out a shaky "Hello, fine, thank you," just as Rebecca reached the counter. "I was just thinking of calling you."

"Well then, how convenient it is that I am here," Rebecca said with a bit of mischief in her smile.

"It is," Onnie replied as she capped the polish bottle. "How're you? Is it still raining outside?"

"Why, dear, hasn't anyone told you?"

Onnie cocked her head to the side.

"This is Washington. All it does here is rain." Rebecca smiled and winked at Onnie, "But I'm quite well, thank you. Your Grandfather, too, and he sends his love. He requested that I check in on you today." She ran her hand softly over the marble counter as she looked around the store.

Onnie smiled. Despite her initial misgivings, she was beginning to like Rebecca, even if the woman was a bit odd. "Oh, it's all good, I've been fine."

"I know we have rather left you to fend for yourself these past few days, so I hope you haven't had too much trouble."

"The customers are friendly, and when I'm not cleaning, there's plenty for me to explore on the shelves," Onnie said, affection in her voice for the shop unmistakable. "I have a few questions about the day-to-day management stuff the store needs, though."

"Of course you do, dear, and I'll be happy to help you with whatever you don't know how to do yet." Rebecca smiled politely.

"Well, I asked Grandfather, but he wasn't very forthcoming with his answers."

Rebecca's smile faltered before it slipped into a frown, and she placed her hand gently on Onnie's shoulder. "He misses her, that's all. Let's endeavor not to pour salt on any open wounds, alright? I can answer any questions you have. Try to enjoy your time with him in other ways."

Onnie nodded, not wanting to add more pain to the older man's heartache. "Alright."

"Wonderful!" Rebecca exclaimed, clasping her hands together, the sudden shift startling Onnie. "I'll come in on Saturday, and we can discuss anything you want over tea."

"Okay, thanks, Rebecca."

"Of course, dear. Now, then, you're a young woman. You should be out on the town, seeing the sights, meeting people. What would you say about taking a day off and leaving the shop to me? I know a great little coffee shop down the road, and their bakery is divine!" Rebecca slipped the cleaning cloth from Onnie's fingers and set it beside the polish bottle on the counter. "Come now, say yes."

"Ah...yes?" Onnie wasn't sure what just happened, but it sounded an awful lot like Rebecca was shooing her out of the shop. "Are you sure? I don't mind staying."

"Positive, you've been in Alku for over a week and have worked every day since you arrived. I insist."

"Alright, I'll just get my bag then."

Onnie walked into the back room and retrieved her bag from the small couch in the corner. She'd found the piece of furniture buried under sacks of bubble wrap and packing peanuts yesterday, so she spent a few minutes clearing it off and setting up a comfy staff-only lounge area. As she walked back to the front of the shop, she picked her phone up from the counter and slipped it into the outside pocket of her bag.

Rebecca was now pulling books from a box that had arrived that morning. In no time at all, the woman had covered the surface in neat stacks, ready to be put out on the shelves.

Onnie hesitated, "Oh, I was going to put those out this morning. Do you want me to do it before I leave?"

"Nonsense, you go and have a wonderful day. I can manage these." Rebecca said, stroking the freshly printed paperbacks fondly.

"Oh, and enjoy that new chair of yours." Onnie's expression must have shown her surprise, and Rebecca chuckled. "Your Grandfather and I know quite a few people in this town, and gossip travels quickly. It sounds like you are perfect for each other."

"Yeah, it was, and thanks again for the day off. It's being delivered tonight, and now I can be home to let them in."

"Of course, dear, think nothing of it." From somewhere in the shop, a phone rang, its chime barely audible, and Rebecca made a shooing motion at Onnie, "Go on then, enjoy the day."

"Thanks again!" Onnie nodded before turning and walking to the coat rack by the door. She heard Rebecca answer a phone that Onnie didn't even know the store had, adding another thing she apparently needed to ask the woman about.

"Hello. No, not yet, Gabriel. I told you I would call." Rebecca's voice sounded exasperated, and Onnie could only assume the caller on the other end was the same man from Onnie's first day in Alku. She stopped and looked over her shoulder, recalling the conversation she'd overheard and then having promptly forgotten. She never did get a chance to ask if another clerk had been working at the shop recently.

Rebecca was still waving at Onnie and smiling. Onnie felt she was correct in her assumption that it was the same Gabriel, seeing as people kept telling her Alku was a small town, and she doubted there were two Gabriels. Rebecca nodded once before walking into the back room to continue her phone call.

"She hasn't found it yet…." Rebecca's voice trailed off, and Onnie shook her head.

Apparently, the man had a rapport with Rebecca, so Onnie would stay out of it unless asked to help. Besides, she figured if Rebecca couldn't find it, there was no way Onnie would after only working there for a week.

She stepped out of the shop and smiled at the misty sky. She knew it was strange that she needed a few hours off this afternoon, and now she had them, but she'd started to accept that her new town was a bit odd and chose to ignore it.

Alku was beautiful, and Onnie hadn't had much time to herself since her explorations on her first day, so today, she would do a few things she'd been itching to do since moving.

The first thing on her list was to get that coffee Rebecca dangled in front of her. The coffee shop seemed to be the hub of all Alku's gossip, and Onnie had gotten into the habit of stopping there mornings before work. She found it amusing to sit and listen to the early risers discuss all the comings and goings of the town.

She'd seen Dany several times, though they hadn't spoken again since that first morning. The woman had been right, though. It felt like everyone was aware that Onnie was a recent addition to their town. Everyone she met was friendly and welcoming to her, and she was still amazed and slightly uncomfortable with how Alku already felt more like home than anywhere she'd ever lived. Even though she returned to her empty, quaint apartment, at the end of every day alone, it was becoming a home. She was slowly filling it up with the necessities and, surprisingly, was enjoying the process.

Onnie noticed movement across the street and saw the woman at the flower shop, who had twigs in her hair and dirt on her arms, carrying out a small pot of blush blooms. She waved as the woman set down the plant and waved back with a bright smile. Onnie pulled her hood up and crossed the street in the other direction.

Now that she had a full day to enjoy, she decided to go home after a stop at the library for a new book. Instead of cutting through City Center Park, she skirted its perimeter and passed the school. It must have been a mid-morning break because there were kids everywhere of all ages. Groups of teenagers stood around, no doubt gossiping, while the younger ones played sports and tag. A soccer ball bounced over to Onnie, and she stopped it with her boot.

"Excuse me," a young man's voice came from across the field, "can we have that back?"

"Sure," Onnie said and kicked it back. The ball went wide, and the boy had to run after it. "Sorry!"

"No problem, thanks!" The boy kicked it back to his friend before rejoining the game.

Onnie continued her way down the sidewalk and chuckled when a teacher called the end of recess, and a collective group of moans followed.

She turned the corner and stopped to look up at the library. It still amazed Onnie how something with so much knowledge and potential stood behind such an imposing building, the fire station hiding it from view. She went up the steps and through the nondescript door next to the bronze plaque on the wall.

As Onnie stood in the library's doorway, light spilling in around her, she couldn't help it when her breath caught. The entryway of the building was beautiful and nothing like what the outer facade had implied. When Onnie saw the rectangle of light with her shadow cast upon a large inlay in the floor, she realized she'd been gawking and quickly shut the door behind her.

She stepped further into the expansive space, and her eyes roamed the glossy mahogany floor. An inlay of ebony wood filled the center with a crest she'd never seen before. The circle was lined in gold and depicted three women, their arms intertwined and raised to the sky where a book lay open and emitted golden light. The words, "By the Sisters shall the knowledge of old be found, for when sight shines upon Keeper and Kin, antiquity will be the savior of forever," bordered the crest. Onnie found the image captivating even without knowing its history, and she treaded softly when crossing the foyer.

The rest of the library was drab by comparison. Industrial metal shelves filled the single room on each floor, feeling more like an army store cupboard than a place for contemplation. As Onnie passed the front counter, a clerk greeted her and then refocused on the patron she was assisting.

Now, Onnie just needed to decide on what she felt like reading. From her cursory glance, it looked like the first floor was dedicated to trade skill books and the coursework for the school across the road. The second was primarily non-fiction, and the third was where the fiction and children's sections were. The fourth floor was closed off for repairs, and Onnie's heart grieved for the so obviously withering library.

Being a fiction reader, Onnie headed up two flights of stairs. The second and third floors looked like the first: bland, clean, and clinical. The only place that had any life to it was the children's section, and even that was slight and primarily due to a colorful rug and a few pictures hung on the walls.

Onnie spent a few minutes skimming book spines on a shelf holding classic novels and picked a worn copy of Peter Pan. It looked well-loved over the years, and she was happy with her choice. She skipped back down the stairs, headed to the counter to check out the book, and then wanted to grab that much-desired coffee before heading home.

While Onnie appreciated Rebecca's intention, Onnie was more of a homebody than a night-on-the-town kind of gal and intended to read the afternoon away.

The clerk from earlier was no longer at the desk, and as Onnie set her book on the counter, she noticed a bell with a small card in front of it that read; *shift change, please ring.*

Onnie gently tapped the bell, its shrill chime echoing off the expansive atrium. She winced at the sound's intrusion on the calm quiet and opened her purse to pull out her wallet.

"Onnie, is that you?"

Onnie looked up and saw Dany as she stepped into the doorway of a small room behind the check-out counter.

"It's so good to see you!" Dany said, coming over and leaning over the table to hug Onnie quickly.

"Hey, Dany," Onnie said, taken aback by the woman's level of familiarity.

"Checking out?" Dany said, picking up the book and reading the spine. "Nice, this was always one of my favorites as a kid." She gently turned the book over in her hands and examined the cover and the edges of the pages. "I really did a number on it over the years. I should probably find a new copy."

"I think it's perfect just the way it is. It feels loved." Onnie held out her driver's license for Dany to scan it, "Here."

Dany smiled and placed the book back in front of Onnie on the table. "Oh, nice try. Our system is too outdated for that. We're old school here." Dany pulled out a chair and sat down, slipping a book and pen from the keyboard tray hidden under the desk. "Good old-fashioned bookkeeping."

Onnie cocked her head to the side, but when she glanced around, she didn't see any computers, so Dany was obviously serious. "Really?" She shook her head and replaced her ID in her wallet before staring at the logbook. "What info do you need then?"

Dany flipped to the page labeled October 27th and uncapped the ballpoint pen. "Name and signature. You can keep the book for seven days. After that, you can renew it up to two more times. Just call us or come by, and we'll mark it." She swiveled the book to face Onnie and passed her the pen.

"Ah.... Okay." Onnie filled out the line while Dany updated the due date on the yellow card she'd retrieved from the book's front cover.

"How do you hold people accountable with this system? Wouldn't it be effortless not to return something?"

"Actually, no." Dany scoffed, slipped the card back into its sleeve, and handed the book to Onnie. "You'd be amazed what a good tool gossip can be. One word from me into the right ears, and the whole town will be on your doorstep until you return it."

Onnie's jaw dropped in shock, "You're kidding!"

"Hell no! I do it all the time. Mrs. Radcliff is the worst. I expect her this time tomorrow to return the gardening book she borrowed. I keep telling her just to buy the damn thing from your Grandfather's shop."

"Remind me who that is?" Onnie asked, straining to place a name with one of the many new faces she'd met recently.

"Florist. Across from your Grandfather's shop."

"Ah," Onnie chuckled and slipped the book into her bag. "Wow, that's cold. Does she even remember it's a library book at her age?"

"You're not the one who has to waste half her morning talking to all the blue-haired ladies of Alku to get Mrs. Radcliff to behave and to answer your question, yes. She most definitely remembers. Don't let her appearance fool you. That woman's sharp as ever."

"I'll make sure to remember that," Onnie said honestly.

Dany stood and looked at the clock across the room, "It's coffee time. Wanna join?"

"Coincidentally, I was headed to do that myself."

"Perfect! Give me one sec to switch the guard and grab my purse."

"An awful lot of coincidences today," Onnie muttered to herself as Dany dashed off to the back room.

She returned a minute later wearing a long red trench coat and a leather bag slung over her shoulder. As she came around the counter, Onnie saw she was wearing denim jeans tucked into black leather boots that came up to her knees and had wicked-looking metal spiked heels.

Dany's dark blue hair was pulled back in a loose braid and pinned with a silver clip at the base of her neck.

Onnie suddenly felt underdressed in her wellies and baggy canvas coat. "Don't you need to…." She trailed off, indicating with her wiggling fingers at the shift change sign.

"Huh?" Dany said, looking at the sign, "Oh, no. That's not for me. I manage the library. That's my two librarians switching. I just picked up the slack while she was finishing her breakfast. She'll be out in a minute or two."

"Oh, if you're sure."

"Yup! Ready?" Dany said before linking her arm with Onnie's and leading her out the library door.

Chapter 5: Comfortable

October 2021 - Alku | Onnie Moore

After four hours of coffee and gossip, Onnie was finally draped over her new leather chair and wrapped in her quilt. She had a goblet-sized mug of apple cider between her hands to warm them up, and she was utterly exhausted of people.

Onnie was learning that Dany wasn't just energetic; she could power the entire town off of her vigor and spark. Their conversation had been fun, and while Onnie enjoyed it, she had been looking for a way to politely sneak away when the store owner had called about delivering her chair. The two high school kids he employed for deliveries were off school for the day and ahead of schedule. Onnie assured him she'd be home, grabbed another coffee, said her goodbyes to Dany, and made her way home as fast as possible. As she hung her keys on the hook, the young men knocked on her front door.

Now she was content, and Onnie snuggled further into her chair and inhaled the spiced cider that reminded her so much of Christmas with her family. She dug around under the quilt to find her cell phone and called her Mom, hitting the button for speakerphone before placing the phone on the arm of the couch.

A few rings later, a peppy voice flooded the small apartment. "Hey, it's my baby girl!"

"Hi, Mom."

"What're you up to? Are you at work?"

Onnie could hear running water and then her Mom's old kettle being placed on the stove. "Nope, Rebecca gave me the day off to go out and do something young. So obviously, I am at home curled up in my quilt on this new comfy chair."

"Naturally. Do you have a good book, at least?"

Of course, her Mother would ask if she had a book. She knew her well, and Onnie smiled. "Duh, I checked out Peter Pan from the library this afternoon. It's not much of a library, though, honestly."

"Yeah, I remember that. Even as a kid, that library felt old and run down."

Onnie reached behind her and lifted the library book off the window sill she used as a side table, "It feels… I don't know, sick somehow." She sat the book on her knee and gently flipped through the yellowed and cracked pages.

"Mmm…." A loud crash from the other end of the phone broke Onnie's concentration, and her Mother cursed. "Crap."

"Are you okay?" Onnie said, closing the book and replacing it on the window ledge.

"Yeah, I dropped a damn glass. I swear the little sucker jumped right out of the cupboard." Onnie smiled. Her Mom's klutziness was a running joke in their family. "While I sweep this mess up, why don't you tell me about your week so far? Have you made any friends? Met any men?"

Onnie rolled her eyes and sipped her cider before answering. "It's great here. I've made a couple of friends...I think. Well, there's this one woman who I don't think I have much of a choice of whether I want to be her friend or not. She's pretty energetic." The sound of a kettle's whistle made Onnie warm and happy inside. She and her Mom had spent many nights drinking tea together since she was a child.

"Is energetic a bad thing?"

"Nope, not really. Dany's just…outgoing."

"Good, you could use a little outgoing. Call Dany up and see where it takes you."

"Yeah, maybe." Onnie agreed while fiddling with the hem of her quilt.

"How do you like the weather? Your toes frozen off yet?" Her Mom chuckled before slurping her tea.

"Meh, it's okay, more damp than cold, though."

Sadness laced her Mother's voice. "I worry about you. I know you love the heat."

"Mom, it'll be okay. I don't miss it that much. I mean, really, who can miss one-hundred-degree weather? You don't."

"I know I don't, but you're not me. You're like…a cactus, and you need it."

"Honestly, I'm fine. I have my cider and my quilt, and now this comfy chair. I'm all set. Besides, I'm close to Seattle, which has endless tea and coffee shops for me to try."

"I guess."

"Besides, I think I'm coming to love boots and legwarmers."

Tory snorted, "Did you just say legwarmers?"

"I did," Onnie grinned. "What about it?"

"Nothing, nothing." Tory giggled, and it made Onnie smile.

"Really though, stop worrying, Mom. It's not like I'm alone up here. I have Grandpa."

"I know. That's why I can sleep at night, even with all his faults. He loves you and will watch out for you."

A deep voice came over the phone, breaking the tension. "What're you two up to in there?" Lewis, Onnie's stepdad, said as she assumed he had entered their kitchen.

"Hi, kiddo. How are you doing in your new place?" Lewis asked before Onnie heard him kiss her Mother's cheek.

"I'm doing alright. Mom, on the other hand, may end up bald by the new year from all her worrying."

"Hey!" Tory exclaimed with mock outrage.

Lewis' hearty laugh filled both houses, and Onnie felt her face glow with that feeling of connection only family could give.

"You cut that out!"

"Oh no, she's pulled out the mom finger! Save me, Lewis!" Onnie laughed as she clearly saw her Mom shaking her finger in her mind.

"That she did, but you're on your own, kid. Even I won't go against the mom finger."

Snorting, Onnie began to untangle herself from her quilt and choked out, "Yeah, me too, but Anthony did it to me the other day. I think he learned from the best."

"You bet he did," her Mom chuckled, "Though Lewis has been known to use the Dad finger when the situation arises."

Onnie missed them, and even though she was enjoying their familiar bantering, her heart ached. "Alright, Mom, go finish cleaning up your rogue drinking glass. Besides, I think I will head out for a run."

"If you're sure, sweetie." Her Mom replied, choking back laughter, "Well, you call me this weekend, okay? Let me know how Grandpa's doing. I worry about him and you. Don't you catch a chill on your run."

"I won't, Mom. Oh, and Anthony says hi to you both."

"I'm glad you spoke with him. He was anxious about you. We talked last week, and he did not like the idea of you driving yourself up there alone. Lewis calmed him down, though. I think if he didn't have Elizabeth and the kids, you'd have had a co-pilot."

"That man is crazy, Mom. You raised a crazy bunch of kids."

"Yes, I did, but you're all *my* crazies. Alright, you enjoy your run. Make sure to text me when you get back home, okay? Oh, and Jace and Tyler called looking after you too. Call them this week, all right?"

"Yes, Mother…." Onnie whined with a smile. She loved her family, but having three older brothers as protective as hers could get tiring quickly. "I love you. Thanks for talking."

"Anytime, sweetheart, anytime. Love you too. Say goodbye, Lewis."

"See ya, kid!" He shouted through the phone.

"Talk to you soon, sweetie."

Tory hung up, and Onnie looked down at her phone.

Her screen had a picture of her, Jace, and Tyler covered in marshmallow cream as its wallpaper. The photo was from when the boys had taken their first vacation to see Onnie after they had opened their restaurant. After a few drinks and too many rice krispies, the war started. All three of them had ended up covered in marshmallow, and Onnie had found dried bits on her carpet for weeks after that night.

Jace and Tyler were the youngest of her brothers, and at only two years apart, they were the troublemakers of the family. They ran a five-star restaurant in San Francisco, which had been an enormous success for them. Jace managed the place, while Tyler was the head chef in charge of the kitchen. The two of them were a dream team, which showed in their achievements, but it had been a hard road for them to get there.

Tyler had been in college with his major undeclared for two years when things started to go downhill for him. He had begun drinking more and stopped caring about his school work, and when their Mom found out, she freaked and gave him the lecture of the century. It had been Jace, though, to turn Tyler around. Jace stepped in with a plan for a restaurant they would one day own and run. Apparently, when Tyler was in high school, he confided in Jace that cooking was his dream, and Jace hadn't forgotten their conversation. So, when Jace heard Mom lecturing their brother, he drove over to Tyler's dorm, pounded on the door, and laid out the ground rules. Tyler would clean up his act and go to culinary school, and Jace would change his major to business management. Then, after college, they would open a restaurant together.

Five years later, both had graduated, outlined a solid business plan, and made a deal with Lewis for some startup money. Six months after that, Dreamers opened. In the four years since then, their business hadn't slowed down in the slightest.

Onnie's cell phone screen went dark, and she sighed and stretched her legs. She missed the boys and would have to make it a point to call them on her next day off. Today, she was out of extrovert.

She got to her feet, stretching her back before crossing the room and placing her cup on the breakfast bar. As she made her way into her bedroom, she rubbed a kink in her neck. Now that Onnie had told her Mom she was going for a run, she would feel guilty the next time they talked if she didn't. Besides, she had a long list of trails she wanted to try, and there was no time like the present.

Five minutes later, Onnie's feet hit the cobblestone street. She tucked the ribbon around her neck and into her sweatshirt that carried her house key for safekeeping. Ever since she started running in college, she used it as a form of meditation. She could empty her mind and think of nothing but the wind in her hair and the feel of the ground beneath her feet. She stopped to bend down, double-checked that her shoes were tied, and then took a deep breath of fresh air. The rain had subsided, and the air smelled sweet and crisp. It was the perfect weather for a run. Onnie stood, popped in her headphones, and clicked on her favorite playlist before taking off down the path.

She ran to City Center Park, cut across the grass, and went to the field behind the school. Since her first day in Alku, when she'd seen all the bike trails and footpaths that led into the forest, she had been excited to try running some of them. Her Grandfather had mentioned that some of the most significant houses in Alku lay within that forest or skirted the town's southern edge. Evidently, the southern portion of Alku was primarily agricultural, and some residents had large barns that housed a wide variety of animals. A few bred horses and occasionally took them for rides through the forest on sunny days.

As the ground blurred beneath her feet, Onnie giggled at her running shoes' squelching noises on the wet grass. Never having had that problem when she ran streets, she skipped back to a mulch path that seemed safer. The forest came into view, and Onnie tilted her head back, attempting to see the tops of the trees. Dew lined their branches and twinkled in the sun as if they were waving at her in greeting.

Usually, Onnie kept her head empty when she ran, and nothing mattered except the path in front of her, but today, she couldn't zone it all out. Every little thing drew her attention.

She was two miles into her run when she wished she'd remembered to bring a water bottle. Dehydrated and unable to ignore it, she slowed to a jog. She removed one of her earbuds and lowered the volume of her music, observing the forest around her.

The trees were thick, and thin shafts of light twinkled down from the canopy above. Small animals skittered into the underbrush as she passed, and she had to skip over a few slugs that looked like something out of a storybook or maybe a horror story. With the rain paused, birds sang and flitted around from place to place, taking advantage of the sunshine. Everything smelled alive and vibrant. Life teemed around her, and Onnie couldn't think of a time when she'd been this entrenched in it.

Over the years, Onnie had managed to piece together that one day, Grandpa admitted to no longer being able to give her Grandmother what she deserved, so they divorced. Her Grandmother decided to take her only child somewhere new to start over, so they moved to southern California when Tory was only fourteen.

When Onnie was growing up, it was rare that anyone would talk about the time they'd lived in Alku, but when her Grandmother mentioned it, she always had a melancholy voice that made Onnie grieve for her. Her Grandmother had always said she and Abbot weren't the right fit for each other and that he deserved to be happy with someone he could fully love. Her Grandmother, however, had never gotten over him, and everyone tried not to bring up the woman's only love. Even though Abbot had kept in touch with her Grandmother over the years, Onnie's Mom never really forgave him for breaking up their family, and she never visited him in Alku.

Now, as Onnie jogged through the towering trees and the clean-smelling leaves, she wished things had turned out differently for her Grandparents. In Alku, Onnie felt like she could enjoy the company of herself without feeling the need to explain her reasoning or make excuses to other people. The freedom to be who she wanted to be was intoxicating, and she knew her Grandmother would have been proud of her, including for reconnecting with the man who broke her heart.

Onnie jogged around a bend in the trail and stopped at a fork along the path. A smaller footpath branched off from the main one she'd been on and headed in another direction. Blackberry vines covered the rarely used trail, but it looked as though someone had pushed past them recently.

"Why not take the road less traveled?" Onnie said, chuckling as she picked her way carefully through the thorns and followed the path as it swerved between trees and shrubs. A few hundred feet later, it opened into a large clearing surrounded by a ring of pine trees.

Onnie stopped short and blinked from the sudden light that streamed through the canopy, blinding her. The ground was soft, and the bright green moss covered it as a blanket would a freshly made bed.

Onnie sucked in her breath, overwhelmed by the magnificence before her, and slowly turned in circles as she looked up at the treetops and tried to take it all in.

"Oh, wow...it's breathtaking!"

Mushrooms the size of tea saucers clumped together near the base of the trees, and moss crept up their trunks in every shade of green imaginable. The trees were so tall that when Onnie craned her neck back, she could see their tops, and they seemed to be leaning in on one another as if for support. Even their branches were intertwined, woven together, holding hands as if they danced in a circle. All of the life around her completely overtook Onnie. She sat down on a large rock in the center of the ring and continued to stare, her eyes darting from one spectacular sight to the next.

She leaned over and ran her hand atop the moss at her feet, feeling the cold dampness and inhaling when her touch released the plant's crisp, earthy smell. When she looked up to dry her palm on her running pants, a squirrel chittered at her from the base of a tree before picking up a nut and running off. Above the squirrel was a family of tiny birds that chirped at Onnie before flying to the branch nearest her. She looked up at them and giggled when they flew in lazy circles above her before landing back on their original branch and settling down for a nap.

"I wish I had my book. This is an excellent spot to read. I wonder if Grandfather knows about this place?" She took out her cell phone from her sweatshirt pocket to take some pictures to show at dinner, but a rustling noise from across the clearing stopped her hand, and she held her breath. She stood and prepared to run if needed, but when she looked over her shoulder for the path where she entered the clearing, she realized it wasn't there. All the trees seemed to look the same, and when she looked carefully at the moss on the ground, her footsteps had disappeared as the supple material had rebounded quickly.

"Crap! Leave it to me to enter a forest and not mark my path." She turned back to the direction the commotion was coming from, bracing herself for whatever was making the sound as it came towards her. "Here's to hoping whatever can make that much noise is friendly. Please don't let it be a bear. Or a giant cat. Cats are bad, too."

She took a few deep breaths, trying to calm her racing heart, the rustling nearly upon her, then as quickly as it started, it stopped. The silence felt out of place, and the clearing suddenly felt smaller. The air stilled, and the trees held their breath with her.

Onnie broke the thick silence, "Hello? Is anybody there?" She fidgeted from one foot to another, ready to sprint. "Hello?"

The rustling began again, but quieter, and she assumed whatever it was must have started walking. It still moved towards her but no longer sounded like it was bumbling around. Onnie tensed as a man in running clothes stepped from behind the tree across from her, headphones in his ears and utterly oblivious to her presence.

"Oh, thank god! You scared the crap out of me!" Onnie said with a deep breath, doubling over in relief and resting her palms on her thighs.

The man across the clearing stopped walking, and when he looked up and saw Onnie for the first time, he jumped back and ripped out his headphones before clutching his heart. "Shit!"

"Whoa there!" Onnie said with her hands out before her, warding off the stranger. "You stumbled into me, remember? Breathe." As Onnie spoke, she took a few steps closer to the runner. "Are you okay?"

The man was breathing raggedly, and Onnie could see the flush on his face even with him bent over, attempting to catch his breath.

"I didn't mean to startle you. I had no idea you had headphones in, but now it makes sense why you made so much noise." When she was close enough to see his face, Onnie stopped, "Gabriel?"

The man's eyes shot up to hers, and now that she was standing directly before him, he took the time to look at her. "It's you!"

Embarrassed that he not only remembered her but recognized her from her stint of eavesdropping, Onnie stepped backward and crossed her arms in front of herself. "You don't have to shout at me."

"You were the one listening through the shelf of scrolls when I was talking to Bec."

"Sorry, yes, I work at the bookstore. My Grandfather owns it."

"No big deal. Wait.... Did you say the old man is your Grandfather?"

Onnie curled her hands into fists and put them on her hips. "Yes, isn't that what I just said?"

"You're Onnie."

"Yeah, I am. Did you hear that from Rebecca or someone else on the town gossip circle?"

Gabriel ignored her and stared at her for long enough that she became uncomfortable. Then he brushed past her to sit on the boulder she'd been on earlier. She turned and watched him as he sat down roughly and cradled his head in his palm, suddenly pale.

She stepped forward and knelt next to his knee, bracing herself on the soft forest floor. "Hey, are you alright? I didn't mean to snap at you. I'm just a little overwhelmed at all the welcome wagon stuff."

Gabriel met her eyes with his own, a slight smile straining on his lips. "Welcome wagon?"

Onnie snorted and looked down to where she was playing in the moss with her fingers. "Yeah, everyone in Alku is friendly. It's kind of creepy that everyone knows who I am. I'm much happier being invisible."

"I doubt you could ever be invisible," Gabriel mumbled under his breath, but Onnie heard it clearly.

She recaptured his stare and glared before biting out, "You don't even know me." Then she stood and turned away from him, pulling out her other headphone and acting busy.

"You're right. I'm sorry. Truce?" He stood and walked around her and held out his hand. "I'm Gabriel, and you are?"

Onnie rolled her eyes but decided to play along. "Onnie. Pleased to meet you." She shook his hand firmly and forced herself to ignore his warm palm against her icy one.

"Likewise. So, Onnie, what brings you to Alku?" Gabriel said, slipping his hands into the front pockets of his jacket.

"Ah, well, my Grandfather is getting older, and he asked me to come to help him run his bookshop, and I said yes."

Gabriel raised one eyebrow questioningly. "Just like that? 'Yes, I'll move and run your shop for you?' No questions asked?"

"He's family," Onnie muttered and shrugged.

"Hm, I wish all families were like that."

Onnie frowned, a crease wrinkling between her brows. "Well, in my opinion, they should be. Blood-related or chosen. Mine hasn't always been here for Grandpa like they should have been, but I'm trying to change that. So yes, when he called, I came. No questions asked."

"He's a lucky man to have you then." Gabriel ran a hand through his sweaty hair and searched the ground with his eyes. "So…."

Onnie crossed her arms and rolled her eyes, his posture clearly screaming that he wanted something. "What?"

"Ah…. Do you run here often?"

"What?" Onnie said, stunned at the one-eighty shift in conversation. "No, this is my first run since I moved here. I found this place by accident and forgot which way I came in. I was just about to go home when your thrashing around stopped me. I thought maybe you were an animal that needed help or something."

"Thrashing around?" He raised one eyebrow at her observation.

She scoffed and smirked at him. "Yeah, you sounded like a bear. Or a wild cat."

"A cat? I thought cats were supposed to be stealthy. I think that makes you more of one than I was. Standing there, waiting for me, ready to pounce on your prey." Gabriel chuckled to himself, and Onnie could feel a flush of embarrassment creep up her neck.

"Oh, trust me, I will not be pouncing on you. You or anyone else, for that matter."

"Ouch! Sheath the claws, little Cat. It was a figure of speech." Gabriel said, raising his hands in a gesture of surrender. "I didn't mean any offense."

Onnie crossed her arms in front of her, and it was her turn to raise one eyebrow. "Yeah, well, you did."

"Fine, Cat, have it your way." Gabriel looked over her shoulder at the ring of trees and attempted to lighten the mood. "Come on. I'll show you home." Gabriel gestured forward with his hand.

"No, thank you. I don't make it a habit of bringing men I don't know to my doorstep. Feel free to point me in the correct direction out of this place, though. That, I would appreciate."

He looked behind and to the left of Onnie, chuckling to himself. "That's a wise precaution, though I assure you, it's wasted on me. I would never harm you. Head that way. Make sure you don't look over your shoulder, or you'll end up right back where you started. Lost."

"Thank you for the advice." She said, relaxing a little. "I'm not used to running on anything but city streets."

Gabriel shook his head, smiling gently at the corners of his lips, "Well, you're in for a treat then. I'm sure you've noticed, but Alku isn't much of a city, and we have quite a few forests."

She smirked, "Somehow, I must have missed that, huh." She tapped her finger against her chin in fake contemplation.

"Well, if you ever need a running partner or are looking for route advice, I'd be happy to help."

He looked genuine, and she softened a bit toward him and nodded. "Thank you. Truly."

Gabriel cleared his throat, "Now that I've helped you, may I ask for your help in return?"

"It depends on the favor you ask of me. If you ask me to pounce on you, the answer is still no. Other than that, yes, go ahead," she teased.

Gabriel snorted but looked like he knew better than to comment. "I'm looking for a book."

"Is this the same one you asked Rebecca about last week?" Onnie said, cutting him off.

Gabriel smiled back at her with a twinkle in his eyes. "Yes, the same one you heard me discussing with Rebecca. It's vital I get it."

Onnie shook her head. "Nope, sorry. It's obvious that you two have a history, and I'm new here and need all the help I can get from her. I am not in a position to piss her off."

"Trust me, you won't piss off Bec, that's practically impossible, but you will make me one thrilled man."

"Tell me why Rebecca won't find it for you herself."

"It's not that she won't find it for me. She says she's tried, but so far, she's not been able to, but it's imperative that I find it. The sooner, the better."

Onnie squared her shoulders and crossed her arms, looking at Gabriel skeptically. "What is it you're not telling me?"

"Nothing. I need a book, and you run the bookshop. I'd get the damn thing straight from the shop, but she won't—"

Onnie's cell phone began ringing so unexpectedly that she jumped. She fumbled it out of her pocket and read the screen before holding up one finger to pause Gabriel. "I'm sorry. Can you hang on a second?"

She stepped back a few paces, putting some distance between them, and answered her phone. "Rebecca, hi. Is Grandfather okay?"

Gabriel Vansand

Gabe could hear mumbling on the other end of Onnie's phone call, and he couldn't help but chuckle at Rebecca's all-too-perfect timing. He should have known better. After a minute or two, he crossed his arms and shook his head. His conversation with Onnie was over. Rebecca had seen to that.

"Yes, of course. I can be there within the hour. Thank you for telling me. No, it's not a problem at all. Okay. Goodbye, Rebecca." Onnie turned and faced him again. Guilt was written subtly into her posture.

"I'm sorry, I have to go. Rain check on that favor? Come by the store, and I'll see what I can do. I'm not making any promises, though."

"Fair enough. It was great to meet you, Cat."

Onnie gestured with her thumb over her shoulder. "This way out, right?"

Gabe nodded before quickly adding, "The old man's alright, right?"

"Yeah, he's okay, just needed a change of scenery, I guess." Onnie turned, jogged towards the section of trees Gabe had indicated previously, and shouted over her shoulder without turning around. "Thanks again for your help!"

Gabe stood and watched Onnie's back as she disappeared into the foliage. Dumbfounded, he looked to the sky, closed his eyes, and let the sun wash over his face. She'd changed a lot from the picture he'd seen of her from her graduation. Eight years was no short time, but even so, he hadn't realized it was her with his cursory interest.

"Looks like your shop found a smart partner for itself. Cat's got good instincts. She didn't turn around." Smiling, he jogged back from where he came, not looking over his shoulder as he left the clearing.

Chapter 6: Peace

October 2021 - Alku | Onnie Moore

Onnie looked up at the sign above the door of The Book Nook and smiled. She'd only been gone less than a day but still missed it. She slipped her phone into her bag and retrieved her keys. Before putting the key into the lock, she hesitated, pressed her palm against the worn wooden door, and pushed it open. Since it was just after closing, Rebecca must have lowered the front lights because it was nearly dark inside the shop, and Onnie had to squint to keep from stepping on the books piled around the door as she entered and stowed her keys again. She closed the door behind her, locked it, and then called out into the shop's quiet, "Rebecca, Grandpa, you here?"

"Back here, dear." Rebecca's voice drifted from deeper within the shop.

Onnie went to the register, slid her bag under the counter, and flipped through the day's inventory log. Apparently, they had received two deliveries of stock a few hours earlier. There were three cases from a well-known publishing house and a single book from a private source. Onnie frowned at having unknowingly missed a perfect opportunity to ask questions about their supply ordering process. She closed the log book before going to the sitting area with the wingback chairs. When she rounded the corner, she smiled, seeing her Grandfather tucked into the largest one with a steaming cup of tea in his weak hands.

He looked up and grinned ear to ear. "Why, hello beautiful, how are you this evening?"

"I'm fine, Grandpa," she said before crossing the room and kissing his cheek gently. "How're you?"

"Oh, nothing to complain about. Felt like getting out of the house for a bit, and Rebecca suggested that dinner here with my girls would make for a pleasant evening."

"A change of scenery never did anyone harm," Onnie said with a smile as she curled up in the chair beside his. Rebecca emerged from between two shelves carrying her usual delicate serving set.

"Exactly. My lovely Rebecca here packed me up, and now here we are. My home away from home." He looked up at Rebecca and snatched a cookie off her tray as she passed.

Rebecca smirked at him from beneath her lashes. "Fiend."

Abbot waggled his eyebrows and threw her a flirtatious wink before biting into the cookie.

Rebecca placed the tea tray on the overstuffed ottoman and refilled Abbot's cup. "Would you like some tea, Onnie? You mustn't catch a chill after your run."

"Yes, please."

Rebecca carefully handed a cup to Onnie. "I hope we didn't ruin any plans you had this evening. Here, I told you to take a day off, and then I called you to come in anyway."

"Thank you," Onnie said warmly. "No, you didn't interrupt anything. I was just going to re-read Peter Pan. I stopped by the library this afternoon and checked it out." She took a small sip of her tea, which was, per usual, the perfect temperature for her. "Do you need help with dinner?"

"No, thank you." Rebecca smiled fondly. "You stay here and keep Abbot company. That's help enough." With a pat on Abbot's shoulder, she left the sitting area.

"I didn't know you were a runner, my dear," Abbot asked while blowing on his tea to cool it.

"Yeah, I haven't had a chance since the move, but I was talking to Mom, and it reminded me of an area I wanted to explore near the school."

"We have some lovely trails in the area, and if I remember correctly, we even have a book or two in here that has maps and the history of the trails. Rebecca could point you to the right place to look for it."

"Thanks! That sounds like fun. I'll make sure to ask her." Onnie watched her Grandfather's hands shake slightly when he lifted his teacup to his lips. "I was talking a bit about the forests with Dany this afternoon, and she mentioned you might know of some good places to try."

"Oh, so you've met our resident librarian, have you? Dany is a spirited one and quite a smart young woman as well." Abbot leaned forward and picked up two more cookies from the plate on the ottoman.

"So, I've noticed." Onnie giggled. "Dany cornered me at the coffee shop my first morning here and was rather enthusiastic about meeting me."

Abbot sputtered into his tea before filling the store with his bellowing laughter. "Yes, that sounds like our Dany. Forthcoming and overly excitable. I'd best apologize to you then, my dear, for her excitement was my doing. She's a special young woman to me, and when I knew you were coming for sure, I couldn't help but share in my happiness."

Onnie blushed but couldn't fault the older man for his

oversharing. "Grandpa…just how many people did you tell I was coming?" she said teasingly.

"Oh, just everyone who would listen, dear," Rebecca said as she came around the bookcases. She carried a fresh plate of cookies and sat them on the tiny table by Onnie, well out of reach of Abbot. "These are for Onnie," she scolded, pointing her finger at Abbot. "You just wait for dinner, mister."

Abbot pouted and bent his head to blow bubbles in his tea.

"See if I let you out of the house anymore," Rebecca grumbled as she left the sitting area.

Onnie giggled at the pair as she lifted her teacup and inhaled the familiar aroma. "What kind of tea is this, Grandpa? Rebecca made it for me the first day I came into the store, too. It smells amazing, but there's an underlying ingredient in it that I can't seem to place."

"This is a unique blend. She makes it herself. I didn't realize you knew so much about tea."

Onnie picked up a cookie for herself before sneaking one to Abbot, who winked before he bit into it. "Well, I can't really say I know much about it. I just drink a lot of it. I don't like being cold, so I'm not very picky."

"Another interest both you and Rebecca share." Abbot reached over and gently pat Onnie's knee. "It warms this old man's heart to see you two get along so well."

Onnie sipped her tea silently. She didn't know how to respond to that. Sure, she liked Rebecca, but the woman made her feel strange. Being near her felt like seeing something out of the corner of your eye, but when you turned, there was nothing there. There was just something...off...about her. She was too perfect, too polite, and too… calming. Onnie's head felt like it was full of cotton when Rebecca was nearby, and it felt like she was forgetting something.

On top of that, Onnie never really knew how to act around the older woman. It was evident she and Abbot had a romantic relationship, and Onnie didn't mind that part. But Onnie had a Grandmother, and she wasn't looking for a replacement. Rebecca was kind to her Grandfather, helpful and patient, and that's what mattered. Onnie could try to ignore the rest.

"Where did you drift off to, Onnie? I lost you for a moment." Abbot said, dragging her focus back to the dimly lit bookstore.

"What? Oh, sorry, Grandpa, just a daydream. Do you need more tea?"

"No, I'm fine, thank you. Finish yours up. I think I smell dinner coming this way," he said, smiling, closing his eyes to breathe in the aroma drifting in the air.

Sure enough, Rebecca strode around a bookshelf carrying a larger tray than they used for tea. It had fold-out legs, with three bowls, flatware, and wine glasses atop it.

"I hope you two are keeping out of trouble," Rebecca asked, directed at neither of them in particular.

"Absolutely not. What's the point if not to get into a bit of trouble!" Abbot smiled with a mischievous glance at Onnie. "It smells delightful, darling." He added, leaning forward and breathing in the steam that wafted before him.

"Good, I'm so glad," Rebecca chirped while popping the legs out on the bulky standing tray.

"Would you like any help?" Onnie offered politely.

"No, thank you, dear. This will take but a second." Rebecca began setting up smaller, personal folding trays and passing out their meals.

Onnie resigned herself to being waited on, and while her Grandfather quietly chatted with Rebecca, it allowed Onnie to observe him relatively unnoticed. The little old man had seemed so frail a week ago, all wrapped up in blankets to keep some warmth in his bones.

Today, he appeared to have a rosy color to his cheeks, and his clothes fit him more snugly. He had ditched his flannel pants, sweatshirt, and slippers for a vest and trousers from a three-piece suit complete with a pocket watch and cufflinks. He had even tucked a small yellow silk square in his breast pocket. Onnie glanced down and saw his shoes shined and dress socks peeked from under his pant legs. If Onnie hadn't known better, she would have thought the man in front of her was the healthy twin of the one she'd met the week prior.

"Onnie dear, here's your soup," Rebecca said, placing a folding tray neatly in front of Onnie.

She looked down at the beautiful china bowl that matched her teacup and grinned at the clam chowder that filled it. "Thanks, Rebecca. This is one of my favorites."

"I know, dear. Now eat up before it gets cold."

Onnie was suddenly famished and attributed it to her earlier run. Each bite of the creamy soup she took seemed better than the last, and the warmth drifted down to her toes.

"You've outdone yourself, Bec. This is superb," Abbot said before patting his lips with a cloth napkin.

Rebecca smiled as she began to eat.

Onnie couldn't disagree with her Grandfather's statement from earlier. It was nice to get a change of scenery, and seeing him inside the bookshop had settled Onnie's anxiety. The anxiety she hadn't realized she'd been carrying. Hopefully, he'd be up to more nights like this one in the future. Onnie felt her brow crinkle, and she frowned, "Ah… Rebecca?"

"Yes?" The woman answered as she swirled her spoon in her soup and cleaned off the back of the utensil before popping it into her mouth delicately.

"Where did you cook the food?"

Onnie saw Abbot's fork stop halfway to his mouth, and he looked over at Rebecca, the nervous flash in his eye unmissable.

"At home, of course. I simply reheated it when we arrived. We have a small hot plate in the back that your Grandfather used to use for his lunches." Rebecca replied as she prepped another spoonful of soup. "Why do you ask?"

"Ah, no reason. Curiosity, I guess."

"Would you like some wine, Onnie?" Her Grandfather abruptly interrupted as he picked up the uncorked bottle from the larger tray.

Onnie nodded spoon still in her mouth. "Yes, please," she said after she'd swallowed.

Abbot filled her glass, Rebecca's, and then his own, replacing the bottle on the tray. He lifted his glass and smiled. "Toast!" His eyes twinkled in the dim lamplight, and Onnie rushed to raise her glass with his. "To finally having all my girls in one place! May there be many more evenings spent together!" Abbot raised his glass to the ceiling and reached across the ottoman to clink with Onnie's and then Rebecca's.

The three of them each took a sip, and Onnie closed her eyes. Her whole body began to tingle, and a warmth started in her chest and radiated outwards.

"Mmm…this wine is excellent. I think it's doing a better job warming me up than the tea did." Onnie's eyes widened with worry as she realized how that might have sounded. "Sorry Rebecca, I mean your tea is excellent…"

Rebecca reached her free hand over to clasp Abbot's, smiling back at Onnie. "Think nothing of it, but I have a feeling the warmth you're experiencing has more to do with the toast than the wine."

Onnie felt herself blush, and she hid a smile behind her wine glass.

"Perhaps you're right," Abbot said, placing his glass on the tray before him and closing his eyes.

Onnie watched him as his expression slowly softened, and a smile crept into his features.

"Yes, perhaps you're right," he mumbled again, his eyes still closed.

Chapter 7: Questioning

November 2021 - Alku | Gabriel Vansand

Gabe rubbed his neck to work out a kink he'd acquired from watching Onnie across the school field. She was out for a run, and today was the only bright day in weeks, so he was envious. The sun glinted off her jet-black hair, a braid running down the middle of her back. She was fit and athletic, and her energy suited her witty personality. He had enjoyed teasing her when they'd bumped into one another in Wayward Clearing, and he knew if he weren't careful, life would get far more complicated very quickly.

He watched her as she ran down the path that bordered the back of the school fields, passing his students with a smile and a small wave. When she passed a young girl named Miranda, sitting on the grass alone, Onnie stopped and walked back over to her. While he knew that anyone Abbot trusted wouldn't hurt any of his students, Gabe observed them nonetheless.

Miranda held up her shoelaces and stuck her bottom lip out to pout. Onnie nodded in understanding of the little girl's plight and sat down on the grass beside her. For the next fifteen minutes, the two of them giggled together while Onnie taught Miranda how to tie her shoes on her own.

When they finally reached their feet, Miranda hugged Onnie and darted across the field and toward him with a broad smile. He'd never seen the girl this expressive before as she plonked her butt on the cement and untied her shoes in front of him.

"Miss Onnie taught me how to tie my shoes. Wanna see!" She said in a small, soft voice that Gabe was unaccustomed to hearing, but he somehow managed to keep his expression neutral.

"Sure, show me," Gabe said, playing along and squatting beside her.

She'd only gotten through step one of her explanation when the bell rang, signaling the end of morning recess. Miranda quickly tied both shoes expertly and then happily hopped up and ran off.

Gabe stood there with his mouth hanging open as he watched Miranda's back until she disappeared into her classroom. He turned to see if Onnie had made it to the tree line yet, guessing she had but wishing she hadn't. When he saw the empty field, he was annoyed he'd not thought to ask for her number. Abbot would undoubtedly have it, but Gabe was sure that Onnie would freak out if he called her out of the blue. Even if he only wanted to ask her what had just happened.

Gabe scanned the school grounds to check for straggling kids, trying to delay their return to class, but was pleased to see the nearly one hundred children seemed to have granted him a reprieve that morning.

He pulled out his phone and checked it, more out of habit than expecting a missed call. He'd called Bec the day before, but not unsurprisingly, she'd still not found the book he needed. With indeed zero missed calls, Gabe sighed and slipped his phone back into his pocket, only to jump when it began vibrating. Abbot's home number was displayed on the glass screen, and he answered as he walked to a moderately sized building off to one side of the field that functioned as the school's gymnasium.

"Hey, old man, how's it going?"

"Gabriel, my boy, is that you? I've forgotten what your voice sounds like." Abbot's low rolling laugh came through the phone.

"Hey, now, that's not fair. I hear you've been mighty busy with that Granddaughter of yours. What would you need me around for?"

Abbot growled, "Boy, you better not be thinking that. Don't make me come over there and talk some sense into you. I may be old, but I'll never be too busy for you."

Gabe flinched at the pain in the man's voice. He hadn't meant to imply anything or hurt the old man, far from it. "I know, sorry, Abbot. I didn't mean it that way. This whole waiting game has me all upside down. I'm not thinking clearly."

Abbot sighed and whispered thank you to someone beside him, likely Sam, who had probably brought him a fresh cup of tea. "I know this is hard on you, Gabe. She'll get there. Soon enough, you will both be ready, and everything will change."

"So you all keep telling me." Gabe picked up an abandoned football from the grass and then pushed through the gym doors and into its brightly lit interior.

The old man sighed, "Don't go wishing for something that you may not like the outcome of."

"We've been waiting for the Transference to happen for years now. I want to get it over with and move on with our lives."

"It doesn't work that way. You know that once the Transference begins, nothing will be the same. As you so eloquently phrased it, you won't be able to 'get on with your life.'"

"I know, I know." Gabe threw the football across the gym into a large trash can full of other sporting equipment. "How's Bec?"

"She's fine. She's at the shop today since it's Onnie's day off. I swear, Gabe, Onnie would never leave the store if we didn't force her to go home and sleep."

"Oh?" Gabe asked with genuine curiosity.

"She's strong, Gabe. I'm not sure how that will affect the shop, but I am excited to see what comes of it."

Gabe pulled his keys from his pocket and unlocked the door to his office. He flipped on the fluorescent lights overhead and propped open his door before making his way to his desk and lowering himself into his chair with a grunt. "I'm not sure, Abbot. She's smart and seems to have good instincts. I'll give her that, but she seems…young."

Abbot roared with laughter, causing Gabe to hold the phone away from his face and rub his forehead in frustration. "Boy, I love you and may have raised you, but sometimes you're thick."

Gabe rubbed his temples.

"Onnie has not had an easy life. In fact, you may want to ask her about it before you jump to conclusions about her. You might find you have more in common than you think. And though she may look young, she is, in fact, far more mature of spirit than you give her credit for."

"Ugh, you're making me sound like a jackass, Abbot." Gabe placed his feet on his desk and leaned back in his chair.

"Then stop acting like one," the older man said without hesitation.

Gabe growled into the phone and was startled by a knock on his office door. He looked up, and Dany was leaning on the door frame with a crooked grin on her lips.

"And what's different about you being a jackass today than any other day?" She said, crossing her arms. "Hi, Abbot." She called out with a raised voice.

"Oh, is that Dany! Tell her I said hello." Abbot replied.

"Tell her yourself," Gabe placed his cell phone on the desk and hit the speaker button, "I've put you on speaker."

"Hello, my dear. How are you on this rare sunny November day."

Dany crossed the room and slipped into one of the beat-up chairs typically reserved for Gabe's students. "Just dandy, Abbot. Missin' seeing your special face at the library meetings."

Gabe rolled his eyes and smiled. Dany and Abbot were a pair to behold. Dany was an endless flirt, and Abbot was none too shy himself.

"Well, I miss you too. We'll have to get together for dinner sometime soon, perhaps a big Thanksgiving feast!"

Dany smiled, and Gabe could tell by Abbot's tone his own was likely just as big.

"That sounds amazing! I'd love to see you, and I won't complain about spending more time with Onnie either."

"I'm so glad you two are hitting it off. She needs a few good friends in her life."

Gabe tapped his keyboard to wake his computer from sleep mode and checked his email. "I hate to interrupt you two, but I have a class to teach in fifteen minutes that I need to prep for."

Dany stuck out her tongue and made a raspberry sound, and Abbot chuckled. "Alright, my boy, I get it. Well, you teach those youngsters something good and do what I suggested, talk to Onnie. Get to know her, and she may surprise you."

"I will."

"Bye, Abbot!" Dany yelled into the phone while she physically waved at it.

Abbot laughed before saying goodbye and hanging up, leaving Gabe to turn off his phone and look at Dany questioningly.

"What's up, Dany? You never come to visit during the day, so to what do I owe the pleasure?"

Dany leaned back and stuck her leather boots up on his desk

corner. "What? Can't a fellow educator come to chat with her colleague?"

Gabe rolled his eyes and crossed his arms, leveling a look at her that would scare a lesser being. "No."

"What about a sister?" Dany said with a frown.

Gabe only blinked.

"Ugg." Dany scoffed and lowered her feet. "Fine, I wanted to know if you were alright. You've been distant with Abbot, angry with Bec, and I can't remember the last time we went for coffee."

Gabe uncrossed his arms and stood up, locking his computer and walking around the desk. "You're right. I'm sorry." He pulled Dany to her feet and wrapped his arms around her.

Dany frowned and punched him in the arm. "Sometimes you're dense."

"I know. Come on. I've got a few minutes before class. I'll treat you to a bad cup of coffee from the teacher's lounge."

"Blegh, no thanks, that swill is nasty, but I'll help you set up for class." She kissed his cheek and linked her arm with his. "What's the game today?"

Gabe led the way into the gym, closing his office door behind them and locking it. "I figured it's nice out, so I'll give them a break. Tag for the little ones and baseball for the high schoolers."

Dany giggled and jumped up and down next to him. "Tag! Can I join?"

Gabe chuckled at his sister's antics and tugged on her twin blue pigtails. "These kids fight dirty. You may mess up your cute outfit."

Dropping her jaw in mock offense, Dany scoffed. "Pfft, I can take um."

They kept walking until they reached the main campus building, neither speaking until he cleared his throat. "So…Miranda talked with

Onnie today." Gabe saw Dany's head swivel in his direction with raised eyebrows.

"Oh? Where'd they have a chance to do that?"

"Right over there," Gabe said, indicating the edge of the field with his chin, "Miranda was near tears over an untied shoelace, and Onnie stopped to teach her how to tie them."

"Really, and how did that go?"

"Miranda seemed to enjoy it. They giggled, and when the bell rang, she ran over to me and told me to watch as she showed me what Onnie had taught her."

Dany stopped in the middle of the field, causing Gabe to turn and look at her. "She spoke to you?"

Gabe nodded and slipped his hands into his pockets. "And apparently to Onnie, too. I'm not even sure Onnie knew Miranda was mute."

"Wow." Dany closed her eyes and tilted her face to the sky, a shaft of light highlighting her cheeks. "She's the one, Gabe. Can't you feel it?"

He rolled his eyes. "No, I can't."

Dany lifted one eyelid and looked at his brooding expression. "You're hiding something from me."

Gabe turned and began walking away from the field to collect the second-grade students. "Come on, are you playing tag with us or not?"

"You like her."

"I do not," he said, spinning around to face his sister.

She opened her other eye and looked at him directly, "Liar."

He turned around and called over his shoulder, "I'm going to go get the kids."

"I'll be here when you guys get back."

Gabe nodded and entered the school's main building. "Damn, Dany, you see too much." He stopped before a door decorated with brightly colored papers and a dozen painted handprints. "If Onnie is the one, I should keep my distance. She'll need my strength, nothing else." He roughly pulled his hand through his hair and then gently tugged at the ends. "I need to keep my priorities straight."

With a soft knock, he pushed open the door and smiled as the cheers of twelve munchkins greeted him.

Chapter 8: Adjusting

November 2021 - Alku | Onnie Moore

Onnie uncontrollably grinned while unlocking the newly familiar green door to the bookshop. When she pushed it open, she took a deep breath, inhaling the smell of leather bindings and hand-crafted papers that filled the room. A month had passed since Onnie first stepped through the bookshop's door, and every time she entered it, she was thankful it had become part of her life.

The time spent in the bookshop was precious to her, and Onnie hated hearing the antique clock strike seven every evening, telling her to close and go home. Every night, she would reluctantly clean up and prep for the next day, dragging her feet as if to force the clock to move slower. When everything was perfect, and she couldn't find another thing to support her excuse to stay, she would turn down the lights, lock the front door, and begin her walk home, ticking down the minutes in her head until morning.

That morning, for some reason, as Onnie looked around the shop's main room, the typical tranquility she usually felt was replaced with a sense of urgency. When she tried to pinpoint the cause and couldn't, she brushed it off as arrant anxiety with a smile.

"Rebecca, you here?" Onnie called out into the dimly lit room.

Silence being the only answer Onnie received, she walked past the rows of shelves and down the center aisle. "Guess it's just us today," she spoke aloud to the shop, which had become her best friend over the weeks. She wasn't sure when she'd begun talking to it, but Onnie thought it felt right.

As she walked, she began turning on the glass lamps as she passed them and then flopped her bag on the front counter once she'd reached it. All the lamps tucked between the bookshelves were electric and merely look-a-likes to their older oil-burning ancestors. However, the beautiful brass lamp atop the counter was a genuine oil-burning antique, so Onnie reached beneath the counter for a box of wooden matches she'd tucked there.

On her first visit to the shop, the lamp was already alight, and Onnie hadn't realized it was authentic. When she came in the following morning, she searched for the matches for over an hour before finding them buried under an old tea set in the back room.

Lighting the thick braided wick was a highlight of Onnie's morning routine, and she carefully removed the sizable bulbous glass cover. Once it was free of the base, she softly ran her fingers over the delicate etching that flowed around it in patterns of vines and leaves. She set it aside and removed a match, striking it on the side of the box before lighting the near-finger-thick rope wick. After the flame caught, she replaced the glass cover and stuck the matchbox into her back pocket.

Onnie leaned on the counter and spaced out at the flame. Though the lamp gave off little to no warmth, she still felt like it did. The light filled the space around her, and only once it did did Onnie feel like the shop was truly awake for the day.

The soft ringing of the store's phone came from deeper within the back room, and Onnie jogged over and picked it up from its charging dock.

"Hello, The Book Nook. This is Onnie speaking. How may I help you today?"

"Why, good morning, dear."

"Oh, hello, Rebecca. How are you today?"

"I'm just lovely, sweetheart. Thank you for asking. Your Grandfather, on the other hand, is not feeling his best. He'd like for you to close the shop early this afternoon and bring him some of the tea I blended for him. I keep it under the counter in a red tin. Can you see it?"

"Is he okay?" Onnie asked as she made her way back into the main room.

"Oh yes, he's just a bit more tired today than usual, and silly me, I forgot the fresh tea I put together yesterday at the shop."

Squatting down, Onnie lifted the stock logbook and moved aside a few returned Harlequin paperbacks and two aging scrolls sealed with wax. "Alright, if you're sure."

"I promise he'll be right as rain after a good cup of tea." Rebecca's enthusiasm helped to put Onnie's mind at ease.

"Alright, I'm at the counter. Umm…I don't think I see—"

"Oh…." sighed Rebecca regrettably.

"Wait," Onnie lifted a black leather-bound book and moved it on top of the Harlequin novels. "Yeah, I think this is it. Is the tin shaped like a cut gemstone?"

"Yes, oh, how delightful! Thank you, my dear. Your Grandfather will be thrilled. We will see you at three this afternoon, then."

"Yes, of course. Are you sure he's alright? Do you want me to come earlier?"

"That's alright. He's got enough left at home to make it until this afternoon. Don't you worry. Have a good day. Goodbye."

"Ah…bye, Rebecca."

Onnie moved the phone from beside her cheek and frowned at it. She set the phone on the top shelf under the counter and slipped the tea tin into her bag so she wouldn't forget it later.

Before Onnie could worry any further about her Grandfather, the clock began to chime by the front door, signaling it was time for her to open the shop. She pushed aside her fears over her Grandfather, trusting Rebecca would have told her if she needed to worry. It seemed like nothing could dampen her mood, and Onnie bounced around the counter and over to the front door. She opened it and grinned out at the gloomy November day.

"Bite me, you stupid clouds. I'm happy, and there's nothing you can do about it!"

"You tell 'em, girlfriend!" Dany said from where she stood, leaning against the brick siding of the bookshop.

Onnie jumped and smacked her hand over her mouth, involuntarily yelping as she did so.

Dany roared with laughter and bent down to pick up two paper coffee cups. "Sorry about that. I'll make it up to you…." She smiled and handed Onnie one of the cups.

"Oh, my god! You scared me half to death!"

"Yeah, well, you shouldn't go around throwing out insults if you don't want people to retaliate."

Onnie growled but stopped to sniff the coffee. "Is this?"

"Cinnamon latte with half coconut milk, yes," Dany said before sipping from her own cup.

Onnie took a sip and sighed as her eyes rolled back. "What did I do to deserve this slice of heaven in a cup?"

"Who said you did anything? Can't a girl just bring her friend a coffee?"

"No." Onnie passed her cup back to Dany for her to hold while

Onnie pulled out a rickety a-frame sign from just inside the shop and placed it outside near the door. When she went to take her cup back from Dany, the woman twirled away and out of Onnie's reach. "Oh, don't play with me." Onnie groaned. "Give it back."

"Fine, I lied. I want something from you, give it to me, and you can have your coffee back." Dany's eyes glinted with mischief as she danced from one motorcycle boot to another.

"It's yours." Onnie crossed her arms and glared at the closest thing she'd ever called a girlfriend. "You're evil. What do you want?"

Dany stopped and stuck out her bottom lip in a pout. "Can I be your friend?" She laughed before handing back the coffee to Onnie and stepping inside the shop.

"Ugg, you're nuts," Onnie smiled before taking one last deep breath of the fresh air and following Dany back into The Book Nook.

Dany shrugged off her cropped leather jacket and hung it on the coat rack by the door before wandering to the science fiction section.

"Give me a second to finish opening up, and then you can tell me why you're bribing me," Onnie said as Dany disappeared around a bookcase.

"Take your time."

Onnie sipped her coffee as she walked over to the rare book section and opened a small stained-glass window nearly obscured by two overbearing shelves on either side. The design was of an owl perched on a tree branch framed by jasmine vines in bloom twisting around itself. The background was clear glass and served to let in the blue sky from outside. This hidden beauty was just one of the many surprises Onnie had found once she began to explore the shop when it was quiet. She found it strange, even though Onnie spent a lot of time in the rare book section, but she hadn't noticed the window the first few times she had opened the shop. She only saw it when she tripped over a stack of botany books and caught herself on the shelf beside it.

Onnie set her coffee on a short table pushed against the wall underneath the window. The table was flanked on either side by two carved wooden shelves, and the size disparity made Onnie think of a child holding hands between their parents as they walked. Inside the tiny drawer at the front of the table, Onnie retrieved a long, thin box and removed a single vanilla incense stick. She placed it into the holder on the window's ledge and used one of the matches from the box she'd stuffed in her back pocket earlier. She shook the match out, her eyes not leaving the swirling smoke drifting lazily off the stick before fluttering in and out of the window.

She felt when Dany came to stand beside her. "Is that the incense we bought last week?" her friend asked.

"Yeah, it smells amazing, doesn't it?"

"It does," Dany said, seeming to join Onnie in her smoke-staring activity.

One day after work, Dany had insisted that the two of them buy some things for Onnie's bare apartment. They had wandered in and out of the stores along one of Alku's main shopping streets and found a small shop that sold candles and body products. Onnie had found a few candles she'd taken home and the incense she'd brought into the shop. She couldn't resist the creamy vanilla scent, and even though she'd never burned incense before, she gave in and bought them, too.

Onnie pulled herself away from the smoke and picked her coffee back up. She used her cup to hide behind as she inspected her friend's faraway expression. "What's up, Dany?"

Full of evident reluctance, Dany sighed and turned to look at Onnie. "Can I stay with you over Thanksgiving?"

"Sure," Onnie answered without hesitation.

"Really?" Dany asked, visibly startled, probably by Onnie's immediate response.

Onnie smiled and turned to lead the way to the sitting area in the shop's back corner. "Duh."

"No questions asked?"

Onnie sat in the emerald green wingback and shook her head. "Nope, not unless you want me to ask questions."

Dany sat down in the chair next to her and shrugged. "Ah…not really?"

"Okay then, but while I appreciate it, coffee wasn't necessary for the record." Onnie had never seen Dany blush before, and for some reason, it made her worry for her friend even more. It was apparent Dany didn't want Onnie asking questions, and she wouldn't, but she was still worried. She couldn't help it.

"I told you I wouldn't ask, and I won't, but you know you can tell me if you want to, right?"

Dany smiled and snuggled into the chair, "Yeah, I know. Thanks, Onnie."

"Mmhmm," Onnie said, closing her eyes and savoring her coffee.

They chatted briefly about local gossip until the shop's phone began ringing.

"Damn, I'll be right back." Onnie groaned, quickly getting to her feet.

Dany nodded and pulled out her phone as Onnie returned to the counter and retrieved the shop's phone for the second time that day.

"Hello, The Book Nook. This is Onnie speaking. How may I help you today?"

A delicate feminine voice began asking about the latest historical romance releases, and Onnie answered the patron's questions as she walked back to the sitting area.

"Unfortunately, we will not be stocking that author until the paperback release date."

Dany raised her eyebrows and smirked when Onnie rolled her eyes.

"I agree. If you'd like, I can place your name on our waiting list and call you when that book becomes available."

Onnie sipped her coffee and smiled. "Next week."

Dany's phone began vibrating, and she frantically started texting back whoever had messaged her, causing Onnie to frown.

"Perfect, I'll see you next week then. Have a good day." Onnie hung up the phone, set it on the ottoman, and then took another gulp of her coffee.

"Another satisfied customer?" Dany said, still texting.

"Yup, coming in next week to buy a new release. What's up with you?" Onnie said, indicating to the phone with the tip of her chin.

"Ugh, nothing. Someone screwed up something at work, and I should go in. I'm trying to get out of it."

Onnie snorted.

"What? It's my day off," Dany whined, "besides, we're busy."

"We are?" Onnie asked with a raised eyebrow.

"Yes." Dany's phone vibrated again, and she frowned yet again.

"Honestly, go deal with it. We can meet tomorrow for drinks or something after work."

"Yeah, I don't think I have a choice. Damn," with one last message sent, Dany stood and slipped her phone into her pocket.

Onnie walked her to the front of the shop, where Dany pulled on her coat. "Crap, I left my empty cup."

"Don't worry. I'll chuck it." Onnie stepped forward for a hug before opening the store's door. "Ew."

The loud pattering of the rain hitting the sidewalk filled the quiet bookshop, and Onnie shivered. "That's some nasty rain."

Worry had creased Dany's brow, but she quickly shook it off. "I'll see you later." She stepped out into the rain and turned around, "Thanks again for letting me stay next week."

"Any time." Onnie waved as Dany pulled up her hood and dashed into the storm.

Chapter 9: Hopeful

November 2021 - Alku | Onnie Moore

When the clock chimed noon, splintering the quiet atmosphere, Onnie returned to the front counter and set the box of new stock on the floor behind it. Her back was stiff and protesting from all the bending over she'd done while shelving that morning. With a deep inhale, she reached over her head and stretched onto her toes.

After Dany had left, a wet and unhappy delivery man had arrived, bringing Onnie two dozen new boxes of bound adventures to look after, and they had kept her busy for the rest of the morning.

At the apex of her stretch, the base of Onnie's neck began to tingle, so she lowered herself back to the flats of her feet and tipped her head to the side. She rubbed just below her hairline and glanced towards the front of the store. Her eyes closed, and she palpated her sore muscles until the creaking sound of the wooden front door opening interrupted her small respite.

Onnie's eyes snapped open, and she narrowed her gaze at the silhouette of a massive man in the doorway. The stormy sky behind him framed his broad shoulders and exceptional height before he entered the shop and closed the door behind himself. He pulled back his jacket hood and shook out his wet hair, sprinkling water in a shower around him.

"Excuse me, can I help you?" Onnie shouted across the store as she tried to remain polite. Paper and water didn't mix, and she fought the urge to scream at him for his carelessness.

The stranger slipped off his jacket and hung it on the coat rack next to hers before turning to face the front counter. "I sure hope you can, little Cat." Gabriel quipped as he strode forward with a confidence he'd never had in their prior meetings.

"Gabriel?" flabbergasted, Onnie raked her eyes up and down the man before her.

The last time she'd seen him up close was that day in the forest clearing. He had the body of a runner then, lean and trim. Not anymore. His shoulders had widened and rippled with muscles that Onnie could see through his tight thermal shirt. His legs were no longer that of a casual runner but someone who could outrun and destroy their target. All the added girth made him seem far taller than before, even at six and a half feet. "Holy crap…you're huge!"

Gabriel reached the counter and looked down at Onnie with a smirk. "Come on...it's not that different."

Onnie merely nodded, still trying to process the changes she saw. There is no way this could be the same Gabriel from the forest. No one could hulk up that much, that quickly.

Gabriel waved his hand in front of her face and teased her, "Earth to Cat...come in…. Honestly, woman, you're going to make me blush."

Realizing she had been blatantly ogling him, Onnie was the one to blush and look away. "Can I help you with something today? Or did you just stop by for an ego boost?"

"I really hope you can." He said, leaning on the counter mere feet from her, causing Onnie to turn a deeper shade of red and step back. "You still owe me a favor, little Cat."

"Yes, well, it's been a month, and it looks like quite a lot has changed for you. I'm sure someone else can help you with whatever it is you desire." She crossed her arms in front of her, angry at him for his unwarranted advances as much as she was at herself for liking them.

"Oh, Cat, snarky does not become you."

Onnie smirked back at Gabriel, "Desperation looks perfect on you."

"I wouldn't doubt it. I've become familiar with desperation recently. That's why I'm here. I need you to find something for me. Unless Bec's hiding in here somewhere." Gabriel looked around the store for any sign of the older woman.

"No, she's not here today, just me. What are you looking for exactly?"

"A book, like I told you that day in the forest." Gabriel returned his focus to Onnie and smiled. "You did well, by the way. You didn't turn around."

She shrugged, "You told me not to."

"And you trusted me. That's refreshing, thank you." Gabriel slipped his hands into the front pocket of his jeans and began pacing the space in front of the counter.

Gabriel's comments had Onnie's emotions all over the place and her mind confused. "Is there a reason I should not have trusted you?"

"No, not at all. I'm not a threat to you, and it's nice to see your instincts agree."

"Uh huh...." Onnie bent down, picked up the box of new stock she'd put down earlier, and placed it on the front counter. "I see your ego increased with your size."

"It's not ego, Cat, it's the truth, and besides, I'm simply being honest."

"Fine, whatever. So, what is it with this book you're looking for? I need more information, and so far, you've given me nothing to go off."

Gabriel frowned, presumably at her abrupt change of topic. He had made her uncomfortable, but she didn't say anything, and he didn't push her further.

"I knew you'd come around, Cat," he drummed his long fingers lightly on the countertop between them and smiled. "It's old, leather-bound, I'd assume, and the text is in Latin."

Onnie held her hand up to cut him off, "Wait, you're desperately looking for a book you've never even seen?"

"Yes." Gabriel nodded.

"You've never held it, never read it, and you know nothing about it," she stated more than she asked.

"Exactly, but I know what it contains," Gabriel said with a twinkle in his eye.

Onnie rolled her eyes and crossed her arms. "That's all you know about it? It's old, in Latin, and might be leather-bound. Do you have any idea how many books in this shop that could easily apply to?"

"Yes, even more than you do."

"What's that supposed to mean?" Onnie snapped.

Gabriel frowned and shook his head, "Nothing, Cat. I wasn't trying to offend you." Onnie found herself relaxing when his voice softened, "I only meant that I've been looking for it for a long time. So yes, I know how many books also have those three characteristics."

Onnie rolled her eyes, the remainder of her frustration falling away at his sudden demure tone. "Do you even know the title?"

"Yes, but it's in Latin."

Onnie continued staring at him, waiting for his reply.

"You wouldn't know what it means anyway."

"Why does everyone always assume I'm an idiot," Onnie whispered under her breath. She fisted her hands on her hips and looked deeply into Gabriel's eyes, trying to pour all her confidence into her gaze. "I work in a bookshop, Gabriel. Try me."

He raised his hands in surrender, stepping back from her, leaving her physical room to be angry at him. "Fine, it's *Custos regni.*"

"The Keeper's Reign."

"Gabriel raised his eyebrows, and a small smile crept across his lips, "I'm impressed, Cat."

"Good. You should be. That's an ancient dialect of Latin."

"Is it?" Gabriel asked with evident fake surprise.

"Ugh, you're impossible. Fine!" Onnie threw her hands up. "I'll help you. Let's get this over with."

"Alright, I'll follow you, but for the record," he leaned on the counter towards her, "you're not an idiot, and I never thought you were."

Onnie blushed as she ignored him, walked from behind the counter, grabbed the store phone, and slipped it into her back pocket. Looking over her shoulder, she headed to the front of the shop and the antique book side.

"You do know my name is Onnie, right?" She sat on the floor beside the shelf.

"Oh, I know, Cat." He said, pivoting to lean back on the counter, but his expression looked pained, and he wouldn't meet Onnie's eyes.

"You're hopeless. Let's start looking over here." She shook her head and smiled, pointing him to the first cabinet by the store's door. "You're on top," she said, indicating above her head before quickly adding, "since I can't reach those shelves and I don't feel like going to get the step ladder."

Gabriel's tight expression loosened, and he smirked as he closed the distance between them. "Then you're on the bottom." he dramatically added, "Only because I don't feel like sitting on the floor."

Onnie's stomach started doing backflips in response to their banter, but she ignored it and stoically nodded, "Sounds more than fair." she winced, adding in a hushed voice, "Are you alright, though? You're not...in pain or anything, right?"

"Hmm?" Gabriel replied, and when she snuck a peek at him from the corner of her eye, he was diligently scanning the books on the top shelf as she'd asked.

"Your...body, I mean. That much change to your physiology that quickly must have been painful."

Gabriel tipped his head to look down at her, and when she saw his slightly surprised expression, she felt like a jerk. She was ordinarily friendly to everyone. It was an easy way to stay in the shadows and out of the way, but there'd been something about the man beside her since the moment she'd first seen him that made her practiced obedience fall away.

"I'm fine, but thank you for asking. I'm through the worst of it at this point," Gabriel answered sincerely and then resumed his spine reading.

Onnie nodded and looked at the shelf before her, "You're sure you've never seen the book before?"

"Nope, sadly, I know nothing more than what I've already told you. Until now, she has refused to share any other details with me."

"Ugg." Onnie groaned before shifting her position on the floor and crossing her legs. "This is going to suck, and I think you may owe *me* a favor after this."

Gabriel chuckled, and she looked up at him and smirked. "Also, please try not to drop any of the books on my head."

"I'll do my best. Besides, the old man would be pissed if I hurt his only Granddaughter." Gabriel teased.

"Yeah, he probably would be, but I think he'd have to wait in line behind my three older brothers to get to you."

Gabriel hissed as if in pain. "Ouch, not something I want to envision. I have to admit I'd forgotten you had so many."

Onnie laughed and began running her index finger along the spines of the leather books on the bottom shelf. "So, how do you know Abbot?" she asked before quickly raising a finger. "And don't tell me 'it's a small town,' that only gets you so far."

"Dany's favorite excuse," Gabriel smiled fondly. "She thinks it covers up the fact that she's just as bad of a gossip as the old women of this town."

"Mmmm. Not even a bit." Onnie agreed fondly but paused, "Wait, are you dating Dany or something?"

Gabriel winced and shook his head, "Fuck no!" his eyes widened, and he grinned, "Sorry, no. She's my sister."

Onnie felt her eyes roll, and she shook her head and laughed softly to herself, "Course she is. Small town."

Gabriel shrugged, and they returned to their task.

Just when Onnie thought she'd not be getting an answer, Gabriel cleared his throat, his voice's teasing tone now absent. "I've known Abbot and Bec since I was a kid. My father did business with your Grandfather, and I used to come in with him."

Gabriel pulled a thick leather-bound tome off the shelf, flipped through it for a few seconds, and then slipped it back into its place. "Bec would give me milk and cookies and read me stories while the two men disappeared to do...whatever they did."

"What kind of business does your dad do?"

"He traded antiques, furniture...mostly. The red wingback in the sitting area was one of his finds." Gabriel sighed and returned the book in his hand to the shelf with more force than was necessary. "Eventually, he lost himself in his work and consequently chose to give little of anything to my sister and me."

Onnie snorted, "Yeah, yours and mine both." She looked up to see Gabriel's posture stiff and his face tight with anger.

"Gods damn stupid," he said through clenched teeth.

"Yes, but their choices made us who we are today." Onnie looked away to give Gabriel some privacy.

Quite a few minutes had passed before he sighed, and Onnie felt the air in the shop relax. "Agreed. Dany found her escape in books, which led to her job at the library."

"That's exactly what I meant. She may not have if he'd been more attentive. See, a silver lining," Onnie said as she stacked leather books around her like a miniature battlement.

She could feel Gabriel's eyes on her as he processed her words. Having gone through a similar situation with her birth father, she gave Gabriel a break and didn't tease him further. There was no reason to add salt to a wound that hadn't yet healed. That much was apparent.

She hissed and dropped the book in her hands to her lap, "Ouch!" She blurted and stuck her finger in her mouth to suck on it. She glared at the scratched and pitted book on the floor before her. "Jerk."

"Are you alright?" Gabriel said, squatting down beside her and picking up the offending book. He flipped it over and frowned.

"Yeah, just a stupid paper cut. What book is it?" Onnie said, reaching for it before Gabriel could pull it away. "*Shades and Shadows of the Afterlife.* Well, book, you suck," she said, scolding it.

Gabriel took her wrist and gently inspected her finger with his calloused hands.

"I'm all right," Onnie said, pulling her wrist free from his hold, "Thanks." She picked up the offending book and shoved it back onto the bottom shelf.

"You're sure?" Gabriel asked, his brow furrowed in concern.

"Yup, come on," Onnie shooed him away, "we've still got lots to go through."

Gabriel still looked worried over her simple paper cut but stood and resumed his book hunt above her.

"So, what about your parents? Dad was a jerk, too, I take it?"

"Yeah, my Dad loved his job so much he didn't even notice when my Mom left him. By the time he realized she and us kids were gone, she'd already met Lewis, and none of us wanted or needed someone who didn't want or need *us.*"

Gabriel's hand stopped mid-air, poised to pull out a book, "Really, he didn't notice?"

"Nope, honestly didn't," she said, shaking her head. "And before you think my mom was a tramp or anything, it was nearly three years before she met Lewis."

"Well, it sounds like it was his loss, and you were better off for it."

Onnie slipped the last book back onto the shelf she'd been sorting and got to her feet.

"Gabriel, you don't even know me." She moved to a new shelf, squatted to open its weighty wooden cupboard doors, and began pulling out stacks of leather-bound books. "Let's just stick to finding your book, okay?"

"Fine, Cat. Whatever you want." Gabriel gestured to the next aisle, "I'm going to look over here. Come get me if you find anything."

"Yeah. The shop isn't that big. If it's here, we'll find it soon enough."

Gabriel frowned again and then disappeared around a shelf, and Onnie returned to sorting through the stacks in front of her.

She wasn't sure why she'd snapped at him like she did. Especially since she'd started the conversation in the first place. Onnie was used to people judging her by her cover, she thought as she caressed the front of a beautifully embossed book in her hand. She had three successful brothers, a loving mother and father, and she excelled in school and had an advanced degree to show for it. On the outside, Onnie looked happy and acted warm and inviting. On the inside, she just wished everyone would leave her in peace. She'd been abandoned by one of her parents, the girls around her growing up had only used her to get to her brothers, and all of her past relationships ended with whoever it was telling her she was a two-faced ice princess and not what they signed up for.

Onnie cleared her throat, tears she didn't want or need threatening to rise up and overtake her. "Stop it," she muttered, "Show them all what they want to see, and they'll leave you alone."

"How's it going over there?" Gabriel asked, breaking Onnie out of her harmful thought pattern.

"Fine."

Onnie returned her focus to their wild goose chase, and one by one, she pulled out each book from the cupboard and checked the titles. Dust floated in the air, thicker and thicker with each book she pulled from its bed. The smell of the yellowing papers and fading inks invaded her nose and made her smile sleepily.

Most of the books she checked, Onnie had never heard of before, and when she thumbed through them, they were in some runic language she couldn't read. It took her ten minutes to search the "fictitious language" cupboard as she began calling it and the shelves above it. Then she moved down the row of shelves one by one toward the front counter and searched each. All the books on the next shelf were in either Italian or French, and after a few minutes and a cursory glance to make sure nothing was shelved incorrectly, she moved on.

Slowly and one shelf at a time, she and Gabriel spent the next hour and a half combing through leather-bound books, scrolls of crumbling parchment, and case after case of dusty texts.

Chapter 10: Relief

November 2021 - Alku | Onnie Moore

Onnie leaned forward, laced her fingers around her toes, and pulled out her sore muscles with an audible groan into the otherwise quiet space.

"Any luck yet?" Gabriel's deep voice came from behind her. "Oh," he cleared his throat, "well then." He smirked as he walked down the aisle and leaned against a thick, hand-carved mahogany shelf to admire her backside in a way he couldn't have thought was covert.

Exasperated, Onnie let out a groan. "Gabriel, you do know you're leaning on a shelf full of religious texts, right?

"So?" the man had the decency to blush, at least.

"So…stop checking out my ass." She rolled her eyes and stood up, pulling her sweatshirt down further past her hips. "Well, it's obvious that whatever book you're looking for isn't here."

"So it seems," he said, dragging his fingers over his eyes. "It should be here. It *needs* to be here."

"Look, I could use a break. We've been hunting for a needle in a haystack for over an hour. I'm going to grab some water." Striding past Gabriel, she weaved back through the shelves and to the register counter. Instead of staying where she'd left him, Gabriel followed right behind her. Onnie snorted with amusement.

"Are you a duck?" she teased.

"Not last I checked."

Onnie reached under the counter, pulled out her water bottle, took a big gulp, and closed her eyes with a satisfied smile. She heard Gabriel whimper, and her eyes popped open. "Did you just whine at me?"

Gabriel shrugged.

"Ugh, fine." She bent down, pulled an unopened water bottle from under the counter, and tossed it at him. "You can have my spare."

"Thank you." He winked at her playfully even though his smile was genuine. He uncapped his bottle, and they both took long, slow pulls in silence.

"Ah.... So much better. Thank you, Cat, honestly."

"You're welcome," Onnie said, "It's probably all the dust we kicked up going through those cupboards."

Gabriel nodded, leaned closer to Onnie, and cocked his head to the side. "I'd say you're right," he reached forward, and before she could stop him, he'd drug his thumb over her cheek, "You're covered in dust."

Onnie choked on her water. "Does that crap usually work for you?" she said between coughs.

"Does what?" Gabriel's brow furrowed, and it looked like he was trying to help, not come on to her.

"Never mind." Onnie shook her head and took another swig of water. Gabriel frowned and pulled out his cell phone, giving Onnie a chance to straighten out her head. She watched as he typed on his glass screen, his brow creased with unease. His jawline was dusted with a day's worth of stubble, and his hair lay across his forehead in a slightly messy but 'I meant to do that' kind of way. He was ruggedly handsome, just as Dany was beautiful, and Onnie wondered why she'd not connected them before he'd told her they were related. There was no room for doubt that their mother and father must have also been beautiful.

She sighed, angry at herself for studying him more closely than she should have. Men were no longer allowed on her to-do list. Onnie was nearly the same age as her mother when she'd been born, and her biological father had already been worthless. Onnie did not intend to make the same mistakes as her parents. She had no business checking out Gabriel, no matter how much fun he was to look at. Onnie turned around, placing her back to him and forcing herself to stop.

She heard him put his phone back into his pocket, and she fussed with something on the shelf behind the counter. He cleared his throat, and she looked over her shoulder at him as he picked his water back up, uncapping it and placing it to his lips.

"So.... How'd the old man convince you into running a place like this?"

"He didn't have to convince me. I told you before my Grandfather's sick, and he asked. Simple as that."

"Yes, you've told me that part of it, but why did you say yes? You had a life in California, friends, and a boyfriend...probably. Why give it up?"

She turned around and narrowed her gaze at him, trying to read whether he was lying. When she saw that Gabriel seemed genuinely curious, Onnie smiled, happy that everything she'd talked to Dany about had stayed between them. It said a lot to Dany's character that she hadn't blabbed to her brother, and Onnie respected her even more for it. She was starting to realize how close the two siblings were as she talked more to each of them.

Onnie leaned on the counter and tried to make herself a bit taller, for what little good it did her. "And what makes you think you're an expert on my life?"

"If I'm so wrong, correct me," Gabriel said, moving forward to match her stance, his height forcing him to look down at her. Delicately, he touched the tip of his nose to hers.

Onnie sighed and stepped back quickly, digging in her purse for her lip balm. "Nope, you're right. I loved my life. I had men falling at my feet, a best friend I traded gossip with, and a little dog named Fluffy."

Gabriel scoffed, "I'm sure you did. Which is why I'm so curious because no one who isn't incredibly stupid or remarkably lonely would give up their life at a week's notice and move across the country for a man they barely knew." Gabriel took another swig from his water, and his nonchalant attitude flipped Onnie's anger switch.

"Wow! Why don't you tell me what you really think, Gabriel!" she sneered. "Since we're dissecting my life, how about yours? Let me guess. You're a teacher because you don't have any children of your own, yet you still want to make a difference in someone's life. You live alone in an apartment full of memories you barely remember happening because you were too busy driving yourself to your next goal in life to prove that you weren't as much of a loser as your father was."

Onnie slammed her palms down on the front counter and leaned toward him, this time standing on her toes and getting into his face. "Since you seem so interested in me, let me educate you."

Gabriel's eyes widened, and Onnie felt something surge inside her and then ripple through the room like a lake after a boulder fell into its waters.

"I love books. I'm fluent in three modern languages besides English. I have a bachelor's degree in ancient literature and a master's in Latin linguistic history and usage. My life was solitary, and I liked it that way because I had no other choice. I had no attachments, did what I wanted, and lived how I wanted. But one day, a silly old man called me up and offered me a chance to change that. He spun tales of a town full of people who were more like a family than neighbors and a shop filled with infinite mystery and stories that would keep me busy for eternity. So, you tell me, Gabriel, what about this place *wouldn't* make me want to move across the country for it?"

Onnie took in a deep gasp of air and realized what she had just done. Her skin burned a bright scarlet, and she stepped back. "Crap."

She clenched her fists to stop their panicked shaking and walked into the back room with as much dignity as possible. She sat on the little sofa in the corner and put her head between her knees, sniffling and refusing to cry. She'd lost her temper and then her filter. Precisely what she tried so hard to avoid, it was a good thing she'd sworn off men. Gabriel probably thought she was insane.

When she heard him clear his throat, she looked up to where he stood, leaning on the doorframe with his arms crossed. "You're right," he said, staring at the floor before his feet.

Onnie picked a fuzzy off of her leggings but said nothing. She'd already said enough.

"About me." Gabriel continued, "I am a teacher because I want to be better than my father. I want to be there for that one kid who maybe doesn't have it so well at home, just like Abbot was for me."

Onnie looked up and stammered. "I'm sorry I shouldn't have—"

Gabriel held up his hand to silence her. "And you're right about the other bit too." He crossed the room and flopped onto the opposite end of the small couch, only a few inches between them. "When I go home at night, I am surrounded by stuff that should mean something to me, but I was too busy at the time to enjoy them, so instead, it's all just clutter. Meaningless clutter." He sighed and touched her cheek, wiping off an errant tear she'd not realized had escaped.

"I may be a lonely, pathetic man, Cat, with nothing but my sister, a dying old man, and a bookshop for friends, but at least I'm living. Can you say the same?"

Onnie pulled her cheek away from his touch and squeezed her eyes shut, unsure how to respond to such raw vulnerability.

Gabriel pulled back his hand and rested it on his lap. "You were right to come here. This store will save your life. She'll be the family you've always needed."

"It's just a job, Gabriel, one I love, yes, but in the end, it's just another thing to help hide me from the world."

"Oh, how very wrong you are, Cat."

The store's phone erupted in loud ringing and broke through the tense moment, and Onnie jumped to her feet at the sound.

"Damn! Why is that ringer so high?" She dashed back to the front of the shop to retrieve the phone from under the front counter.

"Hello, The Book Nook. This is Onnie speaking. How may I help you today?"

"Hello, Onnie dear. I forgot to mention something when we spoke this morning. A man is supposed to come past the shop this afternoon. His name is Gabriel."

"Oh yes, he's here now, actually." Onnie flicked her eyes to where Gabriel had stopped in the back room's doorway after following her.

"Oh really, is he nearby? May I speak with him?"

"...ah sure thing, Rebecca, one sec." Moving the phone away from her ear, Onnie looked at Gabriel and held the phone out. "She wants to talk to you."

"I bet she does. Thanks." Gabriel took the phone and turned around to face away from Onnie. "Hi, Bec. Yeah, we've talked. No. I don't think so."

Figuring it was none of her business, Onnie bent down to pull the stock logbook from under the counter. She moved around a few things and, with the shelf eye level, saw the black leather-bound book she'd moved earlier when looking for her Grandfather's tea. She rotated it around and checked the binding for its title. "Nothing. Damn, so much for that idea."

"Yes, Bec, you don't have to tell me that. I know!" Onnie listened as Gabriel took a few deep breaths and seemed to reign in his frustration. "She has a right to know." he paced around the counter and stopped with his back to her.

Puzzled by the conversation taking place on the phone in front of her, Onnie stood up, bringing the book with her. She wasn't sure what about Gabriel made her want to eavesdrop, but she couldn't help it. Onnie tried to distract herself, and she placed the unnamed book on the counter and flipped through the pages casually. Most of the pages were blank, or in another language she couldn't read, though it looked similar to Latin.

Gabriel turned around to face Onnie again and leaned on the counter. "You're right. I don't understand, but how is that his right?" He focused on Onnie as she shrugged and spun the book around so it was right side up for him to read. She held it open to a page with the odd-looking Latin and pointed to a section.

The moment that Gabriel's fingers met the black leather book, the world around Onnie went quiet. She looked up into Gabriel's dark green eyes, her own likely filled with confusion as the air evaporated from the room. Gabriel's eyes dilated and then flashed crystal blue as time seemed to slow to a crawl. Onnie felt like she was hyperventilating, and Gabriel didn't look much better, but just when they both began to panic, a shockwave ripped outward from the book under their fingers.

Onnie saw Gabriel as he was hurled down the center aisle and onto his back, landing with a grunt and a crack as his skull connected with the ground. The store phone rolled out of his hand and stopped a few feet away.

Likewise, Onnie was flung backward only to hit the shelf behind the counter and crumple to the floor in a heap.

The last thing Onnie registered before she lost consciousness was Rebecca's desperate screams, "GABRIEL! GABE! ONNIE! ONNIE!" but Onnie could only answer her with silence.

Chapter 11: Unease

November 2021 - Alku | Gabriel Vansand

Gabe rolled over with a groan, the right side of his torso already sore from his impact with the shop's floor. He could hear Rebecca's shouts from nearby, and he patted the floor in search of its origin. When his fingers finally grazed the phone's edge, he stretched a bit farther to grab it.

"Stop yelling, Bec. We're all right." He reached the back of his head and felt around for a lump. "I guess she figured it was finally time to give it to us."

"Gabriel," Rebecca stated firmly, "Onnie is going to be very confused, but you mustn't tell her anything yet," Gabe could hear the commandment in the woman's voice, and it was really starting to annoy him how much they'd been keeping from Onnie.

"Yeah, I'm aware. Even after the Transference begins, nothing has changed." he ground out through clenched teeth, "We'll see you at dinner. Go tend to the old man." When Gabe was satisfied he wasn't bleeding, he flopped his arm back down on the floor.

"Gabriel…." Rebecca's voice pleaded.

"Ah huh, bye." He hung up, unable to hear any more excuses from the Link for a while. He coughed and dropped the phone on the floor beside him with a soft thunk.

"Cat, are you okay?" Gabe struggled to a sitting position and winced with the effort. As he looked around the store, the fallout was much more significant than he'd been warned about. Three bookcases on each side of the center aisle were lying on their backs, books strewn all over the floor. The log book and a few others from the counter were all over his legs and torso. Scrolls littered the ground, and dust danced in the air, twinkling in the lamplight like tiny stars.

"Damn, this place is trashed. Cat?" A groan came from behind the counter, and he relaxed, knowing she was all right. "We have a lot of cleaning to do."

He slowly reached his feet and lumbered to the counter to lean on it. "Ugg, I didn't expect it to hurt. Cat...." Gabriel leaned over the countertop and saw Onnie lying on the floor, bent at an odd angle.

"Crap, Onnie!" His injuries were forgotten, and Gabe vaulted over the counter, crouching beside her. "Shit. Shit. Shit. Damn it, Rebecca, why didn't you warn me!"

He sat down and carefully straightened Onnie's limbs before sliding her into his lap as gently as possible. "Onnie, wake up. I need you. You need to wake up. Come on, open your eyes for me."

He could have cried when he leaned down, put his cheek to her mouth, and felt her breath. "Oh, thank the gods. Onnie, you need to wake up."

He whispered to her and rocked her gently, smoothing her jet-black hair back from her forehead and praying that after so many years of waiting, he wouldn't lose her or the shop so soon.

Onnie Moore

Onnie groaned and squeezed her eyes shut tighter. She hurt

everywhere, and for some reason, she felt like she was on the ocean. She mentally went over her body and realized her limbs felt heavy, like someone had draped a weighted blanket over her. She tried to open her eyes but only succeeded in fluttering them.

"Onnie!" Gabriel's voice washed over her, "Open your eyes, come on."

"Ugg, what happened?"

"Good girl, Cat, come on, open your eyes." She felt him shift and realized she was in his lap, and then she heard the sloshing of water.

"Here, open your eyes, Cat, and drink some water," he said, putting a bottle to her lips.

It took her blinking a few times before she fully opened her eyes. She looked up at Gabriel and took in his worried expression.

"Am I on the floor?" She tried to look around and hissed when her neck protested.

"Drink this first." He said as he touched the bottle to her lips again and helped tilt her head back. After drinking a few sips, she rested her head against his chest and closed her eyes again.

"Do you remember what happened, Cat?" Gabriel asked, setting the water bottle aside.

"Ah…I think so. You were talking to Rebecca, and I found a book under the counter and pulled it out to look at it."

Gabriel was slowly rocking her in his arms, and she found focusing problematic. Gabriel's worry over her was surprising, and she didn't know what to make of it, but she was willing to put her no-men rule on the shelf for a few minutes and enjoy the warmth he radiated.

"Right. Do you remember what happened after that?"

"I flipped through it. Most of it was blank, and the rest was in some strange form of Latin."

"Yes. It's ancient. Most people don't even know it exists. Not even ancient lit majors or defunct Latin experts," he said playfully.

"I showed it to you…and then it got quiet and hard to breathe… and then I went flying...we," she corrected, "went flying. Are you alright?"

"Yes, thank you," Gabriel stifled a laugh, obviously trying to minimize his amusement while she was trying so hard to wrap her brain around what had happened. "I really think maybe you should have asked Abbot a few more questions before taking over this place."

Onnie frowned and looked up at Gabriel, only to have him smile and shake his head. "Don't worry about it for now. What's done is done, but either way, I'm glad it was you."

"Not even sure what you mean by that."

This time, Gabriel didn't hold back his laughter. "Let's get you fixed up, and then maybe I can answer a few questions. Bec and the old man will tell you the rest at dinner."

"Stop laughing at me," Onnie winced. "Ow, please?"

"Anything for you, Cat. Come on." Gingerly, he slid his arms under her legs and around her back. "Up we get." Gabriel stood up, lifting her with him as if she were a feather.

"Damn, Gabriel... Lay off the steroids, man." Onnie said, raising one hand to pinch his biceps.

"If only steroids would have worked," Gabriel said, walking the long way to the sitting area.

"So, you have used them! I knew it. There was no way you turned into the Hulk without help."

Gabriel snorted and quickly changed the subject. "How's your head feeling?"

"It hurts." Her self-made excuses aside, she was surprised that she felt comfortable in someone else's care, especially after their earlier shouting match. She found herself snuggling closer and starting to relax. He must have felt her wiggle into a more comfortable position as he carried her over to the wingback nook, and sure enough, when she glanced up, he was smirking.

"I could feel you smiling, smartass. I'm cold, and you're like a space heater."

"You think I'm hot. Thanks, Cat," he teased her more. Onnie rolled her eyes but still couldn't help but match his smile.

Gabriel stopped before one of the wing-backed chairs and shifted her in his arms. "Okay, let's get you sitting, and then I can look and see if you're hurt."

He carefully placed Onnie into the plushest of the chairs, and she could tell he was being as gentle as he could manage. He squatted in front of her, resting his palms on either side of her knees.

"Okay, Cat, look at me." He tilted her chin with his finger, so she looked into his eyes. The intimacy of his action made Onnie fidget, and she drew her legs up into the chair underneath her and shivered.

"Yeah, you said you were cold. I'll be right back." Gabriel stood up swiftly before turning back around and pointing at her. "Don't get up." Only after she'd nodded did he finally turn and walk away.

Once he was out of sight, Onnie slowly lifted one hand to the back of her head and felt the bump that was beginning to form. When she pulled away her fingers, they were red and sticky with blood.

"Crap, Gabriel…." she called out weakly but was only answered by silence.

She began taking inventory of her other bumps and bruises. First and foremost, lifting the hem of her sweatshirt, she reached behind her and gently massaged her lower back.

"Ouch, Gabe…." she tried calling again with the same result.

As she moved away from the bruise and continued her self-examination, everything else seemed fine, only sore and minor scrapes. She checked her legs and arms and even wiggled her toes for good measure. Thankfully, nothing was broken. Onnie reached up and probed the back of her skull again, closing her eyes to assess better what she couldn't see. She heard a soft thudding sound and was unsure if she heard footsteps or if the pounding was in her head.

"Onnie!" Gabriel shouted.

Her eyes snapped open. "Yes?"

Gabriel dashed into the sitting area, fear in his eyes. He had one arm full of medical supplies and a blanket, the other carrying a sloshing cup of tea.

"Shit, you're okay." He set the supplies on the ottoman and the tea on a tiny table nearby before he returned to kneeling at her feet and searched her face. "There's blood on my shirt. I didn't notice it until I was getting supplies. Where are you hurt?"

Onnie again removed her hand from the back of her head and held it up for him to see.

"Damn, I'm sorry, Cat. I didn't realize. I wouldn't have left you alone had I known."

She noticed his fear filling his face, and again, she was warmed by his concern. "It's okay," she smiled as best as possible, "it only hurts a little."

"I brought you some of Bec's tea and grabbed a blanket, too. Drink this while I check your injuries and clean you up." Gabriel handed her the teacup and dug through the medical supplies he'd brought back. He picked up a packet of gauze and returned his focus to her, hesitating when he saw she'd not drunk any tea. "Please drink it."

"Why are you being so nice to me?" Onnie said without thinking. Gabriel glared at her, making her instantly regret her question.

"Do you think so little of me?" his glare turned to a frown instead. "Cat, like it or not, you're stuck with me now."

She couldn't help but roll her eyes, but she did as he asked and took a sip of tea. "I don't know you, and I'm done with the riddles, Gabe. Just tell me what's going on."

His frown faltered, "You've never called me Gabe before." He said, and she saw his shoulders relax, and then he smiled.

Onnie blushed and lowered her face to her tea. At this rate, if she kept talking, she'd talk her way into a situation she wanted to avoid. "Please, tell me."

Gabriel sighed and ripped open one of the gauze squares while taking her free hand, the one covered in blood, and setting it, palm up, on his knee. "Bec and the old man will tell you tonight." He picked up a water bottle, uncapped it, and wet the gauze.

Onnie pulled her bloody palm away and looked at him with defiance.

"Give me your hand, please," Gabriel said, exasperated.

"No. Not until you tell me something, anything." she pleaded with him, her voice practically begging. "Come on. I deserve an explanation for what just happened."

"Cat, don't do that." He held out his hand for her to place hers in it, and when she didn't, he started to get angry at her, growling low in his throat. "Stop it. You're bleeding." When he reached for her hand again, she pulled it further away from him. "No wonder you and my sister get along so well."

Onnie smiled, holding out hope that he'd finally answer her.

He sighed and softly rubbed one of his temples with his fingers. "Cat, that's a big question and one you should be asking the old man, not me." He looked deeper into her eyes, raised his voice's volume, and lowered its tone. He was no longer asking but telling her. "Now, give me your hand."

"He didn't arrange our marriage or anything, did he?" Onnie said with a laugh. When Gabriel's eyes darted around the room before finally settling on her, she tilted her head to the side in question. Her stomach was doing flip-flops, thanks to his reaction and expression.

"I would only be so lucky, Cat."

With a heavy sigh, Onnie gave up. She wasn't in the mind space to play games anymore and placed her bloody hand, palm up in Gabriel's, "Sure, whatever."

"That's a good girl," Gabriel said, his voice back to normal as he began washing her palm as if she were porcelain.

Onnie ignored him and instead looked around the shop. Everything looked and seemed normal still, but they were pretty far from the main area, and she'd caught a glimpse of a toppled bookcase when Gabriel had been carrying her.

"This shop is unique, Cat, more than you could have ever dreamed."

Onnie quickly refocused on Gabriel, hoping that wasn't all he would tell her. "Ah…yeah, a book just threw me across the room. I figured that part out for myself, thank you."

Gabriel lifted his head and considered her eyes carefully for a few seconds. Her typical sass was back, and he seemed to like that. She locked eyes with him and studied the flecks of blue she'd never seen within them before now. He smirked at her, and she couldn't help but look at his lips. Thankfully, he'd already returned his gaze to her clean palm as he carefully rested it back in her lap.

"Turn, please. I want to look at that head wound."

Onnie shifted slowly and winced when the arm of the chair dug into the large bruise on her back.

"I'll get to the bruise in a minute. The bleeding has me more worried."

"Ah…okay, thanks. How'd you know I had a bruise?"

"I felt it when I lifted you," Gabriel answered quickly. "Now, lean back towards me just a little bit if you can."

Having learned her lesson, Onnie did as she was told. Gabriel carefully ran his fingers through her hair, parting it into two sections. He slipped them over her shoulders on either side towards her front and gently probed the sensitive spot with his fingers.

"It looks shallow and only about an inch long, probably a scrape from the corner of the shelf when you hit it. You'll be fine, though. No stitches needed."

She tried to watch what he was doing out of the corner of her eyes, but the strain was giving her a headache.

"Head injuries tend to bleed worse than they actually are, but I want to clean it with disinfectant just to be safe."

The rip of a plastic and paper package seemed to echo in the quiet space, and she heard the clicking sound of a bottle top open.

"This won't sting, but it is cold." Onnie felt a cotton swab with cold liquid brushed over her scalp.

"Will you answer me one more thing…please?"

"I'll try, Cat," Gabriel said, dabbing her scalp dry with a clean gauze pad.

"Where do you fit into all of this? I mean, that book hurled you too, right?"

"Yes, it did." He gently placed his hand on her shoulder. "You're finished. Lean forward, and let me see that bruise."

"I picked up that book this morning before you came into the shop, and it didn't do anything, but suddenly you're in the picture, and it reacts." Onnie shifted and braced her forearms on the chair arm so he could see.

"I was lucky enough not to have a wall behind me, though." He flashed his smile and grabbed the hem of her sweatshirt and shirt. "Can I?" Gabriel asked, surprising Onnie with his consideration.

"Yeah, thanks."

Gabriel nodded and lifted the hem of her clothes just high enough to see what he needed.

"You're not answering the question," Onnie said crisply.

"Right, sorry." Gabriel's fingers palpated her flesh gingerly, and she hissed, winced, and then had to stifle a groan as his fingers traveled over differing spots of discomfort. "I'm sort of her protector and, by extension, yours now."

Onnie's brows wrinkled in confusion, "Her protector?"

"Yes, and yours," Gabriel said, not taking his eyes from her back but nodding.

"Who is she, and protection from what? I still don't understand. You're being cryptic on purpose."

There was a pain in his eyes now when he looked at her, "This world is a lot larger and a lot crueler than you realize, little Cat, but those are questions for Abbot to answer. Please, don't ask me again. I can't stand saying no to you."

They stared at each other, Onnie breaking first with a frown and a shrug. "Fine, I'll wait."

After a few more minutes, Gabriel resituated her sweatshirt and sat back on his heels. "Alright, I'm finished. Curl up now and drink your tea." He stood up, unfolding the blanket he'd brought, and drew it around her shoulders. "Better?"

Onnie pulled it up closer to her neck and snuggled into it. "Much, thank you."

Gabriel piled all the soiled bandages into a plastic bag and tied it closed, placing it back on the ottoman. Then he sat in the chair beside her, leaned back, and stared at the ceiling. After thinking for a few moments while she sipped her tea, Gabriel mumbled and cursed Bec, the old man, and even the stupid bookshop. For the second time that day, Onnie attempted not to eavesdrop and let the man rant privately, but she found it exceedingly difficult.

"So, here's the deal." He leaned forward gracefully, and she smiled a big, goofy grin, hoping she would finally get some real answers from someone. "This shop is special...very special."

Onnie settled in and got more comfortable. "You said that."

"Shush Cat, give me a moment," he snapped and then sighed, "I'm about to betray the trust of two people I deeply respect." Gabriel put his head in his hands and pulled his hair in frustration.

Her skin flushed, and Onnie murmured, "Sorry," before she returned to sipping her tea, forcing her to stay quiet.

"No, I'm sorry. I didn't mean to yell. You're cute when you blush, by the way," Gabriel said, causing her to blush more and him to chuckle. "This is not just a shop, and this building doesn't contain only what you see in front of you. It holds a vast amount of knowledge, far more than you or I understand. I'm not sure even the old man comprehends how much this place is hiding, but it's here, and because it's here, it needs a caretaker or a...Keeper, if you will. That's where you come in."

"So, Grandpa is not just a shop owner?"

Gabriel continued to smile at her, amusement in his gaze, but he said nothing.

"Right...." Onnie said, getting the point. "So, I moved here to be like some uber-librarian?"

"Sort of, but you're much more than that. This isn't a library. Libraries are meant to be shared. Books come and go, and their content changes over time. This is a collection, and you are its Keeper."

"Keeper." Onnie tried the title out on her tongue and found it flowed like water as if it belonged there.

"You are a refuge for all knowledge, a safe haven. The archive. Eventually, you will even become part of it, and it will become part of you."

"You talk as if this 'knowledge' were human."

"Why would it have to be human, and what makes you so sure it isn't?" Gabriel said, raising one eyebrow.

Onnie shook her head. "Because it can't be...in all my time studying, not a single myth describes what you are telling me."

"Cat…a book just threw us both across a room, or have you forgotten that grapefruit-sized bruise forming on your back?" When Onnie's brows creased in disbelief, Gabriel just chuckled and shrugged.

"If something like this did exist, there would be a record of it somewhere, and someone would have talked about it."

"You're so sure you've heard every myth in the world?" he admonished her, "That's small-minded of you, Cat."

Onnie sipped her tea, thinking about what Gabriel implied until her eyes shot open in surprise. "It's here! The myth, it's here, in the shop."

Gabriel nodded ever so slightly, but his face gave away his relief at her putting the pieces together. "It's not a myth, Cat, but a history, and yes, it's here."

"Can I read it?"

Warmth filled Gabriel's eyes, and she realized she believed everything he said. "I'm sure Abbot will share it with you, and eventually, you'll get to read it."

Onnie leaned back in her chair and pulled her blanket tighter around her. There was so much to think about, and if what Gabriel had told her was true, then her Grandfather would have more answers.

Gabriel leaned further forward and peeked into her empty teacup.

"I'll get you some more tea." He said before standing and collecting the bag of soiled bandages, the empty teacup, and the unused first aid supplies. He disappeared around the corner bookshelf as he made his way to the front of the store and left Onnie to continue processing.

Onnie lowered her head into her hands and gently rubbed her

scalp, forcing herself not to wince. "Damn, I don't want Grandfather to worry."

She parted her long black strands into three chunks, braided her hair down her back with quick and obvious practice, and secured it with a hair tie. She patted the back of her head where her wound was and checked her hand for blood. When it came back clean, she was relieved. She felt that dinner would be complicated already, and there was no need to add blood to the mix.

A faint tinkling sound came from somewhere in the store, and Onnie looked up, tilting her head as she tried to locate it. She heard low murmurs coming from the area by the register and assumed a customer had come into the shop and Gabriel had greeted them.

"Cat, can you come up here, please, just for a moment." Gabriel's voice called through the store.

Onnie stood with a slight sway and steadied herself with the back of the chair. She untangled herself from her blanket, piled it on the cushion, and straightened her clothes.

"I'm a mess. Right, you hit your head, and it's fine. Just let it go." With one more tug on her sweatshirt to put it into place, she walked to the front of the store.

It didn't take her long to reach the front counter, considering the three shelves on either side were toppled over, shortening her walk time. When she passed the shelf closest to the center aisle that was still standing, she was stunned by the debris scattered around the store. Papers, blank genre cards, the contents of her purse, and six full shelves of books littered the center aisle in front of the counter all the way up to the front door.

Even with all the chaos, what stopped Onnie was not the destruction but the woman standing at the front counter with Gabriel. She had dark brown skin, wrinkled with age, and hair that was pale grey and piled on top of her head with streaks of dirt running through it that matched the soil on her left cheek. It was apparent that the woman had been in the sun a lot during her life and looked weathered because of it. She wore gardening clothes, a leather apron, tools sticking out of the pockets, gloves, clippers, and even a shovel.

Onnie recognized the woman from the flower shop across the street, but she hadn't yet had the chance to venture in to buy anything.

Gabriel met Onnie's eyes and smiled, gesturing to the woman before him, "Elanor, this is Onnie. Onnie, this is Elanor."

The small woman turned and raised her gaze to meet Onnie's. Her woody hazel eyes sparkled, and Onnie was stunned by her beauty.

"What a pleasure it is to finally meet you, my young friend."

Elanor dusted her dainty hands off on her apron and held one of them out. Onnie took it without reservation and was surprised by the strength in the delicate-looking woman's grip. Age had been kind to this woman, for both her beauty and strength remained. Every morning, when Onnie walked to the shop, she saw Elanor hard at work and always with a smile.

Elanor leaned in and kissed Onnie's right cheek, then she stepped back and smiled. "Sorry about that, a side effect of the trade, I'm afraid." She said as she reached up to brush a smudge of dirt off Onnie's cheek that she'd left behind.

As the woman lowered her hand and stepped back, the smell of freshly pruned roses and newly tilled dirt floated in the air and lingered in Onnie's nose.

Onnie brushed her hand over the skin where Elanor's had just been, "No problem." she smiled at the lovely woman, "It's nice to meet you, Elanor. You own the flower shop on the corner, right?"

"Oh, why yes I do, you remember me!" Elanor said with a slight skip of glee.

"Of course, your shop is beautiful and a highlight on my daily walk to work and home."

Elanor smiled so vast that Onnie was sure the florist would faint from happiness. “Well, isn’t that just the sweetest thing? You stop by anytime, and I’ll make something nice up for you to take home.”

“Thanks, Elanor, that would be wonderful!”

Gabriel chuckled unobtrusively, and Onnie saw he was watching the two of them carry on, but he eventually cleared his throat to bring them back to Elanor’s purpose for being at the shop.

“Onnie, Elanor is here to look for a book.”

Onnie rolled her eyes at him. “Duh, what else would she be here for, a massage?”

Gabriel shook his head at her in amusement, but Elanor spoke before he could sass Onnie back. “Silly me, thanks for reminding me. You know how forgetful I can be.” Elanor giggled and pat Gabriel’s hand that was resting on the counter.

Gabriel shook his head, “Never.” He smiled and turned to Onnie, holding out a slip of paper. “I’m not sure where this one is....”

“Here, let me look.” Onnie took the paper, amused when she recognized Dany’s perfect handwriting. “Oh, Growing Herbs for Brews and Tonics. I talked about this book with Dany the other day at the library....” Onnie’s voice trailed off as she turned and walked towards the front of the store and to the rare books section, still mumbling to herself.

Gabriel Vansand

Gabe beamed with pride at Onnie’s back as her connection to the shop took over, and she wandered off, muttering to herself and unaware of what was happening.

“After you, Elanor,” he gestured with a slight bow and an outward sweep of his arm.

"My, this is exciting!" Elanor clapped her hands gleefully and ran to avoid being left behind.

Gabe followed behind Elanor, the smell of carnations invading his senses as he walked. The scent made him smile at the memories that surfaced of him and his two best friends growing up. He, Sam, and Xayn spent hours with Elanor and Xayn's grandmother, Yvonne, in the forests around Alku. The two older women were vibrant and full of life and easily kept up with the three troublemaking boys.

When they'd finally caught up with Onnie, Gabe returned his thoughts to the present.

"...I'm sorry, Elanor, I don't know the store's stock all that well yet. I wouldn't even know where to...."

Onnie stumbled as she stubbed her toe into one of the ceiling-high bookshelves, and Gabe had to restrain himself from asking if she was alright. She was a Keeper and not made of glass, but he was baffled by how quickly his Guardianship affected him.

"Ouch!" She frowned at the bookcase, but her eyes quickly skimmed the book's spines. "...look."

"My word, you found it!" Elanor clapped and pointed to a moss-green leather book just out of her reach.

"Ah...yeah, I did." Onnie carefully extracted the heavy book from the shelf and handed it to Elanor, who immediately began thumbing through the pages with wide eyes.

"Good girl, Cat," Gabe whispered over Onnie's shoulder. She turned and looked up at him, where he was leaning against a large shelf with his arms and legs crossed, nodding.

Elanor took one of Onnie's hands and kissed the back of it, the smell of daisies replacing the carnations, and Gabe breathed deeply.

"Thank you, Keeper, thank you! This is perfect!" Elanor was giddy, and Gabe knew it wasn't just because of the book.

Onnie's eyes widened in surprise, "What did you—" she began to ask before Gabe quickly cut her off.

"Come on, Elanor, let's get you rung up, shall we?" He gently placed his large hand on the older woman's shoulder and guided her back through the weaving shelves to the front counter. "Cat, go back to the sitting area and wrap up. You're shivering again. I'll be right there."

Elanor looked over her shoulder with a grin so wide her cheeks all but disappeared, and she thanked Onnie again.

Onnie nodded and plastered an uneasy smile on her face until she turned and walked back to the sitting area.

Onnie Moore

Onnie wasn't sure what had just happened, but when a shiver gripped her so hard her teeth clattered together, she followed Gabriel's advice and curled back up in her chair under the blanket.

She already missed Elanor's smell. The ever-changing flowers she worked with must saturate her clothes and act as a natural perfume. She seemed like a lovely woman, and Onnie would have to stop and pick up some flowers one day. Her apartment could use some life and excuse or not, she wanted to speak with Elanor again.

All that aside, Onnie was still reeling from when she thought she heard Elanor call her Keeper. She wracked her brain, thinking of what other word she could have mistaken it for, but nothing came to mind. Gabriel probably wouldn't tell her anything if she asked, and Onnie desperately needed someone to talk to. She knew Dany would know what was going on. Her town intel-gathering skills were honestly impressive. At the very least, she would listen to Onnie's bizarre theories.

Onnie was too sleepy and lazy to retrieve her phone, so she pulled the soft blanket to her chin and closed her eyes. She smiled when the sweet scent of her grandmother's perfume tickled her nose. Onnie wasn't sure how she could smell it, but right now, she needed comfort and wouldn't question it. Stranger things had happened to her today.

The bruise on Onnie's back and the others forming on her body were starting to throb, and she squirmed in the chair in an attempt to get comfortable. She realized she was sitting on something and reached underneath her, pulling out her cell phone.

"Oh, Gabriel must have brought you, and I didn't notice."

She smiled, reminding herself to thank him later, and sent a message to Dany.

I met Elanor. Onnie sent the message and then watched the read receipt and little typing bubble pop up.

Awesome! Where?

She came into the shop. I think she bought whatever book she kept getting from the library.

It's about time! Dany responded, and Onnie snorted, sure her friend was cheering at her desk.

…and something else happened.

She hit send and started typing another message before she deleted it and started again. Three more times. Before she could come up with words that didn't make her sound like she belonged in a psych ward, Dany responded.

Onnie…you're scaring me. Tell me what's wrong, should I come over there?

Onnie sighed but decided to tell her what happened and hope for the best. *Sorry, I was trying to figure out how to tell you I was attacked by a book and not sound crazy.*

Like, it fell off a shelf and hit your head?

Onnie shook her head even though Dany couldn't see her do it. *Nope.*

I'm confused. Dany typed back, and Onnie yawned and stretched.

Me too. Your brother was here. He took care of me.

Another yawn escaped her, and she closed her eyes and leaned her head against the chair to wait for Dany's response.

Chapter 12: Curiosity

November 2021 - Alku | Gabriel Vansand

"She's wonderful, Gabe!" Elanor said with an adorable little jump as Gabe rang her up on the old register. "Just perfect!"

Gabe smiled and punched a few more buttons, trying to get the damn thing to open. "She is."

Elanor tapped him on the forearm to get his attention. "She's important, that one. You protect her, Gabriel. Keep her safe. We need her."

Gabe smiled and clasped Elanor's tiny hands in his large ones. "I know, Elanor. Trust me. I'll do whatever I must to ensure she's safe and protected." He lowered his head and kissed the back of her hand before releasing both. "Trust me."

"Oh, we do, Gabe, all of us. You'll do what's needed."

"I will." Gabe nodded and resumed frowning at the register. "If I can get this damn thing open."

Elanor chuckled, and Gabe thumped his fist on the top of it, and it popped open, hitting him in the stomach. He'd never gotten along with that machine, and even after years, their relationship was stubborn.

"You'll need patience if you're to revitalize this place, Gabe. I have a feeling Onnie will need it, too."

Gabe stopped and considered Elanor's words, "You see her more clearly than I do."

She shook her head, closing her eyes and smiling. "No, I see just as much as you. I just see without bias."

He stared into the register, and Elanor noticed his silence.

"Gabe, I've known you your entire life. You're a good kid and a compassionate one. You simply need to treat that young woman like you would Xayn, Marco, or those kids of yours."

Gabe shrugged, wrapped Elanor's book in tissue, and safely stuck it into a waterproof bag. "Thanks for testing her, Elanor. It was good for her to see what she was capable of, and you have impeccable timing."

"I did nothing, but the fates have their own hold over timing." Elanor reached into her apron and removed a single white daisy, passing it to Gabe with a wink. "She is capable of more than that, dear boy. Give her my thanks." She nodded to the flower and skipped to the shop door, her book in tow. "Remind her to stop by my shop. I'd be honored to arrange something for our new Keeper!"

"I will." Gabe slipped one hand into his pocket and lifted the daisy in his other to his nose. A single one of Elanor's flowers always smelled like a field, and it made him want for spring. He was ready to take his runs through the mountains and not the sidewalks. Maybe Onnie would run with him. There were lots of places he could show— He shook his head, dispelling the image and returning to reality.

"I am her Guardian, nothing more," he said with more resolve than he felt. He picked up Onnie's forgotten water bottle, uncapped it, and then stuck the flower into it.

"Her life will be chaotic enough without adding a relationship to the mix." As the words left his mouth, he realized that's what he wanted. A relationship with Onnie. He hadn't known her long, and he'd never been a relationship guy, but something about this woman made him eager to try. The counter under his hand warmed, and the daisy's water rippled.

"Was that your blessing?" he asked the empty air.

His phone vibrated in his pocket, and he pulled it out to see Dany's face staring back at him on the caller ID.

"Hey, Dany."

"THE TRANSFERENCE STARTED, AND YOU DIDN'T CALL ME!" She yelled so loudly he recoiled and pulled the phone away from his ear.

His sister's enthusiasm was like wildfire. Once you got her started, she blazed hot and was nearly impossible to stop. She had always been the positive one out of the two of them. Life was an adventure to her and something to enjoy, even when it was tough.

"Sorry, been a crazy afternoon. Onnie called you, I take it."

"We were texting, but I think she fell asleep. She said Mrs. Radcliff was there."

Gabe chuckled, walked into the back room, and collapsed on the sofa. "Yeah, Elanor finally bought that damn book you've been harping on her about."

"About time she did, but come on, get to the good stuff! I want deets, brother!"

He closed his eyes and remembered the ripple of power he'd felt earlier. The mix of his, Onnie's, and the shop's. "It was...amazing." he ran his fingers through his hair and sighed. "Threw us both across the room."

"Oh, my gods, is Onnie okay? She said a book attacked her, but she didn't tell me that!"

Dany's voice was concerned, and Gabe's chest tightened at her caring tone. While one side of his sister was wildfire, the other was a healing spring.

"In general, she's fine, just a bit banged up. She hit the shelving behind the front counter."

"Damn, but she's fine?"

"Yeah, shallow cut to the back of her head and a few bruises, but nothing life-threatening."

"Why was it so strong? Wasn't it supposed to feel like a static shock or something?"

Gabe laughed at his sister's way of downplaying something so important. "Sort of, Abbot said it was like a bolt of lightning running up your arm to your heart. He said it would be uncomfortable, and we'd feel a spark, but nothing like what happened to us."

"I should have known something was going to happen today with that storm that came about so quickly. So, what's the plan now?" Dany asked, excitement bursting through her concern. Gabe could envision her practically bouncing in her seat.

"She was planning on going to Abbot's for dinner, and Bec wants me to join them. Hopefully, he'll explain more to her. Did you know Abbot didn't tell her anything about the shop or Alku before she agreed to move?"

When silence was his only answer, he growled into the phone.

"I'm sorry, Gabe, I couldn't tell her. Abbot asked me not to."

Gabe flung himself from the couch and paced the tiny back room in furious circles, keeping his mouth shut and trying not to take out his anger on his sister.

"He said she needed to find it on her own. He promised she wouldn't be hurt and that she'd accept it...and us. That it was her destiny."

"And you just sat there? For weeks, you've been having coffee with her, shopping, doing chick stuff, and you've just been lying to her face the whole time!"

"Gabriel!" Dany shouted into the phone. "Don't you dare!"

Gabe heard whispers as Dany apologized and excused herself. She must have been at the library counter and not in the backroom.

"I adore Onnie. I would never intentionally lie to her, and you should know that. Besides, you didn't tell her either. Abbot asked us not to, and we both respect him too much to ignore his wishes."

Gabe stopped his pacing and rubbed his eyes. "You're right."

"I know," she murmured.

"Gods damn it! You're right, I'm sorry, but you didn't see her earlier. If she'd been a few inches to the left, she'd have hit the edge of the bookcase, not the flat of it. She nearly didn't make it, Dany, and if she hadn't, then where would we be?"

"Abbot wouldn't have let that happen, and neither would the shop. I bet he didn't realize the power she held within her."

"No, I think you're right." Gabe sighed, "She's amazing, Dany. I can feel more than flickers of her now, along the Bond, but there's even more there, just out of reach."

"Good, the shop needs her. I love Abbot, but he's had his time." Sadness leaked into Dany's typically cheery voice, making Gabe's heart ache for her. Abbot was as much her family as his.

"I know, Dany. She'll make him proud. All of us will."

Dany sighed, and Gabe could tell he'd lost her to the sadness she always tried so hard to hide.

"Did you ask her about Thanksgiving?" he asked, trying to cheer her up.

"Ah, yeah, she said it was okay. Of course, that girl would give you the skin on her back if you asked for it."

"No, Dany, she'd give it to you. She's been hurt, and I know you know that. She tells you more than she tells me. I'm still a stranger to her."

"She does. It's a girlfriend thing." Dany laughed.

"Good, it sounds like she needs a girlfriend."

"Or two!" Dany said with glee.

"Yes," Gabe said as he rubbed his palm on the doorway to the back room, "now she has two." He felt a steady hum fill the space and caressed the wood affectionately before walking back into the front room. "Dany?"

"Yeah?"

"I have to run. The shop's a mess, and I want to get it cleaned up before she wakes up."

"Do you need an extra pair of hands?"

Gabe smiled, "No, but thank you. I think it looks worse than it is."

"Alright, if you're sure. Call me after dinner and let me know how Onnie does. Let her know she can call me if she wants."

The compassion his sister was full of and more than willing to share was tremendous, and not for the first time, he acknowledged how lucky he was to have her. "Of course."

"Talk soon."

"Bye," Gabriel said, hanging up and staring at the phone in his hand for a few more seconds.

He stuck his phone into his pocket and gazed around the shop before him. The wreckage that triggering the Transference process had left behind was extensive, and he became aware of just how much energy had been sapped from him.

Nothing had turned out as he had intended when he'd finally decided to ask Onnie for help that morning. Gabe had figured he'd come into the shop, beg Cat for her help, and if she refused or they didn't find it, he would go for a run and ask if she wanted to join him. Instead, he was thrown across a room by just the book he was looking for, had to play nursemaid to the same beautiful woman he'd been trying not to think about for weeks, and had the fortune to watch the new Keeper's first real interaction with the bookshop through their newly ignited Bond.

He reached up and rubbed his neck, as it was becoming increasingly stiffer as he stood there looking at what he needed to do instead of doing it. The first thing was to close up the shop. Over the years, Gabe had helped Abbot and Bec with the bookshop many times. Regrettably, he could probably run it better than Onnie could, which frustrated him all over again when he thought about it. He passed the mess, opened the shop's front door, pulled in the sign, and locked the door behind him.

"The day could have gone worse. I guess," he said, turning and looking down the aisle towards the front counter. "Well…maybe not."

He sighed heavily and began picking up the books nearest to his feet. After he stacked a few of them in his arms, Gabe carried them back to the nearest toppled shelf, hoping they still belonged where they were in the past. He'd tell Onnie he did his best, and she could sort it out later. Or maybe he'd tell Bec that sorting them out could be her punishment for not warning them adequately.

He picked up a few more books before noticing that Onnie's bag was also mixed up in the mess. Moving aside a handful of scrolls, Gabe lifted the bag and frowned when he found it nearly empty. No doubt the contents were strewn about the room with all the books. After a quick search, he found an unopened water bottle, a wallet, lip balm, headphones, and a hairbrush. He stuck them all into the main pocket and placed the bag on the counter.

Then he resumed picking up the rest of the backlash.

Gabe entered the cozy seating area in the back of the shop, where he stopped to observe his aptly named little Cat as she slept. She was wrapped tightly in the blanket he had given her, her legs beneath her, and pillowed her head on her arms. Even though she was curled into a tight ball and softly snoring, her position was clearly taking into account the bruising on her back.

He quietly set the fresh cup of steaming tea on the spindly table beside her and knelt in front of her chair. Brushing her hair back from her forehead, he smiled sweetly and whispered, "You're truly beautiful, little Cat."

Onnie's eyes fluttered behind her lids, but she remained asleep.

"I'm sorry to do this to you…." he raised his voice so she would hear him but not be startled by his sudden appearance. "Wake up, Cat. You need to wake up now."

Onnie yawned and blinked a few times before meeting his gaze and smiling. She looked around in confusion and stretched in place. "What time is it?" she yawned again.

"Two forty-five. You've been sleeping for about an hour."

She sat up quickly and tried to extract herself from the blanket that was doing its best to strangle her. "Shit, I have to get to Grandfather's!" Her abrupt and erratic movements must have strained her sore body, and she hissed in pain.

Gabe reached out his hand and laid it on her arm, "Slow down, Cat. I've already called Bec, and they know we're running late. No one assumed we'd have such an eventful day when they woke up this morning." He picked up the tea and smiled when Onnie closed her eyes and breathed in the scent. "I made you a fresh cup. Drink this, okay?"

Onnie took the teacup and leaned in closer to the steam. "Thanks. I mean, for calling them, and for the tea, too. I'm glad Grandfather won't be worried."

"Of course, once you finish your tea, we'll get you cleaned up and ready for dinner."

"Do I really look that bad?" Onnie asked, patting her hair and looking at her clothes.

"Of course not, you're beautiful, but you do appear like you've been thrown against a wall." Gabe winked at her and stood up.

"You're an ass."

He touched his heart, "Ah, I'm wounded. Such harsh words, and from a lady too." he offered her his hand.

"And apparently, you're a drama queen." Onnie placed her hand in his, and he pulled her into a standing position. "Thanks."

Gabe sucked in a breath when she stopped just a few inches from him and looked up at him, her cheeks turning that lovely pink when she was embarrassed about something. When she became aware of how close they were standing, she quickly dropped his hand and took another sip of her tea as she walked to the front of the store.

He frowned and followed behind her, stopping to pick up her cell phone, slip it into his pocket, and grab the blanket to fold as he walked.

"So, with Abbot living along the waterfront, how do you usually get there? You don't walk all that way, do you?"

"Typically, yes. Though sometimes I do drive." Onnie said as she disappeared into the back room of the store.

"Oh, what do you drive?" He followed behind her and set the blanket on the back of the couch.

"A Jetta," she said between sips.

He rolled his eyes, "Jetta, of course, you have a Jetta."

Onnie looked at him with a scowl, "And what's wrong with a Jetta?"

"Nothing. I'm sure it's a great car." Gabe teased as he returned to the front room and gave her privacy. "Did you walk to work today, Cat?"

"Yes," her voice echoed from the back room, "why?"

"After all the commotion today, I don't want you walking. We'll take my car."

"Fine."

Gabe grinned at how easily she'd agreed, "That was easy."

Onnie's upper body appeared in the door frame, "but next time...I get to drive." she smiled and disappeared again.

Gabe ran his hand through his hair and leaned on the counter. "If you insist," he muttered into the cold marble.

"What was that?" Onnie asked from the back room.

"Oh, nothing," he said before adding, quieter to himself, "just my dignity flying out the window."

Chapter 13: Levity

November 2021 - Alku | Onnie Moore

Onnie looked at herself in the full-length mirror on the wall in the back room of the shop. The first day she'd seen it, she had chuckled to herself, wondering who was so vain they needed a dressing mirror at work. Then she remembered Rebecca's consistently perfect up-dos with never a strand out of place.

Today, seeing herself in the mirror, Onnie was thankful it was there. Gabriel was right. She looked incredibly rumpled, and her Grandfather would worry if he saw her like this.

"Do you see my bag out there?" Onnie called into the front room.

"Yes, would you like it?"

"Yes, please."

Onnie leaned into the mirror, looking deeper into her eyes. Her typically emerald green eyes were more blue than usual and seemed to sparkle as if they knew something she didn't and were excited about whatever it was.

Gabriel entered the doorway with her bag and held it out to her. She stepped back from the mirror, taking it from him and plunking it down on the couch.

"I'm going to finish closing the shop while you get ready." Gabriel gestured to the front of the store with his thumb, "I'll give you some privacy."

Onnie looked up and smiled at his thoughtfulness, "Thanks, Gabriel, that's very sweet of you."

Turning, he threw a smile at her over his shoulder before returning to the shop front, and she had to forcibly ignore the butterflies that had suddenly taken up residence in her stomach. She slipped off her hair tie, shaking her braid out, and then dug through her bag for her hairbrush. When she began to comb it out, an involuntary yelp escaped when the bristles snagged on a few clumps of dried blood.

"Everything okay?" Gabriel's anxious voice came from the front of the store.

"Yeah, I just need a shower." She gave up hope of removing all the tangles and set down her brush before braiding her hair again.

"Cat, I'm going to run to my car and grab a clean shirt," Gabriel called from the front.

"Alright!" she replied, hearing the door open and close behind him.

Onnie looked in the mirror, brushed blanket fuzzies off her dark jeans, and straightened her knee-high leather boots lined with fake fur. When she had left her apartment that morning, she figured she'd be walking to dinner after dark, so she'd worn her warmest shoes. Her shirt was twisted beneath her sweatshirt, so she removed it and straightened her long-sleeve thermal, now covered in wrinkles from her impromptu nap. It didn't seem to be helping, so she had no choice but to admit it was a lost cause. A patch of blood was on the hood of her sweatshirt, and she rolled her eyes.

"Damn, guess I'm only wearing my jacket tonight." She folded the bloody garment and set it on the sofa. Tomorrow, after work, she'd take it home to wash.

The shop door opened and closed again, "Gabriel?"

"It's only me," he responded.

She stuck her hairbrush back into her bag and dug around for her cell phone, patting her back pockets and checking her sweatshirt.

"Gabriel…do you know where my phone is?"

His face appeared in the doorway, a sly smile on it. "What do I get if I give it to you?"

She crossed her arms and narrowed her eyes at him.

"Fine, I'll tell you what I want in exchange."

He stepped further into the room and right up to her. She held her breath as he studied her eyes and then glanced at her lips.

"I want..." he said, dragging out his request with a deep-timbered voice, "you, to..." he leaned down, only a breath from her ear. "Smile," he whispered, the word tickling her ear.

Before she could respond, he tucked her phone into her back pocket and turned, leaving her in shock and completely blushing. It took her a few minutes to rouse herself from the spell his voice had wrapped around her, and she checked her phone.

"You ready to go, Gabriel? It's three-fifteen."

"Yup, I'm waiting for you to turn off the main lights, and we can head out."

"Just a sec." Onnie grabbed her bag before she turned off the lights in the back room and took a deep breath to compose herself. When she walked to the store's entry, where Gabriel waited, she was sure the pink in her cheeks was still visible. Halfway through the room, she stopped and inspected the space.

"Wait, what happened to the mess?" The bookshelves that had been toppled were standing tall once more, books stacked neatly beside or in front of them. Everything that had been on the front counter was back where it belonged, and the floor looked swept.

"I did what I could," Gabriel said, and her eyes snapped to meet his before he looked away. "Not sure if you still had things organized the same way, so I stacked stuff where I thought it might go and figured you...."

Onnie listened as the imposing and intimidating man standing before her turned timid and began to mumble. Without thinking, she closed the distance between them and hugged him. Their height difference meant the top of her head barely brushed his clavicle, and she felt silly and small next to him. Gabriel didn't hug her back, and she worried that she'd made him uncomfortable, but before she pulled away, he wrapped his arms around her and gently squeezed her back. Onnie didn't miss that he held on to her higher up her back than expected, and she smiled against him at his concern and consciousness for her bruising.

"Thank you, Gabe. You didn't need to do that, but I really appreciate it." She said and then began to step back from him. When she looked up at his face, his expression was calm and reserved, but his eyes told his real feelings.

"You're welcome. If you need more help tomorrow, let me know."

"I will." Onnie smiled and walked over to the coat rack by the door.

"You're not wearing your sweatshirt," Gabriel said, retrieving her long black coat from the hook before she could and holding it open for her.

"No, it had blood on it. I don't want Grandfather to see it and worry," she replied as she slipped one arm in and then the next.

"Will you be warm enough in just your coat?"

Onnie zipped, fastened the coat closed, and ran her fingers over the coarse wool paneling and oversized metal buttons. "Yeah, no worries, especially with you insisting on driving anyway." She smiled, looking up at Gabriel and catching his boyish grin.

"Alright then, if you're sure." Gabriel opened the door and

gestured for Onnie to lead the way. He clicked off the last lamp nearest them and exited the shop before stepping aside so she could lock up.

"You're sure you don't want to walk there? The weather cleared up." She said, staring at the sky, no longer grey and wild but a bright, crystal blue.

"Not after that bump you got, Cat. We can walk another time. Today, we'll take my car." A mischievous light sparkled in Gabriel's eyes, and a sly grin crossed his lips.

Onnie knew that look. Three older brothers and an endless amount of chaos energy always equaled that expression. "Oh, jeez, my brothers always make that face before doing something to shock me. Should I be worried about what you drive?"

Gabriel laughed loud enough that people on the street turned to stare. "Oh, little Cat, this is going to be fun."

He led her around the corner to the side of the bookshop bordered by a small parking lot. A sleek white Audi sat parked in one of the two closest spots, glistening with a dusting of crystal raindrops. He reached forward with his free hand and opened the passenger door with a soft click.

"In you get, Cat."

Speechless, Onnie carefully lowered herself into the softest leather she'd ever felt. Gabriel closed the door gently, and while he walked around the front of the car to the driver's side, Onnie inhaled, savoring the scent of the car's leather interior that had meshed with Gabriel's.

He opened the door and lowered himself into the deep bucket seat, sighing with a contented smile.

"You drive a sports car?" she said, looking at him in disbelief. "On a teacher's salary, you drive a sports car."

Gabriel's laugh reverberated through the car, and Onnie was overwhelmed by how truly unguarded and carefree it was. "No, Cat," his eyes sparkled with excitement, "I drive a fast car."

Gabriel started the engine, and they both clicked their seat belts before he shifted gears and pulled out of the small parking lot.

Abbot's house wasn't far from the bookshop on foot and by car, and it seemed nearly a waste to drive. It was the first time Onnie had been a passenger, not the driver in Alku, and she was content to watch the city pass by her window.

"Would you like to pick the music?" Gabriel asked while they waited for a group of kids to cross the street.

"Ah…not rap. Other than that, I'm not picky."

Gabriel clicked a button on the steering wheel, filling the car with the soft plucking of cellos, violins, and a piano.

Onnie turned to look at him, surprised by his choice, "Classical?"

"Not really, just instrumental. There's something beautiful in the simplicity of only having a few instruments."

"I didn't take you for a 'beauty' kind of guy," Onnie said honestly.

"There's quite a lot you don't know about me, Cat."

"Yet here I am in your car. I must have hit my head harder than I realized." Onnie groaned.

Gabriel removed his right hand from the steering wheel and, with one long finger, turned Onnie's chin towards him and pleaded with his eyes. "If there's one thing you can know for sure, it's that I will never hurt you."

"I bet you tell all the women stupid enough to get into your car. Eyes on the road, mister." Heat crept into her cheeks, threatening to betray her true feelings, so she turned to look out the window again.

Gabriel removed his hand and replaced it on the steering wheel, "I have never meant anything more in my life, Cat. You'll realize that soon enough. I can wait."

Onnie closed her eyes and rested her forehead on the glass. She really hoped he meant it because it was starting to look like she'd made a promise to herself all those years ago that she wouldn't be able to keep

.

Chapter 14: Clarity

November 2021 - Alku | Onnie Moore

The rest of the short drive passed in relative silence, and only a few minutes after leaving the bookshop, Gabriel graciously opened Onnie's door, and she stood outside her Grandfather's home.

"Damn, now I remember why I walk everywhere." Onnie teased, even though Gabriel had been an impeccable driver. "What is it with men and sports cars?"

"It's not a sports car." Gabriel chuckled as he closed her door and followed her up the walk.

He placed his hand on the small of her back, still avoiding her sore spot, and even though she liked his palm there, she shrugged her messenger bag across her body to force his hand to move. Unphased, Gabriel wrapped his arm around her shoulders instead.

"I'm an incredible driver. I'll have you know, not one accident on my record, thank you very much."

"The way you drive? I find that hard to believe."

Before they had reached the front door, Rebecca had it open and gestured for them to hurry inside. Onnie seized the opportunity to slip from Gabriel's grasp and skipped past Rebecca and into the entryway.

Gabriel leisurely followed her up the front steps and stopped to kiss Rebecca on the cheek.

"You're an evil boy." Rebecca teased. She looked over Gabriel at arm's length, "My my, doesn't Guardianship suit you. Congratulations, dear. I'm so proud of you, and Abbot is too."

Gabriel's eyes met Onnie's, and she forced a smile before he ushered Rebecca back into the house and closed the door behind them. Onnie took the opportunity to get some space from Gabriel and searched for her Grandfather.

"You're going to tell Onnie tonight, right? Everything?" Onnie heard Gabriel ask as she left, her frustration over everyone's colluding behind her back growing by the minute.

A warm, roaring fire was crackling in the living room, and her Grandfather was cradling a cup of tea while he stared into it, clearly lost in his thoughts. When Onnie cleared her throat softly, he turned to see who made it, and his eyes lit up when he saw her.

"Onnie, my dear, come here and give me a hug." he placed his cup down and held his arms open wide.

She sat down next to him in the second chair, leaned over, and hugged him fiercely, "Grandpa, how are you feeling?" He rubbed her upper back, and she released some of the tension she was carrying.

"I am alright, my dear. How are you?" He pulled away and held her out so he could inspect her, just as Rebecca had to Gabriel a minute earlier. "Rebecca tells me you had some excitement at the shop today."

Onnie nodded with wide eyes, and he chuckled at her but didn't respond. Instead, he looked past her, and she knew Gabriel had joined then. After looking over her shoulder and confirming it, she saw Rebecca smile and then head to the kitchen. Onnie stood and switched to the couch opposite Abbot, making room for Gabriel to say hello.

He walked over and held out his hand to his sick friend, "Hello, old man, been a while."

Abbot took Gabriel's hand but clasped it between his own instead of shaking it. "Gabe, my boy, you've grown since I last saw you."

"Yes, so it seems. Your mistress finally provided the boost I needed to fill out a bit more, and I guess all the training paid off."

"What's that, you say? I was right all along.... Hmmm." Abbot smiled and patted Gabriel's hand before letting it go.

"Don't push it, old man," Gabriel said playfully, grumbling before stepping back and winking at Onnie.

Abbot laughed and gestured to himself, "Well, no need to worry now. As you can see, she has wasted no time beginning the Transference."

"Nonsense, you look fit as a bull." Gabriel tucked the blankets higher around the older man before sitting next to Onnie.

Rebecca reentered the room carrying a tea tray with all the fixings and a pot of hot water. "Onnie, my dear, may I have the tea you brought from the shop, please?"

"Oh, I'm sorry, I forgot all about it." Onnie dug through her bag for the red tin and began to panic when she couldn't find it. Gabriel rested his hand gently on her arm to still her. He reached into the outer pocket, removed the tin, and handed it to Rebecca.

"I must have forgotten I put it there.... Wait, how did you— Were you in my bag?"

"Calm down, Cat, yes. While cleaning up the shop, I replaced everything thrown across the room with us, including your bag and everything in it."

"Oh...." suddenly ashamed for snapping at him, she looked away and apologized, "I'm sorry...."

Gabriel squeezed her forearm, "Look at me, Cat. There's nothing to forgive. You've had one hell of a day."

He smiled at her, and out of the corner of her eye, Onnie saw Rebecca and Abbot watching her interaction with Gabriel closely. Rebecca had her hand on Abbot's shoulder, and he patted it gently while they both shared a glance that told of a shared secret.

Eventually, Abbot cleared his throat, and Onnie pulled her arm from Gabriel's grasp, fire creeping up her cheeks.

"I know you said you were okay, but is there anything I can do?" Onnie leaned forward to accept the cup of tea that Rebecca handed her and narrowed her gaze at her Grandfather. Abbot did look weaker than usual. His eyes were more sunken than she'd ever seen, and there was a paleness to his skin and a sheen of sweat on his brow as if from a fever. He looked like nothing more than skin over bone.

"You've already done it," he said, accepting his cup, "it's nothing a good cup of tea won't cure." He raised a sturdy green mug to his lips and inhaled deeply. Onnie swore his cheeks flushed almost immediately, and the bags under his eyes retreated slightly. Rebecca squeezed Abbot's shoulder gently and watched over him from behind his chair.

Gabriel picked up the last frilly teacup on the tray and poured the aromatic liquid into it. He set it on its matching saucer and sat back on the couch. Onnie watched as he raised it to his lips, and she chuckled under her breath at how absurd such a large man looked with such delicate china. Gabriel noticed and stuck out his pinky, taking a long, loud slurp, which caused Onnie to snort into her drink.

The soft clattering of fine china drew her attention back to Rebecca as she slipped from the room, her own tea in hand.

"I'd like to hear more about what happened today." Abbot asked, "Would you tell me about it?"

"Ah…sure," Onnie said, glancing at Gabriel, who didn't seem to notice. "Although, I'm not really sure what happened."

"Just do your best, dear," Abbot said reassuringly.

"Alright." she lowered her cup's saucer to her lap. "So, Gabriel came into the store looking for a book. We scoured the shop for about an hour trying to find it without luck. When we were taking a break, Rebecca called and wanted to talk to Gabriel. While they were talking, I found this old leather book under the counter that didn't have a title. I showed it to Gabriel, and the next thing I knew, I was on the floor behind the counter."

"Hmmm...." Abbot said, his brow furrowed, not in concentration but in amusement, "And you, my boy, anything you want to add?"

Gabriel tipped his head back and drank the last dregs of his tea before setting his cup and saucer back on the tea tray. "When both of us were in contact with the *Custos regni,* the air around us felt charged, and everything went quiet as if something had removed all of the world's sounds. There was no oxygen, and at the moment before it had us gasping for breath, a shockwave tore us apart. I woke up with a bump on my head and Rebecca screaming in my ear."

"I was most certainly not screaming!" Rebecca scoffed as she emerged from the kitchen, carrying a plate of fresh scones.

Abbot chuffed and looked over his shoulder, "You were screaming, dear."

Rebecca set the plate on the table and then busied herself by pouring Gabriel more tea and topping off Onnie's half-empty cup.

"What about you, my beautiful Granddaughter? Any bumps for you?" Abbot said, concern in his voice and on his brow.

"Ah...nope," she answered quickly, "I got lucky, I guess...." her grip tightened on her teacup.

Her Grandfather's eyes sparkled, and she knew he didn't believe her. "Well, I'm glad you had Gabriel there to ensure you were alright." Abbot leaned forward, plucked a scone off the plate, and dunked it in his tea. "Now, I'm told you've been rather adamant about getting some answers."

Onnie nearly choked on her tea, and she coughed around her words, "Really? You've never wanted to talk about the shop before now."

Abbot sighed and nibbled the corner of his scone. After a few moments, Rebecca stood behind his chair and rested her hand gently on his shoulder. He reached up and pat it, a weary smile on his pale lips.

"Yes, that is true. I miss my store dearly, and it pains me to talk about her. Everything is changing, but now you'll be there to look after her, which warms my heart."

Onnie frowned and felt Gabriel fidget beside her.

"Besides, as Gabriel has correctly pointed out...." Abbot smirked at him across the seating area, "Many times now, you need to know."

"Past time, Abbot," Gabriel said, his body tense and his tone clipped.

"Perhaps," Abbot said, the sparkle gone from his eyes along with the teasing attitude from seconds before.

"Okay," Onnie said as she set her tea on the tray and scootched to the edge of the couch. "Did I honestly get thrown across the room by that book?"

Her Grandfather's small frame shook with silent laughter. "A great man once said, 'Once you eliminate the impossible, whatever remains, no matter how improbable, must be the truth.' I think in this instance, you'll find he was correct."

"Alright, say I believe you. Now tell me how?" With her elbows on her knees, she leaned her chin on her hands and stared at him with undivided attention. "Gas leak, earthquake, fainting spell?"

Abbot smiled wildly, "No, it's much simpler. It was magic."

She rolled her eyes and smiled. "I figured you'd say that. Pretend I believe you crazy people and follow you down this rabbit hole. If magic is real, how is all this happening? You know my background, and I have never heard of anything like this. How was it such a well-kept secret?"

Finished with her rambling thoughts, she looked at the others in the room and saw that she had stood and been pacing the living room, gesticulating wildly with her hands. All three of them were wide-eyed and attempting to hold back laughter.

"Ugg!" She groaned in frustration and plopped back on the couch next to Gabriel.

Rebecca shook her head in amusement and returned to the kitchen as Gabriel took one of Onnie's hands and squeezed it gently. Her chest warmed, and she felt his reassurance through their slight touch. Abbot wore an entertained smile, and she was relieved that she hadn't offended him.

"Those are some complicated questions, my dear girl, and none I will be able to answer adequately tonight. Let's start with something smaller, shall we? Though your thirst for knowledge will be what makes you a fantastic Keeper."

Onnie felt his dismissal and slumped back onto the couch, suddenly exhausted.

"I believe Gabriel may have already begun this conversation," Abbot looked from her to him, "you may tell her anything you wish now."

Gabriel nodded and released her hand, and she immediately noticed the cold seeping into her skin that had so recently been warm. He picked up the teapot, filled her teacup, and handed it back to her.

"Drink. It'll help." then he filled Abbot's mug and his own. Gabriel raised his cup to his lips and took a small sip before clearing his throat. "Do you remember what I told you about you being the Keeper?" He looked thoughtfully at her, and she nodded while blowing across her tea. "Well, you're not alone. The old man over there is a Keeper too, or he was."

Onnie's eyes flicked to Abbot, and once reassured by his smile, she looked back at Gabriel. "Now that we have begun the Transference, his connection with the store will wane, and ours will grow."

"Wait, ours?" Onnie's brow creased in confusion.

"Yes, ours."

"You're a Keeper too?"

Gabriel looked at the older man, his gaze pleading for help. "You tell her. She won't believe it if I tell her. I'm still practically a stranger to her."

Onnie looked at her Grandfather, a slight frown lining his lips, and he shook his head at Gabriel. "No, my boy, you must do it."

She looked back at Gabriel and waited as patiently as she could manage.

Gabriel rubbed his forehead and swallowed loudly. He shifted in his seat and faced Onnie, his knee pressed softly against hers. "So, as I told you before, the shop is a collection of knowledge, and just as the shop can, the Keeper can access all of the information, too."

Onnie nodded, remembering their conversation from earlier, filing away the part about her being able to access endless information. They were finally answering her questions, and she wouldn't screw it up by interrupting.

"A Keeper is attuned with the shop on a deep level. You'll feel her emotions, her elation, and excitement, but with the good comes the bad. The Keeper also shares her pain, remorse, and fear…and sometimes it can overwhelm a Keeper."

Onnie looked over at Abbot, whose face was neutral, but he just barely tipped his head.

"Sometimes, the emotions are reversed, and what the Keeper feels flows through the connection and can overwhelm the shop too." Gabriel paused, "Are you with me so far?"

She paused for a second before nodding, "There's this entity, a woman," she glanced at Abbot, "she embodies the shop, and we have an emotional connection. I can feel her, and she can feel me."

"Right, basically. Because this connection between the shop and the Keeper is so powerful and so much knowledge and information is in play, there needs to be another person also attuned to the store. The Guardian. A Guardian is directly connected to the Keeper and therefore indirectly to the shop."

Onnie's head whipped around and glared at Abbot, who shook his head and indicated she hear Gabriel out. Rebecca's comment from when they'd arrived replayed in Onnie's mind. "*Guardianship suits you,*" she'd said to Gabriel.

"It's the Guardian's job to support the Keeper in whatever way necessary to uphold their pledge. Every Keeper has one, and only one Guardian and their Bond is sealed when both are fit to protect the shop, and she feels comfortable that they can carry out their oaths."

Onnie held up her hand, silencing Gabriel, "You're my Guardian." she stated.

Gabriel looked over at Abbot again.

"No secrets now, Gabriel. You may tell her as much as you wish."

He returned his gaze to hers and nodded. "Yes, I am, and as long as I am breathing, I will be there to protect you. Both of you."

"That's what you meant in the car." She put her head in her hands and pushed the heels of her palms into her eyes to stop her tears. She internally chastised herself for letting a man get to her. She knew better, and she'd made a promise to herself. "Here, I thought maybe you cared about me, but I'm just a job, someone for you to babysit."

"Do not take his oath lightly, child!" Abbot thundered, the windows rattling. Onnie looked up into his red face, his anger palpable. "I have known Gabriel all his life, and he has been preparing for your arrival for many years."

"Years!?" Onnie shouted out in surprise. "Why am I the last to know all of this? Do I even get a choice, or am I just some puppet you all get to push around? Poor loner Onnie, she'd be perfect for saddling with this job, the stupid sap! Who decided I'd be okay with all this anyway? What if I don't want it!"

"Onnie!" Rebecca scolded as she reentered the room with a fresh pot of tea. Onnie could smell the aroma, and what usually relaxed her turned her stomach.

She looked around the room into the three faces staring back at her and saw a mixture of shock and sadness. Once again, she'd gotten to her feet, fists clenched at her sides, and she was yelling at a sick old man and his companions.

She unclenched her fists and closed her eyes, taking a deep breath. "I need some air."

She grabbed her coat from the hook and dashed out of the house onto the back deck. Her mind was all over the place, and she paced back and forth furiously. Her breathing was ragged, and her hands flailed as she shouted to herself within her mind.

How could they do this to her? Why would they do this without asking? She loved the bookshop, sure, but to be some mystical Keeper, didn't she get a choice? They all knew this was unavoidable when they asked her to move.

A soft, raspy sigh caused her to be still. When Onnie turned around, she saw her Grandfather wrapped in a thick woolen scarf and a long black pea coat, shuffling out onto the deck in his slippers. He walked past her wordlessly and, with frailty she'd not witnessed from him before, rested his hands on the railing and looked out over the water. He didn't speak, just stood there and watched the waters shift.

Onnie felt a mental calm settle over her, and the silence that enveloped them helped sweep the angry bees from her head. Her irritation slowly left her body until, finally, she felt like she could talk without screaming.

With a heavy sigh, mirroring Abbot's earlier one, she leaned on the railing beside her Grandfather. "I—"

"Don't apologize to me, dear girl. You have every right to be angry with me. I should have told you what was happening from the beginning."

Onnie turned her head to look at him. "So, you did know this was going to happen."

Her Grandfather nodded.

She returned to watching the boats, and the companionable silence grew between them as they watched people drifting lazily on the water.

"It's beautiful here," Onnie said after a few minutes. "I like Alku."

"Yes, it is, and I'm very glad." She saw her Grandfather's sad smile from the corner of her eye. After a few minutes, he cleared his throat and spoke again, unshed tears thickening his voice. "I'm dying, Onnie."

Onnie lowered her head and squeezed her eyes shut. "I know."

Abbot chuffed softly beside her, "I know, you know, my brilliant Granddaughter. Our shop is wise, and you will make a perfect Keeper."

"So, I really have no choice?" Onnie said more out of curiosity than a desire to refuse.

"No, you don't," Abbot shook his head, "and though you won't believe me, you wouldn't have been chosen if there was even a small chance that you'd have rejected the opportunity."

Onnie picked at the peeling paint on the wooden railing to keep herself from yelling again, her stiff posture apparent to the intelligent man beside her as he continued, "Would having a choice make a difference?"

"Of course!" she exclaimed, her control slipping momentarily.

The older man slowly turned his gaze upon her and raised an eyebrow in question, and Onnie winced under the scrutiny.

"Maybe?" she threw her hands up, "Oh, I don't know."

"Being the Keeper is a magnificent honor, and our bookshop does not choose Keepers on a whim. She looks long and diligently for the right spirit and character to aid her and help in protecting her secrets."

"But, why me?"

Abbot turned and placed his papery palm on her cheek, "My dear girl, why wouldn't she choose you? You seek out learning wherever you go and have a sense of adventure in you that she can relate to. You're witty, honest, and compassionate. When she found you, she knew immediately that you were who she wanted."

Onnie closed her eyes and breathed deeply. When she opened them again, they were filled with tears. "What's going to happen to you? I've only really just gotten to know you, and now."

"My girl, everyone has to die. I have lived a long, full life, been loved, and have loved in return. Having you come here and get a chance to see what a kind-hearted young woman you have grown into has given me the greatest gift any old man could want."

He removed his palm and tucked his hands into his jacket sleeves. "Let me tell you a story, and then I will share something with you."

"Okay." Onnie sniffled, wiped her tears, and returned her gaze to the waters.

"As you know, when your mother was young, your Grandmother and I realized we were not suitable for each other. I loved your Grandmother deeply, but I had the shop to tend to and a destiny to fulfill. I could not give your Grandmother what she deserved. So, Lon and I parted ways.

Your Grandmother moved her and your mother to California, where she remained my best friend until the day she passed. Tory was too young to understand why they were moving away and why I stayed behind. Try as we might, neither your Grandmother nor I could ever convince her that we separated on good terms.

Only on her deathbed did your Grandmother convince Tory to return here and reconnect with me. I believe she hoped our little girl would finally forgive me. So, your mother came to see me, and after a few days of small conversations and heated arguments, she finally understood why I did what I did."

"Mom came to Washington? She never told me."

"I don't think she wanted you to know. Your brothers might, though. I have no idea. Your mother asked to replace me as the next Keeper."

"Really?"

Abbot nodded, "I think she wanted to experience the connection I had with the shop and understand why it was so important that I would give up my family. Rather than lie to her, I told your mother the truth. She was not destined to be the next Keeper, and there was nothing she or I could do to change that. She demanded to know who it was and was extremely upset when I refused to tell her."

"It was me," Onnie stated emotionlessly.

Her Grandfather smiled so warmly that Onnie felt like the sun had broken through the clouds. "All those years ago, our shop knew you would be the next Keeper, but you were too young, and I wasn't finished yet. So, she waited, and when you came of age and were ready to take up the Keeper's mantle, she drew you here, and you came."

"She did?"

"Yes. I may have been the one to ask, but it was her will and, once you were here, her influence and spirit that you grew to love."

"What if I had said no? Then what would she do, look for someone else?"

"No, only one Keeper is destined to inherit the honor. You would not have said no. As I said before, you wouldn't have been chosen if there were a chance you'd refuse or regret your decision. A Keeper cannot be forced onto their path, so she waited until you were ready to accept it."

Onnie broke their eye contact and returned to watch the water again, her mind spinning.

Abbot took her hand in his, "Let me show you something. Close your eyes." she hesitated, and he smiled, "Please."

Obligingly, she closed them.

"Now, I want you to take a few deep breaths and clear your mind."

Onnie inhaled a deep breath of damp air through her nose and out through her mouth and tried to focus on a clear head. After a few minutes, Abbot spoke again, and his voice sounded distant and foggy.

"Good. Now, focus on me. Feel my hand holding yours, my skin, my bones." Abbot gave Onnie a few minutes to focus and then continued. "Now, I want you to ignore my body, instead feel for my mind. Reach out and try to touch it."

Onnie struggled and felt foolish, but she tried to remember that a book kicked her ass earlier that day. After a few moments, a blue thread of colored light materialized in her mind, its light glowing in a sea of black.

"That's it. Follow that thread to its end."

Onnie flew down the thread of light, mentally soaring and weaving around it.

Grandfather chuckled, "Do you see where that thread splits?"

Onnie stopped as the blue thread diverged into two smaller, more vibrant streams of light. One seemed to blend from blue to yellow, and she reached cautiously for it and felt a rush of pride wash over her.

"That light thread leads to Rebecca, and I'll explain where she fits in later. Try the other thread."

Doing as she was told, Onnie followed the strand back to the split and then down the second one, a shimmering opalescent color.

Instantly, Onnie was overwhelmed with emotions, and she coughed and sputtered.

She opened her eyes and looked at Abbot, and his eyes were filled with tears pouring down his cheeks in silent rivulets. His face was lit with happiness as she struggled to pull air into her lungs. Onnie lifted her hand to her cheek, stunned to find they were also damp.

Abbot patted the back of her hand and released it. "Those threads of light are called the Bond, and that last thread was our shop. I think I'd be correct in saying she's happy you're finally here."

Still unable to talk, her heart full to bursting with emotions not her own, Onnie rested her head on her arms and closed her eyes.

After a few minutes of silence, while Onnie tried to settle herself, she felt her Grandfather shiver beside her. Onnie turned her head and studied the older man's profile. "Thank you."

Abbot nodded, but Onnie felt another wave of pride wash over her, much milder this time. It didn't rip the breath from her body.

"That was the shop. She'll become stronger and clearer the more your Bond grows. You'll both become more skilled at communicating with practice."

Onnie nodded and rested her head on his shoulder. "I'm sorry for overreacting, Grandfather."

"You did nothing of the sort. Do not apologize. There is nothing to forgive." Abbot carefully stroked her hair, and she smirked when she realized he was being intentionally mindful of her injury.

"Let's go back inside. Rebecca must be worried." Onnie offered her arm to help guide him.

Abbot chuckled and accepted Onnie's arm. "And your Guardian must be frantic."

"Grandfather, how well do you know Gabriel? How am I supposed to trust someone I barely know?"

"I have known Gabriel since he was but knee high. He has grown into an honorable young man and one worthy of your trust."

Onnie frowned, "But—"

"Your Bond with Gabe will also strengthen over time, just as you saw how brightly mine burned with Rebecca. Guardians are chosen just as carefully as Keepers. You would not have been paired if it was not a fit. Rarely does she make mistakes."

"But my emotions, will he...." she stopped, unable to put her confusion into words.

"Over time, you will each be able to anticipate the other's emotions and understand them without needing words. Never second guess what you feel. Trust yourself."

The back door creaked open, and Gabriel's head emerged. "Am I interrupting?"

Grandfather's roaring laughter broke the tension. "You can come out. I'm going to go in and try to weasel some tea out of Rebecca and mayhap one of her biscotti." He turned to wink at Onnie and started for the door.

"But Grandfather...."

"Trust your heart, dear. What does it tell you?" The older man shuffled past Gabriel and patted his arm on the way by. "Don't stay out here too long, you two. You'll miss dinner."

After letting the older man pass, Gabriel closed the door behind him and stuck his hands in his pockets. "So...you and the old man work things out?"

"Ah, yeah," Onnie said, fiddling with the button on her jacket.

"Good."

The silence stretched between them until Gabriel shifted and leaned on the railing beside her. Onnie returned to leaning on the rail and rubbed her temples with her fingers. Her head hurt and felt heavy.

Gabriel shifted closer, his warmth washing over her when he leaned into her shoulder. She rotated her face and looked up at him, her eyes filled with tears of her own this time. He didn't hesitate, sweeping her into his arms, softly rubbing her back in tiny circles.

"I'm sorry, Cat. What can I do to help?"

Onnie sobbed quietly into his chest, "He's dying, Gabriel, and I've only started to get to know him. I don't want to lose him already."

"Shh.... I know, but you still have some time with him." Gabriel stroked her hair softly and held on to her tightly.

"It's a poor comparison for the life I've missed."

Gabriel cooed, "Abbot has been happier since you've been here."

Onnie hiccuped, and Gabriel chuckled. It made her smile, and she could feel some of the tension releasing from her shoulders. The two of them stayed that way, Gabriel letting Onnie cry and her finding comfort until darkness fell and the crickets sang their night song.

Eventually, Onnie pulled away and wiped her eyes. "I'm sorry, I'm not typically the kind of person who cries."

"What, who cried?" Gabriel teased her, and she couldn't help but smile at his silliness.

She quickly turned away, "I'm sorry about earlier. It was uncalled for, and I barely know you. I had no right—"

Gabriel took one of her hands in his and placed his other hand's index finger softly on her lips. "I know you're sorry, and you do not need to be. You don't know me yet. I plan to change that, but for now, can you do one small thing for me?"

Onnie nodded behind his fingertip.

"Trust me when I say you are not just a job."

Onnie squeezed her eyes closed and nodded.

"Thank you." Removing his finger, Gabriel leaned down and placed a feather-light kiss on her cheek, "Let's head back inside. Bec's probably losing her hair over dinner going cold."

Onnie opened her eyes and smiled, "Yeah. Gabriel…thank you… for everything."

"Anytime, Cat," he ushered her to the door. "In you get."

She took a few deep breaths and entered the house.

Chapter 15: Shock

November 2021 - Alku | Onnie Moore

No one at dinner mentioned Onnie's earlier outburst or her puffy eyes when she and Gabriel reentered the house. Instead, the four of them sat down for dinner. They discussed the differences between the Day Night Cafe and A Shot in the Dark's pastries, the winter snowstorm that had her brother's family sledding instead of schooling, and Onnie's favorite new running route since moving to Alku.

Their light-hearted conversations continued for two hours until Rebecca finally shooed everyone back into the sitting room with promises of more tea and freshly baked goodies. Onnie offered to help clear the table while Gabriel settled Abbot back into his chair by the fire, but after only helping with one plate, Rebecca waved her off and sent her after the others.

Onnie entered the sitting room to find Gabriel and her Grandfather's heads together, exchanging whispers. Gabriel noticed her and blushed a deep crimson before sitting back quickly.

"Gabriel, is that…a blush I see? I didn't know you had it in you." It was Onnie's chance to tease him, which only made him blush more.

"Oh, child, do not pick on your Guardian." Abbot stated, "You'll find they gain great insight into what annoys you as your Bond grows."

Rolling her eyes, Onnie placed a kiss on her Grandfather's forehead and returned to her seat on the opposite couch. "Yes, Grandfather."

Abbot smacked his lips, rubbed his hands together, and looked towards the kitchen. "Where's my Rebecca? I could sure use a spot of tea and some of her delectable edibles!"

Gabriel and Onnie both chuckled at the old man's insatiable sweet tooth. Onnie wiggled deeper into the couch, trying to get comfortable, but her bruising hindered her regular pleasing positions. Gabriel noticed and put his arm behind her on the back of the sofa.

"Dinner was excellent, and I think I could curl up here and sleep for days," Onnie said, extremely satisfied and with a full stomach.

Gabriel smirked at the old man, "See, she's a Cat."

Onnie playfully swatted at Gabriel, "Oh, shush you."

"Just like her mother, my boy." Abbot laughed, "I wish you luck. My little Tory would cuddle up with her blankets and picture books and fall asleep within minutes."

The familiar clinking of china came from the kitchen, and Rebecca set the tea tray on the ottoman. Onnie inhaled the spicy scent of the special tea she'd grown to love, relieved when it no longer made her stomach turn. Rebecca had the grace and poise of royalty as she began serving everyone, and Onnie watched the woman with newfound interest.

With half-lidded eyes, Onnie yawned, "So, what's the truth about the tea, Rebecca?"

Rebecca's hands froze, and she slowly turned to look at Onnie. "Whatever do you mean, my dear? I thought you liked tea?"

Grandfather cleared his throat, getting Rebecca's attention, and she sighed with a subtle nod from him. "No more secrets, Rebecca." Abbot scolded gently.

"Oh, alright." Rebecca poured a cup, placed two freshly baked biscuits on the saucer, and passed them to Onnie. "Here you go, dear."

"Thank you. So, why am I drinking so much of this tea?"

Rebecca sat into the chair next to Abbot's, "It's a unique blend. The proportion and ingredients have been passed down since the time of the first Keeper. Only those who are either Keeper or Guardian may drink it."

Onnie narrowed her gaze and looked at Rebecca. "I have seen you drink it too. Does that mean you are Grandfather's Guardian?"

Her Grandfather made a rude noise into his tea, and Rebecca gave him a sour look before adding, "No, my dear, your Grandfather's Guardian left him long ago."

Gabriel tensed beside Onnie, and she felt anger roll off him in waves. When she glanced at him, she did a double take and saw that he wore an expression of barely contained rage and wouldn't meet her eyes. She looked over at her Grandfather, who looked equally as uncomfortable.

"Since that was a touchy question, why don't you just tell me who you are?" Onnie asked innocently.

"I am the third part of the Keeper's circle, your Grandfather's Link."

Onnie's confusion must have shown on her face because her Grandfather cleared his throat. "You're getting ahead of yourself, dear," he told Rebecca, "I don't believe Gabe spoke to her of Links at all."

Crestfallen, Rebecca's smile dipped to a frown, and she busied herself with making a cup of tea and then sipped it quietly.

Abbot shook his head and smiled with affection at Rebecca. "We told you before that there was a Keeper and her protector, the Guardian. There is more to it than that, but today, we'll just go over a few of the important things and let you absorb them first. First, let me answer your astute question about the tea."

Sipping hers slowly, Onnie nodded her agreement.

"This tea is a particular blend, and it's a recipe passed down from Link to Link through the centuries." Onnie's brows knit together in confusion, and Abbot raised his hand to stop her from interrupting. "I'll get back to the Link part in a moment."

She held her tongue and her sassy comment about him reading her mind.

"The tea is a stimulant. It opens our minds to our Bond and allows us to communicate with one another."

Onnie stiffened, her thought about mind reading seconds before being spoken aloud, "So, we can read each other's minds?"

Gabriel shook his head beside her, "It does far more than that, Cat. The shop is extensive, far more than you realize or can imagine. Through our Bond with her and each other, she can amplify us, making it possible to communicate as if we were standing next to each other."

"So, telepathy? That's impossible, right?" Onnie questioned.

Grandfather tsked, but his eyes sparkled with his excitement at their conversation. "Never explain anything as strange or impossible when it comes to the shop, dear girl. More often than not, whatever it was, did indeed happen."

She nodded and smirked at Gabriel. "So, can you read my mind?"

"No," he shook his head, "it's not mind reading, but we can feel each other's emotions, and over time there won't be much you can hide. Longer term, we'll be able to speak along the Bond too, even when we're apart."

Onnie raised her eyebrows, intrigued.

"Right now, you're mainly excited with hints of confusion, exhaustion, and sadness."

"Oh," she leaned back onto the couch and tried to digest the new information, "So, my direct thoughts are safe, but if I need a sandwich, you'll know?"

The room laughed, startling her, and she sloshed her tea.

"Dear girl, I think that's the most enlightening way I have ever heard our Bonds explained." Grandfather reached for his handkerchief and dabbed at the tears in his eyes.

Gabriel smiled wickedly and leaned into Onnie's shoulder to whisper in her ear. "There's also another emotion I'm feeling."

Onnie rolled her eyes and whispered, "I think you've got your wires crossed, dude. The only other emotion I'm feeling is amusement at the size of your ego." She lifted her teacup and hid her smile behind it.

Gabriel chuckled and mirrored her motion and lifted his teacup to his lips before she heard his deep voice, low and barely audible, "If you like the size of my ego, you should see my—"

Onnie coughed and sputtered into her tea, "So, about this Link thing?" she spoke in a rush, trying to cover her reaction to Gabriel and hopefully change the conversation enough that he wouldn't notice her emotions. Beside her, Gabriel smiled and bit into a biscuit, and Onnie groaned internally.

"I guess it's my turn to explain," Rebecca said, lowering her teacup. "A Link is a manifestation of the shop that can aid the Keeper in whatever way necessary to uphold their oath. As I said before, I am quite literally your Grandfather's link to the store."

"So, when you say manifestation…you mean what exactly? That sounds like a dictionary definition." Onnie said, catching her rudeness and wincing. Rebecca's delicate laugh eased Onnie's worry over offending her, and Rebecca continued.

"Yes, I suppose it does. Let me see if I can make it easier to understand." She took another sip of tea, momentarily lost in thought. "Alright, a Link is not the spirit of the shop as a whole. Instead, she creates a physical representation of her humanity. I am, as are all Links before and after me, a piece of the living entity that is the shop. I am from her, but not her, and she is partly me."

"Okay.... I think I get it." Onnie said, still confused, but she felt she was reaching her limit for the night and didn't press it.

Gabriel lowered his tea and interjected. "She's not real."

Onnie looked at Abbot, more confused, pleading for clarity. "Not real?"

"Rebecca is not human. She looks human and acts human, but she is an extension of my connection with the shop and, therefore, not real."

"Okay, let me get this straight," Onnie placed her tea on the table and stood up, "you," she pointed to Rebecca, "sitting there, are a figment of my Grandfather's imagination."

Rebecca shook her head, "No, I am not from his imagination. I am from his Bond with the shop, but you have the basic idea."

"Prove it." Onnie challenged, placing her hands on her hips.

Rebecca looked at Abbot, and he nodded.

Rebecca met Onnie's challenging stare, and then, where there was once a living, breathing Rebecca, there was empty space.

"Holy crap!" Onnie shouted, jumping back and bumping into a small end table, which she quickly reached out to steady.

"I hate it when she does that," said Gabriel, exasperated.

"Where'd she go?" Onnie asked, skipping to the hallway and searching the kitchen.

Rebecca reappeared, standing a few feet behind the couch Onnie had initially been sitting on, and she was now holding Onnie's bloody sweatshirt in her hands.

"I know you left this intentionally, but I'll wash it for you while your Grandfather explains." Rebecca's smile reached ear to ear, and she exited the room giggling like a child.

Gabriel looked at Onnie and offered his hand, "Onnie, come sit down. You're going to pass out."

Onnie nodded slowly before walking across the room, sitting back on the couch like a zombie. Her voice was shaky, "Ah...Grandpa?"

Gabriel slid closer to her and began rubbing her back. "Breathe, Cat."

"She doesn't get to do that very often, and you did ask her to prove it," Her Grandfather responded with a grin ear to ear. "A Link is, as she said earlier, a manifestation. For all outward appearances, Rebecca is human. She can run the store when I cannot, communicate with me from anywhere, and function as an interim Guardian should the need arise. When I die, she will rejoin the shop's being as nothing more than a memory."

Onnie flinched at the mention of the older man's death, and she leaned a little closer into Gabriel's touch. "That's so sad."

Abbot shrugged nonchalantly, but Onnie could see the worry in his eyes. "I suppose so. She and I will die together, and I think it fits after all we've been through." Rebecca appeared behind Abbot, and she placed her hand on his shoulder.

Onnie involuntarily jumped and let out a tiny squeak.

Gabriel glared at Rebecca playfully, "Bec, you're going to give her a heart attack."

"Your sweatshirt is being washed, dear," Rebecca said, ignoring Gabriel's sass.

"Th-thank you." Onnie looked at Gabriel. "You knew?"

"Of course, I've known Bec my entire life, remember."

"Yeah, okay, um...."

The grandfather clock chimed in the entryway, signaling it was eight o'clock, though Onnie would have said it was closer to one in the morning if she judged off her energy level.

"I think you've had enough information for one night. Let's let that sink in before we overburden you with more." Abbot yawned and held open his arms, beckoning Onnie to him. She stood on shaky legs and crossed the room to hug him. Gabriel downed the last of his tea, helped Rebecca clear the teacups, and followed her out of the room.

"My dear, I am so proud of you. You will make a brilliant Keeper."

"Thanks, Grandfather, I'll try."

"You have already succeeded. You're a strong woman, and you'll figure this out."

Onnie snuggled her face deeper into the older man's neck and nodded softly.

"Come on now, dear," he patted her arm softly, "I'm sure Gabe is ready to take you home. You two had a long day that neither of you expected when you woke this morning."

Onnie released him and kissed his cheek. "You'll call me if you need anything, right?"

"Of course, Rebecca or I will."

"Thank you for everything. I know how much the shop means to you."

He waved at her dismissively, "She's your shop now. I've had my time with her, many years, in fact. It's time she had a girlfriend to keep her company instead of an old man."

Onnie smiled and looked up at Gabriel as he reentered the room. "Are you ready to go, little Cat?" he said, holding her coat for her to shrug into.

"Yes, thank you," she said, slipping her arms in. "Where's Rebecca?"

"She's cleaning up but said she will come into the shop to check on you in a few days."

"So, no dinner tomorrow night?" Onnie looked down at her Grandfather.

"Why don't you take the night and go do something fun? You've spent enough time with this older man. Go out and be young for once."

"If you're sure? I don't mind coming for dinner. I enjoy spending time with you."

"I know you do, dear," he reached up, took her hand between his, and patted it gently. "But you need a life of your own, too. I'll stay in and catch up on some reading I've been putting off."

"Alright, I love you," she bent and kissed his cheek again.

"I love you too."

Onnie picked up her bag and left Gabriel to say his own goodbyes as she exited the house. She needed to be outside. Everything in her world had just changed, and she needed to ensure the sky was still above her.

At some point during the evening, it started to rain again, and Gabriel had parked in the driveway, which meant she had to walk through the garden. Onnie stepped off the porch and out from under the overhang, tipping her head back and closing her eyes. Droplets peppered her face and made soft plinking noises against her jacket. She could feel her hair soaking the water up like a sponge, and she stood there and let it.

Chapter 16: Shattered

November 2021 - Alku | Onnie Moore

The drive to Onnie's apartment was filled with silence and the occasionally spoken direction. Gabriel found her soaked and staring at the moon through the clouds after he said goodbye to Abbot. He didn't ask her about her impromptu shower, just ushered her to his car and turned the heater on full blast. The night was dark and quiet, leaving her with too much room to think.

Gabriel turned on a beautiful piano piece and stayed silent during their drive. A few minutes later, he pulled up in front of her apartment and helped her from the car.

"Do you want to come in?" she asked, voice devoid of emotion and energy.

He paused before answering, "Do you want me to?"

Onnie's brow wrinkled, and she thought about it for a second before she shook her head, "No, not tonight. Thank you for dropping me off."

Gabriel smiled, slipped one hand into his pocket, and used his other to lift her chin, "You'll call me if you need anything." He pulled a small slip of paper from his pocket and held it between his fingers.

She refused to cry in front of him again, and she could feel the tears pressing against the back of her eyes. Onnie managed a nod and took the paper wordlessly.

"Good girl, get some sleep." He leaned down and kissed her right cheek softly, lingering sweetly to whisper in her ear. "Goodnight, little Cat, sweet dreams."

On shaky legs, Onnie walked to her front door and quickly let herself in. Without a backward glance, she closed and locked the door, leaning into it to hold herself up. She sniffled and sputtered, trying to hold back her tears in an attempt to shut off the pain she was feeling and lock it in the deepest part of herself.

She closed her eyes, but when she saw the faint strands of her Bond glowing in her mind, she couldn't hold back the emotions anymore, and they burst from her body. Her back slid against the door until she reached the floor, where she cradled herself in her arms while she cried. Could she do this? Be some magical Keeper. Was she brave enough? Was she even capable?

Only a few moments had passed when her phone rang from in her coat pocket, and for a moment, she debated ignoring it. She knew by the ringtone that it was her Mom and how late it was in Maine, so Onnie gave in. Weighed down with an emotional lethargy that seeped into her bones, she pulled the device from her pocket and answered it.

"Hi, Mom."

"Your Grandfather called and said you needed me. What's going on?"

Onnie didn't have the strength to be surprised at how the man knew what was going on, and she choked out, "He's dying, Mom," she sniffled into her coat sleeve.

The silence grew between them, and Onnie could hear snoring fading in the background and knew her Mom was probably walking to the living room, away from where Lewis was still sleeping.

"He's told you, then, about the bookshop."

Onnie was thankful that her Mom didn't pretend she didn't know or that she was angry about it. "Yes."

"And, what do you think?" Tory asked, now wide awake.

Onnie didn't know what to think. She had grown to love her Grandfather and didn't want him to die, but it was too much when he added the magical bookshop complication, and a man pledged to protect her for the rest of her life.

"Onnie?"

"...I...I don't think I know what to think, Mom." Onnie admitted with a frown, her mind slow and clouded with grief.

"Hmm...that was my reaction too. Where are you?" Her mother's voice was filled with worry, sparking Onnie's guilt.

Onnie lifted her head and looked up, blinking at the light change. "My entryway. Floor."

"Oh, baby girl." Onnie winced at her mother's tone. "Okay, here's the deal. Pick yourself up. Go put on comfy clothes, grab a glass of wine, and curl up in your squishy chair. Once you're there, call me back, and we'll talk about it. Okay?"

"Yes, Mommy." she sniffled.

"Onnie?"

"Yes?"

"If you don't call me back, I will be on the first flight I can get out there, and I'll be none too pleased about flying."

A small smile crept onto Onnie's cheeks, "Yes, ma'am."

"You've got five minutes. I'll talk to you in a few."

"Okay, thanks."

"Of course, talk to you soon."

They both hung up, and Onnie sat there staring at the umbrella propped against the wall before her, wasting a full minute of her five. She shook the distraction from her head and pulled her phone from where it was, still by her ear. She wiped the tears from it, slowly stood up, and pulled off her coat, throwing it and her bag onto the tiled entry floor.

As Onnie walked through her apartment, she began stripping her clothes as if she were ridding herself of emotions. Boots and self-doubt were the first off, and she left them near the fireplace she and Dany had filled with candles. Then her thermal and the tank top underneath it came off as if she were stripping away her fear and worry, not her clothing—those landed by her bedroom door. Leaning on the door frame, she pulled off her knee-high socks along with her anger and threw them across the room forcefully and into her laundry basket. Lastly, she walked in, sat on the edge of her blowup mattress, and slipped off her jeans, with them, her crushing sadness. She looked down at the pants in her hands, closed her eyes, took a deep breath, and tossed them across the room to join her socks.

Onnie reached behind her and grabbed her pajama bottoms and oversized t-shirt from under her pillows and pulled them on quickly. When she looked at the clock on the floor next to her mattress, she saw she only had two minutes left to call her mom back. She ran out of her bedroom and into her kitchen and put the kettle on to boil. Then she clicked the heater up a few degrees and dialed her mom.

Tory picked up on the first ring, her calm voice filled with a smile Onnie could see in her mind. "Good girl. Do you have your wine?"

"No, I'm making tea."

Tory laughed quietly, "Funny, I also opted for that tonight. Comfort over cover-up, I guess. Probably a wiser choice anyway."

"Something like that," Onnie said, drying a mug with a paper towel. "Lewis sleeping?"

"Yeah, he's got a big day at work tomorrow. I can wake him if you want me to."

"No, it's okay. Let him sleep."

"You sure?" Onnie could hear ice cubes popping from a tray and plopping into her Mother's tea.

"Yeah, no sense in waking up the whole house."

"You know he wouldn't mind. He'd do anything for you."

Onnie smiled as memories of Lewis bandaging up her scraped knees, giving her lectures about boys, and taking her shopping flashed through her mind. "I know."

"How's your tea? What did you pick?"

"Water's just about to boil, but I chose jasmine green." Onnie smiled, lifting the teabag to her nose and inhaling the flowery scent.

"That's my girl, the same one I picked."

The kettle began its shrill song, and Onnie plopped her teabag in her cup as she walked to the stove. "One sec, I need to pull the kettle off. Let me put you on speakerphone."

She placed her cell phone on the counter and hit the speaker phone icon. The worn enamel kettle on the stove was increasing its volume, and she retrieved it quickly and flipped open the spout to silence it. After she poured water into her large coffee mug, she replaced the pot on the stove and leaned in to inhale the floral spirals of steam. "Mmm.... I love this tea."

"I do, too." Her Mom slurped noisily on the other end of the phone, with her drink at the perfect temperature with the added ice cubes.

Both women giggled quietly as Onnie settled into her overstuffed chair, placing her phone on the arm of it.

"So," Tory prompted, "tell me what's going on and what you're thinking."

"Yeah...so, Grandfather's dying. I'm now the owner of some

magical bookshop. Oh, and I have a hunky Guardian with an ego the size of Texas to follow me around like a guard dog. Which would you like to touch on first?"

"Oh, the hunky guard dog, let's touch him!"

Onnie tried to choke back a laugh and ultimately failed. "Mother! I'm serious…"

"Right! Yes, seriously, okay…." More tea-sipping noises carried through the phone, and Onnie grinned at her mother's silly attitude, even in a negative situation.

"Grandfather's dying, and it's all because I came here and started this transition thingy."

"Onnie, stop right there. That's not true." Her mother's stern voice filled Onnie's apartment before it softened. "Your Grandfather and I spoke about his death many years ago, and he made it quite clear. Whoever takes his place will begin transferring the Keepership, but only when it was time to do so."

"But if I hadn't accepted—"

"Stop that!" Her Mom shouted, and Onnie withered. "It has nothing to do with you. It's simply his time, and you're just the lucky one chosen for the honor of replacing him."

Onnie closed her eyes, took strength from the steam swirling with jasmine, and held back more tears. She felt like a well-wrung sponge and refused to cry another single tear. "I know," she paused when she realized what her Mother was saying and added, "Honor? You're not angry?"

"Angry with who, you for being chosen over me? Never. I imagine your Grandfather told you of my trip to Washington when you were younger."

"Yeah, he did."

"The minute you declared your major in college, I knew you were next in line. Never think I am anything but happy for you and proud.

It's a great honor and one you're more than fit to carry out. Besides, I never would have let him ask you to move if I thought it wasn't the right course for you."

"Wait, he asked for your permission?"

"Of course! Your Grandfather is a smart man. He knows better than to come between a Mother and her kids. He learned that one a long time ago. Before he asked you, he called and told me what was going on and said that if I thought it would ruin your life as his choice did to mine, he...would find a way to transfer it to someone else."

Onnie was shocked, "He did?"

"He sure did."

"And you said it was okay for him to ask."

Her mother only hesitated for a few seconds, "I did."

"Thanks, Mom." Onnie hesitated but decided she was tired of being kept in the dark, "Mom, do you really think him being a Keeper ruined your life?"

"Of course not," Tory said nearly instantly, and Onnie relaxed. "My stupid father decided it did. I loved your Grandmother, and she was more than enough for me when I was growing up. Sure, would I have liked things to turn out differently? Of course. Was I angry at him? You bet. But...." Tory sighed, "Mom explained everything to me before she died and asked me to hear him out. So I did."

Onnie smiled into her tea, her eyes glazed over as she spaced out at its blonde liquid.

"I love you, sweet girl."

"I love you too, Mom."

Tory cleared her throat softly, no doubt shoving back her tears. "Now, tell me all about this guard dog that came with the job."

Onnie smiled and began retelling the day's adventures. Her Mom responded with the right oos and ahs in all the right places, and after a pot of tea each, they both yawned and called it a night. Onnie promised to call her mom in a day or two once a bit of the dust settled. Then they said their goodbyes and hung up.

Onnie eventually got up from her chair, her battered body stiff and starting to ache. After a yawn and a stretch, she cleaned her mug, hung up her jacket she'd thrown on the floor earlier, and finally climbed into bed.

The slip of paper that Gabriel had given her was on the blanket, and she picked it up and unfolded it. A smile pulled at the corner of her lips at his blocky handwriting. It only said *day or night* and then his phone number, and for a moment, she thought of calling him to talk.

She checked the clock on the floor and frowned, "One in the morning would probably not be what he meant."

With one last look at her cell phone, she yawned and placed it next to the clock. After rolling over, she cuddled further into the covers and pulled the blankets up to her chin before closing her eyes and drifting off to sleep within moments.

Chapter 17: Aggression

November 2021 - Alku | Gabriel Vansand

Gabe got into his car and watched as Onnie unlocked and shut her door behind her. As he shifted into drive, he felt a searing pain through his chest and struggled to pull air into his lungs. He frantically ripped open his jacket and lifted his shirt, searching for whatever wound could cause that much pain. As his eyes became cloudy and he blinked them a few times, he felt tears fall, spattering his thighs. When he brushed them away with the back of his hand, he realized what they were from and froze. Onnie.

His car was back in park, and he was two steps from her front door with his fist raised, about to knock before he realized what he was doing. Gabe struggled but took a few deep breaths and walked back to his car, each step agony. Their relationship was too new for her, and though he managed to stay calm and level-headed for most of the evening, him pounding on her door while shedding her tears would be enough to send her over the edge. Instead, he pulled out his cell phone and called Abbot.

"Gabriel, is everything alright?"

"She needs her Mother," Gabe said through clenched teeth.

Abbot's concern for Onnie instantly filled his voice: "I'll call her right now. Thank you."

"Yeah." Gabe poked the screen, hung up the call, and looked at the cell phone in his hand. He felt the need to punch something. Anything.

After he dashed away the fresh tears and offered a silent prayer to whoever was listening, he got back into his car, pulled away from Onnie's cottage, and sped off into the misty night.

Gabe drove, and he drove fast. He turned off his stereo, the soft tinkling of pianos more suitable for Onnie than himself in his current mood. He'd left her there, crying and alone, in enough heart-searing pain he thought he'd been stabbed with a hot poker.

The stoplight in front of him turned red, and he skidded to a stop. Anger filled the car's interior, and it was palpable enough that he was concerned it might start affecting Onnie. He tried to calm himself down, taking deep breaths while gripping his steering wheel with white knuckles. Not making progress and unable to breathe in the emotionally charged air that filled the car, he rolled down his windows and leaned back into the headrest. The chilled air danced its way under his collar and across his face as if cooling his fevered brow.

Gabe checked the street sign above the light and realized he'd left Alku at some point. He must have passed through the tunnel and out of the valley in a trance, but now he had a few options. There were a few bars outside of Alku he'd been to in the past, and he could grab a drink and maybe drown out Onnie's sorrow. A luxury convertible pulled up beside him, and a brunet with striking eyes and crimson lips looked at him with a coy smile. As if by instinct, he turned his head away. At that moment, he only wanted Onnie, even if he knew he couldn't have her. When he looked back, the woman was driving into the distance.

The light turned green, and he slammed his foot on the peddle, needing to get away from himself. There was one more option.

Gabe pushed a button on his dashboard, "Call Dany," he shouted into the silence. A few seconds later, ringing filled the car, and when Dany's sleepy voice answered the phone, he nearly wept with relief.

"Dany, I need you to meet me at the school."

"Gabe?" Dany said through a yawn, "Do you know what time it is?"

Gabe glanced at the clock and groaned. Apparently, he'd been driving for a few hours and hadn't even realized it was eleven o'clock.

"I'm sorry, I wouldn't have called had I not been a dumb ass and looked at the clock first."

With another yawn, he heard Dany click on her bedside lamp. "Yes, you would have still called, or I'd have to kick your ass. How long do I have?"

Gabe breathed a sigh of relief and smiled at his sister's no-nonsense attitude. "I'll be there in thirty, forty-five at the most."

"Good, I have time for coffee. I'll bring you some. See you there."

"Thanks, Dany," Gabe said, loving his sister more than life itself.

"Umm hmm," Dany said as she turned on her bathroom taps. "See you soon."

"Yeah, bye."

"DRIVE SAFE," she shouted before hanging up.

He eased up on his steering wheel, switched on his blinker, made a U-turn, and returned to Alku, his sister, and all his problems.

"You owe me big time for this one. I was out of coffee." Dany said, leaning against her car, two travel mugs in her hands. Her hair was slicked back into a tight ponytail, and she wore a complete set of workout gear with her long red trench coat thrown over the top to stay warm.

Gabe locked his car door before slipping the key into his pocket and approaching his sister, arms open. "You have no idea." He crushed her to him and buried his scratchy jaw in her hair. With her hands still full, Dany had no choice but to hug him awkwardly with her elbows.

"Gabe?" she asked, worry evident in her voice.

"Yeah, I'm sorry." He stepped back and took the mug she offered him. "I thought you said you were out of coffee?"

"I am. It's black tea, brewed strong."

"Ah, okay." He led the way across the school's field and into the beam of the gym's flood lights.

"I won't ask if you don't want me to," Dany said with a small smile.

Gabe pulled his work keys from his jacket pocket and unlocked the gym, keying the lights on and inundating the ample space with warm light. When Dany had entered behind him, he pulled the heavy door closed and locked them in.

"Wanna give me your coat, and I can throw them in your office?" She asked, sipping from her thermos and holding out her free hand.

Gabe nodded and passed her his mug before taking off his coat and swapping it back for his tea. "Thanks."

"Yup," Dany said, pulling his keys out of his pocket as she walked to his office.

"Bag, self-defense, and then light yoga?" Gabe called out to her back as she walked away.

Dany raised her hand in thumbs up, mug to her lips, too in need of caffeine to stop drinking.

Gabe pulled out the bags, mats, and sparring equipment before unlocking the stereo box and hooking up his phone to the speaker system. He checked his missed calls and, seeing none, checked his texts. He knew Onnie wouldn't call him tonight, but part of him wished they were past that awkward, get-to-know-each-other phase and already comfortable. Relationships didn't work that way, but he could still dream.

"You keep frowning like that, and you'll wrinkle young," Dany said, coming up behind him, coats and tea absent.

He nodded, turned on his workout playlist, and stepped in front of his bag. Dany mirrored his stance with hers, and they both fell into a well-practiced rhythm of choreographed kicks and punches. Gabe tried to keep his focus on the smack of flesh on leather and the smell of sweat filling the air, and eventually, he forced the last remnants of Onnie's pain from his veins. When he glanced at Dany, he smiled at her ability to keep up with his pace.

Forty-five minutes later, they both stopped, breath ragged and bodies drenched in sweat.

Gabe folded his legs beneath him and sat on the floor, aware his muscles would cramp but instead welcoming the added distraction of the pain it would bring.

"Drink," Dany said, tossing him a water bottle when he looked up. "I stole them from your fridge."

He nodded and downed the whole bottle before tossing it across the room and watching it roll into a darkened corner.

"Ready for more?" He asked when Dany had capped her water and began stretching out her calves.

She nodded at him, and they both pulled on their sparring gear and took their places on the mat. Anger and frustration clouded his patience and his practiced tactics. He swung at her clumsily and missed as she gracefully danced out of his reach.

"Are you going to talk to me, or is the plan to kick the crap out of each other and then crawl to our respective homes in pieces?" Dany asked, swiping under his legs with hers, only to have him jump over them and land in a crouch, ready to spring.

"You know what happened," Gabe said through gritted teeth. He feigned left before kicking out to the right, but Dany ducked and jabbed him in the stomach before maneuvering out of reach of his parry.

"Yeah, the Transference you've been working toward and griping about for the last six months. So, what went wrong?"

Nothing." He ground out before finally catching her and locking her arms to her sides.

"Oh, okay," Dany said and went limp, slipping from his grasp and knocking him to the ground with an elbow to the top of his foot and then kicking his other leg out from beneath him. "So, then, what the hell is your problem!" She shouted as she pinned him to the ground.

"I COULDN'T HELP HER!" he screamed.

Dany recoiled. He was not typically prone to outbursts of anger, and now he felt guilty for scaring her on top of everything else. She let go of him and lay on the mat beside him, her head pillowed on his shoulder.

"Talk to me, Gabe."

With one hand covering his face, he pounded his free fist into the mat, making Dany jump and only pissing himself off even more. He counted slowly to ten and reached along the Bond as Abbot had taught him in the months leading to Onnie's arrival in Alku. Onnie's emotions were even, and he suspected she was peacefully asleep. He took a few deep breaths and opened his eyes.

"Sorry, sis, you don't need this crap. I didn't mean to scare you."

Dany shifted beside him and bit his bicep, "Ouch!" he bellowed, glaring down at her, her brow lined with worry.

"Don't be an idiot. Now talk to me." She said before returning her head to his shoulder.

"She's just…amazing. She learned so much tonight and held herself together so well, but when I took her home…." His voice trailed off, the memory of her pain lancing through his heart with a fresh vengeance.

Dany squeezed his forearm, and he swallowed his phantom pain.

"She let it go. All of it. The grief, confusion, feelings of betrayal, and there was nothing I could do to help her."

Dany sighed and shook her head against him. "You did do something. You gave her the space she needed. Onnie's a tough girl, she'll get through this, and when she does, she'll be better off with you by her side."

"You don't understand," Gabe said, sitting up and tugging his hair, dripping into his eyes. "It's my job to help her, my responsibility. She shouldn't have to do it alone, but I just walked away instead of knocking on her door and helping her through her pain."

"Gabriel!" Dany said, sitting up and pulling his hands from his face, effectively forcing him to look directly into her eyes. "First off, she's managed before you. One more day won't kill her, but your pity might have. Secondly, what did you do instead?"

Gabe glanced away, "Ah…called Abbot."

"Why?" she asked, a small, knowing smile on her lips.

"Onnie needed her Mom."

Dany's smile grew, and she nodded. "Yup, that was exactly what she needed, and you made it happen. Then you came back to Alku in case she needed you, and what did you do to release your tension?"

Gabe shrugged.

"You beat the crap out of your sister. See, you were even training to protect her."

He sniggered, wrapped a sweaty arm around his sister's neck, and ruffled her ponytail.

"Hey," she squirmed, "not fair, you big oaf. Lay off the roids, man!"

Gabe stilled and released his hold on Dany, who sat up and looked at him, worry on her face again.

"Onnie said that to me this morning, too."

"Did she? She's an observant woman," Dany said, teasing him, and when he didn't smile, she bumped her shoulder into his larger one. "She'll see you, Gabe, don't worry. She's been hurt in the past and has some pretty big scars, but she'll heal. Then, with your help, you'll heal the shop. Together."

Gabe looked down at his sister, proud of her that even with their rocky childhood, she'd grown into a fantastic woman. "When did my sister get so wise?"

She bounced to her feet and slipped into her defensive stance. "Well, one of us had to be the brains, and you clearly chose to be the brawn."

Gabe laughed and lightly spun up onto the balls of his feet, "Well, if that's the case, I have a reputation to uphold!"

His tension wasn't altogether relieved, but it was lessened by his sister's level head and inability to see anything but the glass half full. They renewed their workout, continuing for another hour until they were both sweating and falling over with exhaustion. After a break that threatened to turn into an overnight sleepover, they managed to get their feet under them, and Gabe walked Dany to her car before watching her drive off in the direction of her apartment. He slid into his cold leather seat and drove home, clicking on the stereo and resuming the soft piano music from earlier.

By the time he pulled up in front of his apartment, he was weak and ready for bed. The emotional day had sapped him of more energy than he realized, and the sparring session with Dany took what had remained. His adrenaline was finally fading.

When he reached his front door, he unlocked it, and the hair on his neck stood on end. Feigning distraction, he turned around and locked his car again, taking the chance to look around, squinting into the shadows. While the morning light was still far off, his home was well-lit, and nothing was there.

As he entered his apartment, he rolled his shoulders. He hung his jacket on a hook by the door and headed straight to his bedroom, not even bothering to turn on the light. Wrapped in the darkness of early morning, he undressed quickly, forgoing a shower for more sleep and collapsing on his crisp sheets.

Before he closed his eyes, he grabbed his phone from where he'd tossed it and checked his messages. There was still nothing, and he thought that Onnie's Mother must be a miracle worker, which made him smile.

Dany was right, and it eased his mind, knowing he'd helped Onnie even a little. Drunk on exhaustion, he sent her a quick message, hoping her phone was on silent, and then he was asleep before his screen went dark.

Chapter 18: Lonely

November 2021 - Alku | Onnie Moore

"Who's there!?" Onnie shouted into the darkness as she bolted upright.

Her heart raced as she blinked away sleep's relaxing veil, still clouding her eyes, and squinted to look around her bedroom. The room was still full of shadows, and she studied them for something out of place but found nothing. Everything seemed to be just as she'd left it the night before.

When she tossed off the blankets, the room's chill made her shiver as it caressed her skin. She rubbed her arms, trying to smooth out the goosebumps, before quickly grabbing her socks from the end of the bed and tugging them on. Her clock only read four-fifty, meaning she didn't need to wake up for work for almost two hours. Whatever had poked at her subconscious had been enough that now she was wide awake and slightly annoyed about it. She stretched and bent forward to touch her toes, loosening the muscles in her back.

Outside her window, something rattled on her back patio, and her breath stilled as her heart started to race.

Onnie always kept a large metal flashlight beside her bed for reasons like this one. Some people used a baseball bat, but she preferred her violence with a side of disorientating blinding. She grabbed the makeshift weapon and raised it over her shoulder, creeping to her bedroom doorway and cautiously peering into her living room.

One squishy chair, three cheap bookcases filled with books, and her laptop bag leaning against one of the shelves. Nothing seemed out of place or moved, and she was confident no one was in her home besides herself.

A different noise caught her attention and seemed to come from outside her patio doors this time. She tiptoed over to the doors in her kitchen that led out onto her empty outdoor space and held her breath.

In her mind, Onnie had the coordination of a super spy, but in reality, she pulled down the cords for the blinds unevenly, with a loud zipping sound, and they clattered against the glass before stopping at an odd angle.

"Ah!" Onnie shouted and jumped back.

A small, wide-eyed, furry face peered through the window at her. She clutched her heart to still its attempted escape from her chest and slowly pulled the cords again to raise the blinds properly. The cat was perched on the patio railing, and surprisingly, Onnie hadn't scared it away with her raucous. Instead, it yawned, stretched, and jumped down, reaching up with its paw to pat the glass door.

Onnie crouched down and considered its deep yellow eyes. The cat didn't move. Instead, it just…stared back at her. After two minutes of their staring contest, it raised one of its front paws and shivered slightly.

"Oh, come on, that's cheating!" She'd say the cat seemed to smile at her outburst if she didn't know better. It replaced its paw on the ground, never breaking eye contact with her, and Onnie threw her hands in the air.

"Fine, I give in!"

She set the flashlight on the floor before pushing herself to her feet and unlocking the door. With the door open, the cat arched its back exaggeratedly and started to purr. Onnie stepped aside, and the cat sauntered past her before it glanced over its shoulder at her and nodded. Now that it was in the house, it went directly to Onnie's wall heater and began to groom.

Onnie laughed and closed the door, locking it behind them.

"You, my friend," she said, shaking her finger, "are one entitled animal."

The cat ceased its grooming, stared up at her, and blinked.

Onnie crossed the room, sat down against the wall, and admired its sleek silver-blue fur and wise eyes.

"You're a Russian Blue, aren't you? My brother, Anthony, has a Russian Blue named Skitter."

The cat closed its eyes and shook its head.

"What? My nephew named him." Onnie said with a grin.

The cat shook his head again with the same smile-like expression as before.

"He was five. Give the kid a break."

The cat cocked its head to the side and stared at her, unblinking.

"Fine, Mr. Grumpy. Do you need anything? I'm not sure I have anything for you to eat, but I can get you some water."

To answer her question, the cat entered the kitchen and jumped up to the countertop next to the sink.

"I'll take that as a yes," she said lightheartedly. It took some work, but she heaved her sleeping muscles off the floor and walked into the kitchen. She rummaged through the cupboards, found a shallow bowl, and filled it with cool water from the sink. When she placed it next to the cat, it began lapping it up while still looking at her.

A rumbling erupted from her stomach, and she grimaced. "Well, I guess I'm awake now." She popped two slices of sourdough bread into the toaster and poured herself a glass of orange juice.

"So, what's your name? I can't refer to you as 'cat,' especially if Gabriel keeps my silly nickname." She raised her glass, hiding a smile behind it, a blush creeping into her cheeks.

The feline lifted its head and regarded her with its unblinking gaze.

"Well, the first question is, are you a boy cat or a girl cat?" Onnie chuckled, "I am so not checking." When the cat shook its head, she bent to look it in the eye, "Boy?"

The feline blinked once.

"Ah.... Is that a yes?"

One blink.

"Right." She stood up straight again and ran her fingers through her hair, snagging on a clump of blood. Frustrated, she tugged her fingers free and hissed when a few strands came with it.

"I'm talking to a cat and imagining its blinking answers back to me. I haven't even had a full twenty-four hours with magic, and I'm going insane."

The tiny bowl was nearly empty, so she crossed the kitchen and attempted to refill it. When she reached for it, the cat swatted at her with the pad of its paw, stopping her movement and sloshing the remaining water onto the counter.

"Hey, what was that for?"

The feline stared at her and cocked its head to one side in that cute, 'wonder what you're doing' kind of way.

"Do you want more or not?" She asked in a clipped voice.

The cat blinked once and nodded.

"Fine," she ran the water and replaced the bowl once it was filled. "I'll play along. You're a boy. So...what about a name? How about... Bruce?"

The cat shook his head.

"Okay…um…Jethro?" Onnie said, drying the counter with her shirt.

Another shake.

"Picky, picky. Okay…how about something more meaningful."

The cat nodded and settled into a more comfortable position.

Onnie paced the kitchen floor, "Okay, meaningful, um...Latin?" she looked at the cat.

Two blinks.

"Okay, well, German's out. Too angry sounding for you."

He nodded in agreement.

"Hmm…." Onnie's toaster popped, and she pulled out the butter from the fridge and began spreading it on her toast. "Welsh? That could be fun," she said, looking over for his reaction.

Instead, he stood, walked over to the counter her plate was on, and looked at the toast expectantly.

"Okay, Welsh it is."

One blink.

Onnie shook her head and chuckled. "Yeah, I'm talking to a cat… Well, I suppose I've had stranger days, at least recently."

He nodded.

"Alright," she returned the butter to the fridge and munched on a slice of toast, thinking intently. "How about…Maldwyn? It means 'brave friend.'"

The cat stood, walked to the edge of the counter, and stuck out his neck, his nose sniffing the air in front of him. Onnie crossed the distance to him and once again met his eyes. He reached out to her with his paw, softly touched her cheek, and then blinked once.

Onnie smiled and ripped off a section of the soft white interior of her toast, "Maldwyn it is. Hungry, my friend? If today turns out to be half as much of an adventure as yesterday was, we'll need the sustenance."

He blinked once, and with his claws extended, he reached out, took the offering of toast from Onnie, and nibbled on it contentedly.

"Well, I guess maybe that's already happened." She smiled and watched her new roommate munch on his breakfast. "You are one strange beast."

Onnie finished her toast and juice and placed her plates into the dishwasher. She checked the microwave clock and frowned. "I have to go to the shop today, Mal. Can I call you Mal for short?"

Mal blinked once.

"Great. You're welcome to stay here. Please… Please, don't claw the chair, though."

Mal rolled his bright cat eyes at her and quickly jumped off the counter, padding into Onnie's room. Onnie followed behind him and dug through her suitcase for a clean set of clothes. Mal jumped onto her windowsill and watched her dig through her bags. She pulled out a deep purple thermal, a black knitted scarf, and a thick pair of black leggings. Then she grabbed a clean set of underwear and added them to the pile before looking up at Mal, who was still in the window.

"I'm going to jump in the shower, okay?" She clicked the heater's dial a few degrees warmer. "If you're cold, you can get under the covers." She froze and crossed her arms in front of her. "You don't have fleas, do you."

Mal hissed and turned his nose up at her, his tail twitching erratically.

"Hey, I'm just making sure," she raised her hands in surrender, "I don't want them any more than you do."

Mal chuffed at her before jumping onto the mattress and disappearing under the covers.

Onnie leaned over and softly pat the lump of a cat under her blankets and then left the bedroom in search of a hot shower.

Twenty minutes later, Onnie stepped from her bathroom in a cloud of steam, red-faced and smiling. Mal was now curled up on top of the blankets, diligently licking one of his front paws, but he stopped and looked up when he saw her.

Only dressed in a towel, Onnie blushed. "Ah…. Mal, do you mind?"

The cat chuffed and closed his eyes.

"Thanks." Onnie quickly finished drying off and slipped into her clean clothes. "Done, thank you."

Mal opened his eyes and nodded.

"Okay, I'll be right back." She slipped into the bathroom to finish her morning routine. Fifteen minutes later, she emerged with a scrubbed face and her teeth brushed. She retrieved her cell phone from where it sat, plugged in, beside the bed, and checked her text messages. There was one from her Mom from last night after they talked, saying she loved her. One from Jace said he would fly up there and hold her at marshmallow point if she didn't call him soon. But the third message was from an unknown number.

Cat, I'm here if you need me. Put my number in your phone. I'll call you tomorrow. Dress warmly. It's supposed to storm. - G

Onnie looked up and smiled sweetly at Mal. "He's a bit overbearing and kind of an ass, but I guess he's trying to be agreeable." Onnie shrugged.

Mal stretched with a yawn before patting the bed next to him, asking for Onnie to sit.

"Bossy little thing you are." She said before sitting on the edge of the blow-up mattress and running her palm along the feline's back. "Wow, you're one soft cat."

Mal purred and carefully climbed his way onto her lap to sit. He reached out, placed his front paw over her heart, and looked into her eyes. Onnie looked down at the tiny paw resting on her chest. "Listen to my heart?"

Mal nodded and pulled his paw away.

"You sound like Grandfather."

Mal puffed up and barred his teeth while he purred, then smiled a crooked cat smile at her.

She giggled before nudging him off her lap. "You're one hell of a cat, Mal. Alright, I'll do my best to listen to it." she stroked him one more time and stood up. "I'm going to get going, and I'm early enough that I can pick up a coffee on my way to the shop. I promise I'll stop and get some cat food after work for you."

Mal shrugged but jumped off the bed and followed as Onnie walked into the living room and picked up her tennis shoes. She plopped into her chair and quickly slipped them on, lacing up the clean white canvas.

"Are you a dry food or a wet food kitty?"

Mal jumped up onto the arm of the chair and stuck out his tongue, blinking twice.

Laughing, Onnie slipped her cell phone into her bag's side pocket and shrugged on her jacket, tucking in her scarf as she buttoned it up. She stood and slid her bag over her head to cross her body.

"You're a crazy cat. Alright, I'm off." She scratched under his chin a few times before giving him one last pat and walking to the front door. "Enjoy your day." She said before unlocking it and slipping outside, closing it behind her with a soft click.

The first rays of dawn were still a few hours off as Onnie sipped her coffee. She'd stopped, picked up a cup and the town's newspaper, and was almost to the bookshop when she realized she hadn't left Mal with a cat box. She cursed under her breath and mentally crossed her fingers that he could wait until lunchtime when she could run back home and set one up for him. Dwelling on it wouldn't change anything, so she refused to ruin her morning over what she couldn't change.

The morning air was so clean and crisp, and the slight pink glow that her cheeks gained from the wind chill woke her up as she meandered the cobbled streets, further increasing her love of walking to work in the mornings. Gabriel's text had said it was supposed to storm, but when she looked up at the crystal-clear sky above her, Onnie found that difficult to believe.

As she rounded the corner that was home to the flower shop, the smell of roses drifted across the street, making her smile.

"Good morning!" Onnie said, greeting The Book Nook's warm brick building when the sign and door came into view.

With her new role and relationship with the shop, she was unsure how to treat it. There was no harm in trying, so she laid her hand on the green wood of the front door, her palm pressed flat.

"We should start over, I think. I'm Onnie, and it's nice to meet you finally." The door warmed up and vibrated softly, and Onnie wasn't sure how she'd missed such vibrant energy before.

"Let's see what this day has in store for the two of us, shall we?"

Onnie unlocked the front door, stepped over the threshold, and squinted into the darkness. She stopped to inhale the smells of the shop with a smile before she removed her bag and hung her coat on the antique coat rack. The matches for her incense were still on the sill from the day before, so she opened the window a crack and struck a match, the bright yellow glow flaring up and temporarily blinding her in the dim light.

Once the stick was lit and the flame out, she grabbed her bag and headed for the front counter, turning on lamps as she passed them with satisfying clicks, splitting the silence in succession. With all the lights leading to the front counter turned on, it was still relatively dim away from the shelves. Onnie removed a match for the oil lamp from the box and struck it. A slight glint of yellow caught her eye from the area above the register when it reflected the flame. If she squinted, Onnie could make out a little silhouette, and she cautiously stepped forward, holding the match closer to the shadow.

"Meow."

"Yipes!" Onnie screeched, dropping the match, extinguishing as it tumbled through the air.

There was a gentle thump, and then the shadow began to wind its way between Onnie's feet, purring loudly and filling the quiet space.

"Damn it, what's with all the cats today!"

Onnie lit another match while being as careful as possible not to step on the enthusiastic feline dancing between her feet. As the lamp's wick fully caught and the shop was entirely flooded with light, Mal jumped back onto the counter and looked at Onnie with wide eyes and a grin.

"Oh, man!" she said, pointing at him in surprise. "How did you get… Wait!" Frantically, Onnie dug through her purse and pulled out her cell phone. She pulled up the text from Gabriel the night before and began to reply.

Gabriel, there's something—

The phone in her hand rang loudly, and Gabriel's number popped up on the screen, her text message now rendered useless.

Onnie pressed the answer icon as she tried to figure out how she would explain the talking cat story to Gabriel. "I was just text—"

"What's wrong?" Gabriel's voice said, short and clipped.

"How'd you know—" Onnie said, pacing the floor before the counter.

"I'm your Guardian, your emotions spiked, and I felt your fear. What happened?"

"There's someone here at the shop."

"I'm on my way," he said, the sound of car keys clattering in the background.

Gabriel's voice was filled with panic, and the last thing she needed was him rushing over and freaking her out more. "Whoa there, calm down. I'm all right."

"You don't feel okay, Cat." Gabriel ground out between gritted teeth.

"Breathe, big man, and I'll explain."

Gabriel let out a few exhales, and Onnie heard a heavy door close. "You have two minutes to explain, or I get into my car."

"Sheesh, I just have a question," Onnie said, rolling her eyes and trying to release some of the tension from the conversation.

"You're down to one minute thirty."

"Fine," she said, giving up, "Are Links always human?"

"Are what?"

"Links, like Rebecca. Are they always human when they...manifest?"

"Ah.... No, I supposed they don't have to be. Why?"

"Well, a cat was at my back door this morning." Onnie looked at Mal, who blinked once at her. "And I let him in, and we...sort of... talked?"

When Onnie was satisfied that Gabriel had calmed down enough not to barge into the store and throw her over his shoulder, she recounted her early morning and shop opening excitement.

"Uh huh.... Go on," skepticism was thick in his voice.

"And I left him at my apartment, but when I got to the store, he was here waiting for me."

"So, he got out." A car door closed in the background, but Gabriel didn't start the engine.

"Ah, no, he was waiting for me in the store...on the register, Gabriel."

"Hmmm.... Put the phone up to his ear."

"What!?" Onnie said, pacing halted midstride.

"You talked to him this morning and think this is a strange request? Just do it, please."

"Ugg!" Onnie returned to the front counter and looked down at Mal. "Gabriel wants to talk to you." she put the phone to his furry ear and yelled, "Alright, he can hear you!"

Onnie watched as Mal's ears twitched in response to what Onnie could only hear as the deep hum of Gabriel's voice.

After a few minutes, Mal meowed in response and pushed the phone away with his paw. Onnie returned it to her ear and didn't bother hiding the surprise in her voice.

"You've got to be kidding me. That worked?"

Gabriel chuckled, his voice tickling her ear. "Yes, it did, and yes, he's your Link."

Onnie just stared at Mal.

"Don't worry, he's only there to help you, and since he's shown up a little early, I wouldn't bet on him being overly useful at this point."

"I'm not sure I understand, but...okay?" Onnie said with hesitation.

Onnie could hear the smile in Gabriel's voice as he started his car. "Enjoy your day, little Cat. Bye."

Onnie slowly lowered the phone from her ear and set it on the counter. Mal stood on his back legs, his front paws on her chest, and stretched up to put his nose against hers. He sniffed her once, and she ran her hand down his silky back.

"I guess it was smart to have you close your eyes while I dressed this morning, huh?" Mal answered her with a quick lick to the tip of her nose, causing Onnie to laugh. She scratched behind his ears and then patted the top of his head.

"Alright, I need to get back to the shop. I'm sure she would like some attention this morning, too. Not to mention," she looked around at the organized chaos from the night before, "I need to finish cleaning up. Gabriel did a lot, but I've still got my work cut out for me."

With a chirp and a nod, Mal jumped from the counter and disappeared behind a bookcase. Onnie chuckled and shook her head before returning to opening the store.

Chapter 19 Discomfort

November 2021 - Alku | Onnie Moore

The rest of the day passed slowly after all the morning's excitement. Everything was back to where it belonged, and the shop looked no worse considering the explosion the previous day. Once she was finished, Onnie busied herself by dusting, restocking, and polishing the ornate wooden shelves, but overall, she'd been bored most of the day. They had a steady stream of customers, which meant she didn't get a chance to talk more to Mal, but considering her mind was still all over the place while it tried to process, any conversation would have probably been jibberish anyway. Mal had been restless, and after sniffing, or sleeping on, every surface in the store, as he dodged patrons trying to pet him, he curled up on the front counter and settled down.

Gabriel had been right, and it had indeed started to storm, which meant that Onnie made an awful lot of tea and mopped up an awful lot of rainwater. Compared to the excitement and hubbub from the day before, today was putting her to sleep.

The only break in the monotony of it all had been her Grandfather calling her at lunch to remind her to drink a few cups of Rebecca's tea.

He had sounded weaker than the night before, but he'd been in good spirits otherwise. They talked for a few minutes, Onnie mentioning Mal, and she was not surprised to find her Grandfather already knew about the newest addition to her crazy life. Their conversation drifted lazily around other topics and was eventually cut short by a customer with a question, so they hung up, and she promised to call him the next day.

Gabriel hadn't texted her since their discussion that morning, and she was surprised to find that she wanted to talk to him. Even though she knew she was lying to herself, she decided she wanted to pepper him with questions. To be fair, she had so many, and her Grandfather still seemed sad when she brought up the store. The last thing she wanted was to make the transition more painful for him. If that meant she needed to rely on Gabriel for answers, so be it.

Onnie thought about Dany and wasn't sure how she would react to the new Keeper-Guardian relationship Onnie now had with her brother. Either way, Onnie felt she should have that conversation sooner rather than later. As it neared closing time, she texted Dany and began to flit around the store anxiously, waiting for a reply. Dany responded a few minutes later, agreeing to a late-night coffee fix and maybe a movie afterward. After reading the message, Onnie deflated and leaned on the front counter in relief.

Once her anxiety calmed down, Onnie peeked at the clock and groaned. "It's five forty-five, Mal. I know I need to talk to Dany, but...I'd rather get it over with."

Mal rolled his yellow eyes and blinked at her once. He lifted his front paw and pointed it at Onnie's chest.

"Yeah, yeah, yeah, follow my heart. My foolish heart is distracted by the unwanted butterflies in my stomach, but I owe it to Dany to at least be upfront and honest with her."

Her butterflies were forgotten as the back of Onnie's neck began to tingle, and she looked up from the counter as a tall, thin man in all black entered the store.

"Hello, Sir. Can I help you find something today?" She said as she stood up straighter and put on her best customer service face.

The man walked forward slowly and pushed back the hood of his sweatshirt. Once closer, Onnie saw a thick black wool coat layered on the sweatshirt and buttoned to his neck. His pants and shoes were solid black, and only his skin offered a contrast with a ghostly pale shade of white. When he reached the counter, Onnie saw that the man had dark eyes that felt endless but the kind you instinctively fought to avoid. Onnie shivered, a cold settling deep in her bones. Mal stood on all fours beside her, with his tail fluffed up in defense.

"Ah...Hi. Can I help you find something?"

The man sneered and glanced around the store, his eyes lingering on each tall bookcase in turn.

"Oh, I do hope so." His voice was silky and washed over Onnie's skin like a gentle caress. "I am looking for a book, a rare one, in fact."

Onnie bit her tongue and spoke as politely as possible even though her body had nearly forced her to run from the strange man as fast as she could. "Do you know the name of the book?"

"Yes. It's gone by many titles, but I believe it was most recently called *Custos regni.*"

The man's grin widened at Onnie's suddenly stiffened posture. Onnie gripped the counter, knuckles white, breath catching in her throat.

"Well, I do apologize then, Sir. We actually sold our last copy yesterday. Might I take down your name and phone number in case we come across another copy? Or perhaps there's another book I could interest you in."

"Pity." he clicked his tongue and shook his head slowly. "But no. You see, this book is one of a kind, and I must have it." The man took another step closer to the counter and looked down at Onnie. "You wouldn't happen to know who purchased it or where I can find them, would you?"

The man's closeness irked Onnie, and goosebumps raised on her skin in a wave. She shifted back and out of the grasp of the man's bottomless eyes and crossed her arms protectively in front of herself. The stranger removed his right hand from his coat pocket and raised his long, delicate fingers in front of Onnie's face.

From somewhere at her side, Onnie heard Mal hiss, and then he jumped in front of her, swiping with his claws at the man. The stranger snatched his hand back and returned it to his pocket. Onnie's eyes had glazed over, and she felt as if she'd started to space out but somehow gotten stuck doing it. She continued to stare at the man in black in front of her but began to tremble.

Mal continued to guard her atop the countertop, and she worried about what a small animal could do against a human if he genuinely meant to hurt either of them.

"My, what a remarkably protective feline you have here."

"He's nothing compared to me," a deep voice rumbled from the front of the store, finally breaking Onnie's staring.

Onnie shook her head and saw Gabriel silhouetted by the Seattle gloom in the shop's front doorway. Mal didn't move, and the stranger didn't even flinch at Gabriel's sudden arrival. Instead, the man merely raised his hood.

"Thank you for your time, Miss." The man in black turned and walked leisurely to the front door, where Gabriel still blocked the exit. "Excuse me." The man in black said politely with his head down. Gabriel hesitated but stepped aside reluctantly.

Without a backward glance, the stranger stepped from the store, and Gabriel watched him from the doorway for a few minutes.

Mal looked away from Gabriel and back to Onnie, and she smiled weakly at the feline before picking him up and nuzzling his fur. When Gabriel approached the front counter, he leaned on it to be level with Mal's tiny face.

"I guess I now have two cats to prioritize, huh?" Gabriel said, reaching out his right pointer finger in a mini handshake position.

Mal blinked once, twisted his front paw out of Onnie's hold, and placed it on Gabriel's finger.

"Nice to meet you, fur ball."

"His name's Mal," Onnie interjected with a roll of her eyes.

"Oh, but you know how much I love my nicknames." Gabriel winked at her and scratched behind Mal's ears. "As the beautiful woman requested, nice to meet you…Mal."

Onnie smiled and reached down to tap her phone's screen to check the time and distance herself from Gabriel's stare.

With one last pat on the head for Mal, Gabriel stood and crossed his massive arms over his chest. Onnie watched as his body language shifted from being the man gently shaking hands with a cat into the firm stance of someone ready to kill anything in his path he saw as a threat. His eyes looked at her with more force than she had ever seen, and she took an involuntary step backward, squeezing Mal a bit tighter.

"Who was that man, Cat?" he asked, tense and angry.

"I… I don't know. He came in asking for help finding a book. He'd only been here a few minutes when you got here."

"What did he want?"

She scratched under Mal's chin, trying to distract herself from his threatening tone. "I told you, a book. Why are you so angry?"

"This is a bookshop. I figured that much out for myself." The corner of his mouth quirked up into a smile that Onnie was sure had been a slip. "What book did he want?"

"I don't know, and he didn't say. You interrupted us before he could tell me." Mal began to squirm in Onnie's arms, and she set him back on the counter.

Worry creased Gabriel's brows, and he placed both his palms on the marble and leaned forward, looking deeper into Onnie's eyes. It made her uncomfortable, and she watched Mal brush against Gabriel's arm with urgency.

"I know, Mal, one second." Without shifting his eyes from Onnie's, Gabriel lifted one hand to pat the distressed cat on the head.

Gabriel's scrutiny continued, and Onnie fidgeted without breaking eye contact with him.

"Why are you looking at me like that, Gabriel?" She put her hands on her hips and glared at him, "I was only doing my job. You don't have to be such a jerk."

Gabriel leaned back with a sigh and recrossed his arms in front of his chest. "What are your plans tonight?"

"I'm going out," she stated.

Gabriel rubbed his eyes and growled. "Look, I know you're pissed, but I'm trying to protect you. It's *my* job."

"Oh, well, in that case!" Onnie threw up her hands before picking up her dirty teacup from the counter. "Since it's your job, I guess that gives you the right to be an ass. Carry on, then. You are so very good at it." She turned her back on him and stomped into the back room but shouted over her shoulder, "I have plans with your sister. Figured I'd let you know since you asked *so nicely*."

She stomped some more and went over to the small sink to wash her teacup and dry it with a delicate tea towel. At some point, she'd have to return to the other room to pick up the rest of the serving set, but right now, she felt more like killing her Guardian than working with him. She was half surprised he hadn't followed her into the back room to yell at her more.

Onnie stopped drying the cup in her hand, realizing she'd wear a hole in the fine china at the rate she was going. She set it down on the drying shelf and took a deep breath to steady herself.

Gabriel meant well, and she knew that, but she hated being referred to as a job. It made her feel more like a child who needed their babysitter than an all-important magical being whose partner was a protector. His fear and anger when seeing her with that customer surprised her. Even though she hadn't felt him through their Bond yet, his emotions were clearly displayed. It still didn't give him a reason to question her like she was some sort of criminal.

Onnie rolled her shoulder and stretched her neck, her body still sore from the day prior. There was still work to be done, and if she wanted to be finished in time to see Dany, Onnie needed to get back to it. She squared her shoulders and left the back room to do her job.

Gabriel Vansand

Gabe watched as Onnie stormed off into the back, furious at him for being a jerk. Mal tapped Gabe's forearm with one paw, but Gabe couldn't take his eyes off the doorway to the back room.

"I know, Mal. I didn't mean to upset her, but what was I supposed to do?" He looked down into the bright yellow eyes that stared back at him. "He wanted the *Custos regni,* didn't he?"

Mal nodded, and Gabe returned to staring at the back room.

"Damn. We should have had more time before anyone realized the Transference had begun. We're going to have to be more vigilant."

Mal dug his claws into Gabe's arm, which got his attention. When he looked down, the cat blinked twice.

"You won't be able to watch her, and Abbot will need Bec tonight. We're already being careless, leaving him vulnerable right now."

Onnie emerged from the back room and ignored them, walking straight to the sitting area and disappearing behind a bookcase.

"I'd stay with her tonight, but she won't like that."

Mal shook his head.

When Onnie walked back into the front area of the shop, she carried the serving set in her arms and didn't look at either of them.

"I'll ask Dany. She'll know what to watch out for." Gabe said, pulling his cell phone from his pocket and quickly messaging his sister. "I'll sleep at Abbot's tonight. Between the two of us, we should be fine."

Mal chirped, and Gabe saw Onnie standing behind the counter, tapping her foot and wearing a frown. "I'm almost ready to go. Are you babysitting me on my coffee date, too?"

"No, Cat, you don't need a babysitter. Can I wait with you until Dany gets here? Or I can walk you to the coffee shop if you're meeting there."

Onnie sighed, and much to Gabe's relief, the fight fled her posture and voice. "Fine, you can walk me if you insist. I'll let you know when I'm ready to go."

Gabe nodded, and she left him to finish up her chores. Mal grabbed onto Gabe's arm and flexed his claws again.

"I know, I'm sending Dany after her as a babysitter, but if she doesn't figure it out, then I don't care. It's for her own good. She doesn't know what's out there yet." Gabe indicated with his head to Onnie, who was now closing and locking the front window.

"She and the old man both need protection, whether she believes so or not. Let Bec go to Abbot tonight. I'll watch over him, and Dany will watch over Onnie. Tomorrow, we'll regroup and figure out how to make this easier for the Keepers."

Mal retracted his claws and jumped onto Gabe's shoulder to nuzzle his stubbly cheek with his soft fur.

Gabe smiled, lifted his hand, and scratched behind the cat's delicate ear. "Of course, her Link is a cat, just my luck. At least I don't have any allergies."

Gabe was rewarded with a wavering purr in his ear, and he was sure he was being laughed at.

Chapter 20: Calm

November 2021 - Alku | Onnie Moore

Onnie closed the shop in record time. She'd washed the tea set until it sparkled, straightened the few books that had been removed throughout the day, primarily by her, and began turning off all non-essential lights. When she reached the front of the store to close and lock the stained-glass window, she looked at Mal and Gabriel out of the corner of her eye. He and Mal seemed to be deep in conversation.

Onnie wasn't sure when her life had changed from reading about magical worlds to living in one, but she was beginning to think she had fallen down a rabbit hole somewhere. If she thought about it, yesterday must have only been the day she finally saw it. Her entire time in Alku, she'd been surrounded by it and blind to it.

She observed Gabriel as he delicately petted and scratched Mal until the feline jumped to his shoulder and began to purr. Seeing the two of them interact put Onnie at ease after their earlier exchange, and she walked past the two of them and back into the back room.

As she passed him, Onnie inhaled Gabriel's scent, and she smiled as the smell of his soap followed her. She'd tried hard to stay angry with him, but if protecting her was his job, then that was all there was to it, and she'd try not to be a hindrance. So, when he asked to walk her to her date with Dany, she'd decided to cut him some slack and agree. It seemed like this situation was new for both of them, and while she didn't like it, she would set some boundaries and try to behave.

Onnie pulled her phone from her back pocket and messaged Dany with the updated plan. Gabriel would walk Onnie to coffee, and then she and Dany would enjoy their caffeine buzz and talk about girly things. Once her text was sent, Onnie looked at Gabriel while grabbing her bag from under the counter.

"I'm ready when you are. I just need to grab my coat."

"Okay," Gabriel said as Mal jumped off his shoulder and back onto the counter.

Mal reached out a paw, waving it at Onnie, and she smiled before lowering herself to his eye level. "Are you coming with me or staying here?"

Mal blinked twice and stretched.

"Alright, go curl up on one of the chairs. I'll bring you some toast in the morning. Will you be okay for dinner?"

The feline's eyes sparkled, and he meowed at her with a smile.

"Alright." Onnie stood and kissed him on the top of the head. "Have fun tonight."

He head-bumped her forehead and stayed on the counter as she walked to the front of the shop and shrugged on her coat. She followed Gabriel outside, but when she went to lock the door, he put his hand over hers.

"Wait, I want to try something…if you're willing?"

"Ah, sure. What do you want me to do?" Onnie's eyes narrowed with skepticism.

"Put your keys away and place your hand on the lock."

"Okay…" Onnie slipped her keys back into her bag and rested her palm on the door's deadbolt. "Now what?"

"Ask her to lock it," Gabriel said, slipping his hands into his pocket and smiling.

"What?" Onnie asked, confused, "Ask who?"

"The store. You know she can hear you. I want to see how strong your connection is."

Returning her wide-eyed gaze to the wooden door, Onnie looked at it and asked. "Lock, please?" Nothing happened. Feeling silly, Onnie pulled her hand back and looked at Gabriel like he was crazy, "Well, that was effective."

"Try again, Cat."

With a roll of her eyes, Onnie tried again. "Nothing."

"Here," Gabriel placed his palm over the back of her hand, and they immediately felt the lock click into place.

"What!" Onnie pulled her hand from under Gabriel's and inspected it. "Did we really just do that?"

"Yup," Gabriel said with a grin. "The world around you is changing, be open to it. It's going to get even better."

"Ah, that was so cool!" Onnie jumped in excitement and threw herself at him for a hug. "How did I—" She blushed and cleared her throat quickly, letting go and putting some distance between them. "Thanks for that."

"Damn, if I knew you would react that way, I'd have shown you sooner. Wanna see something else?" he waggled his eyebrows at her with a big grin.

Onnie playfully smacked his chest, "Fiend."

Gabriel smiled and gestured with a flourish toward the sidewalk before them. "Lead the way."

They walked down the soaked street beside one another, and yet there was so much distance between them. Each of them was in their head and not truly present. Onnie, for her part, was still back in front of the bookshop, hand on the door, making it lock. She couldn't believe they'd really done that. Gabriel implied there was more, that *she* could do more, and she couldn't deny that she was intrigued.

The smell of lavender tickled her nose, and she looked up from the cobblestone street and over to the flower shop at the corner. Onnie waved to the front windows, and Elanor's little wrinkly face peered through, waving back at her. Rain or shine, somehow, that woman was always there to greet her, and it made Onnie feel special every day.

"She likes you," Gabriel said, smiling at Elanor and joining in with a wave.

"She's sweet," Onnie said, pulling her coat tighter around herself and returning her hand to her pocket. "She always makes me feel welcome."

"You are welcome here, Onnie," Gabriel said, stopping her with a gentle hand on her shoulder. "Why would you think otherwise?"

Onnie shrugged, turning to continue their walk.

She tried to break the tension and began talking about lighter things, more rambling than any form of structured conversation. She learned that Gabriel had never lived outside of Washington and that he seemed to enjoy listening to her gush over the heat of Southern California. She told him of the beautiful sandy beaches with their dark, frigid water and the boardwalk with the carousel all lit up at night. With a light laugh, both admitted to wanting some of that warmth at that moment instead of their soaked toes and damp faces.

Onnie spoke of her past enthusiastically and hoped Gabriel would believe her tall tales of her life before Alku. Her face lit up as she talked about her experiences, but the deep hollow feeling that pulsed in her core, she tried to hide from their Bond. She didn't even know how to do it, but she hoped it worked. Loneliness ate at her soul before coming to Alku. Some days, it still did, but she didn't want to share that with him. She'd given this speech to others many times before, trying to convince others of her happiness, but Gabriel frowned as she spoke, and she knew her exaggerated truths weren't fooling him. However, Gabriel nodded and interjected with comments where it was appropriate.

When Onnie brought up her brothers, her longing for her family almost overwhelmed her, tears catching in her throat, and she changed the subject quickly.

When the coffee shop finally came into view, Gabriel reached out and laid a hand on her arm, stopping her.

"Here." He pulled out an envelope from the inside pocket of his coat and handed it to her.

Onnie crinkled it and then lifted it to her nose. It smelled like Rebecca. "More tea?"

Gabriel nodded. "Try to drink a cup before or after your coffee and at least one before bed. Please?"

Onnie stared at Gabriel's hand on her arm, his thumb rubbing tiny circles on her jacket sleeve. "You told me it was to strengthen my Bond with the store, but what does that actually mean?"

"It means lots of different things. Actions, like locking the door as we did earlier, will become much easier, and you won't need my help to do it."

"Okay, but besides parlor tricks, why is that important?"

"The stronger your Bond with the store is, the better off you'll both be. She will be able to help you become more powerful, and you'll use what you've learned to protect her knowledge." Gabriel hesitated but took a deep breath and said, "You will also be able to protect one another should someone wish to do either of you harm."

"So, this tea is a life link between the two of us, the shop and I?"

"Yes," Gabriel said with a quick nod.

Onnie retracted her arm from Gabriel's grip and slipped the envelope into her bag. "How much of this tea am I going to have to drink?"

Gabriel lifted his shoulders. "As much as it takes. You'll also strengthen your connection through interaction, but this is a way to boost it. While you and the old man are transitioning, you need all the strength you can get."

"And you also drink this tea?" she asked, and Gabriel nodded in response. "I'm assuming the same way that the Bond between the shop and I is affected, the tea does the same for you and me?"

Gabriel avoided her eyes and looked at the coffee shop, "Exactly."

"So, this morning, when you called and were out of breath?" Onnie asked nonchalantly, smiling at Gabriel's unwillingness to meet her eyes.

"I was already on my way to you when I called."

"But why?" Onnie said as she moved to stay in his field of vision.

He met her gaze, steady and unwavering. "I told you, I felt your fear."

"Fear?" Onnie's brows knit in bewilderment. "I wasn't afraid. Mal startled me, but I just didn't realize it was him."

"Our Bond is new, fragile…" he paced in place, "not yet fully formed. While you may have only felt startled, it hit me like fear. The more we trust one another and work as a team, the better I will be able to gauge your moods, just as you will assess your store's."

Onnie swallowed roughly. "Oh, um…so last night after you dropped me off…" she lowered her head and peeked up at Gabriel in shame.

Gabriel stopped pacing, his spine rigid, his fists clenched at his side so firmly that his knuckles turned white. "Walking away from your front door last night was the hardest thing I have ever had to do."

Onnie stepped back in front of him to see his eyes, even as a blush crept into her cheeks. "I'm sorry. I would have held it together had I known." Suddenly, realization filled Onnie, her shock surely written on her face, and she smiled. "You called my Mom."

Gabriel laughed softly, "No, but I would have had I had her number. I called your Grandfather, and he called her at my suggestion."

Onnie had a hard time breathing with the emotions filling her lungs. She stood up on her tip-toes and awkwardly used his hand as leverage to kiss him lightly on the cheek. With her that close, it would be easy for Gabriel to see the subtle glistening of tears in her eyes, mirroring the gratitude that was probably rolling off her in waves.

"Thank you," she whispered, returning to stand before him.

"Of course, Cat." Gabriel smiled.

"Oy! Are you comin' in or not, you two lovebirds!" Dany shouted from the coffee shop doorway. "The sky is about ready to open up again."

Gabriel laughed, and Onnie rested her forehead in her hand. "I guess I won't have to worry about telling her about our relationship now."

"Oh, we have a relationship now?" Gabriel said, eyes reflecting the streetlamp behind her.

"Brat," Onnie said, playfully punching him in the arm.

"Enjoy your coffee, Cat." he leaned down and pressed a kiss to her forehead. "Don't forget to have some tea too."

"I won't," she nodded as he stepped back. "Do you want to join us?"

He shook his head with a smile and a glance at his sister. "You need some girl time."

"Alright." Onnie turned and walked over to Dany and was immediately wrapped in the young woman's warm hug.

"Though maybe another time you'll let me take you to dinner?" Gabriel called from the street.

Onnie blushed deeply, the color likely visible in the lamplight, and her heart started racing.

Gabriel laughed softly, smiling, "I'll take that as a yes. Enjoy your night, ladies." He said with a wave before turning and heading back the way they'd come.

"Now I see why you wanted coffee. It's to butter me up for 'the talk,' isn't it?" Dany said with a giggle, "Come on. Let's get you inside. I'm just teasing you."

Onnie smiled and let herself get pulled along behind Dany. Warmth flooded Onnie's body, and she grinned. She knew it wasn't coming from the coffee shop's heaters this time.

Chapter 21: Determined

November 2021 - Alku | Onnie Moore

The smell of spiced cider filled the air, tiny pumpkins sat on every free surface, and the voices of friends and family filled the space with a steady hum.

It had been a week since Onnie had found out about the bookshop's real purpose, the magic it held, and that she did as well. Since then, she had spent a lot of time reading, studying, and trying to absorb as much history about the shop and the Keepers as she could. Her Grandfather had been helping, and so had Rebecca, but Gabriel had been the most forthcoming with information. They'd spent countless hours poring over ancient scrolls and texts, him tutoring her on all the history she never knew existed.

"Onnie, would you care for some cider?" Rebecca asked, holding a tray down to Onnie and breaking her musings.

"Oh, sure, thanks, Rebecca," Onnie said warmly before removing a thick earthen mug filled with the aromatic drink.

"Of course, dear."

She watched Rebecca make her way in turn to each person within the room, offering cider and stopping at Abbot to give him a cup of tea instead. Onnie couldn't help but smile at the two of them. Even with a house full of people, they could look at each other as if they were the only two in the room.

Gabriel cleared his throat and sat on the hearth next to Onnie, a cup of cider in his hand and a smile on his face. "Hey."

"Hey," Onnie said back, bumping her shoulder into his.

"Bec's cider is legendary," Gabriel said before sipping with his eyes closed in bliss.

Onnie raised an eyebrow but couldn't fight the upturn of her lips. "Oh really?"

"Mmmmhmmm…" Gabriel said around the edge of his mug.

Onnie raised her cup and took a deep breath, inhaling the spices into her lungs and nodding. "Smells amazing." She blew over the surface once and took a sip. Her eyes popped open, and Gabriel burst into laughter.

"Told you so."

Onnie smiled and took another sip, looking around the living room in her Grandfather's home. Dany and Abbot sat on oversized chairs in the corner of the room, playing chess on an antique chess table, smack-talking and giggling between themselves. Occasionally, one of them would make a move, and the game would continue, but from where Onnie sat, it looked like they did more strategizing than playing.

Across the room, Sam and his mother, Vanessa, were sitting on one of the couches, chatting with Rebecca about what they were having for Thanksgiving dinner. A bell sounded in the kitchen, and when Rebecca stood to tend to the food, Sam and Vanessa followed to help.

"Vanessa and her husband, Stephan, own the Day Night Cafe in town," Gabriel said, inclining his head at the three of them walking away.

Onnie turned to look at him, "Wait, the one in the town center?"

Gabriel nodded. "Yup, Vanessa runs the day cafe, and Stephan the night cafe."

"That's cool," She agreed, bringing her mug to her lips, "their food is incredible."

"It should be. Those two have spent the last seven hundred years perfecting those recipes." Gabriel said with a sideways glance and a smile.

Onnie coughed and choked on her cider, sputtering as tears filled her eyes.

"My boy, is she alright?" Abbot asked with concern.

Onnie waved him off as she continued to cough back up her cider. She glared at Gabriel and grabbed a napkin off the coffee table beside her.

"She's fine, Abbot. I'm educating her on the age of some of the recipes at the Day Night Cafe." Gabriel winked at Dany, who snorted and hid a smile in her mug along with Abbot.

"You…" Onnie said, pointing at Gabriel, "Are evil!" she managed to croak out.

Abbot and Dany burst into laughter and, with smiles and shakes of their heads, they returned to their game.

"Okay, maybe that was a bit evil," Gabriel rubbed her back softly and handed her another napkin to cough into, "but it is true."

"Explain," Onnie said, skepticism in her eyes, along with a twinkle of laughter.

"Sam and Vanessa are day walkers. Do you remember reading about them?"

"Ah, yeah," Onnie nodded, "um, a sub-race of humans, cursed, I think?"

Gabriel nodded, but his eyes dulled, and his shoulders drooped slightly. "Why?"

Onnie nibbled on her lip, recalling all the races she'd read about a few days before. "They were…banished." Gabriel smiled and continued to sip his cider, letting her continue. "There was a group of humans, afraid of a group of sanguiste, I think."

"Yes, 1000 CE, roughly," Gabriel interjected.

"They lived together with non-sanguiste. In peace." She coughed again and sipped her cider.

"Yes, and when they had built up a sizable community, local humans began to fear them. A nearby village burned their colony to the ground," Gabriel added while Onnie drank.

"Except, the humans only managed to kill anything that wasn't a sanguiste since they are immortal and quick to heal," Dany added before picking up her mug and crossing the room to join them.

Onnie nodded, and her brow creased in concentration. "The sanguiste retaliated and cursed the humans."

"Correct, my dear," Abbot said, joining them before the fire. "With the help of another settlement of magical beings, the devastated sanguiste banished the village of arsonists from the darkness and exiled them into the day. Every night, at sundown, they must be in their homes. Under the impression of safety, like the sanguiste and their families, friends, and companions had thought they were. When a day walker sleeps, it's a deep sleep, filled with troubled dreams they cannot control, ones of fire. The same flames that burned the many innocents burn the murderers every night, if only in their nightmares."

"Haunting them," Gabriel said.

"For eternity," Dany added solemnly.

Onnie shivered, and a tear ran down her cheek that she quickly dashed away with the tips of her fingers. "And if they're not home at sundown?"

Gabriel took her free hand within his own and gently squeezed. "Then they burn like their victims."

Dany sniffled and took a deep breath. "In the beginning, many day walkers would purposely leave their homes and use the flames as a sort of suicide."

"But as the years passed, the elderly learned they never sickened. Never died." Abbot sipped his tea quietly. "It was revealed that they had also become immortal in their punishment."

Gabriel squeezed Onnie's hand again. "Now, most of them suffer through the nights and live ordinary lives during the days."

Onnie looked towards the kitchen, her voice catching with emotion. "And Sam…" She looked back at the three of them, who just nodded at her with accepted sadness.

"He and Vanessa are both day walkers, and Stephan is a sanguiste. A rare pairing, but a loving one nonetheless." Abbot said, voice filled with pride.

"You've probably not met him yet, but there's another sanguiste, Marco. He works nights at the cafe." Gabriel frowned.

Abbot nodded, "Stephan and Vanessa also consider him a son, even if not by blood."

Sam walked in from the kitchen with a smile and a piece of ham between his fingers. "Hey guys, dinner's—" He stopped, noticing the room's silence and tears on everyone's cheeks.

Onnie placed her mug on the hearth and crossed the room, hugging him and crying into his neck. Sam slowly wrapped his arms around Onnie to hug her back, but she could feel his confusion at her sudden emotional outpouring.

"Come now, Dany, I see young Sam here has ham," Abbot said teasingly as he stood up from his chair and plucked the piece from between Sam's fingers as he walked by. "You know how much I love pork." Abbot and Dany left the living room, and Gabriel stood to follow.

"I'll be just in the other room if you two need me." He nodded to Sam and slipped from the room.

"I'm sorry," Onnie said, stepping back and sniffling. "I just… They just told me."

Sam blushed and put his hands into his large pants pockets. "Ah, they told you I'm a day walker finally."

Onnie nodded and leaned on the back of the couch behind her.

"But why does that make you cry?" Sam asked, using his sweatshirt sleeve to dry her tears.

She shook her head and shrugged. "It's just so...barbaric." She met his eyes, and tears welled up all over again. "You're so young, too young to deserve that."

Sam sighed and sat on the back of the couch next to her. "I'm over a thousand years old, Onnie. I'm not young," he shook his head and looked at her, his face lined with pain, stress, and fear, "and we were the barbaric ones."

Confusion crossed Onnie's brow, "But surely you didn't…"

Sam nodded once, "I was there, Onnie, I did. We were so ignorant back then, nothing more than silly humans pretending to be protectors."

"Protecting what?" Onnie asked.

"The Keeper."

"What?"

Sam shifted and picked at a patch sewn onto his pants. "I guess you haven't gotten to that."

She shook her head.

"My village was settled to protect the Keeper and one of the past locations of the archives. The sanguiste settled nearby because they could sense the magic, and our Keeper allowed it, said there was safety in numbers." Sam sighed and closed his eyes tightly. "It was alright for a while, but they were different, not human, and even with all the magic my people had seen, we couldn't help but think they were evil."

Onnie slipped her arm under his and rested her head on his shoulder. "Difference is often seen as the enemy."

Sam chuckled. "Yeah, that's what the Keeper said after we'd been cursed. Stated that we didn't deserve our punishment, just as the people we'd killed hadn't deserved to die. But now we would be as they were. Different. United forever against what others saw as *normal*. Always cast out, always apart."

"You're not different, Sam. You're special." Onnie squeezed his arm and kissed his cheek. "You'll let me help you if there's anything I can do, right?"

He softly patted her hand and hugged her tightly. "Thanks, Onnie, but there's nothing. I have to live with what I've done."

"Will you tell me of living in that time, of that Keeper?" Onnie asked tentatively.

"Sure, someday I'll give you a history lesson from someone who lived it." Sam tried to smile, but it didn't quite reach his eyes.

For a few minutes more, they sat together, Onnie clutching her friend close while the horror of the last night of his human life flickered in his eyes. Gabriel eventually appeared in the doorway, hands in his back pockets, and Onnie could feel him pressing on their Bond with his emotions. She smiled at him before untangling herself from Sam and messing up his hair.

"You didn't eat all of the ham, right?" she goofed.

Sam laughed and ducked under Onnie's arm. "Nope, but Abbot may have. I swear that man is made of bacon."

"Oh," Onnie said with mock fright, "go rescue me some ham!"

Gabriel winked at Onnie and squeezed Sam's shoulder as he saluted her. "Yes, ma'am!" Then he dashed past Gabriel and into the kitchen.

Onnie stood and walked over to Gabriel, eyes puffy and feeling wrung out like a sponge. "I don't care if he did it. He or Vanessa. I will find a way to help them."

"Many have tried, Cat," Gabriel said, catching a stray tear as it rolled down her cheek.

"But they weren't me." She stood straighter, scrubbed her face with her sleeves, and nodded once before heading into the kitchen to join the others.

As she walked away, she was sure she'd heard him whisper, "No, they weren't. And this time, that may make all the difference."

Chapter 22: Lost

November 2021 - Alku | Onnie Moore

A roll flew past Onnie's face.

"Oof," Sam said, winded. "What was that for!" He pulled a black olive from the bowl in front of him and threw it back at Gabriel.

"Sam!" Vanessa scolded, a smile on her face but no spine in her voice.

"What?" he said with a shrug. "Gabe started it."

"Very mature, Gabriel," Onnie said, her own form of scolding.

"Oh, don't bother," Dany said with a grin. "This is a tradition. I'm surprised they were this well-behaved for so long, actually."

"Really?" Onnie said, glaring at Gabriel.

Abbot and Rebecca both chuckled. "Yes, my dear," Abbot said, watching the pair's antics. Gabe and Sam grew up together. Along with another young man, Xayn."

"Always into trouble," Rebecca added.

"Never giving me a moment's peace," Vanessa said, pulling Sam to her for a loud smacking kiss on his cheek.

"Ah, gross!" he squirmed.

Dany pointed her fork at Gabriel and squinted her eyes at him in disapproval. "Yeah, it doesn't matter that Sam is older than dirt. Gabe still manages to bring out the seventeen-year-old in him."

"And you wouldn't have us any other way," Gabriel said, chucking another roll, this time at his sister, who caught it and flung it at Rebecca instead. She shrieked and disappeared, reappearing in her chair, rolling with laughter and blushing profusely.

"Much better, you almost had me!" She said, placing the roll on the table and smiling at Onnie. "One day, she'll manage to actually hit me with it."

Onnie smiled and popped a piece of ham into her mouth. Her friends were an energetic bunch, but they kept her entertained, and she was smiling most of the time she spent with them.

Her thoughts drifted back to her conversation with Sam, and the more she thought about it, the angrier she became. It had been over one thousand years, and still, he was paying for his crimes, while those sanguiste who'd cursed them had probably forgotten what happened after so long. Wasn't Sam's father, a sanguiste, proof enough that old prejudices had long since died? She had to do something. What good was being the Keeper of all knowledge if you couldn't help the people who mattered?

"Onnie!" Gabriel growled beside her, his voice raised.

"What!" she shouted, looking up at the table. Everyone was silent, and Abbot wore a worry on his brow that caused her to pause. "I'm sorry, what were you saying? I was spacing out."

"We know, child," Abbot said with a small smile. "Are you alright?"

Onnie shook her head, clearing her thoughts. "Yeah, sorry."

Slowly, the table began to talk among themselves again, and Gabriel leaned over and whispered in her ear. "If you really want to try and find a way to break it, I'll help you, but let it go for tonight." He kissed her cheek and sat upright, stabbing a carrot on his plate.

Onnie blinked a few times as her brain processed his comment, and she sighed. Her control over the Bond was still in its infancy, and clearly, she'd failed to keep her anger to herself.

"I'm sorry," she whispered to Gabriel, who took her hand that had been resting in her lap and squeezed it gently.

In a matter of seconds, her body started to warm up, her hand he was holding being the origin. Gabriel had become proficient at reading her in a short time, and she ignored his blatant use of their Bond. Instead, she smiled and returned to her food and the conversation around her, but she didn't release his hand.

"Bec, you've done it again," Gabriel said, leaning back and rubbing his stomach.

"Thank you, dear," Rebecca said as she stood and cleared the table. "Would anyone care for some tea? I've made a fresh batch of biscotti and scones."

Sam and Gabriel groaned.

"Don't feed them anymore, Rebecca. Gabriel has to be conscious enough to drive us home." Onnie chuckled and poked Gabriel in the side.

"Oof, careful Cat," Gabriel whined, "I think I'm going to explode."

"Me too," Sam added.

"Ho!" Abbot bellowed. "Well, if you young men are so full to bursting, that means there's more for us."

"Can I help with the dishes, Bec?" Dany asked, pushing back her chair and stacking plates.

"Nonsense." Rebecca removed the dishes from Dany's hold and shooed her off. "You ladies get these men out of my kitchen, and I'll handle the dishes."

"You sure?" Onnie and Dany both asked at the same time.

"Yes." Rebecca set the plates into the sink and returned to the table to collect more.

"Alright, then, you two," Dany said, wiggling her fingers at Gabriel and Sam. "You heard her. Out. Let's go, move it."

"Need help, Grandpa?" Onnie asked as the rest of the table scooched their chairs back and made their way into the living room in response to Dany's nagging.

"No, my dear, I'm all right. Go on, and I'll be right there." he raised his teacup, "I'll just finish the tea in my cup first."

"I'll stay and bring the tea set out when the water's boiled." Vanessa offered to Rebecca. "Surely you'll let me do that much, at least."

As Onnie left the kitchen, Abbot's laughter and Rebecca's tsking followed her into the other room, where it joined with Sam's laughter and Dany's shout of warning. Something streaked towards Onnie's face, and she ducked at the last minute, a pillow flying close enough to ruffle her hair before colliding with the wall behind her. Onnie picked up the pillow and looked into the living room, where Dany and Sam were practically rolling with laughter, and Gabriel was whistling and tapping his steepled fingers together. Narrowing her gaze to Gabriel, Onnie walked around the couch to stand in front of his chair.

"Damn, dude! You're so gonna die." Sam chuckled into the crook of his arm.

Onnie stopped and looked down at the man before her, now trying to choke back his laughter that bubbled just below the surface. Onnie held out the pillow and winked at him, a sly smile on her lips.

"Payback's a bitch, Guardian." She turned her back on him, plopping onto the sofa between Dany and Sam.

"Taking the high road, I like it," Dany said, draping her legs over Onnie and onto Sam's lap.

"Oh, there will be retaliation," Onnie said, still looking at Gabriel, amusement written in his brows, "just not tonight."

"Oh, that's cold, Onnie," Sam said, trying to tickle Dany's feet. "He'll be looking over his shoulder for days."

Onnie broke her staring contest with Gabriel and smiled at Sam. "If he's lucky."

Dany snorted with laughter, "You're good." She lifted a foot and poked Sam's full abdomen, where he groaned in discomfort. She smirked and looked back to Onnie. "So, what's the plan for tonight? A movie, coffee shop, devious plots against my brother?"

"Sam, how's it going not having to go school for the twentieth time? I'm still shocked Vanessa let you bail." Gabriel asked, giving Onnie and Dany some privacy for their conversation.

"Actually, I bought stuff to make s'mores if you want. I have a fireplace I've never used." Onnie said with a grin from ear to ear.

"Really!" Dany said, sitting up straighter. "That sounds awesome!"

Onnie smiled at her best friend's enthusiasm. "You've never roasted marshmallows, have you?"

Dany shook her head, "Nope! I'm so excited!"

"Me too, I miss s'mores. Oh, and Mom wants to have a video call. It's a Thanksgiving tradition, and she said it would finally give her a chance to meet you."

"I'd love to meet her!" Dany was buzzing with energy, and when Abbot walked into the room, he looked from Dany's grin to Onnie and nodded slightly.

"So much excitement, it's enough to put an old man to bed early." He said before taking a seat next to Gabriel.

"Sam?" Vanessa said, poking her head around the doorway from the kitchen.

"Yeah, I know," he said over his shoulder. "Thanks, Vanessa. I'll be ready to go in five minutes." Vanessa returned to the kitchen, and Sam squeezed Dany's ankle gently. "Okay, ladies, half an hour until sundown."

Dany pulled back her feet and let Onnie stand up. "We should head out too, Onnie, especially if we are calling your mom."

"Yeah, I guess you're right." Onnie stood and hugged Sam tightly. "I'll find a way, I promise." She whispered into his ear.

"Thanks, Onnie." He said, lifting her off of her feet with a squeeze. He repeated the hug for Dany and then shook Abbot's hand. "Wanna come warm up the cars?" Sam asked Gabriel after a quick fist bump.

"Sure, let's go say goodbye to Bec." Gabriel squeezed Abbot's shoulder gently, "I'll stop by Monday and check in on you."

Abbot waved him off with a smile, "I'm fine, my boy, but if you insist, I'll never turn down spending some time with you."

Gabriel nodded, and the two men walked into the kitchen to finish their goodbyes.

Dany sat down next to Abbot and hugged him before kissing his cheek with a smile. "Thank you for having us again this year."

"Hush with that. You're family." Abbot said, patting Dany's hand in his own. "Now, you girls stay out of trouble tonight, okay?"

"Oh, I can't make that promise, Abbot. Onnie's got s'mores on the books."

"Well, in that case." His eyes sparkled with humor, and he winked at Onnie.

Dany gave him one last kiss on the cheek and stood up, "I'll go make the rest of the rounds, too," she said, making space for Onnie to say her goodbyes before leaving the room.

"Come here, my girl," Abbot said, patting the spot Dany had just vacated.

Onnie sat down next to him and rested her head on his shoulder. "Thanks for lunch, Grandpa. It was nice to spend Thanksgiving with family."

"You've been alone too long, my dear. You have a family here who loves you and another spread over the country." He wrapped an arm around her shoulders and squeezed her closer. "Never forget that. There's safety in numbers, and you have an army willing to fight alongside you."

Onnie nodded her head and sat back to look at him. "Thank you for giving me that army, Grandpa."

"Oh, my dear," he placed his palm on her cheek softly, "They have always been here. You just hadn't met them yet."

Onnie nodded, and her eyes met Gabriel's as he and Sam exited the kitchen, arms laden with food and both with smiles to match. Gabriel nodded, and he and Sam went out the front door to pack the cars and warm them up.

"Onnie," Abbot said, her attention returning to him. "I must warn you, the connection between a Keeper and their Guardian runs deep. As your Bond with the shop grows, so will your Bond with Gabriel."

"I know, Grandpa." Onnie nodded. "I've felt it."

"You need to be careful. I raised Gabe as if he were my own, and I trust him with my life, but I don't want to see either of you hurt."

Onnie frowned, "Alright."

"That said," Abbot's smile returned, "Do not close yourself off to love, even with your Guardian."

His words made her blush, and she glanced away, "Grandpa, I'm not really the right person for love."

Abbot shook his head, eyes closed, a smile on his lips. "My beautiful Granddaughter, you have never been more wrong." He opened his eyes and looked deeply into hers, holding her hand softly. "Do not let your family's past ruin the future you were meant to have."

Chagrined, Onnie shrugged and patted his hand in hers. "I'll try."

Abbot lifted her chin with his free hand and smiled. "That is all I can ask of you."

She nodded and hugged him. Being gentle, she opened her Bond to the store, hoping she would pass on the love Onnie was pouring into her.

Abbot laughed and kissed her hair. "I love you too."

Onnie pulled back with a smile as Dany, Vanessa, and Rebecca came in from the kitchen.

"I am so ready for s'mores!" Dany said with her arms also filled with food.

Onnie laughed and crossed the room to say goodbye to Vanessa and Rebecca in turn. "Thanks for lunch, Rebecca, it was wonderful."

"Of course, my dear, anytime." She hugged Onnie with a light squeeze and handed her two bags filled with food. "I packed leftovers, a new tin of tea, and some dessert. Though from the way Dany's been prattling on, it sounds like sweets may be a bit redundant."

"What?" Dany asked with a smile, "I've always wanted to try s'mores. I'll meet you in the car, Onnie." She turned and gave Abbot a high five. "Catch you later, Abbot!"

"Good night, dear," he said with a smile.

Dany left through the front door and closed it behind her. Once she was gone, Onnie shook her head and laughed. "I'm in for quite a night, aren't I?"

Vanessa and Rebecca nodded with smiles, and Abbot giggled to himself from the couch. "When are you not when it comes to Dany?" he quipped playfully.

"Fair enough," Onnie said with a shrug. "Well, I better go rescue Gabriel. It's my fault she's so excited."

She slipped on her coat and said one more round of thanks before she and Vanessa left and climbed into their cars. As Gabriel backed out of the driveway, Sam hung out of Vanessa's front window and waved excitedly. The three of them laughed at his impression of a puppy dog, his tongue lolling in the wind, as they rounded the street corner and disappeared.

"Home please, Wadsworth!" Dany called from the back seat up to Gabriel.

Onnie snickered and leaned back into the headrest, watching the streets pass by and listening to the siblings chatter between themselves.

A few minutes later, they arrived at Onnie's cottage, and Dany gathered as much food as she could while Onnie let her into the apartment. Gabriel came up behind them with the last of Onnie's bags, mainly the one holding the desserts. When Onnie reached for it, he pulled it out of her grasp with a smile.

"Alright," Onnie asked, hands on her hips. "What do you want for the biscotti?"

Gabriel lowered the bag and smiled. "A date."

Shocked, Onnie snorted, "Right, what do you really want?" She held up her hands, showing no crossed fingers, "I promise I won't retaliate for the pillow."

"Cat," Gabriel said, taking another step closer to her. "I want. A date."

Onnie shivered, looking up into his eyes, and saw no sign of a joke. "Why?"

"Why not?" Gabriel said with a crooked smile. "I'll pick you up from the shop tomorrow. I assume you'll be open."

Onnie managed a nod.

"Say yes." He asked, reaching up to rest his knuckles on her cheek.

Onnie couldn't look away, his gaze pulling her in, but her brain shouted a dozen different responses. "Yes."

"Perfect," he bent down and kissed her cheek, "I'll see you tomorrow then."

When he stepped back, the bag of desserts was in her hand, and a blush crept up from her toes.

"Night, Dany!" Gabriel called into the house before returning to his car, never taking his eyes off Onnie. "Get inside, Cat, enjoy your s'mores."

She nodded and turned, looking over her shoulder at Gabriel one more time before she walked into her house and closed the front door behind her.

"Well, it's about damn time he asked you out!" Dany said from the kitchen, smiling ear to ear, marshmallows in one hand, chocolate in the other.

Chapter 23: Envious

November 2021 - Alku | Onnie Moore

“Oh no, you heard that?” Onnie asked, mortified, and hid her face in her free hand.

“Afraid so, the front door wasn’t latched.” Dany swapped the s’mores supplies she carried for Onnie’s bag of leftovers and pranced back into the kitchen to stick them in the fridge. “Honestly, he should have asked weeks ago. It would have saved him quite a few headaches,” Dany rolled her neck, “and me quite a few bruises.”

Onnie giggled nervously and went to sit in front of the fireplace, ripping into the bag of marshmallows and sticking one in her mouth. Dany looked over at Onnie, who made a face, puffing out her cheeks and crossing her eyes.

“Don’t look so sour about it. You should have said no if you didn’t want to go.” Dany turned on the tap and filled the kettle before setting it on the stove to boil.

Onnie murmured around her marshmallow, shook her head, and shrugged her shoulders. When Dany laughed at Onnie’s horrible attempt at communication, she chucked a marshmallow at her.

“What,” Dany said innocently, “you look like you’re playing

chubby bunny." She popped the marshmallow into her mouth that Onnie had thrown and joined her on the floor.

Onnie swallowed and rolled her eyes. "I have a weakness for marshmallows."

"mmmI mmSee mmThat." Dany hummed before swallowing and grinning ear to ear. "Sorry, couldn't resist." She winked and reached for a chocolate bar, unwrapping it and breaking off a square. "So, what's first on the agenda?"

"Well, my mom wants to video at ten Maine time, and then we have junk food, junk food, oh, and desserts from Rebecca!" Onnie snagged a chocolate square and bit into it with a loud snap.

"Oh, I can feel the stomach ache and cavities already," Dany said, cradling the second unopened bag of marshmallows against her cheek like a swaddled baby.

"Don't forget the hangover!" Onnie said, standing up and bounding for the kitchen, "I've got wine, too!"

"She's trying to kill me," Dany said to the ceiling. "Well, when in Rome. Pour me a glass and get me a coat hanger. We got s'mores to make and hangovers to be had!"

"I'll drink to that!" Onnie cheered while uncorking a bottle of red wine.

Nearly three hours later, they were in their pajamas, lying on the apartment floor, staring at the ceiling. Two empty bottles of red wine were on the mantle, two empty glasses on the hearth, one empty bag of marshmallows, and another half-full sat next to Dany. Onnie nibbled on a graham cracker as she read a chocolate bar wrapper.

"I have to work tomorrow," Dany mumbled, playing with a gooey marshmallow between her fingers.

"Did you know this chocolate was made in Pennsylvania?" Onnie asked, spinning the bar between her fingers before fumbling and dropping it on her face.

"I don't remember the last time I had a day off," Dany said to her messy fingers. "Well, today doesn't count. Thanksgiving is a holiday. Who goes to a library on Thanksgiving?"

"I've never been to Pennsylvania. I wonder if it looks like Maine? Mom loves Maine."

Dany stuck her fingers in her mouth to eat the marshmallow goop, her loud, happy, lip-smacking noises filling the room.

"I miss Mom," Onnie said before biting off another square of chocolate.

"Maybe I should ask for some time off," Dany said around her fingers.

Onnie snapped off a piece of chocolate and held it out to Dany. "Aren't you the boss? Play hooky."

"Yum, thanks!" Dany nibbled at the sweet with a smile. "I can't play hooky. Not all of us own our jobs."

Onnie rolled her eyes and glared at Dany, "I don't own my job. Grandpa does and besides tomorrow's Black Friday. I have to work too, and it's going to be a madhouse."

Dany shook her head, "Nah ah," she liberated the chocolate bar from Onnie's grasp. "Alku doesn't really do Black Friday. You'll be fine. Just another typical day."

Onnie scoffed.

"Right, as normal as it can be with your life." Dany giggled and poked Onnie's side.

"Ugg, but I have a date." Onnie covered her eyes with her arm.

"Ooooh!" Dany shifted and rolled onto her stomach, stopping right next to Onnie. "I forgot! Where are you guys going?"

"I don't know. He didn't say." Onnie muffled into her bent elbow.

Dany tsk-tsked, "Well, we can't have that! How will you know what to wear?" she reached over Onnie and grabbed her abandoned cell phone from the carpet. "I'll ask him."

"Wait, what?" Onnie uncovered her eyes and saw Dany typing away on her cell phone.

"What? It's a valid question." Dany rolled her eyes, "Fine, you ask him. He texted you anyway."

"He what!" Onnie said, snatching the phone and navigating to the message screen.

Dany snickered and rolled back over to the hearth. "Want more wine?" When she saw the two empty bottles on the mantle, she frowned. "Well, maybe not. I'll make some tea then."

"Sure, thanks," Onnie mumbled in agreement when Dany stood and, on shaky legs, made her way into the kitchen.

Gabriel had texted her over an hour ago, and she must have missed the notification sound.

Are you frunk? Runk? Damn it! Drunk! Are you DRUNK!

Onnie roared with laughter, tears rolling down her cheeks—no idea why Gabriel's text was so funny.

"What? What happened?" Dany said, turning on the stove and coming back over to Onnie, who held up the phone, still rolling with laughter. "Frunk? Did he ask if you were frunk?"

Onnie nodded, snorting and laughing even more, going silent as she did when she laughed too hard.

"What the hell is frunk?" Dany asked with sincerity.

"He meant drunk." Onnie wheezed.

"Well, obviously." Dany said, gesturing to the phone, "I can read, you know."

Onnie replied with a simple, *yup!,* when her Mom's face appeared on the screen. She sent the text to Gabriel and answered her Mom's video call.

"There's my baby girl!" Tory's voice boomed, making Onnie wince. "Oh my, my baby has had a bit to drink, I see."

"Can you stop yelling, Mom, please?" Onnie said, sitting up and combing her fingers through her hair.

"TORY!" Dany shouted from the kitchen. "Yeee!" she ran in, flopped down next to Onnie, and stuck her face in the camera. "Hi, Tory! I'm Dany!"

Onnie smiled at her friend's enthusiasm and draped her arm around Dany's shoulder.

Onnie's Mom smiled politely and waved. "Hi, Dany. It's so nice to meet you finally! Onnie's told me so much about you."

"We made s'mores, Mom," Onnie said, eyeing the half-full bag across the room.

"Oh! I'll make more, and tea should be done soon, too." Dany waved at the phone before scooching out of Onnie's grip and over to the marshmallows.

With Dany no longer able to see the phone's screen, Onnie's Mom gave a thumbs up and whispered, "I like her."

Onnie smiled and nodded in agreement.

"You two girls aren't getting into too much trouble, I hope?" Lewis said from off-screen, where he was holding the phone. "You're not driving, right?"

Tory smiled fondly at him before raising a brow at Onnie.

"Oh, all sorts of trouble." Onnie grinned. "But no driving, no. We're safe."

"Good, I'm glad," Lewis said, affection thick in his voice.

"Where's everybody else?" Onnie asked.

Tory waved her hand dismissively, but Onnie saw the sadness her mom couldn't entirely cover up. "The boys are still dealing with the Thanksgiving rush at the restaurant, and Lizzy has the flu, so Anthony is busy putting the kids to bed."

"Oh…" Onnie said with a frown.

The kettle whistled in the kitchen, and Dany and Onnie looked at each other. Dany had one marshmallow halfway to her lips and two coat hangers in the other hand, sticking into the fireplace.

"I'll get the tea," Onnie said, gracelessly getting to her feet and making her way into the kitchen. She set her phone on the counter and propped it up so she could still see her Mom. "We ran out of wine."

Tory rolled her eyes, and Onnie could see the camera shaking as Lewis laughed, too.

The four of them chat for a little longer, Dany and Onnie each a sticky mess by the time they were done, and Tory and Lewis yawned from a full day of cooking and visiting with friends.

"Alright, girls," Tory said, knocking back the last of her tea, "I think it's time we were off to bed."

"Aww…" both girls whined, looked at each other, and broke into laughter.

Tory smiled and shook her head in amusement. "Dany, you get my number from Onnie. You text me, and we can girl talk sometime."

Dany's face lit up, and she nodded vigorously. "That would be awesome!"

Onnie smiled and waved at the phone. "Love you guys. I'll call you this weekend."

"Sounds good, honey," Tory said before looking over the camera to Lewis.

"By kiddo!" he called out.

"Bye!" Onnie and Dany said in unison.

Tory reached forward and turned off the camera.

"Your family rocks!" Dany said before bumping her shoulder with Onnie. "Thanks for sharing them."

Onnie chuckled, "You may regret that. Just wait until my brothers get a hold of you. They are some seriously overprotective bears."

"All the same, I think I could do with some more bears. My family just has the one," Dany said with a sigh. "Did he text back, by the way, Mr. Frunk?"

"I forgot," Onnie said, navigating back to her messages. "Yeah, he did."

Dany leaned in over Onnie's shoulder and read the message out loud as it appeared. "You're projecting onto our Bond." she looked sideways at Onnie, confused. "What does that mean?"

"I don't know. He may—" Onnie blanched, her mouth opening in surprise. "Oh, wow."

"What?" Dany asked, slightly panicked.

Onnie shook her head. "Nothing, well, nothing bad, at least," she smirked at Dany. "I think he means that I relaxed my hold on our Bond, and he's now feeling drunk, too."

Confusion colored Dany's face but was quickly replaced with understanding. "No! Really?"

Onnie nodded.

"Shit, that's good!" Dany giggled.

Sniggering, Onnie stood and headed for the kitchen. "I think I'm marshmallowed out, but I'd kill for one of Rebecca's biscotti and a fresh cup of tea, you want?"

Onnie heard Dany mumble no thanks, but after that, Onnie lost focus. She brought Gabriel's message back up on her phone and hit reply.

Sorry, I didn't know. I'll be more careful, and if you tell me where we are going tomorrow night, I might not share the hangover. :-)

She slipped her phone into her pajama pocket and pulled out the bag of desserts from Rebecca. Dany joined her in the kitchen, carrying an empty bottle under each arm and a wine glass in each hand.

"Thanks." Onnie said, "Just set them in the sink, and I'll wash them tomorrow."

"Okay, and hey, thanks again for letting me crash here," Dany said, pulling the whistling kettle off the stove and refilling each of their mugs.

"Anytime." Onnie popped a bite-sized biscotti in her mouth and frowned while she chewed. "Not that I mind, it was nice not being alone for the holidays again…but when you asked me the other day, you seemed kind of…I don't know, sad about it."

"Ah, nope, not sad," Dany said, replacing the kettle on the stove and grabbing her mug of tea before retreating into the living room a bit too quickly.

"I promised you I wouldn't pry, but…" Onnie picked up her mug and the small container of cookies and followed her friend.

"So, don't." Dany snapped.

Onnie held out the container without looking at Dany, and they chewed in silence before Dany finally sighed and hung her head.

"Has Gabe told you anything about our family?" Dany said in barely more than a whisper.

Onnie shook her head before sipping her tea.

Dany nodded once and bit into another cookie. After a few minutes, she swallowed and let out a deep breath. "My Mom died a few years after I was born. Some freak accident, I don't remember any of it, and I don't remember her."

Listening intently, Onnie felt her phone vibrate in her pocket but ignored it.

"Gabe remembers her. Two years made all the difference, I guess. Lucky jerk."

Onnie sat down the cookies and linked her arm through Dany's.

"Our dad, on the other hand, worthless piece of shit that he is, is still alive and kicking somewhere."

Dany's posture was rigid, and Onnie laid her head on Dany's

shoulder. "The only thing Gabriel said was that your dad spent more time doing his job than with you guys."

Dany leaned forward and pressed the heels of her hands into her eyes. "My dad was Abbot's Guardian."

Onnie's spine went stiff, and for a moment, she let her anger slip through her Bond and towards Gabriel. "I thought you said your Dad was still alive."

"He is. He didn't just abandon *us.*" Dany leaned her head back against the wall and sighed. "He abandoned everyone."

"But why?" Onnie asked, the pitch of her voice raising and a frown creasing her brow.

"We don't know. He and Abbot had a huge argument one day, and the next day, he was gone."

Onnie sat up and looked at Dany, "So, you wanted to stay over because…" Onnie's phone vibrated again in her pocket.

Tears shimmered in Dany's eyes, but she blinked them away quickly and broke eye contact. "Gabe would rather brood alone over our lack of family, and I'd rather be with people."

"You know," Onnie said with a smile, "a great man once told me, 'Do not let your family's past ruin the future you were meant to have,' I think maybe you should listen to his advice too."

Dany closed her eyes and smiled, "Yeah, he's a pretty wise one."

"Yes, he is," Onnie said, pride gleaming in her eyes. "Well, you're welcome here anytime."

"Thanks," Dany said with a small smile before a yawn interrupted her. "Damn, it's only like ten."

"Been a long day, though."

"Yeah, I guess." Dany picked up her and Onnie's mugs and hoisted herself to her feet. "I'll wash."

"Sounds good," Onnie said, closing the cookies and stretching. "Where do you want to sleep? Floor, big chair, or blow-up with me?"

"With you, if that's okay."

"Yup, it'll be comfier anyway." Onnie slipped the cookies into the cupboard and grabbed two water bottles from the fridge. "Oh, but you may wake up with a cat on your head. Apparently, Mal likes sleeping on the pillows."

Dany laughed light-heartedly and cheerfully. No traces of her sadness were left. "Strange beast, that one. I didn't realize he and Rebecca could exist simultaneously."

Onnie shook her head and clicked out the kitchen light, leading Dany back into the bedroom. "They can't, but he comes to check on me while Abbot's sleeping."

"Ah, so he's over-protective too," Dany said as she picked up her bag from inside the bedroom door. "Mind if I use your bathroom to beautify myself before bed?" she batted her long eyelashes at Onnie playfully.

"Oy, no, take your time," Onnie said, flopping onto the mattress and slipping her hand into her pocket.

"Sweet, thanks. Be right out."

Dany closed the bathroom door, and Onnie pulled out her cell phone. There were two messages from Gabriel. The first one was in response to her earlier flirting.

That's blackmail, and I don't have to work tomorrow, so it's tempting to suffer. ;-) I'm considering the Day Night Cafe since you've never been there after dark.

He was right. She'd only been during the day and blushed, liking the idea and hoping the cafe became more romantic at night. During the day, it was generally packed full of people in a hurry and tourists from out of town.

His second message was not as playful.

What happened, are you hurt? Dany?

Onnie was surprised Gabriel wasn't already beating down her front door in worry, so she assumed when she'd calmed down, it must have reassured him that they were alright.

We're okay. Dany told me about your dad and his connection to Abbot. You'll tell me tomorrow, not as your date but as your Keeper.

She hit send and immediately realized her mistake.

And don't bother Dany. She's had enough trauma telling me about it, and she doesn't need you growling at her, too.

Onnie set her phone on the bed beside her and combed her fingers through her hair. "Dany, what time do you need to be up for work?" she called to the bathroom door.

It squeaked open a quarter of the way, and Dany's green goop-covered face peered out, blue hair pulled back into a bun, and eyes squinted nearly closed.

"Damn swamp thing!" Onnie teased.

"Shut up you." Dany stuck her tongue out and smiled. "I can be up whenever you are. I'm the only one there tomorrow."

"Okay, seven work?" Onnie said, turning her alarm on again and jumping when the phone vibrated in her hand, and a message popped up.

We'll talk. I won't say anything to Dany. Today's already been difficult enough for her. Thanks for tonight. She needed it. Sleep well, little Cat.

"Ugg, yeah, perfect." Dany groaned and returned to the bathroom to dunk her face in the sink's running water.

When Dany finished, she swapped with Onnie, who gave her hair a quick brush, braided it down her back, and washed her face and teeth without utilizing any green sludge. When finished, she turned off the light and crawled into bed next to Dany.

"Thanks again, Onnie," Dany said, lethargy thick in her voice.

Onnie smiled, "Anytime."

They both closed their eyes and were softly snoring within minutes.

Chapter 24: Surprise

November 2021 - Alku | Onnie Moore

Onnie was leaning on The Book Nook's front counter, tracing the marble's swirling pattern, when Mal appeared at her elbow.

"Hey, Mal."

He nudged her arm, and she lifted her hand to scratch behind one of his silky ears.

"You're sure it's okay for you to be here?" Mal nodded, so she continued to scratch. "You didn't come home last night."

Mal purred and bumped his head against her shoulder and then yawned.

"Did Rebecca need to stay with Grandpa?"

Mal nodded again, and Onnie sighed, "Well, I missed your furry butt on my pillow this morning, and I secretly think Dany was disappointed you weren't on her head when she woke up."

Mal looked at her and cocked his head to the side, and Onnie chuckled.

"That woman may look like she stepped from a magazine, but she sure doesn't seem to let it stop her."

Mal cocked his head again.

"She's crazy about you, silly purr machine," Onnie said, scratching under his chin and bopping him on the nose.

He sat up straighter and puffed out his chest, a goofy cat grin spreading ear to ear.

"My day has been dull. Dany was right. No one has come in. This is by far the slowest day I've had so far." Onnie sighed and reached for her cell phone. "I'm even half tempted to catalog the romance section."

When Mal shivered and shook his head, Onnie couldn't hide her laughter. "How has your day been?"

Mal stared at her and blinked before rolling onto his back, closing his eyes, and draping his tongue out of his mouth.

"Maldwyn! That's just wrong!" Onnie scolded half-heartedly. "It's not like you're actually dead when Rebecca's with Grandfather. More like…sleeping." He shook his head at her, and Onnie put her nose against his.

"Don't tell me that, Mal. You'll make me sad."

He reached up and swatted at a piece of her hair that had loosened from her braid and swung forward past her cheek. Onnie grabbed her braid and proceeded to tickle his tummy with the end of it.

"I have a date tonight." Mal stopped chasing her hair and looked at her. "Oh, don't you act surprised. Privacy doesn't exist in this family."

Mal smiled and resumed chasing her hair.

"Grandfather gave me a mini-lecture last night." Mal caught his claw on the braid's tie and tugged at it gently, no longer playing, his eyes locked with Onnie's, unblinking. "I'll be careful, Mal."

The cat shook his head and rolled to his feet before rubbing his chin on Onnie's.

"Hey, would you be up for helping me with some stock? We got some new books in that I could use some help with."

Mal stretched and arched his back with a yawn before jumping off the counter and padding into the backroom.

"I guess that's a yes." Onnie smiled and followed the feline. "So, there's a box on the couch..."

When she entered the backroom, Mal's back end was in the air, tail swaying as his nose sniffed everything in the box. "I see you've found it."

Onnie crossed her arms and leaned on the door frame to watch Mal. "Everything up to scratch?"

A tiny meow came from inside the box, and Onnie chuckled. "I'll let you continue your inspection."

She returned to the front counter and retrieved the uncapped bottle of water with a daisy in it that Elanor had given her nearly a week earlier. The flower looked the same as the day it was gifted to her, so Onnie took it to the back room and refreshed its water. "Magic, I'm sure," she muttered to the friendly floral and returned it to its place. When she smiled down at it, its fragrance filled the area, and she closed her eyes and enjoyed it for a few minutes before heading back to Mal.

She pulled her cell phone from her purse on the spindly table beside the door frame in the back room and called Dany.

"Hey, girl! How's the Black Friday rush going?" Dany said with a grin that Onnie could hear through the phone.

Onnie scoffed. "Yeah, you win."

Dany's giggle made Mal's ears twitch from the sound, and Onnie smiled. "How's the library?"

"Slow, same as you, but I'm working on a lesson plan for the little ones at the school."

"Really? That sounds like fun."

"Yeah? I guess it is." Dany said, pride in her voice. "So, what're you up to? Mal with you?"

"Yup, he's currently giving a new box of stock the sniff test."

"Probably a good idea. Never know what'll show up from Abbot's suppliers."

"Really?" Onnie said, pressing the phone to her ear with her shoulder as she crossed the back room to a pile of empty boxes. "Like what?"

"Oh, you know," Onnie could hear Dany get up from the front desk and walk into the backroom, "dark areas of magic and stuff. They need to be handled a bit more carefully."

Onnie picked up the box cutter from where she had left it and began flattening the cardboard. "So, why does he accept them if they're dangerous?"

"Where else would they go? It's a far better plan for the Keeper to have control of who can access them than anyone else."

"I guess that makes sense."

"Yeah, there's too much darkness in this world, and evil often tries to sell their souls for it. I know—" Dany's voice cut off, and Onnie could barely make out a deeper male voice in the background. "Onnie, I've gotta go. I'll text you later."

"Sure thing, bye." Onnie heard the line go quiet, and she pulled the phone from her ear, frowning at it. "Hmm..."

Mal meowed from the couch, and Onnie looked up, "I guess she had a customer." Mal shrugged and patted the box with his front paw.

"All safe?"

He blinked once.

"Thanks. Would you mind helping me stock before Gabriel comes to pick me up?"

Mal responded by jumping into the box and tapping the lip of the opening.

"Oh, I'm carrying you, am I?" Mal grinned as Onnie hefted the box into her arms. "Alright, spoiled, point me in the right direction."

The two of them fell into a companionable rhythm where Mal

directed her to the appropriate shelves for the rare books, and Onnie would settle them into their new home with care. When the box was nearly empty and only two books remained, Onnie slid it onto the front counter with her hip and stopped for a water break. Mal jumped out and onto the floor, heading to the china dish by the wall with his water.

"Thanks for your help, Mal. That's getting easier. I think I can feel her guiding me to where the books go. It's almost like I know where you will tell me they belong before you actually do."

Mal swished his tail and sat back to clean his face.

The clock started to chime, and Onnie's eyes widened. "Oh, man… it's already five."

Mal purred and jumped back onto the counter to look at her.

"Gabriel will be here soon. Let's get these last few books shelved."

Mal jumped back into the nearly empty box, standing on his back feet, front paws on the flap.

"I think not, feline. You can walk. I'm ditching the box." Onnie ruffled his ears and dug out the three remaining books. "Huh," she said with a frown, "I swore there were only two left a minute ago." Mal chuffed and jumped back out onto the counter and down the floor.

"Lead the way, little master. The first book is a modern romance, front section, new releases."

Mal did a little skip and padded quietly in front of Onnie to the proper shelf, where she slid the book into the open space before reading the second title.

"Classic Shakespeare, Hamlet, hand calligraphy and…" she flipped the cover open, "French."

Mal walked to the center aisle of the shop and stopped to look at her.

"Hm…classics." Onnie crossed to the right side of the store and skimmed the shelves with her eyes. "Hand inked," she walked three shelves down the row, "French," she looked up at the top shelf and the space, conveniently the correct size for the book in her hand.

Mal rubbed his body against her shins, and she smiled before slipping the book onto the shelf.

"Last one." She bent down and scratched behind Mal's ears while reading the cover. "Looks like some runic language, antique, leather-bound." she lifted the book to her face and inhaled. "Smells amazing, like campfire smoke."

Mal nibbled on her hand, and Onnie looked at him as he nudged the book toward her with his nose.

"A test?"

He nodded.

Onnie stood and took a deep breath. "Okay, well, I have no idea, so…"

Mal meowed quietly, and she looked down at him, where he closed his eyes and breathed deeply.

"Bond?" Onnie said, confusion in her voice.

Mal nodded again.

Onnie closed her eyes, took a deep breath, and reached for her Bond. She found Gabriel's first, and her heart fluttered a bit. Pushing past it, she found Mal's and gently fed it affection before moving on and reaching the shop's strand.

It pulsed, sharp and bright. She pulled her focus back to the book in her hand and waited for the subtle humming that indicated the shop's response. Any chance she'd had, Onnie spent practicing her communication with the shop along their Bond, and Gabriel said her progress was astounding. Onnie was sure he was making a big deal out of nothing but warmed at his praise anyway.

Her Bond vibrated, and Onnie returned to her practice. She opened her eyes and looked at Mal, watching her closely.

"This way, Mal." Onnie returned to the shop's back corner, where the tea area was, and stopped. Mal jumped onto the back of the wingback chair nearest to her.

"This is where I think I need to be," Onnie said, looking around at the shelves. "None of these seem right, though. Did I make a mistake?"

Mal reached out a paw and rested it on her arm when she tried to walk by, stopping her.

"Mal?"

He removed his paw and closed his eyes again, taking another deep breath. Onnie did the same. She quickly focused on her Bond with the store and felt the intense vibrations from their little game of hot and cold. She held her hand in front of herself and felt the vibrations increase. Without opening her eyes, she took a step forward. The vibrations increased. She took another step. Increase.

Onnie opened her eyes and scanned the bookcase behind the sitting area. "These are Latin, 1500s, it looks like, but why is she telling me to go here?"

Onnie looked over her shoulder at Mal, who was loudly cleaning his paw and apparently ignoring her. His action clearly indicated she was on her own. She rested her palm on the shelf before her and closed her eyes. The vibrations were definitely there, and she took a few steps to the left, further behind the sitting area, hand still out in front of her and running along the wall of shelving. Half a dozen steps later, the vibrations in her mind were practically humming, and she stumbled forward when the bookcases beneath her palm ended. Her eyes snapped open, and a gasp escaped from behind her lips.

"Mal! Come quick!"

Mal flashed to the floor next to her feet with a meow.

Onnie never took her eyes off the space in front of her but managed to stutter, "Mal, is this a doorway? There's no way. There has never been a door here."

Mal rubbed against her leg, and Onnie's eyes widened. "Oh, man!"

she blinked and looked down at Mal. He was sitting on the edge of the rug from the sitting area, but his tail bounced lightly on the hardwood floor in front of them.

The floor was glossy and vibrantly red, running into the wall's baseboards that matched the rest of the shop. Onnie's eyes traced their way up the opening, following the creamy paint to a stunning archway that eventually disappeared into the darkness of the room beyond.

"Mal?" Onnie's voice shook.

Mal pushed her legs from behind, and she took a tentative step forward. He pushed again. She took another few steps.

"Mal, where did this room come from?" In the distance, Onnie could hear her cell phone ringing, but it sounded farther away than it should. "Mal?"

The cat pushed her one more time, and Onnie took one more faltering step into the room. A whisper of fresh air blew in from the bookshop behind her and danced in her hair, twisting the strands and playing with the hem of her shirt before continuing deeper into the darkened room. A breath later, Onnie gasped and looked above her as a glass chandelier winked on, dozens of small candles lighting all at once. With only a few seconds to gawk at it, wall sconces in a row on either side of her roared to life, two candles in each. Mal raced forward past her, the room now filled with light and the soft sound of flames. Onnie turned awestruck, eyes roaming over everything. The wood floor gleamed and looked to be on fire from the reflection of the candlelight on the lacquered redwood. Waist-high, carved wooden bookcases lined the edges of the room's brick walls, paintings hanging above each shelf. Onnie stepped forward, twirling around, and looked at the ceiling above her head. Aside from the sparkling chandelier, two beams ran the length of the room from the doorway to the far wall and painted curling vines roamed the smooth surface and meandered down the first few rows of bricks.

Mal meowed, and when Onnie looked at him, he gestured with his paw to the table he was now sitting atop.

"What is it, Mal?" she asked, crossing the room, eyes still roaming. Three stacks of books were haphazardly arranged atop the oak slab table, and a few lay open next to them. "They look like someone was in the middle of reading them."

Mal meowed.

"Wow, I haven't seen this room in ages."

With a yelp and a jump, Onnie spun to face the doorway where Gabriel stood stroking the door frame like a lover's greeting. His lips curled at the corners in the smallest smile, but she watched as he traced the wood grain in the beams lining the doorway, and his posture shifted. Gabriel stood taller, straighter, and when he turned and finally looked at Onnie, she shivered. His irises glowed a crystal blue so vibrant it took her breath away.

"I see you've had a busy day, Cat." He said, slipping his hands into his pockets and approaching her slowly.

Onnie stepped back, the back of her thighs hitting the table behind her. She held out her hand in front of her. "Stop."

Gabriel froze, his features hardening. "What's wrong?"

"Your face, your eyes."

He reached up to touch his cheek and smiled just before his hand got there. "Ah, I see we've missed an important lesson." He took another step forward but stopped when Onnie leaned back further. "Cat, it's me." When she didn't move or say anything, Gabriel sighed, "My eyes are blue, aren't they?"

Onnie merely nodded.

"Eyes hold power, Cat, and in our case, a sign of our responsibility."

"Being a Guardian, you mean?"

"Yes, but it's not just me. Yours and Bec's, Mal's, and the old man's turn as well. All of us." Gabriel put his hand back in his pocket and took a few unhurried paces around the room, his back to Onnie. "It's partly a sign to others to give us the respect we are due. Right now, it's involuntary since we're not controlled enough yet. However, once our control grows, we will be able to regulate our eyes shifting as well. You've probably never seen Abbot's eyes turn, have you?"

Onnie shook her head and used the table to brace herself before she slid onto it and sat cross-legged. "No."

"The old man has remarkable control over his gifts. I've only seen his shift a handful of times over the years." Gabriel turned back to face her, and his eyes returned to their usual vibrant green shade. "Better?"

Onnie nodded, and he crossed the remainder of the room and scratched behind Mal's ears.

"So, why did yours change?"

Gabriel looked up and smiled, "Lack of control. My emotions got the better of me for a second. Seeing this place…" he looked up at the painting on the ceiling, and his smile grew even more prominent, "I hadn't realized how much we'd lost over the years."

"What's that supposed to mean?" Onnie said, opening her arms for Mal to crawl into her lap.

Gabriel looked at his watch, pulled out one of the dark wooden chairs, and lowered himself into it. He leaned back into it and steepled his fingers in front of his face. After a few breaths, he dropped them and leaned forward to rest his elbows on his knees.

"Have you and the old man talked at all about how the Keeper is connected to the physical space of the shop?"

Onnie played with one of Mal's ears and shook her head, "Not really."

"Okay, I figured as much. So, you know the knowledge of the shop is vast, far larger than that single room out front."

"Yes, I always wondered where it was stored. We've just had other things to talk about."

"Right, I'm not criticizing you, just making sure we are clear." Gabriel took a deep breath and rubbed his forehead with his fingers. "The knowledge is kept archived in lockable rooms that are kept safe by the Keeper who protects them. The information is never far away, only hidden from view until needed. Just like this room."

Onnie cocked her head to the side, "Hidden?"

"Yes, able to be accessed by the Keeper at will...with enough control."

"Does that mean my control is getting better?" Onnie perked up and smiled.

"Partly," Gabriel's hand reached out to rest on her leg, "and partly, the old man's is slipping."

Onnie stiffened, and Mal meowed, looking directly into Gabriel's eyes. "Relax," Gabriel said to the feline. "Cat, your Grandfather is sick. We both know that. What you don't know is how long he's been sick and how it has affected the shop, their connection, and, honestly, this town."

"What are you talking about? Sure, he can't run the store like he used to, but Rebecca's been helping. It's not like it's been neglected."

"No, Cat, that's exactly what happened. Abbot has done none of it out of malice, but his strength and control have been waning over the past few years, and slowly, room by room, the shop has been getting smaller. Preserving its strength, going into a sort of hibernation."

"What does that mean?" Onnie shifted Mal further into her arms to cuddle him, taking comfort in his warm, furry body.

"It means that with a new Keeper having begun the Transference..." Gabriel looked up and into her eyes, and she knew he'd felt her sadness ripple through their Bond.

"How long, Gabe?" she asked quietly.

"Not long."

Onnie closed her eyes and cuddled Mal closer, burying her face in his neck and kissing him. She heard Gabriel stand up and the chair slide along the floor before she felt his arms around her and Mal.

"It'll be okay, Cat."

Onnie nodded and hugged a little harder, a squeak coming from Mal. Gabriel gently kissed the top of her head and released her a few minutes later when she'd pulled away.

Onnie sniffled but tried to hide her grief, "You said you knew this room. What is it, and why did this one appear first?"

Gabriel chuckled and stepped back, one hand brushing his hair from his eyes. "I guess this is the last room the old man was in. This was where he spent most of his time. Bec would take care of the customers up front, and he would hide away in here."

Gabriel walked around to the other side of the table and picked up a book from the top of the stack, more modern than the rest. "Yup," he laughed, "*How to Get to Know Your Adult Grandchild.*"

"No way," Onnie said, moving Mal off her lap so she could lean over to take the book from Gabriel.

"He was really nervous," Gabriel said with a smile and looked down behind the stacks. "Okay, that's funny."

Onnie looked up from where she was flipping through the self-help book, "What?"

Gabriel lifted a teacup from behind the books, swinging it back and forth on his finger. "Thankfully, empty."

"Um, ew," Onnie said, wrinkling her nose.

Mal rolled his eyes and stretched.

"Yeah, we should wash that," Gabriel said, replacing it on the saucer with a slight clink.

"With bleach." Onnie laughed before returning her attention to the book in her hands.

"Cat," Gabriel said, breaking her concentration.

"Hmm..."

"You still up for dinner?"

"Oh!" Onnie closed the book and placed it back on the pile. "Sure, what time is it?"

"Near to seven."

"Crap! I'm sorry, yes." She scooted herself off the table and picked up Mal. "Let me get my coat and bag." She had taken a few steps before her eyes rested on the flaming wall sconces. "Um, how do I..."

"She'll do it," Gabriel said, falling into step behind her.

"Okay then."

The three of them walked back into the sitting area, Gabriel stopping again to rest his hand on the doorway's frame.

"Why do you do that?" Onnie asked as she walked away.

"I've spent countless hours in that room. It tore me apart when I found it gone." Gabriel said solemnly as he followed.

"Oh, I'm sorry, Gabriel," Onnie said with a frown as she sat Mal on the front counter and headed into the back room.

He said nothing but gave a tiny shrug as he meandered the rows.

Calling over her shoulder, Onnie asked, "So, what's the Day Night Cafe like at night?"

"Quieter and with an entirely different menu. Why?"

"Am I underdressed?" Onnie asked with a quick look in the mirror.

"No, you look perfect, but you have a coat, right? I'd planned on us walking."

"Of course," she said, warming from his compliment and attentiveness. In her bag, she found her pink-tinted lip balm and mascara. She reapplied both and examined her sparkling green eyes, a few more flecks of blue throughout than she'd had in the past. With one last finger comb of her hair, she grabbed her bag and clicked off the light.

"Ready?" Gabriel asked, lowering Mal back to the counter as she emerged.

"Yeah, I just need my coat. You're sure the rear lamps will be fine?"

Gabriel nodded, "I promise."

"Okay, what are you going to do tonight, Mal?"

Mal jumped down from the front counter, followed Onnie down the center aisle to the coat rack, and sat in front of the door.

"Heading out then, be careful, okay? I'd offer to leave a window open for you at the apartment…but something tells me you wouldn't use it anyway."

Mal smiled a crooked cat grin and, with one last look at Gabriel, disappeared.

"I don't think I'll ever get used to them doing that," Onnie said with a shake of her head.

"He did that just to tease you." Gabriel reached around Onnie and plucked her coat from her hands with a grin. He opened it for her, and she shrugged it on, picked up her bag, and threw it over her shoulder. "Great, now I have two more men whose goal in life is to tease me."

"Basically."

"Get in line. I have three brothers who will willingly fight you for first chair."

Gabriel winked. "Come on. I'm hungry." He offered her his arm, and without hesitation, Onnie slipped hers into it.

Chapter 25: Emotional

November 2021 - Alku | Onnie Moore

Together, they stepped out into the lamplight and the Washington evening gloom. Onnie spun and looked at the sky while Gabriel gently placed his hand over hers, still resting in the crook of his elbow.

"Rain?" Onnie asked casually.

"Always," Gabriel answered as they started walking. "It's only a few blocks. Are you okay to walk?"

"Sure, I'd prefer it."

Onnie smiled at Gabriel's attempt at being a gentleman when he placed her on the inside of the sidewalk. They waved to Elanor as they passed and carried on idle small talk as they walked. They talked about nothing important, but Onnie enjoyed his company. Most of their interactions up to this point had been Keeper-Guardian related, and she found herself listening to him speak with a different attention to detail as just a woman.

Their light conversation also allowed her to admire him further, and she smiled as she tried to keep her inspection of him from his notice. His dark-washed jeans fit his style perfectly, and his modernized military coat looked like it had been made especially for him. She loved the feeling of the coarse wool and the contrast of the soft leather panels running tandem down his sides and arms. She couldn't resist running her fingers over the section on the arm she held while they walked.

Onnie couldn't hold back her stare as they approached the Day Night Cafe, her eyes wide and smiling. During the day, the café's double doors were never closed for long as someone was always going in or out. Tonight was completely different, and the regular flurry of activity was mellow and soft. The trees that lined the cobbled sidewalk were draped in white twinkle lights to match the crisp white linens that now covered the weighty iron tables. Three delicate red roses in a crystal vase topped each table and were flanked by two small candles. The soft lilting of a violin flowed out and onto the street through the two propped-open front doors and past the maître d' in a dark suit.

When the man saw Gabriel, his eyes twinkled with mischief, and he winked at Onnie.

"Gabriel, how nice to see you!" He turned and held out his hand to Onnie, clasping her free one and bringing it to his lips for a kiss. "You must be Onnie, our new resident Keeper. I've known your Grandfather Abbot for going on sixty years now."

Onnie's brows raised as she not so subtly gave the man in front of her an up-and-down glance. He smiled under her scrutiny and released her hand. "Oh, stop, you'll make this old sanguiste blush."

Gabriel caressed her hand still on his arm and laughed, "Come on now, Marco, we're here to eat, not flirt."

Marco snorted at him but grabbed two menus from the podium in the doorway. "I think there's a lot of fun in flirting, aren't I right, my lovely lady." With another smile flashed at Onnie, Marco spun on his shined dress shoes and escorted them into the restaurant. Onnie laughed at the two men and their friendly rapport while Gabriel gently pressed his palm into her lower back and guided her to follow Marco.

The inside of the little cafe had also been updated for the night crowd. More white linens lined the tables, with candles and roses atop them. Standing vases were nestled in the corners of the room and filled with even more roses, and a corner in the back had been cleared out for a lone violinist on a stool. The normally bright and cheerful wallpaper was even covered by thick red curtains that had been unfurled from the ceiling. It felt like the typically busy cafe changed into an entirely different and delightfully cozy spot at night.

Marco led them both to a table opposite the musician, where he pulled out Onnie's chair for her. He helped her from her coat and settled it on her chair back. Gabriel shrugged off his jacket and revealed a deep blue dress shirt unbuttoned at the top and relaxingly untucked. He draped his coat along the back of his chair and slid into it with the grace of a panther.

Marco tsked and shook his head approvingly, "Why can't they make one of you for us lonely men."

"Marco," Gabriel said with a small smile playing at the corner of his lips and a light blush.

"Yeah, yeah, I know. Straight." Marco smiled at Onnie and passed her a menu. "Shame, I tell you." He handed Gabriel his menu and clasped his shoulder. "Enjoy your meal, you two. Let me know if I can get you anything."

Gabriel reached up and pat Marco's hand, "Of course, thanks, man."

Marco nodded and left them.

Onnie watched as Gabriel smiled fondly at Marco as he walked away. "Friends?" Onnie asked with a smile.

"For most of my life. He's who I mentioned at Thanksgiving. Related to Sam and the others."

"Oh, I hadn't realized. That's great. How did you two meet?"

Gabriel snorted. "I was about five years old, and Abbot took me to one of the community gatherings. Everyone else was too busy to spend time focused on a child. Marco walked right up to me and held out his hand. I shook it, and we've been friends ever since."

Onnie didn't know what to say. Gabriel's life growing up sounded so lonely and, at the same time, full of love and chosen family.

A young waiter approached their table with water glasses, and when he looked at Onnie, he blushed. She tried to stifle her laugh and keep a straight face as he leaned closer than necessary to hand her the glass. He stepped over to place one before Gabriel but faltered when his eyes met with Gabriel's now crystal blue and disapproving stare. After a muttered apology, he set down Gabriel's glass, the young man's cheeks now burning, and he rushed off.

Onnie chuckled and opened her menu.

"What's so funny, Cat?"

"I'm pretty sure our waiter just wet himself."

Gabriel snorted and lowered his menu to level a gaze at Onnie from across the table. "And why do you think that?"

"Because you practically flayed him alive with your ice-blue glare just now." Onnie returned to her menu.

"Did I?" his voice sounded slightly surprised, and she'd bet he hadn't fully controlled that. "Perhaps if he'd shown a little more respect, I wouldn't have to glare."

From behind her menu, Onnie tsked Gabriel. "Oh, he's just a kid. You're such a caveman sometimes."

Gabriel grinned, "Onnie, that *kid* is older than you and I. Combined. By a lot."

Onnie lowered her menu and jaw before quickly shaking her head in acceptance. When she looked under her lashes at the diners two tables over, the woman winked at Onnie with an approving smile, and Onnie burst into laughter.

Gabriel joined in with her infectious amusement, and their waiter returned with two glasses and a bottle of the house wine. He set them on the table with a quick nod and retreated again as if he were on fire.

Onnie cleared her throat and eyed Gabriel over the menu in her hand. "So, tell me why you scared the crap out of our waiter?"

Without removing his eyes from his menu, "You're his Keeper. No matter how beautiful you are, his hormones come second."

"Sanguiste, I assume," she asked, red flushing her cheeks.

"Mhm."

"I wasn't sure. I assume there are other...beings with long lives that I don't know about yet."

Gabriel smiled at her softly, "You will."

They resumed looking at their menus, but Gabriel was still quietly laughing. "How have you not been here before?"

"I haven't been out much since I moved. Well, except for my runs, but I don't typically run in the more populated areas."

"Is it the forest itself or the lack of people that draws you there?"

She lowered her menu and thought about it for a minute, "It's a little bit of both, I think. California didn't have the trees and greenery like here, but that's not all of it."

Gabriel lowered his menu and laced his fingers together, ignoring their unordered food and waiting for her to continue.

"Since coming to Alku, everything has changed in my life. In California, I could blend in, be the girl in the back with a book nobody gave a second glance to. But here…everyone watches what I'm doing. They want to be involved, and even my spare time is watched with interest. Sometimes, it's just nice to escape it all and hide among the trees."

"That will stop eventually, once the novelty of a new Keeper has worn off."

"Really? It doesn't seem like it has for Grandfather."

Gabriel smiled, the corners of his mouth lifting but not quite touching his eyes. "That's because the old man is almost finished with his duty. Now they revere him and want to pay their respects and to thank him every chance they can."

"I missed a lot of time with him," Onnie said, tracing the condensation on her water glass.

"You did, but he's happier now than I've seen him since Dany and I were kids. You've put his heart at ease, I think."

"I'm glad."

Silence drifted through them, not stifling or suffocating, just resting atop them like a lovingly placed blanket on a cold night.

"She's happy." Onnie finally said, rubbing her hands up and down her arms.

"She is. I can feel it, too." Gabriel's smile shined, and he nodded before cocking his head to the side as if listening to something too faint for Onnie to pick up. "And you need a sandwich," he teased, referencing her comment when first learning of their Bond.

Onnie laughed and jabbed her finger at the menu, "It all looks so good."

Gabriel reached over, pulled down Onnie's, and pointed to an Ahi tuna salad. "That's my favorite right now. They get their fish fresh from the Seattle market every morning. It's the perfect texture, and how their seasoning on the fish contrasts with their dressing makes it one of their bestselling dishes when it's in season."

Onnie read the description and smiled, "Well then, with that much praise, I think I'll try it. Thank you for the suggestion."

Onnie closed her menu, and their waiter darted over to take their order nearly instantly. Gabriel ordered a salad for each of them and a pot of water for tea. As their waiter took his leave, Gabriel leaned his elbows on the table and pressed his fingers together, his brows furrowed.

"So, what's got you tied in knots?"

Slightly confused, Onnie just stared back at him.

"Cat, we're linked now. I can feel your emotions, and right now, I'm pretty sure you want to barrage me with questions."

Onnie sat speechlessly. She was both impressed at how well he could read her in such a short time and annoyed that she couldn't do the same.

Gabe smirked, "Fine, let's start with the tea. I felt your emotion flare when I ordered the hot water."

Onnie leaned forward, mirroring his position, "It's nothing, really. I've just had a lot of tea lately. I'm kind of tea-ed out." she rolled her eyes. "I never thought I would say that."

"I know, but to grow your Bond, we need you to drink it a bit more for a little longer. Eventually, you'll be able to have just a cup a day or so, but for right now, you need all you can get."

"So, what you're saying is I should drink the magic tea and shut it."

"Basically," He said with a smile as he sat back in his chair out of their waiter's way.

"Thank you," Gabriel said as the young man placed two simple white mugs and a matching teapot on the table. Then he bowed slightly and walked away. Reaching into his jacket pocket, Gabriel pulled out two teabags and dropped one in each mug. He slid one to Onnie and poured the hot water in each.

"Drink up."

Onnie reached forward and warmed her hands on the milky white china while blowing on the liquid's surface to cool it. "Can I make you a deal?"

Gabriel lifted his cup and took a sip of the steaming liquid. "I'm listening."

"I drink one cup of tea, and then I can have a glass of wine."

He laughed at her and shook his head, "Two cups."

She narrowed her gaze and looked over her mug at him, "One for one."

After a short staring contest, he lifted the wine bottle and poured them both a glass, "You drive a hard bargain, Keeper."

"You're a smart man for knowing when you've lost." She swapped her mug for the wine glass, lifted it for an unspoken toast, and sipped it slowly before placing it behind her still-full cup of tea.

"Tell me more about you. All these months have been more focused on getting to know my Guardian than the man behind the… sword, as it were."

"There's not much to tell, really. You were correct in your assumptions and accusations that first day."

Onnie winced, "I'm sorry about that. That was horrible of me."

"Don't be too hard on yourself. I was an ass."

"That doesn't excuse my behavior, and I'm sorry. Can we start over?" Onnie smiled, inhaling the steam from her tea.

Gabriel laughed, "Please, no, I've waited too long to have you. I don't think I'd live through doing it again." Her eyes widened, and he must have realized how that sounded because he cleared his throat and started again, "Ah, thanks for taking care of Dany last night."

"I didn't do much taking care of. It was more like I let her get me drunk," she smirked, "and us, I suppose. Were you okay last night? I didn't even think our Bond would—" her face paled, "were you driving?"

Gabriel blinked at her a few times without responding, and she realized she'd dropped what little control she had over their Bond. Closing her eyes, she clamped down on her thread connected to Gabriel as quickly as possible, and she heard his sharp intake of breath.

"It's okay, Cat, stop." he said, reaching for her hand, "I'm sorry, you just overwhelmed me for a minute." His smile made her breath catch, "I'm flattered that you worried about me, but no, I was not driving. Though I think a little warning would be a good idea next time."

Onnie tried to hold a straight face, but her lip quivered, and she clapped a hand over her mouth as she started to laugh so hard her eyes started streaming.

"I'm sorry," she sputtered between giggles, "of course, I'll give you a warning next time," she laughed more, "We wouldn't want you to be frunk and drive." She leaned back and held her sides while her diaphragm screamed at her to stop the torture.

Gabriel rolled his eyes but started to laugh with her until they were both a teary-eyed mess, and people started staring. "Would you believe me if I told you that was an autocorrect error?"

"Not a chance."

"Now, what fun is being had over here?" A good-looking pale-skinned man said, putting his palms on Gabriel's shoulders.

Gabriel looked up and wiped the tears from his eyes as Onnie answered, "Just life's bloopers." She smiled and held out her hand, "You must be Stephan."

The newcomer raised an eyebrow and smirked, "How correct you are, Keeper," he answered with a bow.

"Okay, you can stop that right now," she stood and offered her hand again, "I'm not sure how Grandfather handled these types of situations, but no one will bow to me, and certainly not my friends."

"Cat…" Gabriel said in warning.

"It's alright, Gabriel," Stephan said without taking his eyes off Onnie. "Well, little Keeper, I see you are just as Sam said." He broke into a grin and took her hand, gently shaking it before kissing the back and holding it between his own. "It's a pleasure to meet you finally, and from what I hear, we are a lucky town." His white teeth gleamed in the candlelight.

Onnie shook her head, "Are all sanguiste such flatterers, Gabriel?" she asked in mock curiosity.

"Only the smart ones," Stephan said, releasing her hands.

"He means yes," Gabriel said, shaking his head, "though Stephan and Marco have known each other a very long time, and Marco may be rubbing off on him finally."

Stephan winked at Gabriel, "He's quite right about that. Marco is a bit of—"

"Did I hear my name?" The man of the conversation said, appearing at Stephan's elbow.

"—a flirt." Stephan finished, "He also has the best hearing, second only to myself."

Marco beamed, "Well, that and I have food to deliver and just happened to be right behind you." He placed Onnie's plate before her and smiled, "Enjoy, Onnie." When he put Gabriel's plate down, he blew him a kiss and winked, to which Gabriel gave a fake eyelash flutter and a small wave, the action ridiculous coming from the large man.

"Come now, Marco, enough flirting with our Keeper's date." Stephan flashed one more beautiful smile before pushing Marco across the room and shooing him back to his podium.

Onnie locked eyes with Gabriel over the table, and they both burst into laughter. "Well, now you've met Stephan," Gabriel said, digging into his dinner.

"I have. I see why Vanessa and Sam were drawn to him. He seems sweet, otherworldly."

He nodded at her, "He's a big softy under his commanding exterior. They all are, but it's not easy to remain so approachable when you've been around that long."

"True," she sipped her wine to wash down her food, "but imagine what their lives have been like. They've seen all the history I have studied. They've lived it! I bet they were at some of the biggest events: Vesuvius, the Titanic, and the pyramids. I can't even imagine."

"You should ask Sam about it. He has some amazing stories I've heard over the years." Gabriel grinned, "Granted, for the first part of my life, Xayn and I thought they were fairy tales."

Onnie giggled. She felt lighter. Her mood and her body. Wine perhaps being the cause of the latter.

"But I do agree with you. The way their minds work is different than ours. They are just as antiquated as their bodies are sometimes."

"You really don't think Sam will mind me asking?"

"Absolutely not, the kid lives for the dramatic, and besides, he'd do anything for you."

Onnie sipped her wine and thought about what Gabriel had said, eventually losing herself in her thoughts. He didn't seem to mind and let her be. They ate their food and drank their wine with enjoyment, and eventually, the conversation restarted.

"Can you tell me what happened to you between the day in the clearing and the day with the book?" Onnie asked, swirling the last bit of wine around in her glass.

"Would you like more wine?" Gabe asked, tipping the bottle to her glass.

"Ah, a quarter of a glass, please. I still have to walk home."

"Don't worry. I'll make sure you get home safe." He emptied the rest of the bottle into their glasses. "What do you want to know?"

"How you went from Bruce Banner to the Hulk in a few days," she said dryly.

"No wonder you get along so well with Dany."

She shrugged, and he continued.

"It's part of the Transference. Well," he paused, "kind of. It's almost pre-transference. The Guardian must be able to protect the Keeper from physical confrontations. Because I was a special case and knew that I was to be your Guardian years ago, I was able to start training early."

"I want to come back to the part of you knowing years ago," she held up her finger, "but go on."

He smiled but continued, "I'm not sure why myself, but no matter how hard I trained, I didn't seem to be making progress. I was faster, stronger, and nimbler, but my body didn't reflect that. I stayed looking as I always did, average. Two days before I came into the shop, I woke up in agony. I imagine I felt like I'd been stretched on the rack. Everything hurt, and when I dragged myself to my bathroom for a shower, I understood why I hurt so badly. All my years of training hit me all at once. I looked as I do now."

"I'm sorry you had to go through that alone." She looked into his eyes and projected warmth through their Bond.

"I wasn't alone, Cat. You just didn't know you were with me. My Bond with you and the shop opened that day, and I could feel your excitement when you were working and your sadness when the day was over. You're what got me out of bed in the morning." He reached across the table and took one of her hands, "Thank you."

"For what," she replied with confusion, "I didn't do anything."

"You did. You were living life and being your unique self. That positivity and spirit reinforced why I was going through the pain and how much it was worth it."

They locked eyes over the candles, and Onnie was sure her skin was pink and her eyes glassy, but when she felt Gabriel brush against their Bond, she smiled. Then he signed the check, stood, and offered his hand, "Are you up for a walk?"

"Absolutely." She pulled on her coat, waved goodbye to Stephan, and followed Gabriel back to the front, where Marco was busily taking reservations.

"Behave, you two, and go do something I would do!" Marco said with a wink and a wave.

"Well, we have an extensive list of options then." Gabriel leaned down to whisper in her ear, and she playfully smacked him and shook her head.

"Where are we going?" she said, threading her arm in his.

"Well, I thought we'd walk through City Center Park, and then, if you're up for it, I know a quiet place to watch the stars. It is a bit of a hike, though."

"That sounds perfect, on one condition," Onnie said, grinning.

Gabriel responded without hesitation, "Name it."

"Can we grab something warm to drink for the hike?"

He smiled and nodded, "Anything you'd like, and I think that's a fantastic idea."

"Will you tell me how you knew about being my Guardian for so long?"

"Ah," Gabriel sighed, "you haven't forgotten about that, have you," he said, teasing her. "Sure, there's not much to tell, though. My father was already Abbot's Guardian when Dany and I were born, so we didn't see the Transference or anything, but I saw him and how he interacted with his Keeper. At least in the beginning. When he left, I demanded Abbot explain everything to me."

"How old were you?"

"Young. Far too young to understand what Abbot was telling me or the gravity of my father's betrayal, but to Abbot's credit, he did as I asked. He told me the complete history of the Keepers and Guardians and explained how Keepers were chosen and how the Bond worked."

"Did he know then that you would be a Guardian?"

"Not entirely. Years later, Abbot went to visit you for your graduation." Onnie nodded, "Do you remember taking a picture with him?"

"Yes, he said he only had ones where I was alone, and he wanted one of us to take home so he could show his friends."

"He did. When I saw it, I knew I was your Guardian."

Onnie pulled her arm from his and stared at him, "What?"

Gabriel slipped his hand into his coat pocket, "Let me explain. Do you know the concept of love at first sight?"

She couldn't help but narrow her eyes at him.

"I'd imagine it's that same feeling. I can't explain it better than seeing you, and my soul knew I was meant to be your Guardian. Everything clicked into place."

"I—" She wrinkled her brow and continued walking through the park. "How did—" Gabriel chuckled beside her, but she ignored him as her brain worked overtime to process what he was saying. "Okay, so you thought 'protect her' at first sight when you saw my photo. I get it, but what if we hated each other."

"I couldn't hate you if I tried, Cat," Gabriel said lightly, pulling her arm to slow her down. They were now deeper into the small cluster of trees at the park's center, with only the light that shone through the leaves to guide them.

"But what if you had? It's not impossible, right? I could have been the biggest bitch on the planet. You had no way of knowing."

"Cat," he brushed the back of his knuckles against her cheek, "there is no way I would ever hate you. You're the heart of Alku, and one day…" he trailed off and looked away without removing his hand.

"Gabriel?" she whispered.

When he looked back, she saw a tenderness she hadn't expected. "One day, I hope you'll be mine too."

She watched as he slowly lowered his gaze to her lips before he leaned down. His lips were soft and gentle, and he kissed her with a hesitancy she hadn't expected. She gave in and allowed herself to feel, and when she did, their Bond flared in her mind. Longing and affection rushed into her and stole her breath. Gabriel must have felt it, too, because he pulled away from her slowly and lay a chaste kiss on her forehead before resting his against it.

"Sure. Alright...wow," Onnie managed to whisper.

Gabriel smiled and kissed her again, a quick touch of their lips. Then he laced his fingers with hers, continuing down the winding park path. "Do you have any other questions you'd like me to answer, Cat?"

Onnie's head was fuzzy, and she tried formulating a coherent sentence, "Yes, I mean, a ton, but I don't know where to begin. I don't know what I don't know, ah…" she trailed off when she felt him chuckle beside her. "Okay, I have one. Where does Mal go when he's not with me?"

"There can only be one Link at a time. Mal was not supposed to have been created while Bec was still alive, but for some reason, the shop felt that you needed to have your Link earlier, so she created Mal."

"Where is he right now, then?" A touch of worry creased Onnie's brow.

"He is nowhere. Bec is with your Grandfather, and once she dies or disappears again, he will return to you. He's fine, I promise, but right now, the old man needs Bec to protect him."

"Protect him from what?" Onnie asked, more concerned at this point than curious.

"Cat, do you remember the man who came into the bookshop a few weeks ago, asking for the *Custos regni?"*

"Yeah, I remember him, but he didn't ask for *Custos regni,* did he?" She tried to remember what he had asked for but couldn't quite grasp it from her memories.

"He did, and I know you don't remember, but Mal and I both think something was off about him, and we don't like you being alone. Or Abbot, for that matter."

"Well, if Rebecca and Mal can't exist simultaneously, then one of us will always be alone, Gabriel. That's how math works," she teased.

Gabriel smirked, "Sassy Cat. Since that day, Mal and Bec have been trading off in the night, but it's taking a toll. They were also able to shield you when your connection to the shop was still minimal."

"I take it by your tone of voice that something has changed."

"You're stronger now, far more than Abbot is at this point, and we think—"

"Who's we," Onnie stopped, "and why am I not a part of that we?"

"Cat," he growled out at her, "don't do that. You know we were not excluding you. Abbot wanted your transition to be gradual, and he didn't want to scare you. The point is," he tipped her chin up with his index finger, "we want you safe, and to do that we need to have someone stay with you at night."

Onnie pulled her chin from his grip and then her hand, "Gabriel, I don't know about your past relationships, but I don't bring home my dates on the first night."

"Cat," he scolded.

"No, I'm sorry, but you cannot come over and sleep at my house," she put her fists on her hips, "What kind of woman do you think I am?"

Gabriel ran his fingers through his hair and tugged lightly, "Cat, you…" he paced in a small circle, "damn it, Cat."

He stopped and pulled out his cell phone, quickly tapping the screen with rhythmic presses that seemed to echo in the quiet night. When he put his phone back into his pocket and stared at her, she saw hurt in his eyes and was confident that she'd jumped to conclusions. When her cell phone rang a few seconds later, she was positive she had.

"Hi, Dany."

"Cut the man some slack. He doesn't think you're a hussy. I'm coming to stay with you for a few days. If and when you get comfortable with it, Gabe and I may switch off, but there's no pressure. I am staying with Abbot right now, but Gabe and I will swap. I don't mind staying with you, and hopefully, you aren't mad at me for telling you that you don't have a choice…" Dany trailed off and took a breath.

"I'll see you tonight, Dany. Use my spare key, keep it actually, and make yourself at home," Onnie said, not taking her eyes from Gabriel's.

"Oh, thank the gods." Dany sighed in relief.

"Bye, Dany," Onnie said and hung up.

Then she crossed the few steps to Gabriel and stood on her toes to slide her hand around the back of his neck and pull his lips down to hers. Through their Bond, she sent waves of apology as she allowed herself to deepen their kiss. Gabriel gently pulled her to him and threaded his fingers in her hair. When she pulled back, she whispered, "I'm sorry. Again."

Gabriel rubbed his nose on hers, took her hand, and continued walking, "What do you say about that plan of something hot to drink and a night hike?"

She rested her head on his bicep as they walked and smiled when she felt his forgiveness.

"Sounds like heaven."

Chapter 26: Protected

November 2021 - Alku | Onnie Moore

Onnie wasn't sure when she'd ever felt so at peace before. She lay with Gabriel on a bed of soft moss, his arm for a pillow, as they gazed up at the stars. Two empty cocoa cups lay discarded at their feet, and they both breathed on pace together.

Their hike hadn't been a long one, thankfully. Onnie wasn't sure she was ready for a night hike that required her full attention to her surroundings. She found that she was way too distracted by her thoughts. Gabriel had led her, hand in hand, down a small dirt path behind the school, and after only ten minutes of conversation, they stepped out of the thinning tree line and into a field. Moss covered the shadows under the trees, and they'd found a spot dry enough with a clear view above them to see the stars. Onnie hadn't been star gazing since she was little. Big cities were not ideal for that activity with all their light pollution.

"Thank you for tonight," she said, rotating her head to look at him sleepily. "I had fun this evening, more than I have in a long time."

His eyes twinkled at her in the starlight, and when he smiled at her, she couldn't withhold her own smile in response. "You're more than welcome, Cat. I'm glad you had a good time. I did, too." he kissed the top of her head, "Does this mean I get a second date?"

Onnie thought about it briefly before untangling herself from him and sitting up. She rested her forehead in her hands and mumbled to herself, "What are you doing?"

"Cat," Gabriel sat up, "talk to me. What are you thinking?"

"I'm not thinking anything, Gabriel."

"You can't lie to me, Cat. I can feel the turmoil inside of you. What happened?"

"I'm really starting to hate your mind-reading," she hissed. "Can't I keep anything to myself?"

Hurt rippled down their Bond, and she could feel Gabriel tense beside her. "I'll take you home," he said, standing up and holding out his hand. "It's late."

When his fingers wrapped around hers, she shivered. The chill of the night air tickled her neck, and goosebumps rippled over her skin. But that wasn't the cause. Something felt wrong, and she silently fed concern and distrust through their connection. When their eyes met, she widened hers and searched the surrounding forest without moving her head.

Gabriel narrowed his eyes but didn't comment right away. Instead, he pulled her to her feet and released her hand. When the chill dissipated with the removal of his hand, she grabbed it again. He looked at their locked hands, and she felt his curiosity.

"My hands are cold. I have a bit of a chill. Mind if I hold on a bit longer?"

He was confused, but still, he said nothing. Instead, he searched her eyes for some clarity.

"I had a fantastic night, and yes, I think a second date would be perfect." With a gentle squeeze of his hand, she stood on her toes and pulled him down for a kiss.

As she moved her mouth against his, she sent him every emotion she thought might explain her sudden change of heart: confusion, anxiety, distrust, fear. She held him tighter when he tried to pull away, pressing their bodies together.

She whispered around his lips, "Guardian," and she felt him still for a fraction of a second before he shifted into the predatory protector.

He pulled away from her lips and trailed a line of kisses across her cheek and to her ear, "What is it, Onnie?" he whispered so faintly she almost missed it.

The relief she felt at his understanding knocked the wind out of him, and he moaned to cover it up while he continued kissing her. She mimicked his hushed whisper as she threaded one hand into his hair.

"I'm not sure. When we're touching, I sense that something or someone is watching us." When he pulled her hips to meet his, she moaned, telling herself it was just an act.

"Cat, let me take you home." Gabriel said in a normal volume, his voice husky as he leaned down to her ear again, "I feel it. Let's head back into town and see if they follow."

"Alright," she panted breathlessly.

"Don't let go of my hand," he pulled away from her and led the way back to Alku.

Gabriel Vansand

Gabe was essentially running and dragging Onnie behind him, but once she'd pointed out the presence with them, it was time to go. As much as he wanted to stay with her under the stars and finish what they had started, he needed to be her Guardian more. Her improvisation was impressive, even if it left him in not an insignificant amount of discomfort.

When they finally left the shelter of the trees and stepped onto the sidewalk in Alku, he slowed down. "Are you sure about this, Cat? Once we get there," he pulled her to him and bent to nuzzle her ear. "I won't be able to stop," he added with a whisper, "They are still following."

"Yes," she responded to both of his questions.

The cool breeze pulled at her hair, and he ran a few strands between his thumb and forefinger. It was her turn to lead the way and for him to follow behind. He looked casually at the shadows as discreetly as possible but found nothing. To test her theory now that they were out of the forest, he pulled his hand from her grip, the unsettling feeling fading, and he recaptured her hand again.

They continued their walk in silence, and he'd wager that she was searching the night's secrets just as he was. Finally, her cottage came into view, and he felt her relax. Gabe thanked the gods when he saw that there weren't any lights on inside. Dany must already be asleep. Onnie wouldn't want her to worry, and he could feel her anxiety over it.

When they reached her front door, Onnie pulled a key on a ribbon out from around her neck and started to unlock the door. With her back to him, Gabe pressed against her, wrapped his arms around her, and whispered, "Get inside, don't turn on the lights, and quietly go wake Dany. She won't mind."

The lock clicked, and she spun around and pulled his mouth down to hers. He nibbled at her lower lip and reached around her to push open the door as they stumbled inside. Not until the door was locked and they stood panting in the entryway did they stop. His hand was still on the back of her neck, and they could both feel whoever or whatever was following them get closer until it stopped and finally retreated.

Onnie rested her head on his sternum, and the tension leaked out of her. "What was that?"

"I'm not sure, Cat, but whatever it was, it wasn't friendly." He tipped her chin up and smiled into her tired eyes, "You were brilliant, Keeper," he winked, "though, to be fair, I'm not sure I'll ever be the same."

She looked at him in confusion, her head cocking to one side. When he pulled her to him, her eyes widened, and he felt along their Bond when she understood his current situation. "I'm only human," he said quietly, but when she stammered, he shook his head, "Honestly, Cat, you did perfectly. You were quick on your feet, vigilant, and my partner."

"I, I'm sorry," she whispered and tried to step back, "I didn't know what else to do."

She was overthinking things, and he silenced her with a kiss. When he felt her tense, he gently pushed her away and nodded to the bedroom, "Go wake Dany. I'm going to make us some tea."

He gave her shoulder a soft squeeze and walked to the kitchen, relieved when she left the room, and he could finally readjust himself. It was going to be a long night, and now that he would have to sleep under the same roof as her, he needed a cold shower—an ice-cold one.

Begrudgingly, he pushed his thoughts of Onnie's lips from his head and tried to focus on the threat that followed them. He needed to get his priorities straight and figure out who or what had been observing them. Cat had been correct in her observation. Until they had made physical contact, skin to skin, he had been unaware of the presence, and he would have to see if Dany knew why touch had anything to do with it.

Thankfully, a few clean mugs were set out to dry next to the sink, and he poured near-boiling water into each cup. He fished a few of Bec's teabags from his jacket pocket and plonked them into his and Cat's mug. Dany needed a different tea, and he didn't want to snoop through Cat's kitchen to find some. He was saved the trouble when

Onnie walked into the kitchen, over to a ceramic jar on the counter, and handed him a teabag.

"Dany's favorite. She's splashing some water on her face, and then she'll be right out."

He passed Cat her mug and finished preparing Dany's, "What did you tell her?"

"That there was an emergency, no one was hurt, but you were here, and the three of us needed to talk."

She closed her eyes and inhaled the steam, and Gabe had never seen anything more beautiful. Her skin flushed, more tension left her posture, and he'd swear her hair even lustered more than usual. When she opened her eyes, he wasn't surprised to see blue rimming her irises.

"Tonight sapped your strength," he said, selfish and selflessly positioning himself behind her to rub her shoulders, "you'll need more than one cup." When Cat moaned at his touch, he had to clench his teeth to remain in control.

Dany silently walked into the kitchen. Her eyes were nearly closed, and she stopped and raised her hand to gesture for her cup. Gods, he loved his drama queen of a sister, but they did wake her up so he would take pity on her. Reluctantly, he left Cat's shoulders, passed his sister her steaming mug of tea, and kissed her cheek.

"Sorry we had to wake you, Dany."

She held up one finger, took two big gulps of her tea, took a breath, and repeated the process. When she lowered the mug, she blinked a few times and finally made eye contact with him, "What were you saying?"

Onnie snorted, and he could only shake his head, "I was apologizing for waking you, but now I think I'll take it back." He pulled her empty mug from her hand and refilled it for her. "Cat, you want to explain it, you were more…" his mind wandered, and he fought to pull himself away from the thoughts of her pressed against him, "aware of it than I was."

"Sure," Onnie said with a sleepy nod, "Come on, I'm about ready to fall over."

She did look ready to drop, and he couldn't help but frown. The energy and passion pouring out of her just a few minutes ago had been replaced with shock and weariness that he would take from her if he could. While the two women went to sit by the fireplace, he put more water on to boil and turned up the heaters. Cat gave him a sleepy smile as he returned to the kitchen.

"So, why am I awake at this unholy hour for a non-emergency emergency?" Dany asked with a yawn so big he heard her jaw pop.

Gabe refilled everyone's tea while Onnie explained everything that had happened. When she got to the point where she had to explain how they communicated so covertly, she hesitated for a split second before deciding not to mention it. He saw her gaze flick to him briefly, and he sent the feeling of approval to her. Dany didn't need to know how they made it home and didn't tip their follower off, just that they had.

"You have no idea who it was?" Dany asked when Onnie had finished.

"Nope," Onnie answered.

"Or what it was," he added hastily, "I'm not sure it was entirely human." Onnie paled, and he sat down beside her and took her hand. "Don't worry, Cat, many beings in this world are not human, and not all are nefarious. Think of Marco and Stephan. Perfect examples."

Gabe had an idea who their mystery lurker was, but with Onnie so adamant that the man in black was just a standard customer, he didn't bring it up. He'd tell Dany later when Onnie wasn't around.

"So, to recap," Dany said, laying on her back and pillowing her head on her arms, "something or someone followed you two out into the forest. Watched you but didn't approach and followed you home, all while feeling unfriendly."

"Yup," Cat said with a sigh, "but when you put it that way, we sound nuts."

"Nope," Dany said quickly, "You can't be nuts in this town. I think it's physically impossible."

"Don't forget the part where we needed to be touching to feel the presence." he interjected, "Do you have any ideas about that?"

Dany was silent for a few minutes, and he let her think. Onnie must have known to leave her be because she closed her eyes and rested her head on his shoulder. He leaned down to kiss the top of her head, but Dany sat up and narrowed her gaze at them before he could.

"Was it skin-to-skin?"

Cat blushed, and he nodded with a smirk.

"Hmm…" Dany trailed off and closed her eyes while simultaneously rubbing her temples. "I think I've read about something like this. About five hundred years ago, a Keeper was killed, and the new Keeper was only a baby."

"I thought the shop waited until the person was ready?" Cat interrupted.

"They do, and either this baby was ready, or the shop had no choice for some reason. I'm not sure, but the point is, the Guardian for that Keeper was its mother, and because the child needed to be held, they found that their Bond amplified their abilities."

"The mother acted as a conduit," he asked, "and because Cat and I were touching, we experienced the same thing? Why hasn't this been documented and become a common practice among Keepers? Wouldn't it be a useful defense tactic?"

Dany shook her head, "No. I mean, you're right, except that other than that one instance and...now yours, it's never happened again."

"What's so special about us then?" Cat asked, yawning on Gabe's shoulder.

Gabe's stomach sank, and he glanced at his sister, who was too asleep to notice. With the amount of power Onnie had already gained and now their odd nuanced Keeper-Guardian ability, he was even more sure that Onnie was the one they'd been waiting for.

"No idea, but I can research at the shop with you tomorrow if you'd like." Dany offered.

"Yeah," Onnie answered with another yawn. "Thanks."

He knew he'd only rouse Dany more if he told her what he was thinking, and he'd already disrupted her sleep enough for one night. "Alright, you two, it's time for bed," Gabe announced, collecting the empty mugs. "Both of you."

"I was sleeping, asshole," Dany snipped.

Gabe kissed his sister on the cheek, "I know, and we owe you one. Now, go get your beauty sleep before I never hear the end of it."

"I would never," Dany said with a lazy smirk.

"Go on, Dany, I'll be right in. I need to get Gabe situated."

He watched as Dany's eyes twinkled when Onnie called him Gabe instead of Gabriel, and he had to admit, he was positive he did the same.

"Night, Sis." He said as she stood and stretched before trudging off to the bedroom. "She'll be asleep in five." He leaned down to help Onnie to her feet.

"Lucky her, I think I'm too freaked out to sleep still," Onnie said, rubbing her arms.

"Cat, come here," he pulled her to him and softly ran his fingers through her hair, "You have nothing to be afraid of. Dany and I are here with you, and we will do anything to protect you."

"I know, but that also scares me. I don't want anything to happen to either of you."

"Cat," Gabe said, lifting her chin, "first, it's our choice to protect you. Secondly, you won't lose us." Moisture twinkled in her eyes as unshed tears, and he could feel her tamping down on their Bond. "Now, you go get some sleep. I'll clean up here and be fine."

"You can use my quilt." She said, pulling away and retrieving the handmade item from the back of the only chair in the room. "My Mom made it for me."

He could tell it was special to her by how her smile lit up the night when she cuddled it.

"I'll take good care of it then." Gabe took the blanket and bent to kiss her cheek, "I'll be alright. Now go." She looked at him shyly with sleepy eyes and lowered lashes, and he shifted to hold the blanket in front of his waist. "Good night, Cat."

"Good night, Gabe." She whispered before leaving him in her living room with her mother's quilt, her scent, and the need for that ice bath.

Chapter 27: Vulnerable

November 2021 - Alku | Onnie Moore

Onnie woke up from the best night of sleep she'd ever had. Dany was snuggled up beside her, quietly snoring, and the sunlight was diffused and soft as it came in through the bedroom window. Even when the previous night's concerns reentered her mind, Onnie still felt refreshed.

It was time for her to get up, and she carefully tried to roll off the blowup mattress without waking Dany. Once off of it, Dany sank closer to the ground, causing Onnie to grumble that it was time for a real bed. Clearly, she wasn't leaving Alku, and if Dany was going to spend the night more, the least Onnie could do was offer a comfortable place to sleep.

As quietly as possible, Onnie freshened up and tip-toed into her living room to see if Gabriel was awake. She felt horrible when she peered around the corner and saw his large body twisted at an odd angle in her reading chair. He must have sensed her watching or felt her guilt along their Bond because he opened one eye and held out his hand, "Come here, little Cat."

She couldn't hide her smile as she walked over to take his hand, "I will figure something out so both of you will be more comfortable next time."

A wicked grin appeared on his sleepy face, and then he pulled her into his lap, "I'd rather you didn't go to all the trouble on my account. Besides, maybe you'll let me sleep with you next time, and Dany can take this monster."

Onnie laughed, a carefree laugh from deep within herself, and she couldn't remember the last time she'd done that. Gabriel's hair was tousled in a deliciously sexy way, and seeing him wrapped up in her quilt made her heart clench. "Perhaps."

"That's not a no," he said, pulling her down toward him.

"If you're good."

Gabriel's eyes flared, and he proceeded to kiss her breathless. Dany wandered out a few minutes later and teased them to get a room, and Onnie stammered while Gabriel answered calmly that he'd have one if his sister weren't already sleeping in it. Onnie smiled, watching the two of them word fencing back and forth while she made tea.

"Alright, you two. I'm already late opening the shop. Dany, you coming in with me?"

Dany nodded around her tea.

"Perfect. I'll be ready in ten." With that, Onnie left the two siblings to their shenanigans.

"We need more coffee," Onnie said, resting her head on the parchment on the table she sat at.

Dany groaned in presumable agreement from nearby on the couch in Abbot's office, where the two of them tried to find any mention of a physical connection between a Keeper and their Guardian. So far, they had found nothing.

"You've never been more right," Dany said, flopping the book she was searching through on her chest and laying her head back against the couch.

"Mind watching the store? I'll run and grab us some and lunch." Onnie rolled up the scroll she was finished with and slid it back into its protective tube.

"Are you sure?" Dany asked, unmoving.

"Of course, your usual and a turkey club?" Onnie said as she grabbed her credit card and phone.

"You're a god." Dany smiled and began to unbury herself from the books around her. "I'll walk you out and stay up front while you're gone. Maybe I'll grab one of those new romance novels you just got in."

"Oh man, the new book by Andi Lark looks amazing," Onnie gushed on her way to the door. "If you read it, tell me what you think."

"Well, I know what I'm doing now," Dany said, heading straight for the bookshelf it was on. "Take your time," she waggled her eyebrows at Onnie.

Onnie shook her head and laughed, "Be back soon."

It was one of those rare winter Washington days when the sun was out, and there wasn't a cloud in the sky. Which meant it was freezing, but after she pulled the shop door closed behind her, Onnie raised her face to the sun and absorbed its faint heat into her skin anyway.

The walk to the coffee shop wasn't too long. It was closer to the bookshop than her cottage, but she and Dany had been pouring over dusty tomes and scrolls for hours, and Onnie's muscles felt like she'd been running instead of reading. So far, they hadn't found anything. Dany was frustrated because she knew the history was there and couldn't find it. Gabriel was just as frustrated because Onnie had told him to scoot and leave her alone with Dany. And Onnie was confused…about everything.

Her date with Gabriel had her on edge, from how much she enjoyed herself, how they fit together, and where they went from here.

She had made a promise to herself of no men, but now she had Gabriel and his sharp wit, intelligence, and their deep connection to think about. He was her Guardian, and while she was new to the whole Keeper thing, she knew how a conflict of interest could spell disaster in any situation. What would happen if their relationship soured? How would she be able to share a Bond with him for the rest of her life?

"Why hello, Onnie!" Elanor's sweet voice said from her shop's porch.

Onnie looked up and returned the older woman's smile and wave. "Hello, Elanor," the florist was up to elbows in a large green pot filled with dirt, "what plant are you working your magic on today?"

"Why, I'm just prepping for some transplants. I have to ensure my babies are warm and have a bed inside for the winter."

"Enjoy the sun then." Onnie smiled and crossed the cobbled street.

She took a deep breath and briefly reached out to rest her palm on a tree trunk. If she cut through City Center Park, she would get to coffee faster, and she loved walking through the mini forest, so she decided on the scenic route. The sun seemed to have brought everything out for a day of frolicking. Birds chittered and chirped as they dove between the treetops, and squirrels darted along the ground around Onnie's feet. She lost herself in the little one's antics as she followed a well-worn path through the trees.

When she was about halfway to the other side, she felt the presence from the night before and shivered. Her eyes widened, and her heart tried to beat its way out of her chest, but she forced herself not to change her walking speed. With great effort, she plastered a fake smile on her face and pretended to be entranced by the birds as she covertly looked for anyone out of place. A cute couple sat on a tucked-away bench reading, and a few kids were running through the trees, their dad following behind at a jog.

Just as abruptly as she'd felt it, the presence disappeared. She exited the trees on the other side of the green space and turned around to look at the beautiful park that now scared her. Anger pulsed through her veins, and she stiffened her spine. When she stomped around a cluster of trees to finish the short distance left to the coffee shop, a man in all black caught her eye as he walked away from her. He felt familiar, and she started to run toward him, but he continued into the trees.

"Hey!" she shouted after him. When he didn't acknowledge her, she forced her way through the exact spot where he'd entered. There was no path, and she pushed branches and bushes out of her way.

A few minutes later, she stepped between two trees and saw the man she was following leaning against a tree just down the path. "Excuse me," she asked as she approached him, "who are you?"

The man in all black looked up, and Onnie froze in place. His eyes pierced her, and her clattering teeth sounded loud in her ears. Her stomach curled, and when the stranger smirked, it made her skin crawl.

Suddenly, the only thing she could do was run. Onnie didn't hold back. She ran as fast as her feet would carry her, and when she reached the cobbled street, she dashed across it and into the coffee shop without stopping. She put both hands on her knees and bent over, gasping for breath. When she looked up, much to her horror, the baristas and patrons were all staring at her. Red crept up her neck as she walked over to a vacant leather chair and tucked herself into a corner slightly hidden from the room's view. She pulled her phone from her pocket and saw ten missed calls and several texts from Gabriel, but before she could reply, he called again.

"Cat, I swear," Gabriel growled into the phone, "what the fuck is going on?"

She winced at the tone of his voice, possessive and angry. Their Bond pulsed with rage, and she swallowed loudly. "I felt him again."

"Where are you?" he spitted out.

"Coffee shop getting lunch for Dany and me." As soon as the

words left her mouth, she realized her mistake. The rage she felt before was nothing like what she was now experiencing. Onnie doubled over in pain and put her head between her knees, "Gabr…iel..." she whimpered.

Gabriel was so enraged she knew he hadn't heard her. "Where is Dany? She was supposed to stay with you. I'm going to kill her." She could hear his keys in the background, "What was she thinking? I'm on —"

"Gabe," Onnie said a bit louder but still barely more than a whisper. It was enough because Gabriel stopped his tirade to let her speak. "I can't…breathe...Bond," was all she could mutter.

"Fuck," Gabriel said before the anger he radiated pulled back, and she gasped for breath, "I'm sorry, Cat, I didn't realize."

"It's fine. Give me a minute." Onnie took a few deep breaths and slowly sat upright. Now she was doubly thankful she'd chosen a spot in an out-of-the-way corner.

"Cat?" he asked tenuously, and Onnie heard his car start.

"Yeah, sorry. I'm sorry I didn't pick up when you called. My phone was on silent." She would have to rectify that, especially if Gabriel expected her to pick up on the first ring.

"We'll talk about it later. What happened?"

She could hear his blinker clicking in the background, "Please don't come here. I'm all right."

"Cat, I am your Guardian," he said through clenched teeth.

Onnie rubbed her temples, "Gabriel, I'm fine. Can we talk about it tonight? Maybe you can come over, and we'll have dinner?" Gabriel wasn't quick enough, and she felt his sudden surprise and arousal before he regained control.

"Cat," his voice said huskily, "are you trying to distract me with a date?"

Onnie snorted and tried not to laugh, "Sure if you are okay with

Dany being there and ending the night digging through dusty books." He didn't answer immediately, and she opened her mouth to soothe his ego.

"That sounds perfect, Cat," his voice was calm and professional, and Onnie couldn't help the sadness she felt at his retreat, "then you can tell me what happened today."

"Deal," she said, defeated.

"I'm calling Sam to walk you back to the shop, and before you think to argue," Onnie clapped her mouth shut, "you won't win this battle."

"Fine," she snapped, "I've got to go." Gabriel's mood swings were grating on her already stretched nerves, and his dictating threatened to push her over the edge. "Talk to you later."

She couldn't hang up fast enough, and when her phone rang with a text message a few minutes later, she was tempted to ignore it.

Cat, don't push me when it comes to protecting you. I'll protect you from yourself if I have to. Sam is on his way.

The armchair was soft beneath her as she leaned back and closed her eyes. Disappointment tugged on her heart, and she knew now that she and Gabriel could never be more than Keeper and Guardian.

What she didn't expect was the anguish she felt over her decision.

Chapter 28: Confessions

November 2021 - Alku | Gabriel Vansand

Gods give him strength.

His Keeper was going to be the end of him with her sassy mouth and defiance. When would she realize how important she was and stop taking everything on by herself?

Gabe pulled his car into a parking spot a few buildings from the coffee shop and turned off the engine. He had to know she was okay, and he would worry until he saw her with his own eyes. It didn't take long for her and Sam to step out on the street. She looked weaker than she had that morning, and he made a mental note to buy Sam a beer when he took her bag from her. They walked off toward the shop, but when Sam started for City Center Park, and Onnie shook her head and brought them the long route, he couldn't shake the feeling of dread.

It was almost two, and he would be late to see Abbot at this rate. Cat worried him, and he pulled at his hair and groaned. He had screwed up again. He wrote her a quick text apologizing for being an ass and started his drive to Abbot's house.

When he arrived, the older man was on the dock with a shaking cup of tea in his hand. Gabe could never sneak up on Abbot, and nothing had changed with the man's age.

"Come here, my boy. I think you and I need to chat."

Gabe sat in the chair waiting next to Abbot's and put his head in his hands. "I screwed up. Again."

"My boy, you have done nothing of the sort. Look at me, son." Abbot's gentle voice said, and Gabe slowly lifted his head to find the older man smiling at him. "I know what happened, all of it, and you acted as her Guardian should."

"But—" Gabe started to say when Abbot shook his head.

"No, Gabe, as her Guardian, you have made all the correct choices, but as a man, and someone who," his eyes twinkled in delight, "wants to be a different sort of guardian as well, that is where you fell flat."

"I don't know what to do." his voice broke, and he resumed sulking. "You know I've never really been in a relationship with anyone. I just…"

A thin, wispy hand was in his hair and gently caressed him, "You love her." Abbot stated.

Gabe squeezed his eyes shut. Did he love her? "I think I could, Abbot." The last thing he expected was to hear the old man chuckle.

"Let me tell you a story, Gabe." Abbot stopped patting Gabe's head and cleared his throat, "Have I ever told you how I met my Lonnie?" Gabe shook his head, and Abbot nodded, "Well, I was twenty-three and madly in love." he smiled, and his eyes softened, "The moment I saw my beloved Lonnie that first time, I was drawn to her like a fish on a line. She was beautiful. We were both at a flower market outside Alku, and I was picking up something special for my Mother," he looked over to Gabe and beamed, "It was her birthday, and I was going to buy her a large bouquet of daisies. They were her favorite, and she always said they smiled at her. I had the flowers in my hand, and I was walking through the market headed home when I saw Lon."

Gabe shifted in his chair and smiled at the faraway look in Abbot's eyes. The old man's affection for his wife was written all over his face, even after many decades apart.

"She was walking in my direction, and when she saw me, she froze. My feet walked me over to her on their own, and I held out the daisies to her. I said, 'Daisies are friendly. They smile at you.'"

"You gave her your Mother's flowers?" Gabe laughed.

"I did," Abbot blushed, "she lifted them to her nose and closed her eyes to inhale their scent. When she opened her eyes, I asked her to join me for my Mother's dinner party, and she laced her arm in mine with a smile. It was only a few weeks later that I proposed, and we were married."

"Wow," Gabe said, impressed, "you move quickly, old man."

Abbot laughed, but his smile didn't quite reach his eyes. "Yes, well, I knew I wouldn't be able to live without her." A shadow came over his features, and the anguish was palpable when he looked back at Gabe. "She moved here to join me in Alku. Then I became the Keeper. Staying in Alku was both the best and worst decision I have ever made."

Abbot stared into the distance, and Gabe watched his eyes follow a boat. They sat in sad silence for a few minutes before Abbot sniffled and cleared his throat.

"When Lon left... I died that day," Abbot said, his words hanging between them. "She was my everything, her and my Tory, but the shop was my destiny. I made my choice, and I chose my fate and the fate of the magical world over the love of my life and our child."

"I didn't know," Gabe took the old man's hand and gently rubbed the back of it.

Abbot squeezed it gently, "I know, but don't make the same mistakes I made. You love Onnie, and I know she has feelings for you. I've never seen a Bond burn so brightly than when she looks at you."

"She's so powerful, Abbot. Yesterday, she and I needed to be touching for her to feel we were being watched. Today, she knew without me there."

Smiling proudly, Abbot nodded, "She's the one, Gabriel." The older man closed his eyes. "I can feel it, and so can Rebecca."

When he reopened them, they glowed a crystal blue. "Both of you are, Gabe." Abbot said, resting his hand on Gabe's cheek, "You're so much stronger than your father. You are the man he never was and could never be."

Gabe had no words. He just sat and thought of Onnie, a smile tugging at the corner of his lips.

Abbot clutched Gabe's hand tenderly, "Together, you two will be strong enough to survive whatever your destinies throw at you. You take care of her, my boy. She's going to give you hell and then some."

Gabe met the old man's eyes and nodded once, "She already does, but you're right. I can't live without her." Abbot kissed the back of his hand and then released it. Gabe stood and paced the dock.

"She's in my dreams, Abbot. When I'm not with her, I'm tapped into our Bond like a lifeline, and when she is with me…" he stopped pacing and rubbed his eyes, "I don't see anything but her. I can't let that happen, and last night was too close."

"Gabriel," he turned, and the old man shook his head, "you will find a balance." Abbot turned away, "You will do what I could not with my beloved Lonnie."

Gabe stepped toward Abbot, his shoulders now shaking as he wept silently. The Keeper and husband deserved his privacy, so Gabe collected his teacup, and turning, he left the older man to cry in peace. With one last glance over his shoulder, Gabriel watched as tears continued to fall from the old man's eyes.

Abbot would be proud. Gabe stood on Onnie's doorstep with the most enormous bouquet of daisies Elanor could whip up and two bottles of wine. With no free hands to knock, he closed his eyes and touched his Bond. Gabe plucked it like a guitar string, and a few seconds later, he felt Cat's curiosity flow to him. His response was a cocktail of hunger, impatience, wanting, and half a dozen other feelings, and then he gently kicked the door with his booted foot.

The door opened a minute later, and Cat's eyes greeted him with ice.

"Can I come in?" She stepped aside to let him through but still said nothing. "These are for you. A wise man told me that they smiled at their recipient." He held out the daisies and bent to kiss her cheek only to find her step back.

"Thank you, Gabriel. I'll put them into water." She took them slowly and walked to the kitchen.

With no choice but to follow her, he stepped over dozens of books strewn around her living room and piled up in corners. There were three teacups on the hearth, and he frowned. He placed the two bottles of wine on the counter and leaned against it, crossing his arms. "Tell me what's wrong, Cat." He felt her despair flicker, and then she regained control over it.

"Nothing, it's been a long day, but we still have a lot to go through." She carried the vase to a bookcase and placed it on a shelf with a bare spot. The flowers looked like that place was created just for them, and he shook his head at the strangeness of his life.

"Where's Dany?"

Onnie whirled around, and her eyes flashed, "Why? So, you can yell at me some more because she's not two inches from my side, Gabriel?" He opened his mouth to answer, but she cut him off, "She walked Sam home and is picking up dinner for the three of us." Her anger flushed her cheeks, and she tensed her muscles as if ready to strike out at something.

He wanted to pull her into his arms and beg for forgiveness so badly that it was physically uncomfortable.

"I am not a child, Gabriel. I'm not helpless." It was evident she had been holding all of this in at the rate she spewed it out now. "Once a loner, always a loner. I can handle myself, and if you think for one second I couldn't handle the man in black on my own, then you—"

When he heard her mention the man who had been snooping around the shop for the *Custos regni,* his pulse flared, and he was done being berated. Without knowing what had happened that morning, he hadn't realized that she had actually seen the cause of their unease.

He took two strides, ran his fingers to the back of her neck, and pulled her lips to his. She felt so closed off to him, fresh walls rebuilt where he'd just managed to tear them down. When he felt her relax against him after a few seconds, he deepened their kiss. After his conversation with Abbot, Gabe knew he'd never be able to get enough of her. The way she tasted drove him crazy. Her smell and the way she laughed, all of it. They were both out of breath when he finally pulled back and rested his forehead on hers.

"Cat, I missed you."

"What?" she asked in barely a whisper.

"I'm sorry about this morning, and I'm sorry I hurt you, but I missed you today. You closed yourself off, and I've never felt so alone. You are part of me, Cat, and when I couldn't feel you, I realized something." He bent his knees to be level with her eyes and stared directly into them.

"What did you realize?"

Gabe smirked and stroked her cheeks with his thumbs, "That even if I weren't your Guardian, I would still be lost without you."

She looked confused, "I… Gabriel, I don't think…"

"No, Cat, I'm not telling you so that you feel you need to reply. All

I wanted was to tell you how I feel because I don't want to keep anything from you, and I can't suppress my feelings for you anymore."

"What are you saying?" her eyes were wide.

"I love you, Cat." He kissed her gently and was relieved when she kissed him back. When he pulled away, he tucked a strand of her hair behind her ear and lightly rubbed the end of it between his fingertips.

"Will you tell me what happened today? I'm not mad, and I won't yell. I promise."

Onnie stood there and stared at him for another minute before she shook herself out of her shocked stupor. He contained his glee at how she reacted, and she wasn't running for the hills or throwing him out. For now, that would be enough.

"Well, um," she brushed past him and into the kitchen to open one of the bottles he had brought. "I think I may know who our presence might be."

She poured herself a glass, took a big gulp of wine, and then began recounting the day's events.

Chapter 29: Violated

December 2021 - Alku | Onnie Moore

"Alright, Cat, you're doing great. Try putting your whole body behind your fist," Gabriel encouraged her. Onnie shook the sweat from her eyes and bounced lightly on the balls of her feet.

Their every other-day training sessions were kicking her ass, but she had to admit she saw an improvement after only two weeks. When she had told Gabriel all the details of her experience with the man in the park a few weeks ago, she was shocked when he remained calm. He made sure she was alright, called Dany, and told her to bring her workout gear and dinner and meet them at the gym. Onnie was instructed to change into the same, and the three of them spent the next few hours at the school.

They'd carried on like that every evening for the last two weeks. Sometimes, Dany would join them, and other days, like today, it was just Onnie and Gabriel. The latter of which was currently trying to kill her.

"Are you kidding? What do you think I've been doing this entire time?"

"Cat…" he growled, and she punched the padded glove on his palm. "Better! Alright, I think you've earned a break."

"Thank God!" she moaned and flopped to the mat beneath her. "Where did you learn to be so…"

"Supportive?" Gabriel interjected.

"Vicious." Onnie smiled, "Where did you learn all this stuff."

Gabriel ripped off the Velcro band, its screech echoing off the darkened walls of the gym. "Abbot."

"You're kidding!" Onnie sat upright, her jaw dropped.

"Not a bit," Gabriel swapped the glove with a water bottle next to the mat and sat beside her. "Drink," he said, passing it to her. "When my father walked away from his duties, Abbot needed protection. He wasn't a spring chicken, but he studied to ensure he could take care of himself if he had to. When I was older, he offered to train me, and I said yes."

"So, my pale little Grandfather taught you to do that," she gestured wildly at the boxing supplies.

"He did, and later I trained Dany."

"Dany knows all of this too!" Onnie coughed a mouthful of water.

Gabriel laughed, "Don't sound so surprised. Dany is more than capable of taking care of herself. Some days she even kicks my ass."

"Huh, I'll have to remember that."

Gabriel chuckled at her, "Did you think she was joining us for yoga and endurance because that's all she could manage?"

Onnie nodded sheepishly. "It just didn't occur to me." She groaned and got to her feet to stretch out her tired muscles.

"I wouldn't leave you in anyone's protection if they couldn't actually protect you, Cat," Gabriel said while he pulled his arms across his body to loosen them up. "Ready for more?"

"As I'll ever be. What's up next?" She held out her hand and pulled him to his feet. "And I should say thank you. I know I am complaining a lot, but I've never been one for strength. I'm more of an endurance runner than a sprinter."

"I know, which is why we will get you athletically well-rounded. Besides, I've been going easy on you," he smirked.

Onnie defiantly put her hand on her hip, "No way, don't let me off easy. If you're going to train me, do it—" She let out a squeak as she was smoothly and efficiently tackled by Gabriel to the floor. "right."

Gabriel hovered over her, his nose an inch from hers, her legs pinned, and her arms behind her back wedged there by her own body weight. "I'm not sure you're ready for unrestrained training, Cat." He bounced to his feet and pulled her up to stand beside him once again.

"You win." she said, shaking her head, "What will you teach me next, Master Yoda."

He raised one eyebrow at her and stood shoulder-width apart with his hands up, "I think it's time for hand-to-hand self-defense."

"Couldn't we have done this part in the beginning? Now I'm tired, and you're going to wreck me." She mimicked his stance, and they started to circle one another.

"Do you think whatever asshole wants to hurt you is only going to do it when you're rested?" he teased.

She groaned but saw his point, "I hate it when you're right." Focusing on his left hand, she saw it twitch slightly, and when it came toward her, she sidestepped it quickly.

"Good, Cat!"

When his weight changed to his right foot, she focused on it, preparing herself to avoid it. Her focus was too narrow, and she missed Gabriel's right hand as it wrapped around her neck and pulled her body against his, pinning her against his chest. "Your focus was too visible. You can't let me see what you're thinking."

"Isn't this kind of pointless," she struggled to break free, "I mean, with our Bond, couldn't you—" The blood drained from her face, and her body started to tremble.

"Cat," Gabriel released her and spun her to face him, "What is it?" He looked her over and brought the back of his hand to her forehead. "You're cold."

"Gabriel, something's wrong. Can't you feel it? I feel—" Onnie shuttered, and her eyes rolled back into her head as she collapsed into Gabriel's side.

"Onnie!" Gabriel shouted as he caught her.

Emotions hit Onnie like the waves of a storm-filled sea, each one crashing harder than the next.

Fear.

Pain.

Outrage.

Then, all of them flared and burned their way through her. She screamed in anger, the roar of pain ripping through her. The screaming wouldn't stop. *She* couldn't stop. Finding her Bond, she flew down the cord toward the shop, but when she approached, she was overwhelmed and thrown back.

Her eyes snapped open, and tears streamed down her face. A few seconds later, Onnie blinked up at Gabriel, his eyes crystal blue, no doubt hers matching them.

"She's hurt. We have to get to the shop."

"I'll get our coats." Gabriel quickly released her and dashed to his office.

The pain was increasing, and Onnie's head was pounding, making it difficult for her to get to her feet, "Hurry, Gabe!" Whatever made the shop that angry, terrified Onnie.

Gabriel returned, quickly pulled on his coat, and helped her into hers. "Can you stand?"

"Yes, we have to go. Now!" Onnie sprinted to the gym door and threw it open frantically.

"Cat, wait!" Gabriel ran after her and caught up by the first street corner.

Wind thrashed around them, branches and debris flew past Onnie, and she somehow managed to jump over or dodge most of it. Rain pelted her, and each drop that hit her cheeks felt like a pebble trying to rip through her.

"Onnie, you have to stop!" He grabbed her upper arm and tugged her to his body, where she stood, shaking violently and clinging to his coat. "Look at me." He asked gently.

She shook her head and continued to cry.

"Onnie!" He snapped at her and tilted her eyes up to his.

"We have to—" Onnie saw that Gabriel, too, was crying. His eyes were still blue and now bloodshot.

"Cat, I can feel her too and what this is doing to you, but we cannot charge in there blind. We don't know what happened, and my first responsibility is to keep you safe."

"But we can't just leave her—"

He placed his finger over her lips to silence her. "We're not. But I need you to trust me. Can you do that?"

Onnie nodded.

"Good, now relax and focus on the shop. Hone in on one emotion you're feeling right now, the strongest one, and try to block out the others."

Closing her eyes, Onnie pictured the bookshop in her mind. The reading nook in the back corner that was filled with wing-backed chairs. The front counter with an ornate register and an antique glass oil lamp. Rows and rows of bookshelves filled to bursting. Abbot's study with its welcoming environment she'd grown to love.

In the distance, she heard Gabriel whisper, "Good Cat, keep

going."

Concentrating harder, she pictured herself standing at the front door looking into the shop. It was dark, and some of the shadows she saw didn't belong. She took a step forward and stepped on a splayed book. Bending down, she examined it and then looked further down the aisle. Books lay everywhere, shelves were toppled, cases were smashed, and their glass lay in ruins on the ground.

"No!" Onnie screamed, but the sound was distant to her ears.

"Stay focused, Onnie. Do you see anyone?" Gabriel's voice was further now, but she could still make it out over the blood roaring in her ears.

She stood up and willed the lights on, just as she had been practicing for the last few weeks. The bookshop was quiet, and Onnie knew she was alone. Her bookshop was alone, and it needed her.

She closed her eyes again and focused on Gabriel and the feeling of him holding her on some faraway street corner in the rain.

When she blinked and met his gaze, she saw his tears streaming faster than the rain could hide them, and she knew hers were the same.

"She's alone." Onnie croaked, and Gabriel tightened his arms, holding her close.

"Come on, Cat. It's safe now." She sniffled, and Gabriel lifted her into his arms and began to walk the rest of the way back to The Book Nook as she sobbed into his chest.

Instinctively, she knew when they neared the shop, and she unburied her face to examine it as they approached. From the outside, it appeared as if nothing had been disturbed. Thunder rumbled in the distance, and Onnie flinched and squeezed her eyes closed.

When they reached the door, Gabriel kissed her forehead and placed her gently on her feet.

"Let me go in first, okay? I need your keys." Onnie lowered her gaze to the lock, and Gabriel smiled at the sound of it clicking open.

He turned and slowly opened the shop's ordinarily warm, wooden door that was currently covered in a thin layer of ice. When the bright interior lights flooded the walkway, Onnie tried to look around Gabriel's hulking form that blocked her view. "Did you turn on the lights, Cat?"

"Yes, before. When I was…um…checking."

"Okay, well, that saved some time. Good thinking." Gabriel stepped into the store slowly, his body coiled and ready to strike if necessary. He seemed to ignore the toppled shelves, the shattered glass, and the broken furniture as he stepped over all of it to move throughout the shop. After a few minutes, he called out from deeper in the store, "You can come in, Cat, be careful of the glass."

Onnie stepped into the shop, and her breath caught. The damage was worse than she thought. It wasn't just the main walkway. They had ruined everything. Not a single shelf had been left upright or case unsmashed. The books had been thrown from their shelves and ripped apart as if someone had been trying to find something hidden within them.

When Gabriel returned to her side, she asked, "Who would do this?"

"Just as there are forces for good in this world, there are forces for evil. The who is not important right now. The why is what worries me." Gabriel began lifting shelves back upright and uncovering more and more literary works destroyed beyond repair.

Onnie made her way to the sitting area in a daze and found that the delicate china had been smashed as if someone had flung the whole tray against the nearest wall. Falling to her knees, she placed her head in her hands and wept tears of her own, oblivious to the china and glass shards beneath her.

Gabriel Vansand

Gabe felt when Onnie finally let go and cried for her friend. He continued to pick through the ruins, looking for any clue as to who had done the destruction. His gut feeling told him it was the man who had been sniffing around Onnie, but Gabe needed a way to prove it to her and then find the creep before he could do any further damage. Gabe knew the man in black was trouble. Even her Link knew it. Onnie was stubborn, and now they would need to be even more on guard.

The daisy Mrs. Radcliff had given Onnie the night they'd triggered the Transference lay on the floor beside the front counter. Its bloom had been crushed beneath a fallen book. Gabe frowned at it and bent to pick it up, but he never got to.

Onnie's scream came from the corner where she served tea, and Gabe took off running, vaulting over the rubbish and not caring what he stepped on to get to her. He felt her momentary shock, and then her overwhelming anguish hit him with full force, nearly knocking him to the floor.

"Onnie!" He shouted, nearly falling over the last toppled-over bookcase more than jumping. When he landed next to her, she clutched Mal, whose eyes were closed, and she gently rocked him back and forth.

Gabe pulled her damp hair back from her face and looked closer at the unresponsive feline in her arms. "Cat, what happened? Where'd you find him?"

Choking back uncontrollable sobs, Onnie stroked the side of Mal's face with tenderness. "I didn't find him. He just appeared. He looked at me, meowed, and collapsed."

"You're sure he was awake when he first appeared?"

"Yes."

"Cat, give him to me." Gabe held out his arms.

"What?" Onnie looked up at him in confusion and pulled the feline tighter to her chest.

Gabe could feel her reluctance, but he didn't take his eyes off of Mal, "Give him to me. Now."

After another few seconds of hesitation, Onnie gently passed Mal to Gabe before she closed her eyes to hold back more tears.

Gabe leaned over the unconscious animal and closed his eyes. He followed his Bond that led to Onnie, and where it branched, he chose the thread connected to Mal. It pulsed faintly, but it was enough. After Gabe checked the other Bonds leading to the Link, he confirmed nothing was nefarious. A few seconds later, Mal's thread flickered a few times but then held steady.

Gabe opened his eyes and whispered to the feline, "You owe me one, hairball."

An unfamiliar male voice laughed in his mind, and Gabe knew Mal would be fine. A moment later, that far-off voice spoke via his and Onnie's Bond. *Onnie, open your eyes. Come on, girl. It's okay.*

Onnie opened her eyes and looked at Gabe expectantly, but he smiled and shook his head. "It wasn't me, Cat."

He lowered his eyes to Mal, and they watched as Mal's tiny body began to breathe again, his eyes remaining closed.

"He's breathing!" Onnie sobbed and stroked the cat's head gently.

Yup, though, the man who did this to the bookshop weakened her considerably, and I used the last of our strength to get to you.

"It was the man in black that's been lurking around since Cat and I started the Transference," Gabe said to the sleeping feline's form.

Yeah, we were right. There's more to him than just low-level evil.

Onnie sniffled, and Gabe used his free hand to brush her hair from her face again.

Onnie, I'm okay. Take Gabe home with you and try to get some sleep. We are all going to need it in the morning.

Onnie looked around the shop, sadness pouring down her Bond, "Will it be alright if we leave her like this overnight, Mal?"

Yeah, the old girl will be fine. She'll be good as new soon enough. Oh, and um...take me with you, please. It's going to be cold in here tonight, and I hate the cold.

Gabe almost felt Mal's smile and knew the Link would be a handful.

"Of course." Onnie looked up at Gabe. "I guess we can't do anything else for her tonight. May I carry Mal?"

He gently passed the cat back to her, and she wrapped him up in her scarf and tucked him into her coat. It was better that he had his hands free anyway, just in case. Gabe clenched his teeth, hearing them grind slightly with his frustration.

Thanks, girl.

"Come on, Cat, let's get going." Gabe helped her to her feet, and they carefully maneuvered through the wreckage back to the front of the shop.

"Wait," Onnie stopped him before he could turn off the lights. A split second later, they were in utter darkness. "Come out, and I'll lock the door behind us."

The three of them stepped back out onto the sidewalk, and seconds later, the door swung closed, and the lock clicked into place. Onnie didn't comment on it, just continued walking down the darkened street towards her cottage. When Gabe tested the lock on the door, he wasn't surprised to find it secured.

Onnie was way too powerful, too fast, it was bound to be noticed, and that would put her in danger. She hadn't even reacted when Mal had used their Bond to speak telepathically. A few weeks ago, she would have been terrified. She was obviously getting used to this new world of hers.

Mal's voice echoed in Gabe's head, and reality crashed back

around him. *Abbot's dead, Gabe and Rebecca. She gave the last of her strength to get me back here. Whoever did this shattered the last of the Bond between the old Keeper and the shop. They're trying to weaken Onnie by forcing the Transference to go faster and must be completed before she's ready. This isn't good.*

Gabe shook his head in agreement and jogged to catch up with the newest Keeper and her Link.

Chapter 30: Numb

December 2021 - Alku | Onnie Moore

Their walk had been silent, and Onnie was on autopilot the entire way to her cottage. With glazed-over eyes, she walked through the wet streets. She clutched Mal to her chest, focusing on his breathing. Gabriel was quiet and vigilant by her side, his presence reassuring. With no telling who or what could lurk in the shadows but no energy left to care or fight back, Onnie left her Guardian to do his duty.

They were wrapped in silent darkness. Rain poured down around them, but the sound was muffled. She could still feel the shop's anguish, but it seemed to have regained control of itself, and it was no longer unbearable.

After what seemed like an eternity of sadness, they arrived outside her cottage. Onnie mumbled to Gabriel which pocket her keys were in, and he let them into the dark apartment and clicked on the lights.

Onnie went straight into her bedroom, turned on the light, and laid Mal carefully on her new bed in a pile of pillows and blankets. Stacked neatly in a corner, she picked up one of Jace's hand-me-down shirts and a baggy pair of pants from the top of the pile. She closed her bedroom door, stripped down, and slipped into the shower.

Gabriel was all but forgotten, and she focused on the water. She was entirely out of tears and the will to cry, so she rested her head against the cold shower wall and let the steaming water cascade around her. The water pooling at her feet was pink, and she glanced at her knees. At some point, she'd cut herself, but it didn't look deep, so she ignored it.

She closed her eyes, and with little effort, the Bond flared in her mind. Just like her body, her mind was weary, and she dimmed her view of the Bond. Without the energy to face them, she shut out the answers within her to questions that she wasn't ready to have answered.

Gabriel Vansand

Gabe watched Onnie's back as she walked across the living room and into her bedroom. Removing his jacket, he hung it on a hook by the front door and looked around the sparse apartment that had become a mess in their recent weeks of research. Books about nearly every magical topic and the history of the Keepers were piled up in corners and resting open all over the floor. They had learned so little, and now, without Abbot... Gabe's mind wandered, and he focused on going to the kitchen to put Onnie's kettle on to boil.

The sound of the shower starting drifted down the hallway, and he was relieved to know she was warming up as they were both soaked from their workout and then subsequent treks through the rain.

He closed his eyes and focused on Onnie, trying to latch onto her overriding emotion, but after a few minutes of feeling nothing, he gave up in frustration. He wasn't sure if she was shutting him out or if she was truly so exhausted that she felt empty. It really didn't make a difference at the current moment, so Gabe instead checked on Mal and found the cat in a light restorative sleep state.

When Gabe opened his eyes, he texted Dany quickly, asking her to bring him an extra set of clothes and sweats. Telling her about Abbot and the shop was better done in person, but Onnie was his priority tonight. Dany could wait until the morning. She'd have to. He couldn't take care of them both.

The loss of Abbot hit him again. The closest thing he and Dany had to a family was now gone. Never to share his wisdom and guidance with them again. Gabe was on his own now and had two people to care for alone.

He stripped down to his boxers, his wet clothing starting to soak Onnie's carpeting. Once off, he wrung what water he could out of his shirt into one side of the sink before doing the same with his socks and shorts.

The kettle came to a boil and whistled its harsh song, startling him from his thoughts. When he saw the handful of dirty dishes in the sink, he washed them quickly and then pulled out two of Onnie's clean mugs. Her kitchen was still bare, with most of the cabinets empty, making him heartsick for her and the solitude she chose to live in.

He and Dany had been spending quite a bit of time with Onnie, and she spent a fair amount with Abbot, but sometimes, it felt like she was just going through the motions. Even their relationship had seemed to stall after his confession a few weeks prior. She had continued to keep up some of the walls she'd rebuilt and tried to treat him like nothing more than her Guardian.

Until tonight when she let him hold her.

When the shower turned off in the bathroom, he waited a few minutes and then filled both mugs with tea, making hers precisely how she liked it. He left his own on the counter and took Onnie's to her bedroom, knocking softly.

"Cat, I've made you some tea," he spoke calmly, but only silence answered him. "Cat…"

She's asleep, Gabe, but she's dressed. Mal spoke in Gabe's mind.

Gabe quietly opened the bedroom door and stuck in his head. Onnie was curled up under the covers and breathing softly. He walked over to her makeshift nightstand on the window sill and set her tea down in case she woke up thirsty.

Crossing to the other side of the room, he slid down the wall to sit on the floor, resting his head in his hands.

She's going to be devastated in the morning, Mal thought to Gabe.

I know, and damn it, I have to tell her. She's going to hate me, Mal. Sadness gripped Gabe's heart like a vice.

She's an intelligent woman, man. She'll know it wasn't your fault.

Wasn't it? I'm a Guardian. I should have been there.

Gabe, you're her *Guardian, not Abbot's. Don't beat yourself up for something you couldn't control.*

It's my blood that failed her, my father. I should have done better. I should have known that something was still out there. We should have never left the store unprotected. Gabe ran his fingers through his hair and tugged at it slightly.

Dude, don't make me wake up and come over there. I may not need a cat box, but I'm more than happy to pee in your shoes. This wasn't your fault. Get some sleep. She's going to need you tomorrow.

We can't lose her, Mal.

I know, dude, but she's not going anywhere.

"Fine," Gabe got to his feet and walked over to Onnie. He lightly ran his palm over her hair, the damn strands clinging to his skin. "Sleep well, Cat."

As he walked to the doorway, he picked up her wet clothes and turned off the lights, closing the door behind him.

Her clothes were just as soaked, and he rang them out and placed them in the sink with his. Then he retrieved his lukewarm tea and downed it in one go. He was rinsing the cup when someone knocked softly on the front door. Before he made it over to ensure it was Dany, she used her key and closed the door behind her. If he weren't so exhausted, he would have teased her about her shocked face when seeing him in nothing but his boxers in Onnie's living room.

"Brother mine!" she smirked, "what's this I find?"

He hugged his sister hard and felt some tension leave his body. Dany stiffened and hugged him back, her voice dropping to a soothing whisper. "Gabe, what is it? Is it Onnie?" She understood instantly that something was wrong, and he held her tighter.

"No," his voice cracked, "she's fine. Sleeping." He pulled back, took his overnight bag from his sister, and put on his sweatpants.

"Gabe, tell me what's going on. Why are you soaked to the bone and nearly naked? The woman you're in love with is asleep in the other room, and you're hugging me like you haven't seen me in months?"

"Nothing, Dany, it's just been a rough day." Now that he was in warmer clothes, his energy waned, and he urged his sister towards the door.

"Damn it, Gabe!" Dany stomped her combat boot, "If you don't tell me what's wrong, I'm going to go in there," she pointed over his shoulder towards Onnie's bedroom, "and get Onnie to tell me."

"Dany, it's nothing. We will talk about it tomorrow."

His sister twisted out of his hold and brushed past him, "Fine, if you won't—"

"The shop was attacked tonight." Gabe lamented with his back to his sister. Dany's intake of breath was loud in the quiet cottage, and he closed his eyes.

"What?" She walked back to him and put one hand on his shoulder.

"Can we please talk about this in the morning?"

Her firm but compassionate voice shook, "No, Gabe, tell me."

"The man in black ransacked the shop looking for something, and it's completely wrecked." Gabe held his breath, willing his sister to stop asking questions he didn't have the strength to answer. She was quiet for a long time.

"How's Onnie?"

He could hear the tears in her voice, and he clenched his fists. "She's as fine as she can be. We were at the gym when it happened."

Dany's relief washed over him with the exhale of her breath, "Thank the gods."

Logic was one of Dany's mastered skills, and he knew where her next thought had been headed before she said anything.

"And…Abbot?"

Grief squeezed his heart like a fist, and he opened his mouth a few times to answer her, but no sound came out. Finally, he rubbed his eyes with one hand and managed to shake his head, "Mal is with Onnie right now. Only after..."

Dany's hand gripped his shoulder tighter, and then it was gone, and she slipped to the floor.

"I'm sorry, Dany."

When he turned and saw the anguish on his sister's face, he felt the most helpless he'd ever been. She held back tears in her eyes, and he walked away to give her some privacy. Gabe plucked a pillow and the handmade quilt off the leather chair and made some space on the floor to sleep.

Dany sniffled and got to her feet, dashing tears from her cheeks before turning to face him. "I'll see you tomorrow. I'm going to Abbot's to…" her voice caught in her throat, "I'll be at Abbot's," then she left.

She'll be okay, dude. Mal assured.

With nothing left to do but grieve, Gabe turned off the lights and lay down on his makeshift bed. His eyes roamed the tiny cottage and its bare walls and lack of furniture. The main item in the room was the shop's books, but those weren't Onnie. She locked herself away who knows how many years earlier, and now, with Abbot gone, she would feel even more alone.

Her apartment is so empty. Mal, the Cat I know, is so full of life, but in here, she seems…

Lonely. Mal interjected.

Lost.

She was Gabe. That's one of the reasons why she chose her. Onnie needed to be rescued just as much as the shop did.

But has it rescued Cat or trapped her in a different state of lost?

You already know the answer to that, man, don't worry. She'll come into her own soon enough, and I have a feeling the magical world won't know what hit it.

I hope you're right, Mal.

You worry too much. Chill and let this play out. You'll see.

I hope so.

Get some sleep, my man. You need time to grieve and process today, too. It's not just Onnie who needs to be in top-head space tomorrow.

Gabe slipped his arms under his head and stared at the ceiling. "Night, furball." He whispered into the darkness and felt Mal drift back into his healing sleep.

For hours, Gabe continued to stare at the ceiling as he replayed that day's nightmare in his head over and over until the sun crept over the horizon.

Chapter 31: Denial

December 2021 - Alku | Onnie Moore

Onnie rolled over and into a warm shaft of light coming in from the window. Yawning, she stretched and grazed her arm on a warm, furry body beside her. Mal purred in response.

"Morning, Mal," she said through a second yawn.

"Morning, Onnie."

Scrambling backward on all fours before she realized it, Onnie flopped off the bed, yelped as she hit the floor, and then backed up into the wall behind her.

"You can talk!" she shouted.

Her bedroom door burst open, and Gabriel ran in wearing only an incredible pair of sweatpants and brandishing her metal flashlight as a nightstick.

"What's going on? Are you alright?" Gabriel looked around the room frantically for an intruder.

Onnie pointed to Mal, "He can talk!"

Mal looked at Gabriel from the mattress and smiled. Gabriel lowered the flashlight and rubbed his eyes as he started to chuckle.

Onnie, while still pointing at Mal, glared at Gabriel. "What's so funny!?"

Gabriel clutched his bare side and began to laugh uncontrollably, and Mal rolled on his back with all four paws in the air and joined in the laughter.

Furious at both and angry that no one was taking her seriously, Onnie stood and walked past Gabriel into the living room, leaving the two of them to their hyperventilating. Noticing Gabriel's makeshift bed on the floor, she winced with guilt. As she entered the kitchen, Mal jumped on the counter next to his water bowl and smiled at her.

Gabriel followed behind him, wiping tears from his eyes. "We're sorry, Cat, we didn't mean to laugh at you."

"Speak for yourself, man. I was *totally* laughing at her. Did you see her face? That was priceless!"

Gabriel choked on another laugh and shot Onnie a look of sympathy.

"So, you can talk now, and you didn't think to warn me of this before I went to sleep?" Onnie's eyes darted between the two of them. "Either of you!"

Gabriel walked over and wrapped his arms around Onnie, enveloping her in his warmth, her cheek against the bare skin of his chest.

"Come on. You can't be mad at me for that. How was I supposed to know he could talk?" she felt him tense for a split second before continuing, "Your Bond must have strengthened as the shop is regaining its balance."

"You could have warned me it was possible," Onnie said as she wrapped her arms around his waist.

"I didn't think to mention it. No one has had a non-humanoid for a Link in over thirteen hundred years. I forgot. Besides, you didn't seem phased when he spoke inside our heads last night."

Onnie studied Mal and then switched to Gabe before shrugging. She actually hadn't registered their conversation as being non-audible the night before. "Fine, you're forgiven."

Onnie stepped back and leaned on the sink to be at eye level with Mal. "What's your excuse? You didn't think it was a good idea to warn me?"

"And miss you freaking out like that, no way!" Mal rolled on his back, roaring again with laughter.

"Mal!" both Onnie and Gabriel scolded.

"I'm sorry, she's just so shocked! Even after everything, a talking cat is something she thinks is impossible."

Onnie nudged Mal off the bar, and he landed on his feet with a thump, still laughing. "You're an ass with a voice." Onnie opened the fridge and pulled out a loaf of bread. "Toast, Gabriel?"

Gabriel shot Mal a sympathetic shrug but still chuckled, "Sure, want some tea?"

"Um, actually, I could use a coffee. I was going to get changed and run to A Shot in the Dark and pick some up. Want one?"

Gabriel crossed the living room, pulled a t-shirt from his overnight bag, and slipped it over his head. "I'll go while you make the toast. What would you like?" He smiled and slipped on his jacket and shoes.

"You sure?" Onnie asked as she popped two slices of bread into the toaster.

"Yup."

"Okay, something sweet please and…" she pointed to his bag, "when did you get that?"

"Dany brought it for me. You were sleeping." She noticed his uneasy eye contact with Mal when he answered, "Something sweet, coming right up. Mal will stay with you. Don't answer the front door."

"I'll watch out for her, Gabe." Mal jumped back onto the kitchen counter and sat down, no longer laughing but severe and stiff.

"I'm not a child, you two." Onnie rolled her eyes, and Gabriel stopped with his hand on the front door. Letting go, he crossed the living room in a few strides and lifted her chin to look into her eyes.

"You are not a child, but you are precious. If anything happened to you, both Mal and I would be devastated. Do not take away our right to protect what is ours." Gabriel leaned down and placed a chaste kiss on her lips. Then he brushed her hair back from her cheek and kissed her again.

"I'll only be gone a few minutes. Enjoy your toast." With that, he turned and walked out the front door, grabbing Onnie's key and locking the door behind him.

Onnie stood speechless, the silence only broken by the toaster popping behind her.

Mal purred, "Girl, he's got it bad."

Onnie turned and stuck her nose against Mal's. "I am still not talking to you, and yes, we've already covered that."

"And you're going to leave the poor boy hangin'? Onnie, you're a smart girl. That is one love-sick puppy. Take him home or put him down."

"Maldwyn! What a horrible thing to say." Her voice broke with a high-pitched squeak, but her cheeks flared, giving her real feelings away.

"You're in denial." Mal reached out and licked her nose with his scratchy tongue.

"Ugg, men!" Onnie threw her hands up and retrieved her toast.

"Hey, can I have a slice?"

"Sure, you talk. Why don't I make you a slice of toast, too!" Onnie popped another two slices in the toaster and pushed down the lever with a click.

"Um… Onnie?" Mal muttered.

"What!?" Onnie snapped with frustration.

"Ah, I don't have thumbs…and I'm still kind of weak… Can you make me some tea…? Please?"

Onnie turned and found Mal looking down at the floor in shame. She sighed and filled the kettle, placing it on the stove and clicking it up to high. Then she walked to the silky blue cat, carefully lifted him into her arms, and squeezed him into a hug.

"I'm sorry I snapped at you. Yesterday sucked, and I'm still processing it. And don't be ashamed of not having thumbs. You have a tail, and tails are cool."

Mal purred and licked her cheek. "I'm sorry I laughed at you, but really, you should have seen your face… 'He can talk!' It was perfect."

Onnie laughed and squeezed Mal tighter, "I'm glad I made you laugh."

The two of them stood in the kitchen in a tight hug until the smell of warm bread reached their noses, and the toaster dinged a second time. Onnie moved to place Mal back on the counter, and he clawed onto her sleeve as she started to walk away.

"Onnie? He cares about you, and you should have seen him last night. The guy was a wreck."

She smiled and petted the top of the feline's head, "Thank you, Mal."

Onnie fixed Mal his toast and tea, and the two of them sat on the floor in the middle of the living room, waiting for Gabriel to return with coffee. Mal sat with his shallow water bowl filled with tea and raised on a short box. He lapped at the deep red liquid while Onnie ripped his toast into small pieces.

"Mal, what's going to happen to the shop?"

"She'll be okay. As she and I regain strength and your connection with her increases, she'll right herself. We have some cleanup, that's for sure, but something tells me you're not one to be afraid of a little elbow grease." Mal smiled his crooked cat grin.

"You're sure?"

"Yup, I promise. Don't get me wrong, things have changed, but everything will work out in the end." Mal returned to his tea and toast, closing the conversation for now.

A few minutes later, Mal's ears shifted, and Onnie looked at her front door and held her breath. The scraping of a key in the lock had Onnie jumping to her feet as she frolicked to the kitchen and popped Gabriel's toast into the toaster. He opened the front door, and Onnie closed her eyes and savored the smell of freshly roasted espresso and caramel as it wafted toward her.

"Is that a caramel macchiato?" Onnie asked with her eyes still closed.

"Ah… Yes?" Gabriel said uncertainly as he closed the front door with his foot.

She skipped to him with pure glee, and when she kissed his cheek, she was handed a large coffee in return. "Thank you, this is perfect. I just put your toast in. Do you want me to butter it?"

Gabriel locked the front door with his free hand and went to set down his coffee on the kitchen counter. "Nope, I can manage. Enjoy your coffee."

Smiling, Onnie flopped back on the carpet next to Mal, sipping the warm cup of paradise she now delicately cradled.

Gabriel Vansand

Gabe sipped his coffee and then pulled the butter out of the fridge. He walked past Mal, eating bits of buttered toast next to Onnie.

She's doing better, I take it? Gabe asked Mal while removing his jacket and hanging it back up by the front door.

Mal gave a slight nod. *Yeah, we're good.*

Have you told her about the old man?

Does it look like I've told her?

Mal narrowed his eyes at him, but Gabe turned to watch Onnie staring out the window, sipping her coffee while a small smile played at the corner of her lips. She looked peaceful, and after what happened last night, she deserved some peace.

How do you wanna play this, Ace? Asked Mal.

I have no idea. Onnie's going to be hurt that we kept this from her for this long. Gabe's toast popped, and he buttered it quickly, knowing he wasn't expecting to finish it.

I'll help as much as I can.

Sounds good, man. Well...here goes nothing.

Gabe retrieved his coffee and carried it and his napkin of toast to their makeshift breakfast circle on the floor. Onnie looked in from the window and, smiling, sipped her coffee.

"Sorry about the lack of furniture. I never really had the chance to settle in."

"I don't mind, and Mal sure doesn't seem to." Gabe and Onnie watched Mal roll on his back, scratching on the carpet. "You don't have fleas, do you, furball?"

Mal hissed at Gabe. "Bite your tongue!"

Onnie ruffled the top of Mal's head, "He was playing, Mal."

Mal grumbled and resumed his back scratching.

"How's your coffee, Cat?" Gabe asked as he sipped his own.

You're stalling. Mal sneered at Gabe.

"Amazing, perfect! Just what I wanted. Thank you again." Onnie smiled over the lid of her cup.

"Anytime." Gabe sipped his own, continuing to stall as Mal had insinuated.

Gabe...

"Yes, I know, Mal!" Gabe snapped. Onnie jumped at the sudden exclamation and looked at him in surprise.

"Dude, that was your outside voice," Mal said as he rolled back onto his stomach.

Gabe sighed, set down his coffee, and rubbed his forehead. Onnie sat her coffee next to his and scooted closer to his side. Reaching up, she rested her palm lightly on his forearm.

"Gabriel, what's wrong?"

She's too...happy, Mal. Something's wrong.

Mal sighed along their Bond. *She's turned it off. The Bond. Her emotions, all of it.*

She can do that?

Apparently, Mal walked over quietly and crawled into Onnie's lap. *Come on, man. I'll help.* Mal said only in his mind still.

Onnie looked down at Mal resting in her lap, and Gabe assumed they were having a mental conversation.

Words sped through Gabe's head faster than he could keep up with. But he didn't know the words to ease the pain she was about to experience, and he wasn't even sure he was up to experiencing it himself when she lost control, and it flooded their Bond. He'd shoved the loss of Abbot from his mind last night, knowing that if he thought about it too much, he wouldn't be able to stop his grief, and he didn't want to chance waking her with it.

We're done. I think she's as ready as she'll ever be, man. Mal interrupted Gabe's inner musings.

What did you say to her?

Mal purred. *I reminded her that we love her and would never cause her pain.*

When Onnie looked back at Gabe, he knew his stalling was over. He scratched Mal's chin in silent thanks. The cat was trying to help, and he'd take all he could get right now. His hands moved on their own to cup Onnie's face gently, and he stared into her beautiful green eyes.

"Cat, Onnie… Do you remember last night when Mal appeared in the bookshop after it was broken into?"

"Of course. I was upset, Gabe, not possessed," Onnie nodded as a look of anguish crossed her face, "I thought he was dead."

"Do you remember how he said he'd gotten there?"

"Um… Rebecca had done it."

Mal rubbed his head against Onnie's stomach.

"Yes, she did. Onnie, you need to know something about Rebecca and the old man's relationship." Gabe softly stroked his thumbs over her cheeks, "Your Grandfather's Guardian left him a long time ago, and because of that, Rebecca acted as sort of a stand-in protector."

Confusion slowly creeping through their Bond, she nodded, "I remember. You guys told me that."

Gabe squeezed his eyes closed, and when he opened them, he assumed that by the way Onnie's widened, his were now ice blue as he strained with his emotional control.

"Because Bec acted as the old man's Guardian, she would not have left him while the store was being attacked. She'd have stayed with him…to protect him."

"That's a good thing, right? Gabriel, I'm confused. Tell me where you're going with this."

Gabe, get on with it. I can feel her starting to lose it here. Mal warned in his mind.

"Do you also remember when I told you Mal and Bec couldn't both be in the world at the same time? That there could never be two Links at once?" Gabe leaned his forehead against Onnie's and felt her emotions resurface as she began to connect the dots.

"Gabriel. Where's Rebecca?" her voice sped up in her growing panic.

He sighed and shook his head with what little control over himself he had left.

"Gabriel, how is Mal here? Where's Rebecca?" Onnie pushed back from him and looked down at Mal curled in her lap. "Mal, what's going on? Where's Rebecca? Why isn't she with Grandfather?" Onnie's breath came out ragged and frantic.

"Breathe, Cat," he said, reaching out to calm her.

"No! How is Mal here? Where's Rebecca? What happened to my Grandfather?" Onnie stood abruptly, and Mal jumped to the floor just in time.

"He's gone, Onnie," Mal said, looking up from Gabe's feet. "They both are."

"What do you mean he's gone? He can't be gone. He said he still had time!"

Gabe stood up slowly. "He was fragile, far weaker than he wanted you to realize, and when the store was attacked, the last of his connection with her was broken."

"You're lying. He's alright, you'll see." Onnie stepped around both him and Mal and dashed into her bedroom.

"Cat!" Gabe started after her but only made it one step before Mal walked in front of him.

"Gabe, let her get dressed. She'll have to come back out here soon enough. Focus on her emotions. What do you feel?" Mal said, looking up at him with sympathy in his eyes.

"I don't need to focus, Mal. I can see her. She's obviously upset!" His fists clenched and trembled with anger at his sides.

"Is she?" Mal stated and then walked slowly into the bedroom after Onnie.

Gabe took a few deep breaths and closed his eyes. He found his connection with Onnie in his mind, and what was usually a multifaceted thread of emotions was still and singular. His loving, excitable, passionate Cat was distilled into one base emotion.

Gabe reached out and effortlessly grasped the Bond in front of him.

Anger.

His eyes snapped open as the force of Onnie's anger hit him in the chest. She wasn't sad or upset over her Grandfather's death. She was angry.

Gabe had seen the old man at this level of anger only once, and Gabe would never forget it. Keepers were strong creatures, and an angry one was dangerous. If what Gabe and the others assumed was true, he'd just unleashed the most powerful fledgling Keeper since the first one that had ever existed.

Chapter 32: Anger

December 2021 - Alku | Onnie Moore

Onnie stomped around her room, ripping off her clothes and digging through her stacks for clean ones. Not bothered by which one of her male companions may walk in on her as she undressed, she only thought of getting to her Grandfather. Bending over, she pulled on a pair of black skinny jeans and socks. Mal walked into the room slowly with his eyes closed and sat in front of the bedroom door.

"Onnie?" he said in a whisper, clearly testing her reaction.

"What, Mal? I'm getting dressed and going over there. I need to see him. I need to know he's alright." She pulled a sports bra over her head, followed by a comfortably worn grey t-shirt.

"You know he's gone, Onnie. Focus on your connection with the store and me. It's gotten stronger since the attack, but your Bond to Abbot has weakened, and if you look, you won't find Abbot connected to the shop at all."

"That's just from all the tea Gabriel's been pouring down my throat. He said my Bond would increase from drinking it." Sitting near the bed, Onnie pulled on her shoes and began tying up the laces.

Mal opened his eyes and walked over to sit by her thigh. He placed one paw on it lightly and looked up at her. "Test your Bond, Onnie. I know you felt your Grandfather's Bond with the store as a sort of echo in the back of your mind. Look for it. Can you still feel it?"

"Ugg, fine, Mal!" Onnie sighed and closed her eyes, searching her mind for her connection with the store. She found the colored strand easier than ever before, and her mind followed a yellow glowing tether that led back to Mal.

Good, that's ours. Try the next one.

Onnie watched as the glowing strand pulsed, and she felt a wave of approval coming from Mal. A red strand that connected her to Gabriel was what she found next. She shivered as a feeling of despair washed over her.

He's upset you're hurting and thinks you'll never forgive him. He blames himself even though there was nothing he could have done.

Onnie squeezed her lids tighter and looked at another strand glowing and shimmering in a rainbow of colors and bright in front of her. Her shop. Onnie could see dim sections along the strand, but as she watched, they continued to mend themselves and regain their glow.

Why would someone want to hurt her, Mal? She's just a bookshop. Who else knows she's alive?

There's a whole world of magical creatures and people out there, Onnie, and many of them wish to see her harmed. Mal sighed and slightly extended his claws into her leg. *Now focus, where's your Grandfather's strand?*

Onnie searched frantically, but the dark blue thread that had extended from the shop to her Grandfather and then to Rebecca was barely a flicker. Rebecca's was gone entirely.

"No!" Onnie's eyes shot open, and she stood up. "That means nothing." She grabbed her bag and jacket and quickly pulled both on as she walked back into the living room.

Gabriel's eyes snapped open as she entered the room, and he stepped in her path. "Cat, stop."

She caught herself just before running into the wall Gabriel made with his body. She looked up at him and glared. "Move, Gabriel. I'm going to see him."

"Not until you listen to me." Gabriel reached out and gently grasped both of her upper arms.

"Move out of my way, Gabriel," Onnie said through clenched teeth. "Now."

"He was important to me too, Cat. They both were, but you're still here, and it's my job to protect you, so stop running and listen to me."

Her eyesight sharpened, and she focused her anger on Gabriel, "Let go of me, Gabriel." The words came out far calmer than she felt.

"No, stop it and listen to me!" Gabriel snapped, his fingers pressing harder into her biceps, his patience thinning.

"No, you listen to me!" she ripped her arms free and stepped back. "This is my Grandfather we're talking about. Mine. He was just an old man to you, but he gave me a chance and listened to me. He cared about me. Even after all the shit that happened between him and my Mother, he still loved me. So, no, I will not stop and listen to you because he may be hurt, and I need to help him!"

The anger she'd been bottling up slipped from her control and was replaced with a calm fury. With one last look at Mal walking out of the bedroom, she picked up her keys and opened her front door.

Gabriel's hand slammed it closed above her head, and he leaned down behind her and spoke into her ear, his words no more than a growl. "Your Grandfather was one of the most important people in the world to my sister and me. He was more than an old man. He was like a father. Don't you dare pretend that you are the only one hurting, and don't think for one minute that he meant more to you in the last few months than he did to me in the past twenty-eight years." Gabriel let go of the door and stepped back.

She ripped open the door and slammed it shut behind her, Gabriel's frustrated yell pouring from her cottage.

"Not your best move, my man." she heard Mal scold.

Gabriel let out an animalistic roar as she started to run.

Onnie sprinted as fast as she could to her car, parked only a few spots from the cottage's front door. Yanking the door open, she slid inside, starting the engine and throwing it into reverse. She drove, focusing solely on getting to her Grandfather as she pulled onto the streets with other people.

All the cruel things she'd said to Gabriel were driven to the back of her mind, and she focused instead on navigating the foggy morning streets. Every car she encountered seemed content with driving ten miles under the speed limit, and as the moments passed, Onnie became increasingly frustrated. When she finally pulled up in front of her Grandfather's sleepy little house, she was ready to rip apart the next person she saw.

Onnie stumbled out of the car before slamming the door closed with enough force to rattle the windows. The neighborhood was silent as she ran up the front walk and knocked loudly on the door, the noise shattering the calm.

She waited.

Thirty seconds later, she pounded again. And again. And Again.

There was no reason Rebecca would not have answered the door… unless she was gone. With a sinking heart, Onnie realized Gabriel had been telling her the truth. She'd been horrible to him after he did nothing but try to help her. Completely devoid of emotion and without any tears left to cry, Onnie turned and sat down against the front door.

Mal appeared a few feet away with anguish written all over his tiny face. Slowly, he crawled into Onnie's lap and rested his chin in the palm of her hand. She stroked his soft blue-grey fur and, with glazed eyes, stared off into the distance.

Gabriel Vansand

Gabe was beside himself with anger. He paced the tiny space in Onnie's living room, fuming at their argument and replaying it repeatedly in his head.

He was furious at her, but that paled compared to how he raged at himself. He fluctuated between angry and sad, but he was shocked when he thought of Abbot, and his anger increased.

How had Abbot left them? He and Onnie still needed the Keeper's wisdom, but all of them had been too complacent about the threat of the man in black.

Gabe kicked a paperback, which slammed into the wall before landing crumpled on the floor. He felt when Mal had had enough, and he disappeared, leaving Gabe to deal with his rage. Alone.

Gabe stopped pacing and fell to his knees. His shoulders were hunched, and he took a deep breath to steady himself. The anger coursing through him buzzed along his skin like electricity, and he needed to tamp it down before he hurt Onnie. The last thing she needed was his emotions swirling with her own.

Mal, how is she? He thought along the Bond.

What do you think? Why don't you ask her yourself? Mal sneered back at Gabe.

The Link was just as upset about losing Abbot as they were, but Gabe could feel his anger as they fought amongst themselves. He severed his focused connection with Mal and reached out to Onnie. Their Bond glowed brightly, and Gabe didn't need to expend much energy to feel her pain. The anger was still there, cold and bubbling under the surface, but the pain she felt was now resting on top of it like a grey cloud cover.

Gabe sat slumped in Onnie's living room, wrapped in their mental connection, feeding calming emotions down their Bond. When he felt Onnie respond to his support, Gabe smiled as she sent back a gentle wave of apology and forgiveness. The two of them stayed like that for a few minutes until he felt Onnie's attention waver and her anger skyrocket. Then, she blocked their connection.

"Onnie!" Gabe yelled, opening his eyes and looking around her empty apartment.

Onnie Moore

Onnie felt Gabriel the minute he focused on their Bond, but she waited to see what he would do. She'd already done enough damage to their relationship, but when she felt his attempt to soothe her, she smiled and wordlessly apologized in return.

She knew he was still a few miles away, probably in her apartment, but she was enjoying the feeling of their minds being so intimately connected. Unconsciously stroking Mal's fur, she relaxed and wrapped herself in Gabriel's mental comfort.

Mal's ear twitched, and Onnie cracked open her eyes and followed his gaze. Across the street was a man hidden in the shadows watching them. When he realized he'd been seen, he stepped out into the light, and Onnie saw his face clearly.

Mal growled low in his throat, and Onnie lost control of her anger. The warm cat in her lap forgotten, Onnie jumped to her feet and severed her focus from Gabriel, locking him out entirely.

The man in black turned and walked down the street away from them.

"It's him, Mal!" Onnie yelled as she raced off down the sidewalk after the man responsible for all of her and Gabe's pain.

"Onnie, wait!" Mal shouted at her heels.

She ignored him and continued running, chasing after the stranger when he had started sprinting. When she felt Mal and Gabriel's consciousness tugging on her Bond, she relented and let them in.

Onnie's taken off chasing after the man in black, Gabe.

Stop her, Mal! I'm on my way!

Onnie heard their conversation but ignored it. Mal appeared close on Onnie's heels, his tiny ears flattened from the wind. "Onnie, stop. Wait for Gabe."

"He killed my Grandfather!" She shouted back, picking up speed and following the man in black off the street and into the forest. Mal repeatedly disappeared and reappeared, trying to keep up with her. "Mal, just go get Gabe!"

"No way! He'd kill me if I left you. Just keep running!"

"Keep up then!"

She ran even faster, jumping over fallen piles of leaves and logs. Her lungs filled with the sweet forest air, making her smile. The clean air fueled her running, and she watched as she closed the gap between her and the man in black. When she was close enough to reach out and touch his jacket, the three of them burst through a clearing in the trees.

With one final lunge, she tackled the man's back, and the two of them rolled along the detritus on the forest floor. When their momentum stopped, Onnie was straddling the man's torso, and Mal appeared between her arms, a mess of hissing and spitting.

"Why did you attack my shop!" Onnie yelled in his face.

The man in black leveled his cold, empty eyes at her and slowly began to laugh.

She grabbed his hood and forced his head off the ground only to slam it back down, growling through gritted teeth. "Why!"

With a sneer, the man smiled at Onnie. "To watch you burn."

"Who are you?!" Onnie screamed over Mal's head, his fur rippling from her breath.

The man in black cackled.

Mal hissed and swiped his claws across the man's face…but the man had already disappeared.

"NO!" Onnie bellowed and looked around her, half expecting him to try to stab her from behind or something. "Mal, where did he go!"

Mal sighed, "He's gone, and there's nothing you can do about it now, so take a breath, Onnie."

She screamed up into the canopy, causing a flock of birds nesting to fly to safer perches. She was fuming, scrabbling to her feet and pacing around the clearing.

Cat, Mal, where are you guys? Is she safe? Gabriel's voice worried along their Bond.

We're in the clearing. She's going to lose it, Gabe.

I'm almost there. Keep Cat in the clearing!

Onnie ignored the men's conversation, squatted in front of the feline, and met his warm eyes. "Mal, I need answers."

Mal shivered when he saw her icy blue eyes, and she was clearly drawing a lot of power and barely containing it, not to mention her emotions being out of control. "Sit down and ask."

She stared at him, neither of them blinking. After a few minutes, she felt calmer, and she felt the blue from her eyes slowly slip away. She sat on the forest floor cross-legged in front of Mal.

"Alright, who is he?"

"I don't know much more than you do. You know the man in black has been interested in you and the shop, and he asked about *Custos regni.* He's also been stalking you, and I'd bet, Gabe. Next question," Mal said matter-of-factly.

"How did he disappear?"

"I can disappear. Why shouldn't he be able to? But for the record, he didn't turn invisible. He moved through space."

"Okay, so what species teleport then?" Onnie said, unsure of her question. "You can, and you're a Link. He's obviously not, so what other creatures can disappear?"

"You're wrong, well, at least I think you could be. I believe the scum is a Link. Just not in the same sense that I am, and not connected to the shop. I believe he's a Link to something else..." Mal licked his front paw.

"So, there is more than one type of Link?"

"That's my guess. You have a better one?" Mal asked, still looking at his paw.

"Ah, no."

"I wasn't asking you," Mal said shortly.

"He was asking me," Gabriel said from behind her.

Jumping to her feet, Onnie spun to face him. "Ah…hi." Her gaze fell as she remembered their argument earlier and all the horrible things she'd said to him.

"Cat," Gabriel said sternly.

"Yes?"

"If you ever—" he crossed the clearing in half a dozen slow strides. "do that again," reaching Onnie, he crushed her in his embrace and softly stroked her hair, "I swear I will do something I won't regret."

"I—" Onnie slowly wrapped her arms around his waist, hugging him back. "I'm sorry, that was really stupid, wasn't it?"

"Stupid?" Gabriel snapped, holding her away from him and staring into her eyes. "Yes. It was reckless, dangerous, selfish, and on top of that," Gabriel leaned down and placed his lips on hers. He slowly kissed her while gently stroking her cheek with one hand and her lower back with the other.

Onnie couldn't breathe as he kissed her. He flared their connection in their minds, and she shut out the world around her. Nothing mattered except his arms grounding her and his lips on hers. Her heart was filled to bursting with his feelings—gratitude, happiness, and… praise.

Gabriel pulled back slowly, breaking their kiss, and rested his forehead on hers. "On top of that, Mal said you ran like a girl on fire. I would have loved to see that," he smiled at her.

"Ugg, get a room, you two," Mal said from their feet.

"I'll make you into a slipper, Mal," Gabriel growled in mock anger.

Mal disappeared and reappeared on Gabriel's shoulder. "Just you try, big man."

Onnie laughed and stepped back from the pair, now play fighting with Gabriel poking Mal's stomach and Mal whacking him in the face with his paw.

"Come on, you two. I need to go pick up my car. And break into Grandfather's..."

Onnie's face fell just a bit, and she felt herself slipping back into her cold anger as if it were a well-worn sweater.

"You don't have to break in, Cat." Gabriel pulled out a key from his pocket and tossed it at her. "I've known the old man for a very long time."

Onnie caught the key and blushed, her earlier outburst still nagging her with guilt. "Ah, Gabe, about earlier, I'm sorry. I shouldn't have…"

"Cat, stop." Gabriel put Mal on the floor, placed his hands on her shoulder, and bent his knees so she had no choice but to gaze into his eyes. "It's okay. I forgive you. Nothing to forgive, actually. I know my relationship with Abbot was...difficult for you. It's fine."

Onnie's brow crinkled, "Difficult for me?"

Gabriel stood and rubbed the back of his neck with one hand, "Ah, yeah. I noticed it at Thanksgiving," he looked away from her.

"There were times when Abbot interacted with people, and you'd...go hollow."

It was her turn to look away, and when she did, there was a raven on a tree branch with lime-green eyes watching her. "Damn, I was hoping to have kept that to myself." A hummingbird flew over and hovered beside the raven, and Onnie cocked her head to the side at the odd pairing.

Gabriel sighed beside her and then drew her attention back to him when he placed a quick kiss on her cheek and then wrapped his arm around her shoulder. "Let's tackle that topic another time." He turned them to face a gap in the trees. "Do you remember this clearing?"

Mal jumped into Onnie's arms as she looked around her. "Is this the clearing by my apartment, the one we met in?"

"Yes…and no." Gabriel smiled, "This clearing is special. Once you exit it, it can lead you somewhere else, but the distance is shortened."

"Wait, what?" Onnie's brows knit in confusion.

"Think of a bed sheet. Lying flat from one side to the other, there are six feet of fabric, right? Now fold over the center third. Now, it's four feet across. This clearing is that fold. It's the space that gets bent to decrease the distance."

"So, there is a magical clearing that happens to connect my apartment and my Grandfather's house?" Onnie said skeptically.

"Not exactly," interjected Mal. "The clearing bridges whatever you need it to."

"It's helped me get to your apartment, the old man's, and Xayn and Grandma Yvonne's cottage. For you, it may be different." Gabriel gestured in each direction.

"Okay, so how do I find out where it will lead me?"

"It's already helped you once. The first time we met, you made it back home faster than you'd expected, right?"

"Oh, actually," Onnie thought back to her first run so many weeks prior, "You're right."

"Chances are, we're way *way* out in the middle of the forest outside Alku right now, too," added Mal.

"Well, that's convenient." Onnie smiled at the trees in front of her.

"For now, let's head back to Abbot's." Gabriel took one step and stopped. "Do you remember what I told you last time we were here?"

"Don't turn around, right?"

"Partially. Don't even look over your shoulder. While many things in this world are good or evil, this clearing isn't one of them. Picture an eight-year-old with a bag of pranks. If you turn, this clearing will play one on you, and you'll end up lost forever. Or until it gets bored." Gabriel smiled up into the treetops. "It's a tricky being this clearing and a topic of many of the world's stories about Fae."

"Right," Onnie gulped, "well then. Off to Grandfather's?"

"Carry me. I'm weak," Mal said, turning to dead weight in Onnie's arms.

"You are such a drama queen," Onnie said, tickling him as the three walked forward, led by Gabriel's warm arm wrapped around her shoulders.

"Gabe?" Onnie said as they walked. "What's this clearing called? It has a name, right?"

"Wayward Clearing," Gabriel answered as they stepped through the trees.

Chapter 33: Love

December 2021 - Alku | Onnie Moore

Shafts of sunlight filtered into the room through heavy velvet curtains, spilling onto the glossy hardwood and thick patterned rug atop it. Dust particles floated and twinkled in the light, bouncing to and from around the room. Two walls were nothing but books—shelves nearly eight feet tall, stuffed to the brim with all of Abbot's favorites. Pictures, prints, and paintings surrounded a bathroom and a closet door on a third wall. The only exterior wall had an enormous four-poster bed pushed against it and a cushioned bay window overlooking the back deck beside it.

On any other day, the room would have been warm and inviting. Today, gentle sobs filled the room that had gone cold. Onnie sat on a wooden chair beside the large bed with her head resting on the soft blue duvet. Mal lay curled up on the edge of the bed at Onnie's elbow with wide eyes and a slightly glassy expression. Gabriel leaned on the bookcase behind Onnie with his arms crossed protectively in front of him, tears glistening on his stubble.

Mal reached out and softly rested his paw on Onnie's head,

stroking her hair gently. After a few moments, she shifted to look at him and smiled weakly.

"Thanks, Mal," she said, staring into the peaceful face of her Grandfather.

Mal had explained to Onnie how Rebecca's last act for Abbot had been to help him into his warm bed, where the two closed their eyes together as their life left them. Grandfather would be eternally surrounded by his favorite books, and Onnie silently hoped Rebecca would find her way to him in her own sort of afterlife.

Onnie searched her Grandfather's final expression and saw the joy in his features. The corners of his mouth were turned up as if Rebecca had whispered a joke into his ear, as his eyes dimmed. His left arm clutched the empty space beside him, and his right was over his heart. Onnie could only guess he'd been holding Rebecca at the end.

Sitting up, Onnie wiped the tears from her eyes and cheeks and took a deep breath. She leaned down to look Mal directly in his eyes, "Will he be safe here, truly safe?"

"Yeah, Gabe and I will arrange his funeral." Mal licked Onnie's nose and softly bumped his forehead with hers affectionately.

Then she heard his voice along their Bond. *Take Gabe and get out of here for a while. He's barely holding it together over there. Your Grandfather meant more to him than you realize.*

"Thanks, Mal." Onnie stood and leaned over her Grandfather to kiss him softly on the cheek.

"I love you, Grandpa. Thank you for believing in me." With a last quick pat on Mal's head, Onnie turned and walked to the bedroom door, stopping to rest her hand on one of Gabriel's crossed arms.

"I'll be in his library when you're ready. Take your time." She stood on her tiptoes, then she kissed his cheek, and left the room.

Onnie walked down the hall into a wide-open office filled with even more books and baubles on floor-to-ceiling shelves. The room had no windows, only books, a fireplace, and an ornate desk in one corner. The air smelled of dust, old paper, inks, and fire. Onnie inhaled, fully filling her lungs, and walked to the desk, skimming her fingers on the surface as she passed it. The room looked devoid of life without its flames softly cackling from their bed in the fireplace.

When Onnie had come over for dinner, she and her Grandfather had often sat in his library in front of the fire. They talked about literature, the ancient languages Onnie had studied in college, and the ones she hoped to explore in the future. Abbot had shown her his home collection of books, some rare or hand-painted, but all were his favorites. One of his favorite books was a hand-illustrated copy of Alice's Adventure in Wonderland, and the two of them had spent quite a few hours talking through its many hidden secrets.

She approached the largest bookcases, delicately pulled down the sizable cracked leather volume, and rubbed the front cover. Alice lay sleeping under a large tree embossed into the leather and gold leafing spelled out the title in delicate swirls and curls. Onnie gently set the book on the desk, walked over and lit the fireplace. Returning to the book, she wrapped herself in a throw blanket and curled up on the floor before the fire.

When she closed her eyes and opened the front cover, the slight creaking noise it made put a grin on her face to rival the Cheshire's. She flipped to her favorite passage in the story, but a small envelope tucked into the pages slipped into her lap. Onnie flipped it over to find it adorned with her name in the same curly script as on the front cover. She carefully set aside the book and slowly peeled open the letter flap. Inside was a beautiful butter-colored parchment with her Grandfather's delicate handwriting.

My Beautiful Granddaughter,

If you are reading this, my time has come, and I no longer walk beside you. It gladdens me that you have chosen to honor our memories with one of my favorite stories. While I'm relieved that you have found this letter, I am saddened not to have been able to tell you this in person.

I am so proud of you, my girl.

You are a wildly spirited young woman with a heart of gold and the ability to shine your light onto any situation, no matter how dark it seems. Your mother once told me she wanted to become the next Keeper, and while she would have grown into an honorable Keeper given a chance, you were destined for this and will do so brilliantly.

Do not despair that I am gone, for now is your time with our Lady, and she is so lucky to have you with her. I know you will learn to protect one another, make each other laugh, and one day change the world with your gifts.

I have left you all that I own, including this house. I know you've been living in your cottage apartment, but it makes my heart ache to see how sparse and devoid of life it is. You deserve better than I can provide, but I hope what little I can give will help where it can.

Mal and Gabriel will take exquisite care of you, and I think you will find that they will need your courage and wisdom very much before long. I raised Gabriel as my son and never considered him anything but. He has been waiting for you for many years, my dear. Follow your heart with him, just remember that a life without love is no life at all, and protect each other. He, as your Guardian, and you as his Keeper. Your balance is paramount. That being said, give him a solid kick if he needs it...from me.

As for Dany…I'd ask you to keep her out of trouble, but I'm not sure even a Keeper could manage that. She will be one of your greatest allies in the future, but always remember how fragile even the strongest bridges can be if damaged correctly.

Sam, Vanessa, Marco, Elanor, and everyone who makes Alku our home need you. Just as much as you need them. Remember to be patient with those who need it and lean on others when everything feels too challenging. Nothing can't be accomplished with the help of your family. Chosen or blood.

I love you very much and am so lucky to have had these last few months with you. Protect that outstanding sparkle of life you carry in your eyes and smile for me, beautiful girl.

My love to you, Gabe, and Dany,

Grandfather

Onnie looked up and smiled into the flames. When she clutched the letter to her chest, she closed her eyes and opened her connection to the store, releasing a torrent of happiness and thanks through their Bond.

The sound of water droplets hitting paper drew Onnie's attention, and she opened her eyes. The letter's envelope sat in her lap as water splashed onto it from above. She reached one hand to her cheek, which was wet and sticky with tears. Laughter bubbled past the tears, and she lost herself while sitting amongst her Grandfather's most prized possessions and their memories together.

Gabriel Vansand

Gabe had paid his respects to the old man and was ready to run as far and as fast as he could until he left the sadness behind him. He stepped out into the hall and ran right into Dany.

"Sorry, sis."

"No big." Dany's eyes were wide and puffy, ringed with red and matching her nose. "I didn't realize you were here already. Where's Onnie?"

"Not sure, around here somewhere," he pulled his sister to him and squeezed her tight. "How are you?"

Dany sighed and sniffled into his neck, "About as good as you're expecting me to be. I had just stepped out for some coffee."

"Did you eat?"

"Yes, brother," she kissed his cheek and stepped out of his arms, "as much as I could manage anyway."

"Good." He ran his hand through his hair and tugged it gently, "Are you going to stay?"

"Yeah," she nodded, "I'll keep him safe until we are ready to move him."

"Alright, call me if you need anything?" he leaned in and kissed her cheek.

"Duh. Go take care of Onnie. Alku will need its Keeper soon." she shivered, "There's trouble brewing. I can feel it. The attack on the shop was just the beginning."

Gabe's mouth was set in a thin line as he processed what Dany had said. When he focused, he also felt the strangeness. "Yes, I'm afraid so."

Dany smiled and left him, entering Abbot's bedroom, and Gabe heard her talking to Mal.

Gabe focused on Onnie and was surprised when he didn't feel her sadness or anger from earlier. Instead, she was feeling a mixture of peace, excitement, curiosity, and anxiety. He was coming to learn that this mix of emotions was how his Keeper reacted to books. The house still held her presence, so she must still be in Abbot's library.

He made his way there, his steps slow as his body subconsciously protected his mind. Abbot's library was not somewhere Gabe felt ready to enter yet, but he slowly pushed open the door. A fire was dancing in the fireplace, and Onnie was wrapped up in a throw blanket, rolling on the floor with laughter.

Gabe cleared his throat and took another step into the room. Finally noticing him, Onnie released her control over their Bond, and he was hit with a wave of happiness so strong he staggered back and reached for the wall to steady himself. Wide-eyed and short of breath, he stared at the tiny woman clutching a leather-bound book to her chest, a slip of paper in her fist, and a look of pure glee in her eyes.

Onnie must have felt his unease because her emotions ebbed by a fraction, and she detangled herself from the blanket and rose to her feet. She placed the book she carried on the desk as she passed it and crossed the room to approach him. When she stood before him, she reached out her hand and placed it on his cheek, her soft skin threatening to make him shiver. The green of her eyes was glassy from tears, but the color shifted to a bright blue when she looked deeply into his eyes.

"It's okay, Gabe. *I'm* okay. Grandfather left me this." She raised a letter, and he recognized Abbot's scrawling handwriting. "He loved you and was so proud to have you as his son."

Gabe closed his eyes and felt when Onnie again increased her pressure on their Bond, this time with feelings of love.

"He also told me to take care of you and to follow my heart."

When he heard her words in tandem with their feelings, he opened his eyes and searched her face for answers. Her eyes gave away nothing.

"Trust me. We'll get through this. Together." Onnie smiled at him and wrapped her arms around his waist.

Gabe pulled her closer with one hand on her back and, with the other, traced a handful of her silky hair between his fingertips. Their Bond hummed around him, and he closed his eyes, reaching for it to wrap himself inside it. Onnie smiled against him, and Gabe opened his eyes and lifted her chin to see her face. His eyes darted to her lips and back to her eyes, and when she noticed, she nodded wordlessly to him. The urge to make sure she was really still beside him won out, and he lowered his lips to hers. When she didn't pull away but deepened their kiss, he relaxed, and they both forgot all of the sadness for a few moments.

Chapter 34: Uncertainty

December 2021 - Alku | Onnie Moore

The next few days passed by Onnie in a blur of funeral arrangements and tears. Mal had kept his word, and he and Gabe did most of the planning, which had been both a blessing and a curse. It meant she had far too much time to be in her head. To keep herself and Dany busy, the two of them had sequestered themselves at Onnie's cottage, switching between packing and researching Keeper lore.

Onnie and Mal were moving into Abbot's house and out of the cottage, and for the first time in her life, she had more than two boxes and a suitcase to pack.

"Dany?" Onnie said, breaking their silent studying. A bottle of wine sat empty on the kitchen counter, and a bag of marshmallows sat between them. They each had a hefty tome on their laps, reading on the floor to the sounds of Alku's latest storm beating down on her roof.

"Hmm?" Dany mumbled.

"Can I ask you something?"

Dany looked up, confused, "Of course, what's up?"

Onnie blamed it on the wine, but she needed answers, and she would take the courage where she could get it, "It's about Gabe."

One of Dany's eyebrows raised, and she slowly closed the book in her lap, "Oh?"

"Ah…" Onnie closed her eyes, and when she opened her mouth, the words spilled out faster than she could hold them back. "I just wanted to know, if you want to tell me, I mean, you don't have to, but Gabe, Gabriel, does he, did he," she shook her head, "what is his history…with women?"

Amusement glittered in Dany's eyes, and the corners of her mouth twitched like she was trying to hold back laughter. "What do you mean?"

Onnie threw a marshmallow at her best friend and hit her right in her ripped concert tee, eliciting a smug smile.

"You know what I'm asking, Dany," she was whining, and she knew it. "I told you about my history with men. I have horrible heart direction, and I can't risk…."

"It going wrong since he's your Guardian." Dany finished for her.

Onnie nodded and set aside her book before skewering a marshmallow and sticking it in the fireplace.

"Skewer me one of those, and I'll answer anything you want," Dany said, opening another bottle of wine for them.

Onnie stabbed a second marshmallow onto the end and returned it to the flames. "I don't really know what I want to know. I guess… whatever you're willing to tell me."

"Well, there isn't much to say, honestly," Dany plopped down next to Onnie and traded her wine for a skewer, "Gabe doesn't do the whole women thing. I don't think he's had a girlfriend since high school, and even then…" Dany trailed off and sipped her wine, "It was always like he was waiting for someone."

"But he had, like, one-night stands and stuff, right? I mean, he can't have been celibate since high school."

Dany snorted, "No, he certainly wasn't. He doesn't have that many notches in his metaphorical bedpost, but no, he hasn't been alone this whole time."

"Good," Onnie said, meaning it. She was glad he'd found some comfort over the years. "I guess you answered my unasked question then. Gabe doesn't do relationships."

Dany pulled her marshmallow from the fire and waved it around to cool it, "I didn't say that."

"Well, I know, but I inferred that that's what you meant."

Dany rotated to face Onnie, "Gabe has changed."

"I just can't get hurt again, Dany. I just can't."

"I know," Dany clasped Onnie's wrist gently, "and I would never mislead you. Gabe isn't perfect. Will it be bumpy? Sure, what relationship isn't?"

"But ours is even more complicated than normal."

"Onnie, Gabe is different with you. I've seen the way he watches you. His eyes roam your face, trying to read you while he taps into your Bond. He trains harder than ever to protect you, and when you're not together, he waits for the next time you are."

Onnie held her breath, "How do you know that?"

Dany smiled, "He won't stop talking about you, and if he does, it's only because he's checking his phone to see if he missed you."

Onnie's eyes widened, and she couldn't help the smile that crept into her face, "you're sure?"

"Positive. Sam won't stop teasing him about it." Dany pulled the gooey marshmallow off the end of the stick and shoved the entire thing into her mouth.

Onnie smiled into her wine and pressed on her Bond with Mal. His purring reassurance vibrated in her mind, and she switched to Gabe. He and Mal were off somewhere planning something for the funeral, but she warmed when she felt his happiness. She pressed her curiosity to him gently, and his joy flared brighter, along with a few other muddled emotions she couldn't untangle.

She returned her focus to Dany and smiled, "Thank you for telling me."

The two of them returned to their reading, munching on marshmallows absentmindedly. Onnie was skimming a text about magical and supernatural coalitions when the word "sisters" jogged her memory.

"Hey, Dany?"

"Hm?" Dany said, still focused on the book in her lap.

"What is this reference to 'the sisters' about? I saw it at the library, too."

Dany nodded and grabbed another marshmallow from the bag. "I was wondering when you'd ask about them."

Dany was practically bouncing excitedly, and Onnie just shook her head and smiled, "Why?"

"Because I am one of them." Dany bit off half of the marshmallow in her hand and chewed with a grin.

"Okay…more info, please," Onnie said, closing her book and settling in to listen.

"Okay," Dany chewed, swallowed the other half of the sugary treat, and closed her book. "The Scholarly Light is an ancient organization pledged to assist in archival and curating the knowledge under your protection. Basically, we are the researchers, purchasers, deal-makers, etcetera, that go out and get what you and the shop need. We're less important now that the Internet and international shipping are a thing. Still, before London to Washington postal service was viable, we traveled the world collecting and bringing whatever we could find back here."

Onnie rubbed her eyes, "So, I have minions?"

Dany snorted, "Not exactly. There are fewer of us than in the past, and most are embedded within major publishing houses."

"What does that mean?"

"Ever wonder why you only get a single copy of every book? Excluding ancient and rare ones, I mean."

Onnie's brow wrinkled, "Actually, I did notice that. Every shipment we'd get was only one of everything."

"Did you notice how once you shelved the book within the shop, you never ran out of that book?" Dany grinned.

"I assumed Rebecca was shelving them faster than I could. But actually..." Onnie thought of the shop's tiny back room, "Where was she storing all the extra stock?"

Dany snickered, "You're just now noticing that?"

"Hey!" Onnie playfully shoved Dany's arm, "Not like there wasn't *other* odd stuff for me to pay attention to."

"Fair enough. There is no stock room. The shop makes what it needs. Once a book enters, there's a record of it, and it will be replaceable forever, or until the Keepership and archive itself are no more."

Onnie leaned forward and pressed her fingers to her temples. "So, what you're saying is that when I sell a copy of a book, another one will magically appear where it was out of thin air?"

"Pretty much." Dany grinned, "That's why most of our Sisters are within the publishing industry. There are contracts for how we handle purchases and profits."

"Explain," Onnie said without releasing her temples.

Dany shifted beside her, and she continued once she was more comfortable. "Alright. Basically, when a publishing house is founded, a Sister is sent there for assignment. The industry is relatively small, especially when you're higher up the management ladder, not to mention not everyone is human. A magical contract is created that states all new releases will be sent to the Keeper at publication. That single book is then added to the bookshop, and as copies are made and sold, payment will be made to the publisher on a reoccurring schedule, ensuring they get what they are owed."

Onnie looked up, "Like on-demand printing?"

"Exactly!" Dany nodded, "In fact, that's how the contract refers to it so that anyone non-magical won't see any red flags."

"And the rare books?"

Onnie wasn't sure why an infinitely generating bookstore was making her head hurt, but Mal, the talking manifestation, didn't, but it was.

"These days, anyone not in publishing mostly hunts down the rarer books and travels wherever needed to acquire them."

"Where have you traveled to then?"

"Me, oh, nowhere." Dany picked back up the heavy book she'd been reading, "I am the Alku representative."

Onnie's eyes went wide, "What does that make you? Is that your title?"

Dany cleared her throat and looked down at her book, "Ah, no. That's not my title."

"So, what is it?" Onnie prodded, softly poking her friend in the side.

Dany looked up, a blush coloring her cheeks as she glanced away, "It's Head Sister Danella Vansand, Acting Leader."

"Acting leader!" Onnie gushed, "How have I not heard of this before now?"

With a shake of her head, Dany shrugged, "It's not that big of a deal. Honestly, I'm an uber secretary. Every so often, I hand out new assignments to Sisters, ensure publishers are paid, and handle all the managerial work."

"I think I need more information." Onnie grabbed the book she'd been reading and flipped it back open, "Let me read this, and then I want to know more."

"I'll tell you anything you'd like, Keeper."

Onnie caught the strange tone of her friend's voice and looked up, "Dany?"

"Sorry, it's just a long story and one that started with Abbot." Dany hung her head again.

"Oh," Onnie closed her book and scootched closer to Dany, wrapping her arms around the woman and squeezing her, "I don't need to know tonight."

"I'll tell you. I promise, but can you give me a bit of time?"

Onnie's heart ached at the small, mousy voice her ordinarily loud and boisterous friend used. "Take all the time you need."

"Thanks, Onnie," Dany said, hugging her back.

Onnie was finally settled into her Grandfather's house, and it felt strange to think she would probably never move again. It had taken only a few hours and a long conversation with her leasing office to break her contract with minimal fees. Mal had tried to get her to use her Keeper status to get out of it entirely, but Onnie scolded him and paid the fee.

Gabe helped move the boxes she and Dany had packed to Abbot's house, and while he was picking up the last few from her cottage, she was pacing her new kitchen. After checking with both her head and her heart, she asked Mal what he thought of inviting Gabe to move in with them.

"We've got spare rooms, Mal, and he deserves this house as much as I do. Maybe more. Why shouldn't he move in?"

"I'm not saying he shouldn't, Onnie, just that you should think about it. Abbot left you a house full of stuff, and we may have moved in with essentially nothing, but Gabe has an entire apartment. Where's he going to put everything?"

"Mal, this house is far too big for just the two of us. We don't need four bedrooms. Besides, isn't he supposed to be protecting me? He can do that better by being right down the hall." Onnie said, scratching his chin.

Mal's eyes closed, and he purred, "That's cheating. Fine, but he's not taking my window box and can't sleep in our room. This tomcat wants his privacy."

Onnie laughed and hugged the little furball. "Thanks, Mal. You're the best. We'll have him take the two rooms at the end of the hall that were Rebecca's. That work for you?"

"Fine, fine. You win." Mal snuggled further into her arms and buried his face in the crook of her elbow.

"Let's go tell him."

Gabe was closing the front door with his foot, her last box in his hands, when Onnie and Mal ambushed him with their proposal. At first, Gabe was so shocked by the offer that it took a few minutes of reassurance to convince him they weren't joking.

Once he agreed, he left the house hurriedly to make his necessary arrangements. Onnie stayed behind and spent a few days cleaning out the two back bedrooms that Gabe would transform into his bedroom and office. She'd kept her Grandfather's library and bedroom for her own and even converted the cozy bedroom window seat into a place for Mal.

As the days passed and Gabe's move-in date crept closer and closer, butterflies filled the pit of Onnie's stomach. She would wake up to his intensely chipper mood every morning and fall asleep, knowing he was just a wall away. When she thought about him being just down the hall from her, what little remaining resolve she'd had to keep him as merely her Guardian crumbled away.

Gabriel Vansand

When Onnie had asked Gabe to move in with her and Mal, it had taken him a few minutes to process what she had said before he said yes. Dany was meeting him at his apartment, and they would move what he couldn't live without and leave the rest for a day when it wasn't pouring rain.

They must be crazy to do all this while planning Abbot's funeral and repairing the shop. It did mean that none of them had the time to get lost in their grief.

Mal had kept Gabe busy with funeral planning and the ceremony, and Dany had taken it upon herself to distract Onnie. Things were being checked off of lists, and everyone could grieve, but none of them were alone.

No one had been back to the bookshop since the attack, but Onnie had been checking their Bond and didn't think there was anything to worry about. On his way to his apartment, Onnie had asked him to swing by the shop and post a notice about the closure on the front door. When he got there, he saw a slip of paper already posted.

Closed for repairs and inventory stocking.
Abbot's Archive and Annals
will re-open on December 21st.
-Thanks,
Management

Gabe smiled at the memory of the old man and gently pat the shop's front door. He continued on his way, noticing the quiet streets of Alku and the irregular closures of the town's shops. Word had traveled fast of Abbot's passing among the town's human residents, and many of the magical ones had felt it when it happened. Everyone was grieving, and Gabe would do well to remember that. It wasn't just him and his little family.

"Gabe!" Dany waved from the street corner ahead of him.

Warmth filled his chest when he saw her smiling, and he hadn't realized how much he'd missed it. She was back to wearing her usual funky outfits, even if her long duster and spiked heels were in all black. Her hair was such a deep blue that it was virtually black, too, and she walked with a black umbrella trimmed in pearls that matched the simple strand around her neck.

She wrapped him in her arms with no qualms about his soaked state before kissing his cheek and holding him at arm's length.

"Gabe, where's your car?"

"My apartment. Onnie drove this morning, but she was in the middle of something when I left."

"Why didn't you bring an umbrella, you idiot," she threaded her arm through his and led the way, "at least you're just in jeans and remembered your jacket, though any longer, and I'm sure you'd have been soaked all the way through."

"It wasn't raining quite this bad when I left, but yeah, I've had brighter moments. My head has been a little absent with all the funeral planning lately."

Dany nodded, but neither of them spoke about it.

After walking a block in silence, Dany bumped her hip with his and smiled, "So…you're moving in with Onnie…"

Try as he might, Gabe couldn't hold back the stupid grin from spreading across his face. "I swear the floor dropped from under me when she asked, Dany. Never in a million years did I expect her to ask me that."

"I did."

He turned and looked at his sister's smug expression and confident posture, "Did she talk to you about it?"

"Nope, but she's in love with you."

Gabe froze and turned his sister to face him, "What did you say?"

"Oh, she doesn't know it yet." Dany placed her hand over his jacket where his heart was currently trying to beat its way free, "but you do, and you don't know how difficult that is for her."

"I—" Gabe closed his mouth like a guppy and let Dany drag him back to walking.

Did he know that Onnie was in love with him? How would he know that? Their Bond wasn't that finely tuned yet. He'd know when she was feeling love, but she could be reacting to his shirt, or the weather, or anything else around when they were together. He'd have no idea if it was because of him or not. He slipped into his head and brushed against their Bond, smiling like a fool when she felt him, and her happiness spiked.

"So, lover boy," Dany teased, breaking his mental flirting, "has she told you anything about what she and I have found in our research?"

"No, we haven't spent much time together talking recently," he felt his sister's witty comment before she spoke, "and that's because most of our time together has been physical training or moving boxes. There's not been a lot of time to talk."

Dany laughed, "Oh, yeah, I bet. Only time for grunting."

Gabe groaned, "Sister, mine, don't make me extend your training next week to include swordplay." He smirked at her, and she stuck her lip out to pout. "But really, tell me what you two found."

"Oh!" Her demeanor quickly reverted to the bubbly one she had when discussing research. "After the attack, she asked me to help her learn as much about Keeper history as possible, so we've been pouring over old books and ledgers."

"I hadn't realized she'd been back to the shop."

"She hasn't. I've been bringing anything I can find from the library. She's not ready to go back yet."

"Neither am I," he admitted quietly.

"We've found tons of stuff!" Dany said, her excitement increasing the speed of her voice. "There were some journals and histories of past Keepers and a few practical ritual books, and we even found one on the intricacies of the Keeper and Guardian relationship, though neither of us has read that one yet."

Gabe raised an eyebrow while he pulled his keys from his pocket and unlocked his front door.

"Don't give me that look. I have no idea what's in it, but it's at Abbot's, so ask Onnie for it." She shed her dripping jacket and umbrella by the door before walking into his kitchen and making coffee for them.

"Has she learned anything useful then?" he asked, stripping off his wet clothes down to his boxers. He saw Dany hesitate out of the corner of his eye as she pulled mugs from his cabinet, "Dany?"

"She's frightening, Gabe." Dany's voice shook, and she shivered.

"What do you mean?" he growled.

"I mean, I'm glad she's on our side. I've seen what Abbot could do, but Gabe," she turned to face him, "Onnie is on an entirely different level."

"She's the Keeper of Prophecy, and we knew that," he said, chucking his wet clothes into the dryer.

"No, Gabe, if she were to lose control…" Dany trailed off.

"What?"

When she finally met his eyes, they were full of fear, "no one would be able to stop her."

They stared at each other for a few minutes before Dany looked away and he finished turning on the dryer.

Chapter 35: Unity

December 2021 - Alku | Onnie Moore

Onnie stood in the kitchen up to her elbows in flour. The sound of tinkling keys and the front door shutting informed her of Gabe and Mal's return.

The two had walked back to Gabe's old apartment through the cold December air to pick up a few things he had forgotten the week earlier. Dany would take over his lease and keep most of his furniture, making the spur-of-the-moment change considerably easier. Over time, they would no doubt make changes to the house, but for now, both Onnie and Gabe took comfort in the well-known surroundings.

Onnie had spent the morning in her Grandfather's library, where she stumbled across an old cookbook of her Grandmother's. When she flipped through the cracked yellowing pages and found a sugar cookie recipe that looked easy enough to make, she carefully photocopied it and began making the dough.

The sound of footsteps had preceded Gabe before he came around the corner, and she looked up from the mixing bowl in her hands.

"Hey, Cat." He stood in the doorway with one hand behind his back and a subtle blush on his cheeks.

"Hi, did you get what you needed?" Onnie said as she pulled the wooden spoon from the bowl and set it on the counter so she could knead the dough with her hands

"Yeah, all done." Gabe walked to her and bent to kiss her cheek softly. "Paperwork is all finalized. I officially live here, and Dany will be..." he looked at the clock over the stove, "probably already soaking in the huge tub by now."

Smiling, Onnie detangled her fingers from the sticky dough and wiped them off with a towel. "So then, why are you acting so squirrelly? Are you having second thoughts?"

"Not at all." Gabe pulled a single red tulip from behind his back and rested it against her lips. "Thank you, Cat. The old man would be proud of you, and I know how hard it was for you to invite me here to share a home with you."

Blushing a deep crimson, Onnie took the tulip and looked down towards her feet. "I hope he thinks so. I wasn't sure about changing the bookshop's name, but it seemed to fit."

Tilting her chin up with his fingers, Gabe quickly kissed her lips, "He'd love it."

Onnie nodded and rummaged around under the counter for a vase. "What's the plan for tomorrow?"

Gabe walked around the island and sat on one of the bar stools. "The car will pick us up at nine, and we'll drive to the cemetery first. You'll have as much time as you want with him to say your goodbyes at the end. We can stay as long as you want, and when you're ready, we will come back here, and I've ordered a nice dinner to celebrate his life."

As she settled the tulip into the vase, Onnie looked up surprised, "When did you have time to do that?"

Gabe reached across the counter with a warm smile and rested his hand on Onnie's. "Cat, this is important to both of us. Don't feel guilty, please."

"How did you know I—"

"Our Bond has grown quite a bit in the last few weeks, and your discomfort is rolling off you in waves."

Frowning, Onnie tucked a strand of hair behind her ears, "I just feel like I should have done more to help with the planning."

"You've done enough. The old man would be glowing if he could see what you've accomplished with this house and how much you've learned from what Dany told me the other day. Besides, I know the next few days will be hard on you, and after tomorrow, you'll need to focus on the shop. Think of this as my gift to him, helping you ease into your new role as Keeper."

With a heavy sigh, Onnie covered the cookie dough with plastic wrap and placed it in the fridge to rest. "Where's Mal?"

Gabe snorted, "Hiding, I'd assume."

Onnie cocked her head in a puzzled way.

"Nothing to worry about. He's just embarrassed."

"What happened?"

"Let's just say he had a run-in with a frisky feline and wasn't prepared for it."

Now, it was Onnie's turn to snort.

Shut up, Gabe. I know where you sleep.

Onnie and Gabe laughed, no doubt the sound drifting to wherever Mal was sulking. Gabe opened his arms, beckoning Onnie to him as she crossed the kitchen. He pulled her to him, and they laughed until they were shaking.

You two are both dead. Seriously, it's not funny.

Mal skipped into the kitchen and hopped onto the barstool beside them. "I think you will both wake up with a dead mouse in your beds." Mal turned and sat with his back to them.

"Oh, Mal." Onnie scooped the pouting cat up into her arms and rubbed his belly. "You're one hell of a tomcat. Why wouldn't the ladies throw themselves at you?"

Onnie stopped petting him, and Mal grabbed her hand with his paw to place it back on his belly. "You're not done making it up to me."

Onnie giggled, "Alright, you little Prince," and resumed her petting and leaned back into Gabe's arms.

"What's for dinner?" Mal mumbled with closed eyes through a purr.

Tilting her head back on Gabe's shoulder, Onnie looked up at him. "What do you feel like?"

Gabe's eyes twinkled with mischief. "Hmm..." He began leaving feather-light kisses along the underside of her jaw.

"Oh, gross man, get a room," Mal said as he twisted himself from Onnie's grasp and landed softly on the floor beside them. "I think my eyes are burning."

"Thanks, Mal. Love you too." Onnie grabbed and chucked a dishtowel from the counter at Mal's receding backside.

Hey, you're hot, him…not so much. I saw his bare ass on accident the other day, and I'll have nightmares until I die.

"At least my ass isn't hairy!" Gabe called after Mal.

That's what you think.

Chuckling softly to himself, Gabe rotated Onnie within his arm, "I am so going to shave him in his sleep one day."

"Oh god, only if you're prepared to live with him afterward." leaning on her toes, Onnie kissed Gabe's nose, "Have you decided what you'd like for dinner yet?"

"I've come to find something rare and exquisite that I've grown rather fond of lately. Trouble is…it's a rather hard catch." Gabe gave Onnie a sideways smile and bent down to nuzzle her neck.

"Hard to catch, huh? Sounds like a lot of work." Onnie tried to suppress a shiver, not wanting him to see how much he was affecting her.

"But well worth the effort," Gabe ran his hand up Onnie's back, tangled his fingers in her hair, and gently bent her head back further, "and the wait."

"Mmmm…" Onnie's knees shook slightly, and she inwardly groaned at losing her self-control. "I think…if it's as wonderful as you say it is…" Onnie gently pushed back from Gabe's chest, "Then you should have to work for it."

Onnie stepped from his arms, blew him a kiss, and skipped out of the kitchen. She bounded into her bedroom and quietly closed the door, noticing Mal wasn't in the window and instead was likely in her Grandfather's office.

In one of the books Dany had found a few days prior, a former Keeper had hypothesized that a Keeper's ability to project themselves into the shop spiritually might also be theoretically possible outside of the shop if the Keeper were skilled enough.

Onnie had been practicing, and after a few days, she had finally managed to do it. Only she wasn't just a formless part of her consciousness when she'd succeeded. She was also able to project a visual of herself into the space. It had come in handy when she wanted to prank Gabe or Mal and, as of yet, hadn't gotten old.

She closed her eyes and focused on Gabe. He was still in the kitchen at the bar, running his fingers through his hair in apparent frustration. His eyes glanced at the kitchen clock, and a wicked smile flashed across his features. Even though she felt guilty since she was essentially spying on him, when he stood and had to readjust himself, she bit her lip.

She wasn't sure when it had happened, but Gabe had pushed past all her defensive walls. Their emotions were connected, and he couldn't lie to her that way, but seeing how he thought of her when she wasn't beside him set her mind at ease and reinforced that she'd made the right choice.

Onnie reached for their Bond, *Gabriel,* she called with her mind. She watched Gabe rush to look for her, starting with the library, where Mal was in the process of bathing his nether regions.

"Aw, man!" Gabe covered his eyes. "Dude, can't you do that somewhere else!?"

"You barged in on me, man."

"Gross." Gabe stepped back out of the library.

"Close the door!" Mal shouted.

"Gladly!" Gabe slammed the door. "Where are you, little Cat?"

Onnie projected herself, this time with her body visible, as one of her feet disappeared around the corner leading into Gabe's bedroom.

"Cat, are you playing with me?" Gabe growled.

Onnie returned to her body and shook her head. A bath sounded incredible, and she made her way into the attached bathroom and turned on the bathtub while making sure both doors were closed so Gabe wouldn't hear the water running.

She'd learned a lot in the last few grief-ridden weeks, which made her proud. Everything she'd read about Keepers and their powers indicated that, occasionally, a Keeper could do one of the things she was able to. None of the evidence she'd found had suggested that any *single* Keeper could do *all* of them. So far, she'd been unable to figure out why she was different, but that wouldn't stop her from looking.

After a warm bath.

Gabriel Vansand

Gabe began walking down the hall to his bedroom, fully knowing Cat would not be in there. He was aware that she was playing with him through their Bond, but she was becoming so proficient that most of the time, he couldn't tell what was real and what wasn't. He just knew she was doing it.

When he opened his door, a small part of him hoped Onnie was lying on his bed waving at him with a giddy grin on her face. But he'd learned that nothing was that easy when it came to her. There was no one in his room, as he'd expected, and he pushed the heel of his hand against his groin with a low growl. Their games may have driven him crazy, both body and mind, but he loved them nonetheless.

The woman was clever, and she was getting stronger.

In just a few weeks, she'd grown from being able to observe the Bond and telepathically talk to him and Mal to projecting herself into the world with a visual presence, not just a spiritual one. Dany had a right to be scared. Onnie was stronger than anyone expected, and they would collectively need to discuss that, but right now, she was really starting to rile him up, and that's all he cared about.

Gabe walked to his closet and bent to pull off his shoes and socks.

Gabriel... Onnie's voice whispered along their Bond, *Have you given up?*

Oh no, little Cat, I have far from given up. Gabe focused deeper on their Bond, and from her highly relaxed state, he knew she was in her bathtub. *But you enjoy that soak of yours.... I'll be with you momentarily.*

Cheater, she replied with a soft laugh.

He pulled his shirt off over his head, stepping away from their connection as he did. He emptied his pockets, placed everything onto his dresser, and left his room searching for his all too clever Keeper.

Onnie Moore

Onnie closed her eyes and waited for Gabe to make his way to her room. Even though it was unrealistic, she was ready for their feelings of loss to fade. Gabe had been supportive through everything, and somehow, they had managed to deal with two apartment leases and move two houses into one home, all while he planned her Grandfather's funeral.

Wincing, Onnie felt guilty over how much work he had put into the funeral and how little she had. She'd tried to order flowers, but between her and the bookshop's sadness over Abbot's death, she'd been unable to do it. Elanor had reassured Onnie that she'd take care of everything, and Gabe had finalized the details while she had buried herself in books.

Someone had to tell the rest of the family about Abbot's death, and Onnie managed, but it had been hard. Her Mom had been quiet when Onnie told her, but after three hours, they had finished a box of tissues each and two pots of hot tea.

Even worse than telling everyone of his death, Onnie had to tell them not to come for his funeral. None of them had been close to Abbot, so they'd be coming more to support her than to say goodbye to him. Not wanting to burden her brothers, who had their own lives, Onnie had told them she'd be okay, and they didn't need to fly in. On top of that, with whoever had attacked the shop still a threat, Onnie wanted her family to stay away from Alku until she'd dealt with him. She promised to plan a trip for everyone to visit her in the spring, and they would see her and Abbot then.

That meant that Onnie was going to be alone tomorrow.

She'd had such a short time with her Grandfather, and she knew she was being greedy, but she had wanted more. He had more to teach her. There were more chess games for Onnie to watch or cups of tea to drink with him and Sam. It was unfair, and she was still bitter about him being taken from her early.

There was a soft knock at her bathroom door before Gabe opened it slowly. She quickly wiped the tears from her eyes as she grinned at the man in her doorway. Gabe had removed his shoes, socks, and shirt, leaving him in only his well-worn jeans. His hair was tousled like he'd been pulling on it in frustration, and he was unmistakably aroused. Finding her way to his eyes, she saw his soften as he noticed her tears, and she felt the subtle pressure that indicated he was searching their Bond.

When he found what he'd been looking for, he crossed the bathroom, squatted next to the bathtub, and pulled her forehead to his lips.

"You're getting stronger, Cat. You had me there for a second."

Onnie nodded and lowered her eyes as she reached out to play with the bubbles floating on top of the water.

"Cat, look at me," Gabe whispered.

Onnie swallowed her grief and looked up and saw the unshed tears sparkling in his eyes.

"I miss him too."

Onnie sniffled as Gabe stood up and removed his jeans. When he got to his boxers, he paused and only continued once she nodded. She was heartsick and needed to feel the warmth the man in front of her offered.

Gabe gently slid her forwards in the oversized bath and got in behind her. She turned and snuggled closer into his arms and closed her eyes.

"Are you hungry?" Gabe asked as he began stroking her hair.

"A little, Chinese?"

"Mmm.... You do know how to make a man drool."

Onnie tilted her head and looked up at Gabe, "Over Chinese food? You, Sir, are too easy."

"I didn't say it was the only thing to make me drool."

He lowered his lips to hers and softly claimed her mouth. The tenderness he expressed as he pulled her closer brought fresh tears to her eyes. She didn't know how she'd gotten so lucky as to find him, but Onnie knew she'd do anything to keep him.

"Cat?" Gabe whispered against her lips.

"Mmm?"

"Pass me your washcloth and soap before I can't control myself."

Onnie laced her fingers into Gabe's hair and returned his lips to hers. "What if I don't care?"

Growling, Gabe deepened their kiss for a few more minutes before he pulled back to look into her eyes. "Pass me the soap, Cat, please?"

With a quick kiss on his cheek, Onnie reached to the foot of the tub and grabbed the soap and cloth.

"You know some girls would be hurt by your rejection."

"I am not rejecting you, Cat, and you know that." Gabe reached his hand out for the bottle and cloth she held, "But not many women have a boyfriend who is intimately linked to their emotions and knows when they need pampering versus passion."

Onnie smirked, "And not many men would care if they did. Thank you."

Gabe soaped up the towel and nudged Onnie forward. "We have to go back to the bookshop soon, Cat."

With a heavy sigh, Onnie nodded. "I know, I've put it off too long. She's fine, and I've told her what's going on, so there are no secrets, but she's grieving as much as we are. I'm not sure she'd have even let us in before now."

"I know. She needed the space, too." Gabe draped the washcloth over the bath's side and began kneading the knots from Onnie's shoulders.

"Mmm…." Onnie closed her eyes and let her head fall forward. "That feels amazing."

"Then let's make it feel even better, come on." Gabe stood up and wrapped a towel around his waist. Stepping from the tub, he offered

Onnie his hand. With a shy blush, she stood and stepped into his arms as he reached for a towel to wrap around her back. Gabe carefully dried her off, not missing a drop, and then sent her to the bedroom.

"Let me clean up here, and I'll be right in."

"Okay. I'll check with Mal on the Chinese food plan, too."

Onnie slipped from the bathroom and flopped on the four-poster bed in the middle of the room. *Mal?*

Yeah, girl?

Chinese food for dinner sound good?

Blegh, that crap is too spicy. Can't we do sushi?

Mal, we had sushi two days ago. Not all of us can survive on fish alone.

Aw, come on, fish rocks!

Mal....

Fine, fine, fine. Chinese is good for me. I'll snag some orange chicken, I guess.

Okay, I'll order in a few minutes.

You feel better after your bath?

Yeah, stay out of the bedroom, though...there's a definite lack of clothing.

Gross, yeah, I'll be in here if you need me.

Thanks, Mal. Love you.

Love you too, girl.

"Mal said Chinese is okay," Onnie shouted into the bathroom.

Gabe stuck his head around the bathroom door frame. "Want me to order it now or after your massage?"

"Massage first, please, if you're not starving."

"Sounds like a plan. Be right there." Gabe ducked back into the bathroom.

Onnie snuggled down into the overstuffed duvet and smiled contentedly.

"Tomorrow's going to suck, but at least today hasn't been that bad. Miss you, Grandpa," she said to no one with a smile.

Chapter 36: Pride

December 2021 - Alku | Onnie Moore

Onnie pulled her jacket collar higher around her neck and slipped closer to Gabe's side as they walked up the grassy hill. The gray mist that enveloped Alku on most days was nowhere to be found, replaced with clear skies and a shining sun. This made the air feel freezing, and Onnie could see her breath. Gabe wrapped one arm around her shoulder and pulled her closer to him while Mal bounded along in front of them, gabbing at Dany.

"I'm assuming you know where the mausoleum is, right?" Onnie asked through chattering teeth.

"Yeah, we are almost there. It's just over this hill. You've never seen it?" Gabe asked, slightly shocked.

"Ah, no? Should I have?"

"Well, not necessarily, but all of the most recent Keepers and most of their Guardians have been buried here. Eternally side by side."

"Oh, I guess it just never came up. Grandfather never mentioned it."

Gabe nodded, "It was probably not an easy topic for him. Dany knows more of the history than I do. I'm sure if you ask, she'll tell you."

As the four of them crested atop the hill, they looked out over a spectacular garden. Set away from the rest of the cemetery was a giant hedge maze that, from their vantage point, they could see had a massive stone building at its heart. Rows of rose bushes lined the perimeter of the labyrinth, and a small stone path led down to the entrance and looked to run through it.

"Oh, my, it's amazing!" Onnie gasped.

"Neat, isn't it," Mal said, rubbing against her calf.

"It really is," Dany said with a sad smile.

Onnie looked sideways at her friend. Dressed in all black, Dany wore a long trench coat, belted at her waist, and wedge heels that went to her mid-thigh. She had been quiet most of the day, only stopping to advise Onnie on shoes and borrow lip gloss. Onnie could feel her suffering as if they had their own Bond.

"I see now why you insisted on the flats. Thanks for that. Heels in that maze would have been killer."

Onnie winced at her choice of words. Her Bond with Gabe warmed as he reassured her, and Dany reached over and grabbed Onnie's hand. The four of them stood and looked out over the beauty that was established to celebrate death.

After a few minutes, Gabe sniffled and kissed Onnie's temple, "Come on, we've got a maze to traverse."

Mal stepped forward and led the way as the three of them held hands and followed.

"Wait, do you know how to get to the center?" Onnie said, slightly worried.

"Yeah, the old man used to come here relatively often. He said he liked the gardens." Gabe smiled to himself.

As they passed through the maze's entrance, Onnie felt a deep calm sink into her bones. Following along next to her friends, they passed through twists and turns, going deeper into the heart of the maze. Fifteen minutes later, they emerged into an open clearing filled with twisted jasmine vines and hyacinths.

Onnie took a deep breath and smiled, the beauty surrounding them distracting her. She overlooked the far side of the space at first. A few dozen people quietly bowing their heads blocked a large stone mausoleum.

"Oh," she clutched her chest, their presence startling her from her appreciation of the carefully planned and tended plant life. "Um… hello." Onnie looked over her shoulder at Gabe quizzically, but he just shrugged his shoulders.

Mal?

Don't worry, Onnie. They want to pay their respects to Abbot, too.

She picked up Mal, soaking up his silent support and scratching behind his ears.

"Hello, everyone. I'm Onnie."

A ripple went through the group as they all looked up at her and nodded. Movement caught Onnie's attention on the left as Elanor stepped out from the crowd and approached her.

"Hello, Elanor. It is good to see you again."

Elanor stopped in front of Onnie and Mal and lowered her head. "Hello, Keeper. We have all gathered here to pay our respects to Abbot if you'd let us."

Shocked at her question, Onnie tipped Mal from her arms and pulled Elanor into a hug. Elanor faltered and then slowly wrapped her arms around Onnie and rested her head on her shoulder.

"Elanor, you're most welcome to be here. All of you are. Grandfather would be honored."

A squeak escaped Elanor as sobs started to wrack her petite body. Onnie stroked her hair and patted her back while she whispered words of comfort. With a sniffle, Elanor leaned back and wiped her eyes.

"I'm sorry, Keeper."

"No, don't you apologize." Onnie placed her palms on Elanor's cheeks and tipped her face up. "Everyone has the right to grieve, and I know Grandfather would have agreed, though he would have been sad it was over him."

Elanor nodded, brushed off some dirt she'd left on Onnie's shoulder, and stood up straight. She turned to the group in front of her, who now stood silently with wide eyes and open mouths.

"Everyone, this is our new Keeper. This is Onnie. You all know Gabriel, her Guardian, and down there is Mal."

Gabe stepped up to position himself next to Onnie and nodded to the group. "We'd be honored if you'd join us in saying goodbye to Abbot." Gabe gestured forward and placed his other hand on Onnie's lower back. "Onnie, care to lead the way?"

Inclining her head to the group, Onnie reached back and retook Dany's hand, and Gabe opened his arms for Mal to jump into. The four of them lead the procession into the mausoleum.

Inside the small anti-chamber were alcoves filled with sleeping stone figures. Their faces were lit by candlelight, making them look serene and peaceful. Small brass plaques were under each one, and Onnie glanced at a few as they walked past. She was surprised when she realized the past Keepers hadn't always been human.

You okay? Mal asked.

Yeah, it's beautiful. I just wasn't expecting it.

Keepers are treated with the most respect possible. They are sent into the afterlife wrapped in beauty.

Onnie stepped further inside and admired all the intricate carvings lining the walls. The floor was inlaid with a gold and marble mosaic, and the ceiling was painted to mimic the bright blue sky outside above it. The space seemed to be bigger on the inside than the exterior suggested, and the perimeter walls continued off into the distance farther than Onnie could see, with stone shelves and solemn sleeping stone figures. Too soon, they stepped through an archway and into a side room.

In the center of the second room was a vast stone dais that Abbot's body was resting on with gently crossed hands.

He looks like he's sleeping. Onnie said to Gabe.

Abbot's body will remain as it is now, preserved for a few months. He'll be here for you and anyone who desires his wisdom during the transition period. Then, he'll become stone like the others, remaining in this chamber for as long as you live.

Until I replace him, Onnie stated factually.

Yes.

What about his Guardian?

Onnie felt Gabe tense at her side, and his step faltered for half a second. *He will not have a place here.*

Onnie nodded and approached the dais.

"Hello, Grandfather." Mal jumped softly from Gabe's arms to sit at the old man's feet as Onnie placed her hands on the lip of the stone and traced the carvings. "Gabriel's here too, and Dany and Mal. There are many people I don't know as well, but they are all here to see you. We miss you." Onnie quickly wiped a tear from her cheek as Elanor stepped beside her.

"Would you like Dany and me to handle the ceremony, Keeper?"

With a nod, Onnie squeezed Elanor's hand and stepped back into Gabe's stiff embrace. Onnie looked up at Gabe only to find him closed off and distant.

Gabriel?

Not now, please, Cat.

Onnie stiffened but didn't have the emotional energy to be offended by Gabriel's mood swings, but he was entitled to them. At the foot of Abbot's dais, but still a step above the main floor level, were two slightly warn hollows in the stone floor. They looked about six feet long, and their surface was polished and smooth. Elanor turned and stepped over them and faced the mourners with her back to the dais.

"We've all come today to say goodbye to one of the greatest Keepers this world has ever known. Abbot spent the last sixty-five years being friends with many of us." She gestured to herself by placing her hand over her heart.

"A Father to some of us," she rested her hand gently on Gabe and Dany's cheeks.

"And just as importantly, a Keeper that no one hesitated to stand with. Abbot was a light in this world that all races and species could respect and admire. Knowing our new Keeper, Onnie, has succeeded him," she gestured to Onnie, "gives the whole magical community great peace of mind and hope."

Stepping back, Elanor held her hand out for Gabe. "Gabriel, will you please do us the honors of leading the Transference?"

Gabe squeezed Onnie's shoulders reassuringly and leaned down to kiss her on the cheek.

It'll be okay, Cat. Trust me.

Confusion creased Onnie's brow as Gabe took Elanor's outstretched hand.

"Elanor, do you or another hold the honor to stand as representation for the nymphs?"

"I do."

"And who will stand for the day walkers?" Gabe asked the crowd.

"I will," a small voice cracked, and Vanessa stepped forward.

"And for the sanguiste?" Gabe called.

"I stand for those who cannot." Said a voice from the front row, and Onnie turned to see the owner of A Shot in the Dark, Anton, looking solemn.

Gabe nodded to the man.

"And who from the Scholarly Light?" Gabe asked.

“I stand for the Sisters of Light,” Dany said, squeezing Onnie’s hand before going to stand next to Elanor.

“I will represent the forest and those Kin within it,” a sweet, elderly female voice said from the group. Onnie didn’t recognize her, but her lime-green eyes were captivating, as was the hummingbird fluttering just above her shoulder.

Gabe’s eyes twinkled when he looked at the older woman but then hardened, and he returned his gaze to the rest of the crowd. “Are there any other sanctuary city representatives in attendance?”

A beautiful woman with green hair and porcelain skin stepped forward, “I am here on behalf of the Pacific City.”

She stepped back, and a larger man with a portly belly and magnificently styled mustache took her place. “I have come from the Mediterranean as representation.” His voice was deep and made Onnie’s rib cage feel like it vibrated within her.

“Are there others who wish to act as witnesses?” Gabe asked after the room had been silent for a minute, and it was clear no one else wished to speak up. No one replied, and Gabe nodded.

“Is there anyone here who would oppose this Transference?” he questioned.

Onnie looked towards the crowd of people gathered in the stone building. All but Gabe and the others who spoke for their people remained with their heads bowed.

Gabe turned to face the dais behind him and held his hands out to Mal. “Mal, will you allow us to assist with the former Keeper’s shroud?”

Mal bowed his head, and Dany turned to Vanessa, and the two women unfolded a sheet that shimmered as if it were made of diamonds before draping it atop the sleeping figure.

“Dany, would you please hand me the athame you have carried for Maldwyn?” Gabe requested as Vanessa returned to her place. Dany placed a small dagger covered in blood-red jewels with an onyx blade in Gabe's hand and then returned to beside Vanessa.

Onnie, do you trust me? Mal asked in Onnie's mind.

Yes, Mal, but what's going on?

There's a ritual that must be performed to transfer the remaining power from one Keeper to another. We didn't want to worry you.

You didn't want to worry me? What does that mean?

If you trust us, you will be okay. Please believe in us.

Scowling, Onnie returned her attention to Gabe and the blindfold he now held in his other hand.

"Keeper, step forward, please," Gabe beckoned.

Onnie hesitated.

"Keeper, please." Gabe's eyes pleaded with Onnie's before she took one small step forward. Then another. And another. "Turn around, please, and face your Grandfather."

Onnie did as she was told.

"Place your hands over his shroud on his forehead, please."

Once again, she did what was asked of her.

As Gabe began speaking, he also began to blindfold Onnie. To her relief, he spoke in a dialect of Latin she understood.

"Do you, the incoming Keeper of all knowledge in this world, past and yet to come, good and evil, vow to uphold and honor your sacred calling to safeguard and aid those represented here before you and those not?"

"I do," Onnie replied in Latin, with more fear than she was proud of.

"Do you, Keeper, trust me as your Guardian to protect and care for you? To balance your emotions, anticipate your pain and join you in triumphs."

"I do," Onnie said with less fear in her voice than the previous question's answer. But not by much.

Gabe finished tying the knot that secured the blindfold in place and spoke to Onnie and Mal along their Bonds. *Help her.*

Of course, Mal agreed. *Onnie, you need to open your Bonds. Reach as far as you can towards your Grandfather. Imagine him as he was before he fell. Reach along your connection and wrap his powers around you like a cocoon. Envision him surrounding you in his arms and passing his soul into you.*

I—

Don't think about it. Trust me. Just do it.

Closing her eyes behind the blindfold, Onnie did as Mal asked. She reached out and envisioned her Bond extending through her fingertips and into her Grandfather. Searching, she found the slightest glimmer and gently coaxed it into her hand. As she gently pulled it toward her, she wrapped it around herself tighter and tighter.

When she pulled the last thread and heard it snap, she stood motionless and waited for her next direction.

Instead, she felt Gabe lean down to her ear and whisper, "I love you."

And then she felt the ruby and onyx dagger plunge into her heart.

Chapter 37: Trust

December 2021 - Alku | Gabriel Vansand

Gabe had to stay strong for the woman he was holding on her feet, head slumped forward, a dagger through her chest. He couldn't let his emotions get the better of him, so he gritted his teeth and pushed his fear and tears away.

Mal, watch over her.

Gabe scooped Onnie into his arms and laid her at the foot of the st one dais, mimicking the previous Keeper's position. He brushed a few stray strands of her wild hair from her face and lay beside her in the second stone hollow.

I've got you covered. Bring her back to us. Mal said as he jumped down to sit between Gabe and Onnie's shoulders.

Gabe took Onnie's hand in his own, closed his eyes, and reached for his Bond.

Immediately, he felt Onnie's confusion and anger pouring from her with enough force to knock the wind from him and nearly split his head in two. Gabe focused on the shimmering thread that would lead him to Onnie and followed it across the void. It only took a few minutes for him to feel his consciousness leave his physical body.

Cat? Cat, it's me. Where are you? I've come to take you home. Gabe could feel Onnie's reluctance as she continued to shield herself from view. *I'm sorry, Cat, I didn't have a choice. The Transference is nearly as old as the Keeper's inception. "Thou must forge the Bond between Keeper and Guardian in blood and bone. Together, their solidarity shall be reborn to shine as a light for all who see it."*

Gabe felt a flicker of hope from behind him. When he turned and saw Onnie standing with her arms wrapped around her middle and the onyx dagger protruding from her chest, *Cat I—* he reached out to her, but she vanished.

With a sigh, Gabe realized too late she was a projection. That she could even use her power in this plane was a surprise. *Please, Cat, let me explain.*

Why should I? Onnie's cracking voice drifted through the abyss. *You killed me, Gabriel. I— I don't even know what to say to you.*

I know. Mal and I couldn't tell you about the Transference, or we would have. It represents our Bond, and you needed to give me your life with blind faith. Cat, please, can I at least explain to your face?

Onnie shimmered before him with her hands rubbing metaphorical goosebumps from her upper arms, the dagger still in her heart. *Fine.*

Thank you, Cat. Gabe took one step forward, and Onnie took two back.

Stay away from me, Gabriel. She raised one hand to ward him off. *You've already murdered me once. I won't let you shatter any more of me.*

Dropping his arm, Gabe slid his hands into his pockets to avoid reaching for her.

She looked away from him as unshed tears began to fill her eyes. *You wanted to explain, so do it.*

Gabe looked down at his feet. *The Transference is nearly as old as the first Keeper. Many, many Keepers ago, the duty was given to an older woman who had no one to guard her back. She was vulnerable, weak, and a liability. The entity you know as the bookshop today wasn't fully formed yet, so there was no Link either.*

When the Keeper's death came at the hands of a jealous being, the shop's entity decided to create the line of Guardians.

The next Keeper was located by the same process you were, and the shop found a suitable replacement. Only it had a problem. That replacement wouldn't be born for three hundred years, and they would be even more unable to protect themselves than the previous Keeper.

Why? Onnie interrupted. *Was someone going to stab them in the back, too?* She looked down at the hilt of the onyx dagger. *Oh, sorry, the heart.*

Gabe growled and continued his history lesson. *Yes. The next Keeper would be born blind.*

He saw Onnie stiffen and look away.

So, the entity reached out to find the first Guardian and, in its infinite wisdom, found someone with whom the Keeper would trust with his life. But the entity was young and didn't foresee that while the Keeper had been imbued with the ability to tap into the entity's consciousness, the Guardian had not, so he became greedy.

His judgment became clouded with the need to be just as crucial as the Keeper. That Guardian failed to see they already were, but it was too late. One night, while the Keeper was sleeping, the Guardian snuck into his chambers and stabbed him through the heart. The entity was furious.

It anticipated the evil from the outside world but didn't see it from within its own ranks. Onnie said matter of factly.

Correct. As I said, the entity was still young and, like a child, wanted to believe that beings were inherently good and incorruptible, but it was wrong.

It created the Transference. It is a ceremony by which representatives from various walks of life would gather to witness the transfer of power from one fallen Keeper to another...and the same moment when a Guardian is at their lowest. The moment they murder their Keeper while they have their blind trust.

Onnie began to pace as she ran her fingers through her hair. Gabe struggled not to smile. Her habitual actions while she was trying to solve a puzzle were adorable.

But wait, what good does that do the bookshop? Their new Keeper is now dead. Killed by the hands of their Guardian. She stopped and looked at Gabe. *Right?* Her eyes narrowed at him, and he sighed inwardly in relief.

Gabe smiled at the most amazing woman he'd ever known. *No, little Cat. The rest of the Transference has yet to happen. Right now, we are both in a sort of stasis. Mal is watching over our bodies while our consciousness is mingling. Our Bonds are intertwining, their connection point strengthening.*

To finish the Transference and the bonding process, thereby allowing us both to continue living, I need to trust you now.

Gabe took a few tentative steps toward Onnie, and when she didn't back up, he reached out his hand to her. *It's not enough for you to trust me. I need to trust you, too.*

Onnie staggered back. *No, I know what you're going to say, and I won't do it.* A look of horror filled Onnie's eyes as she finally understood. *You can't ask me to do that.*

Gabe smiled at the brilliant Keeper before him. *You don't have a choice, Cat. You must pull the knife from your body and plunge it into mine instead.*

But why, why is that the test? Wouldn't I want to stab you? You killed me!

Did I? Maybe I'm lying to you right now. Maybe if you remove the dagger, it causes your death to become permanent. How do you know? Maybe I've made this whole story up.

Onnie disappeared and reappeared behind Gabe. *I'm real this time.*

Gabe turned and nodded slightly. *I know. After all this time, you'd think you'd realize you can't hide from me. I'll always find you, Cat. You're part of me, my soul. Always.*

Onnie looked up into his eyes. He knew she was searching him for a lie, but she couldn't find one. With a heavy sigh, she stepped back. *Alright, let's get this over with.*

Gabe nodded and returned his hands to his pockets. *You must listen carefully to me, Cat—the decision to believe me, or not, is up to you.*

What do I have to do? Onnie gestured to the dagger. *Can I just pull it out and stab you?*

When you pull the dagger out, you will save your own life. You have a choice. Do nothing...and I will die for my betrayal, or stab me through the heart, and we will both live, and the Transference will be complete.

That's it? No more lies?

Yes, that's it, but make sure you're committed to going through with it.

Onnie's hand, now inches from the hilt, stopped. *Why?*

Because right now, our bodies are lying on the stone below Abbot. When you remove that dagger, you will set the final piece of the Transference in motion. If you waver… it doesn't end with us having a happy life and a bunch of children.

Oh… Onnie grasped the dagger's hilt and looked up at him. *Promise me this will work. Promise me I'm not signing our death warrant right now.*

I promise, Cat.

Onnie sucked in a big breath and nodded to Gabe once. *Ready?*

I am. Gabe closed his eyes.

I love you too, Gabe. He heard her whisper seconds before a dagger pierced his chest.

Onnie Moore

Onnie's eyes shot open, and the first thing she saw was the crypt's ceiling. There was a feeling, or lack of feeling, of anything beneath her, and she carefully moved her eyes and saw that they were both floating a few inches off the ground in front of the dais.

The room was filled with thick tension; it was tangible as everyone held their breaths. Except something was wrong, Onnie felt wrong. Everything was too bright, too loud. Overwhelming.

Blinking, Onnie looked at her chest, hoping not to see a gaping hole where a dagger had been. Instead, an intense light was pouring from her and feeding into the blade, now protruding from Gabe's heart. The light pulsed and wavered, making her begin to panic.

Don't give up on him now, Onnie. Trust him. Mal's soothed in her head.

Onnie closed her eyes, felt along her Bond to Gabe, and held on to it. She cradled the strand to her and whispered to it how much she loved him. How she couldn't live without him and how she'd never felt at home until she'd met him.

Don't leave me, Gabe. Please.

"Cat, open your eyes," Gabe whispered in her ear.

She blinked slowly, expecting the room to be still bathed in light. The stone felt cold beneath her, and the tension from earlier had left the chamber. Her eyes connected with Gabe's, and he smiled his crooked grin at her from where he had sat up, braced on his forearm.

"You did it, Cat."

Onnie looked down to see that he was holding the onyx dagger in his left hand, which was no longer buried in his chest. Her eyes closed, and her head rolled back on the stone as the adrenaline from the ordeal left her body in an instant.

"Don't you ever do that to me again."

Gabe laughed, and she opened her eyes as he got to his feet and held a hand down to her. Without hesitation, she took it, and Dany took the dagger back, leaving Gabe's hands free to wrap around her.

"I love you, Onnie. You did well."

Onnie snuggled her face further into his jacket and mumbled, "I love you too."

Dude, you are not alone, you know. Mal said to them both.

Onnie cleared her throat and pulled herself away from Gabe's warm embrace. When she looked at the crowd gathered to witness their Transference, she realized she had no idea what to say.

"Um, I'm not sure if there's some sort of protocol for this…but thank you. Thank you all for being here to wish Grandfather goodbye. And thank you for witnessing the Transference. I hope I will make you proud, and in the coming months, I will be able to call you all friends."

A few people nodded, a few cleared tears away, and Elanor grinned so widely that Onnie was slightly worried for her cheeks.

Dany stepped between Keeper and Guardian and picked up Mal to be at eye level with the rest of the group. "May I present your new Keeper, her Guardian, and her Link."

The figures in the room bowed to them in unison and, one by one, made their exits.

Dany hugged Onnie and then Gabe, staying at his side under his arm, "Thank you for trusting him, Onnie," she beamed up at her brother, "I don't know what I would have done if you hadn't."

Gabe kissed Dany's temple, and Mal jumped onto the dais and into Onnie's arms to headbutt her chin.

Elanor approached Onnie warily, the woman with lime-green eyes a few paces behind her. "Keeper, may I have a moment of your time?"

Onnie scratched Mal under his chin and smiled, "My friend, you never have to ask."

Elanor blushed and began to fidget with her apron. "That's very kind of you, Keeper—"

"Elanor," Onnie said with a sigh, "I'm Onnie, just Onnie. Please?"

Elanor froze but quickly recovered herself. "Yes, Onnie," she smiled. "I wanted to tell you that a few of us would like to help rebuild Abbot's…if you'd let us."

"Of course, that would be—"

Onnie shivered. Her eyes passed around the mausoleum and the few people still within it. Something was wrong, and she could feel it, "Can you excuse me for a moment, Elanor."

Onnie looked at Gabe. *There's something here,* she watched Gabe's eyes harden, and he released Dany.

Without waiting for conversation, Onnie led the way out of the mausoleum with Mal in her arms and Gabe close behind. They exited the stone monument and stepped out into the bright sun and the center of the hedge maze. People milled about talking in small groups, but when Onnie's eyes landed on the back of a lone figure walking toward the maze entrance, a shiver shook her down to her Bond.

"You!" Onnie shouted, "Stop!"

The figure ignored her and continued walking while everyone around her went silent and turned to see what the commotion was about.

"I asked you to stop."

When the character kept walking, Onnie's Bond strand that connected her to the shop flared, and she shut her eyes. A new Bond thread flickered to life in her mind, originating in her chest where the dagger had recently been. She reached for the thread and pulled the slight glimmer that connected her to the world. The world exploded into micro strands spreading around her—a glowing tangle of lights and connections that shined in a black sea.

A thread that pulsed a mix of black and deep burgundy caught her attention, and she followed it to the figure.

Then she pulled it.

Her eyes snapped open, and the figure had stopped where it was, mid-stride. Mal jumped from her arms and bounded over to the frozen man.

"Gabe…" Mal said, using his voice for the first time, gasps rippling through the crowd. "This isn't good, man."

Those who remained from the Transference gathered at the commotion as Onnie and Gabe approached the figure's back.

"Mal, what's up?" Gabe asked as he walked around the figure. Once he could see the figure's face, Gabe's body coiled into a fight stance. His eyes flared blue as he reached for the person's throat.

"STOP!" Onnie bellowed and pulled on her Bond with Gabe just as she had the intruder, freezing him in place inches from his target.

"He's mine." She growled with all the anger she'd been carrying for the man in black since the day he'd killed her Grandfather.

Gabriel Vansand

Gabe, this is so not good, Mal said in his mind.

I know, Mal, Gabe growled, *don't let her get hurt. I don't think she can manipulate you like she can me, apparently. We'll deal with that later.*

"Onnie, girl, you need to let Gabe go," Mal said pleadingly.

"In a minute." She stalked a circle around the figure, and Gabe watched the man in black's eyes fill with fear.

Gabe closed his eyes and followed his Bond to Onnie, and when it flared to life in front of him, he gasped. He couldn't believe the vibrancy at which her Bond glowed.

"What are you?" the man spat, and Gabe reopened his eyes.

"I am the Keeper, and you murdered my Grandfather." Onnie's

eyes were crystal blue, and Gabe could feel her on the edge of her control. "That was a big mistake."

The man's eyes widened in panic, "No Keeper should have this much power."

"Well, guess what, asshole, I have more."

Onnie did something, and everyone watched as whatever it was threw the man across the courtyard, where he landed in an unmoving heap on the stones.

"You stole someone from me, and I will never get them back. Do you know how angry that makes me?"

Gabe locked eyes with Dany and flicked his gaze to Onnie. Dany understood and inclined her head before she meshed back into the group.

"Onnie, stop. We can get the information another way." Mal pleaded as he brushed against her legs.

"Give me one good reason why I shouldn't kill you right here in front of all these people. All the people who came to bury a great man. A friend." Onnie began walking toward the man in black like a predator, slow and calculated.

"Because of him," the man in black looked at Gabe.

Onnie faltered. Her hold on Gabe slipped, and he stumbled forward without the man in black to brace himself on.

"Cat, stop this. You're not a killer. That's my job."

"Be quiet, Gabriel, or I'll refreeze you," Onnie said without breaking her eye contact with the man in black. "Tell me how you killing my Grandfather, the man who raised Gabriel, is his fault."

The man in black remained speechless.

Onnie shouted, "NOW," and Gabe felt her emotion spike to brush the edge of her limit, and both he and the man in black coughed and sputtered.

Gabe recovered quickly and slowly stepped closer to his nearly out of control, Keeper.

"Alright!" the man hissed between gasps. "Gabriel killed the old fool the moment he turned his back on my master and sided with the Keepers. Master doesn't tolerate weakness. Gabriel is weak."

Gabe went cold, and without realizing it, his feet had carried him to the sniveling man under Onnie's control. "Who! Who is your master?" he bellowed, "I don't see them here. I see you whimpering on the ground, calling me weak."

The man sneered, and Gabe clenched his fists to hold himself back from ripping the scum's head off right then and there.

"Oh, but if I told you, that would spoil the surprise. We wouldn't want that now, would we." The man focused back on Onnie and spat. "Kill me, little girl, and get it over with."

Gabe held his breath as Mal clawed his way up Onnie's side and onto her shoulder.

If she kills him, she will never recover, Mal.

You think I don't know that?

"No," Onnie said, her voice devoid of emotion and expression blank.

"What?" The man in black asked, confusion written all over his face, "I killed your Grandfather. I killed the *Keeper.* Doesn't that make you want to destroy me?"

That was the point of all this. Gabe's jaw creaked under the strain he was putting it under. They had been set up. The man in black was there for one reason. To break the fledgling Keeper. He was begging for death with his instigation and then with his pleading, and now, Onnie planned on giving it to him. Just as he'd wanted.

You're up. Onnie thought to him, and he nearly jumped, her sudden voice startling him. Then he exhaled and smiled. It was too bad for the man in black. Cat was more intelligent than even Gabe gave her credit for, and he'd need to remember that.

She crossed the last few feet to the intruder and crouched before his face. "Oh, I'm not going to kill you. That's not my job. I am the Keeper, a haven, and a protector. I am not a killer."

"You are just as weak as he is!" The man in black shouted, spit flying from his lips.

"No," Onnie stated calmly, "I'm not, but I wouldn't expect someone like you to understand."

She stood and turned to Gabe with that wicked grin she used when she was going to knock him on his ass. "Hold on tight, and please…try not to get blood on the carpet."

It took a second for Gabe to comprehend the meaning of her words, but he didn't have time for concern. He sneered at the worthless filth on the ground at his feet, "Mal, care to join me?"

Mal looked to Onnie, and with her subtle nod, he disappeared.

Gabe searched for Dany and saw her behind their Keeper as she stepped up to wrap her arm around Onnie's shoulder.

With his next blink, he and his prisoner were in the interior of the bookshop in a room he'd never seen before. It was so dark that all Gabe could make out was the whimpering man on the stone floor beside him. That, and the light blue glow emanating from Mal and Gabe's own eyes in the darkness.

Feelings of support and gratitude caressed his Bond, and he could tell Onnie was giving him, Mal, and the shop her blessing.

Gabe returned his focus to the man in black, who never had a chance to scream.

Chapter 38: Disappointment

December 2021 - ??? | ???

"Damn it!" Shouted the man in black as he stormed into his Master's working chamber and looked down at his translucent body. "What gives boss?" As he walked, his feet made no noise along the stones, and he didn't feel the chill that usually saturated this room.

Black, inky stains covered the floor in patches and splatters. Long, thick wooden tables lined the side walls, and a metal contraption with spinning dials and glass trinkets glittered in the lamplight. Across the dimly lit chamber, a figure faced the full windows that overlooked the city far below them. The figure was draped in a deep red cloak that pooled on the floor around its feet.

"You failed." The figure said, not bothering to turn around and face the man in black.

"What do you mean I failed? I watched the whole Transference just like you asked. It was spectacular, by the way. I know everyone who was a witness, and we can begin our attack." The man in black tried to pinch himself and stomped in silent frustration when his fingers passed through his torso.

The figure in red did not reply and only continued to stare out of the window.

The man in black crossed the stained cement floor and approached the figure, "Can't you do anything about this, boss? I'm not sure why I'm not able to fully form, but it's starting to get annoying." He tried to tap his finger on the button of his jacket, but the action was silent and with no tactile sensation.

The figure in red still did not move or speak.

"Boss?" The man in black came to a stop at the side of the figure, "Hello, earth to bo—"

The figure in red lashed out like a viper and wrapped his left hand around the translucent throat of the man in black.

"You failed," he said, his gaze never leaving that of the city below.

The man in black struggled, kicking his feet and trying desperately to claw at the hand wrapped around his neck. His fingers found no purchase as they passed through his Master's hand, "Boss?" he managed to croak out of his constricted windpipe, "I didn't fail you, I swear it."

The figure in red lifted his right palm, and a glowing sphere manifested within it.

The man in black shifted his attention to the sphere as he watched the Transference just as it had occurred earlier that morning. He watched as the Keeper followed himself from the past to the courtyard and pinned him with her powers, powers she was not supposed to possess. He watched as she bent next to him and spoke to him. Then she surprised him by stepping back and allowing her Guardian and Link to step forward.

"Try not to get blood on the carpet." The Keeper's voice rang into the darkness of the stone room. The man in black watched as the Link disappeared, and then the Guardian and his past self did as well.

With a confused look on his face and a crease in his brow, he looked at the figure in red.

"When was this? I don't remember this." The figure in red tightened his grip and forcibly rotated his head back to face the orb. Returning his gaze to the sphere, the man in black watched as the two figures reappeared in a dark stone room oozing with moisture and lined with lush moss.

He saw himself appear in a chair in the center of the room as the Guardian circled him. "Who do you work for?"

The version of him in the orb said nothing.

The Guardian fired off more and more questions until it was clear that he was getting nowhere, "Mal, care to try?"

"Nope, he's all yours. I'm just here to ensure this slime gets what's coming to him."

The Guardian placed his palms on the chair's arms and leaned into his past self's face. "You've made some powerful enemies, and if you'd like this to go quickly, you'd best answer my questions."

The man in black watched as the sphere version of himself was continually interrogated for hours by the Guardian and his furry pet. When it looked like he was about to become the cat's lunch, the two stepped back and stood against the cell walls, leaving him in the center of the room.

"Finally, you're giving up. It's about time." He watched himself say to the two onlookers.

"No, actually far from it," the Guardian said with a weary shake of his head, "They said I could try my way first, but since you haven't been very cooperative, you've left us no choice."

"No choice in what...." his past said cocking his head to the side.

"It's her turn to try and get some answers," the feline responded.

He watched himself laugh at his captors. "Weren't you fools listening? Your precious Keeper is a lover, not a fighter."

"You're right," the Guardian said as he and the cat walked to the cell door, "she is, but she's not who we are talking about."

The man in black watched as the Guardian and the Link exited the cell, and just when it seemed his show had ended, he watched in horror as he saw himself forced into the air, spread eagle and screaming. Light poured from his body, screams ripped through the chamber, and just when he thought he'd begin to scream along with his past counterpart, he watched as he was torn into a million pieces of light, and the cell was emptied.

The man in black began to claw at his Master's hand, which had tightened and was crushing him with such force that he was sure to die.

He stopped struggling.

The realization took his breath out more than his Master's strangulation.

He was dead.

"Master, Master, I'm sorry I have failed you! You are right, but there's still hope. They don't know about you. I didn't break! You saw it. I didn't break!"

"YOU FOOL!" The figure in red bellowed as he threw the man in black to the floor. "Of course, you broke! Can you still not see what has happened!"

Crawling backward to further himself from his Master's wrath, the man in black pleaded, "I saw it. I never spoke against you. You are safe."

The figure in red took one step toward the man in black. "No, you wretch, the heart of the bookshop looked into your past and saw everything it needed to know."

Horror crossed the man in black's face, "That's impossible."

"I thought so, yes, but it seems our new Keeper is even stronger than I could have dreamed."

"We can still strike the witnesses. Please, Master, give me a chance to redeem myself to you!" His voice pleaded as he crawled to his Master's feet in submission.

"Do not worry. You knew little and still have one use left to me."

"Thank you, Master. I will not let you down again." He leaned down to the stone floor beside his Master's robes and kissed it in place of the hem. "Thank you."

The figure in red turned and walked away from the man in black and across the stained cement floor.

"Yes, you will satisfy me by burning for all eternity."

"NO!" He reached out as the figure in red waved his arm. With one strangled cry, the man in black dissolved, seeping into the concrete, only to be added to the already existing stains.

Epilogue

January 2022 - Alku | Onnie Moore

Onnie stopped on the sidewalk and looked at the worn wooden sign swaying in the soft breeze above her. Lifting her face to the sky, she smiled and hiked her messenger bag higher on her shoulder. The sky was a crisp light blue, and the sun shone on the streets below, bathing them in warmth. Alku was everything she'd hoped it would be, and even after a few months, it still surprised her.

She lifted her palm and traced the word "Abbot's" carved into the smooth wood of the bookshop's door. Smiling, Onnie closed her eyes and reached along her Bond with the bookshop to say good morning. The shop responded with subtle warming through the wood where Onnie's hand was and opened the door for her. With a gentle pat on the doorframe, Onnie opened her eyes as she entered the dark interior.

She closed the door behind her and turned on the lights as she passed each of them, no longer needing the bookshop's help or her own hands. When she was behind the front counter, she slid her bag into its place, smiling at her familiar routine.

It had been three weeks since the Transference and her Grandfather's funeral, and all three had been a struggle.

Once she'd relocated Gabe and the man in black to the shop, she'd collapsed. Thankfully, Dany was there and got her back home. When Onnie had awoken, Dany explained what she knew about a Keeper's powers and what would happen if they were over-taxed. Onnie's eyes glowed blue as she listened to her friend's concern and sipped a cup of Keeper's tea.

A while later, Gabe and Mal returned home to report what happened to the man in black, and Onnie worried that with little new information, they would never find the real villain behind her Grandfather's death. One thing they did learn was that Gabe and Dany's father was involved, which had heightened everyone's sense of foreboding in nearly an instant. Jakob had been smart, though, and his pawn knew little of actual importance.

Once Onnie regained some strength, she needed to go to the shop, as she'd been away for too long. When she arrived at Abbot's to find two dozen of the witnesses from her Transference, along with another dozen people from around the town, elbow deep in furniture polish, dust cloths, and some with hacksaws and nail guns in hand, her heart swelled, and she was afraid it would burst.

Sam hugged her and explained that some of her Grandfather's closest friends and companions in life also wanted to be part of the dedication of the bookshop to their fallen friend.

New faces came and went regularly that day, adding their input or helping to restore the bookshop. Elanor led a building project on the front sidewalk, making new planter boxes with other nymphs, one of Gabe's best friends, Xayn, and his grandmother, Yvonne. Onnie had recognized the woman from the Transference and wasn't surprised to learn that she and Elanor were incredibly close friends. By the time they'd completed their project, the storefront overflowed with brightly colored and fragrant flowers.

Gabe helped to rebuild some of the broken bookshelves, and with Mal's help, new glass panes were relocated into their housings with little effort.

Once every shelf and case was restored, Sam and Onnie spent most of the day sifting through texts and tomes, shelving what they could and salvaging what needed it. They had talked throughout the hours, and Sam furthered her education about the different races and sects in the magical community. When her head genuinely felt like it would burst, Dany arrived with pizza and beer for everyone.

It had taken the group nearly fifteen hours to clean, restock, and repair the bookshop, and after an extremely long day of work, Onnie, Gabe, Mal, Elanor, and Dany were the only ones left.

It was nearly three in the morning when the small band of friends said goodnight and parted ways. She, Gabe, and Mal had collapsed on the couch in the living room and passed out within seconds.

Onnie smiled as she remembered waking up that morning, the three of them in her four-poster bed, a pile of twisted human limbs, and Mal draped over her stomach.

Mal, are you coming in today?

The lazy feline was still asleep in his window at home, but she felt him rouse and then heard him yawn along their Bond. Then he appeared on the counter in front of her.

"What's up, Onnie? I was comfy."

"You didn't *have* to come in. I just wanted to know if you were. But since you're here...." Onnie scratched under his chin and kissed his nose. "Help me figure out what to get Gabe for his birthday?"

"Buy him a blow-up doll so I can have my bed back," Mal said through lidded eyes and a purr.

"Mal!" Onnie pushed him over and began tickling his belly. "You're such a brat!"

Mal disappeared and reappeared on the register, still laughing from being tickled. "What? Ever since he moved into our room, he kicks me off the bed in the middle of the night, and I'm relegated to sleeping in the window box. It was my bed first."

"Maldwyn, are you jealous?" Onnie said with a snigger.

Mal turned away from her, suddenly interested in a dust particle floating in the air. "No, not at all. It's just cold by the window, that's all."

Scooping the blue cat into her arms, Onnie hugged him and planted a loud smacking kiss on his head. "I love you, Mal. I'll talk to Gabe."

Mal rubbed his head under her chin, "Thanks, girl, but I still think you should give him a blow-up doll."

"You're impossible," Onnie said as she gave him one last squeeze and lowered him to the counter. "Making coffee, want anything?" Onnie said over her shoulder as she walked into the shop's backroom.

"Nope, thanks, though."

Onnie felt the soft tingling feeling through her Bond with the bookshop, and she'd come to realize she was telling her they had a customer coming in. The dull thunk of the front door closing came from the central area of the store, confirming Onnie's assumption.

"Be with you in one moment!" Onnie hollered through the doorway while selecting a few buttons on the coffee maker. She slid her mug under the machine, returned to the store's front, and saw Gabe at the counter scratching Mal's ears.

"Hey, I didn't know you were coming in today."

Smiling, Gabe leaned over the counter to kiss her on the cheek. "Nope, I just wanted to come in and steal you away for lunch. You have time?"

"Not really.... The new semester's curriculum books just came in this morning. Rain check?" Onnie said as she rounded the counter and stepped into Gabe's embrace.

"Hm.... I have a better idea. I'll be right back with lunch, and we can eat and sort it out together." Gabe kissed the tip of her nose and smiled down at her.

"Really? Don't you have classes?"

"I do, but not until last period. I'll work on lesson plans after, and maybe we could even go for a run after you close tonight." Gabe kissed her cheek and turned to leave the shop.

"Okay. Pastrami on sourdough, please, extra sauerkraut." Onnie called after him as she looked down at the shipping log on the counter.

When he reached the door, Gabe turned to look back at her. "Cat?"

"Yup?" Onnie said, looking up.

"I love you," Gabe said, gently tugging at their Bond.

Onnie smiled and crossed the room to stand on her tip-toes. "I love you too, Gabe." She reached up and pulled his face slowly to her lips and kissed him softly. She stepped back and caressed his cheek, "Go on, or I may have to eat Mal. I'm starving!"

"I heard that," Mal said from the counter. "Tuna on rye, please, Gabe."

"Spoiled cat." Gabe chuckled back.

Onnie smiled as her heart swelled in happiness. She'd never really fit in anywhere before, and as she looked at the two most important men in her life and the shop around her, she didn't hesitate to pull on their Bonds and pour her feelings into them.

Mal appeared in her open arms and licked the tip of her nose. "We know."

Gabe wrapped his arm around them both and rested his chin on the top of her head. "We love you too."

Onnie closed her eyes and smiled as she heard a woman whisper, *Yes, young one, we do.*

Eliza Leone

Eliza Leone is an author from the Pacific Northwest who specializes is chronicling the stories of her imaginary friends. As a kid, you could find her on the playground with a few kids acting out the stories they'd made up. When she got older and discovered there were entire worlds hidden within the pages of endless books, chances are her nose was in one. Over time, Friday nights were reserved for bookstore runs with her mother and together, they'd resupply for a week of adventures.

Writing had always been a far off dream, her ability to spell and do that grammar thing correctly, severely lacking. It wasn't until her mid-twenties that she decided if she was only writing it for herself, then no one would care about her lack of proper punctuation. Ten years and over a dozen books later, her family, human and fiction, convinced her to finally share her stories with the world.

From short stories and micro-fiction to the entire urban fantasy universe of Alku and its people, Eliza can't wait for you to giggle, sob, and throw your book across the room with her. Just...please don't throw the e-readers.

You can find Eliza Leone on: Instagram @ElizaLeone_author, Twitter @ELeone_author, and at ElizaLeone.com.

Leave feedback, read exclusive bonus content, and support this project at www.campfirewriting.com/explore/ElizaLeone

www.ingramcontent.com/pod-product-compliance
Lightning Source LLC
Chambersburg PA
CBHW020323030826
48979CB00022B/935

* 9 7 9 8 9 8 9 3 9 8 4 2 3 *